Facets of the Nether

The Dissolutionverse:

Novellas and Novelettes:

The Five Hive Plateau

Tuning the Symphony

Merchants and Maji

The Society of Two Houses

Journey to the Top of the Nether

The Dissolution Cycle:

The Seeds of Dissolution (Book I)

Facets of the Nether (Book II)

Fall of the Imperium (Book III)

Facets of the Nether

BOOK II OF THE DISSOLUTION CYCLE

William C. Tracy

Space Wizard Science Fantasy
Raleigh, NC
www.spacewizardsciencefantasy.com

Cover art by Hannah "Spoon" Wilson
Interior illustrations by Cory Godbey
Map by Damijan
Editing by Heather Tracy
Book Layout © 2015 BookDesignTemplates.com

Facets of the Nether/William C. Tracy.— 1st ed.
Library of Congress Control Number: 2020909008
ISBN 978-1-7350768-0-5

Author's website: https://www.spacewizardsciencefantasy.com/

To Writing Excuses:
The first of their podcasts I listened to was "Writing the Second Book."
Well, here it is.

CONTENTS

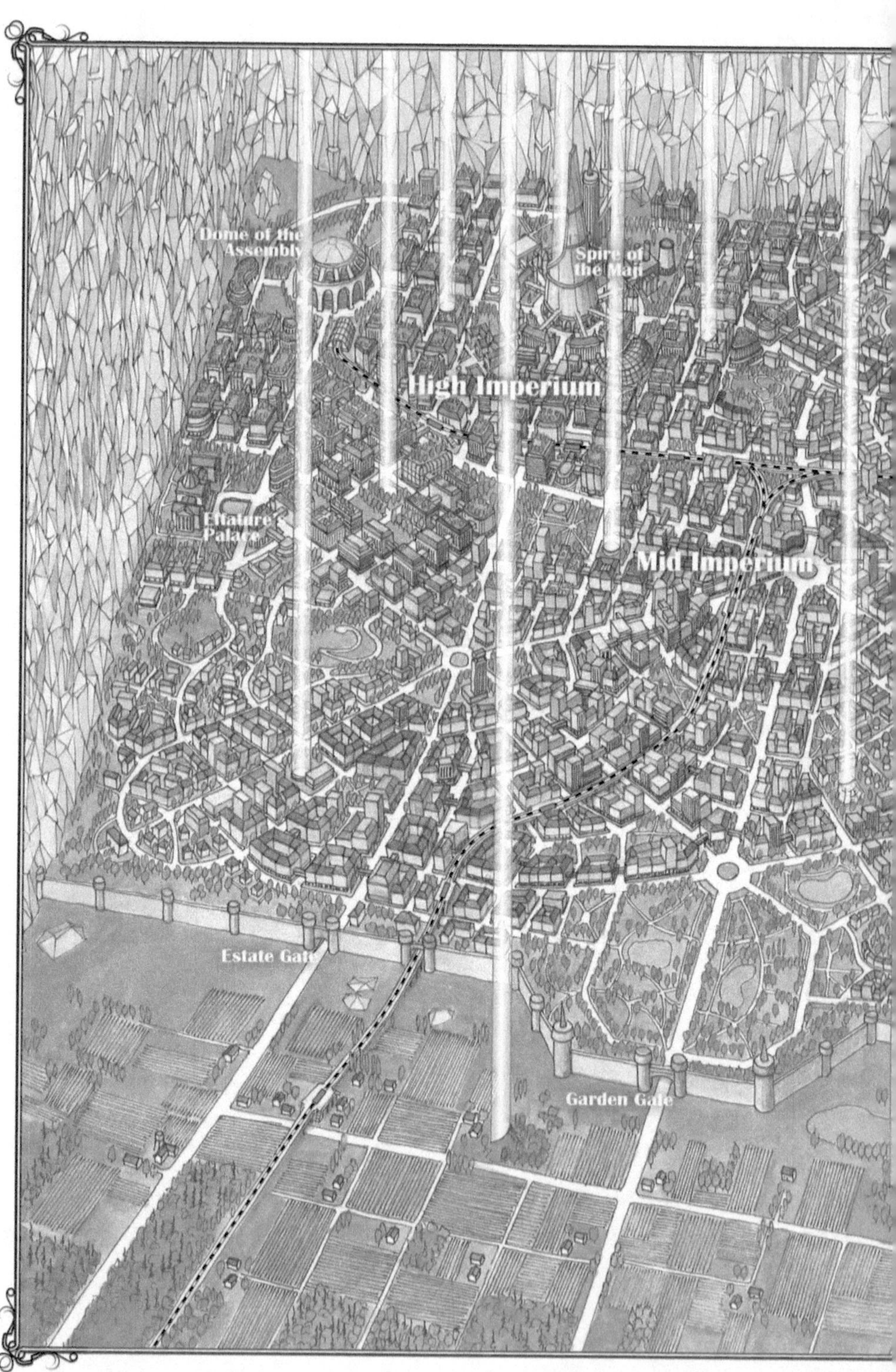

Dome of the Assembly
Spire of the Mall
High Imperium
Eftaire's Palace
Mid Imperium
Estate Gate
Garden Gate

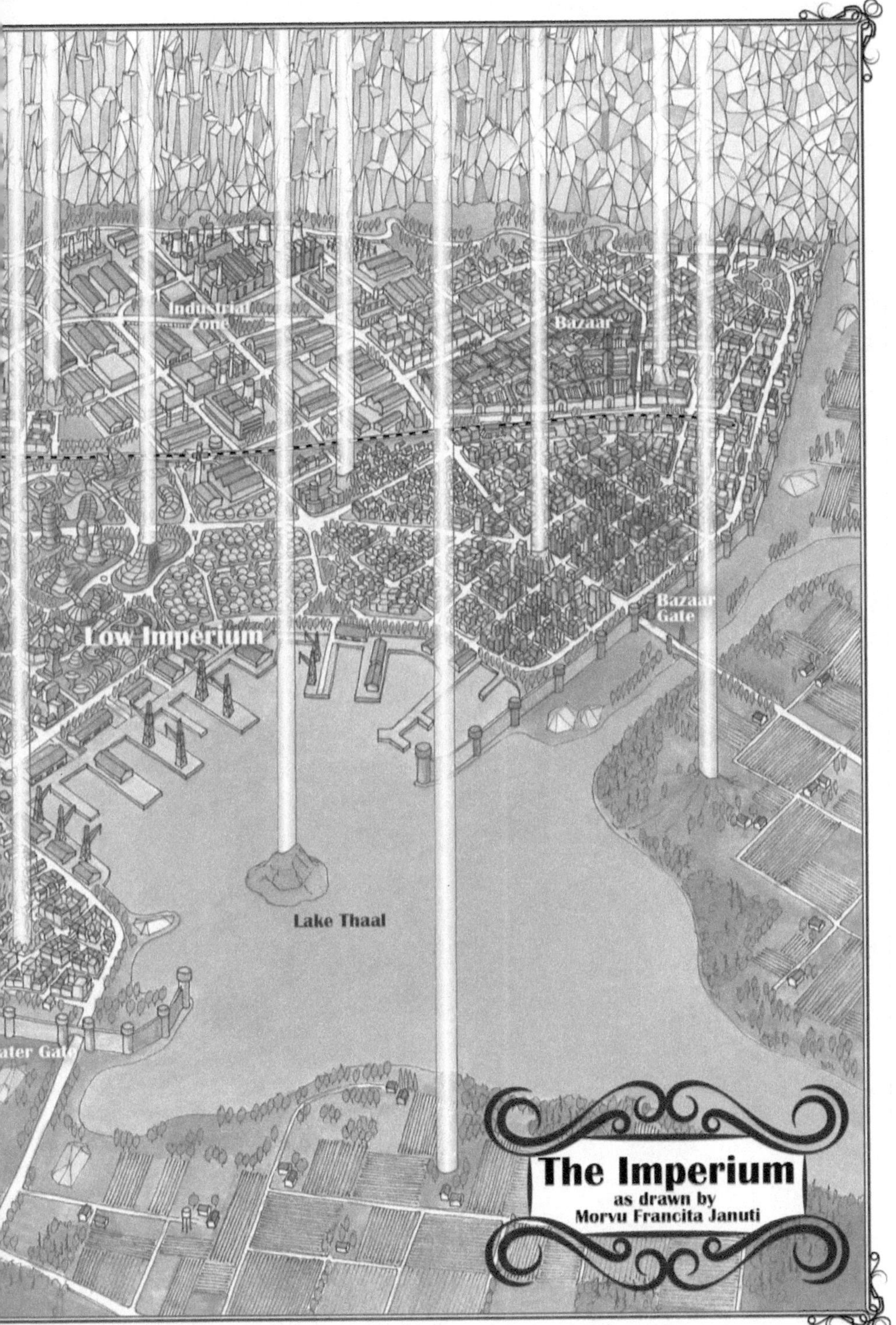

Industrial Zone
Bazaar
Low Imperium
Bazaar Gate
Lake Thaal
ater Gate
The Imperium
as drawn by
Morvu Francita Januti

The Story So Far:

Book 1: The Seeds of Dissolution:

When the sun goes dark in daytime, Samuel van Oen, a young man plagued by anxiety, nearly freezes to death. At the cost of his aunt's life, Sam escapes his home on Earth, fleeing through a strange portal.

On the other side, he learns of the Nether, a hub between ten alien homeworlds, and of the Symphony underlying the universe. Maji of the six houses—Strength, Communication, Power, Grace, Healing, and Potential—hear this music and change its notes to affect reality. Sam meets Origon Cyrysi, of the Houses of Communication and Power, and Councilor Rilan Ayama, the head of the House of Healing. They help Sam overcome his initial anxiety in the Imperium, the capital city of the Nether.

Unable to find his way home, Sam learns he can hear the Symphony and agrees to become Origon's apprentice and to study the phenomenon that almost killed him, which Origon calls Drains.

Sam then meets the twins Enos and Inas, and is attracted to both of them. They help him navigate his anxiety, and share how their entire family was wiped out by another Drain.

Meanwhile, the Imperium is wracked by rumors of people attacked by Aridori, an ancient shape-shifting species thought extinct. At the same time, a faction attempts to secede from the Great Assembly of Species, and a group with anti-maji sentiment attack Rilan on the way to a Council meeting. The Council of the Maji will not let Origon study the Drains, as they insist all maji focus on eliminating the Aridori, real or imagined.

Rilan and Origon rebel, and take the apprentices to the site of the Drain which killed Enos and Inas's family, to determine what caused it. They find nothing, but Rilan learns her home town is under attack by another Drain. Her father, a stubborn man, has likely not left the city.

They travel there, and use the Symphony to keep from freezing. They find machinery stopped, and animals and people dead from exposure. Rilan also finds her father dead, but has no time to grieve.

While escaping, Sam and Enos are separated from the others and captured by cloaked beings who call themselves the Life Coalition. In response to losing her and Origon's apprentices, Rilan is removed from the Council.

Sam and Enos are cut off from the Symphony, and to keep the Life Coalition from killing her, Enos reveals she is one of the lost Aridori.

At the same time, Rilan and company guess at an organization connecting the recent strange occurrences. Origon then receives news that Mandamon Feldo, the head of the House of Power, has captured a true Aridori, and it is held in a prison.

Sam comes to terms with Enos' species, they escape, and he agrees not to turn her in. They meet up with Rilan, Origon, and the other maji as they plan to interrogate the captured Aridori in Gloomlight prison. Sam and Inas have an emotional reunion, and Inas confirms he is also Aridori. The three hide Enos and Inas' species from the others.

However Origon guesses the twins' species and Sam, against his best intentions, confirms. The maji keep the Aridori under close watch. Against Rilan's wishes, the Aridori change their appearance to infiltrate the prison.

Inside they find the Aridori Councilor Feldo captured. Enos communicates with them, though the words and images she receives make little sense until Inas takes over and melds with the Aridori. They discover the Life Coalition will meet in the Nether that night, though the caged Aridori dies. In the process, Inas is injured.

They ambush the meeting and fight the Life Coalition, though Inas is captured in the conflict. Rilan and Origon find the Life Coalition will attack the Assembly itself by creating a massive Drain.

They rush to the Assembly, but not before the Life Coalition succeeds. The entire maji organization attempts to battle the Drain, but it destroys the notes involved and throws the maji into disarray.

During this, Sam is haunted by a voice of another entity in his head, which seems connected to the Drains. It reveals he is not of the House of Communication, like Majus Cyrysi, but is of a new house. Sam, for an instant, sees the flow of time, showing how to defeat the Drain.

He tells the others to leave, and Rilan creates a portal to follow the fleeing Life Coalition. They chase down the attackers, but do not find Inas.

Sam faces the Drain, creating an immense portal linking his current time with the moment when his parents were killed on Earth.

But the voice in his head scrambles his memories, and Sam switches the Drain's endpoint from his childhood to his house directly before he came to the Nether, fulfilling how he originally arrived. When the Drain disappears through the portal, the voice vanishes.

The others return without Inas, and find Sam. He shows them he is not truly of the House of Communication, and asks if the others know of the Dissolution.

Dramatis Personae:

Samuel van Oen: A young man from the outskirts of Charleston, SC, USA. He is affected with severe anxiety, brought on mainly by new places and crowds of people. Sam can hear different music than those of the six known houses, though no one knows why.

Origon Cyrysi (OR-i-gon Ki-RICE-ee): A majus, born into both the House of Communication and the House of Power. He is Kirian, a humanoid with bird-like aspects, especially a mobile crest of feathery hair that adjusts according to his mood. He is arrogant, rash, and Sam's mentor.

Rilan Ayama: A Methiemum majus who determines Sam is suspiciously similar in phenotype to a Methiemum. Rilan is formerly the youngest Councilor for the House of Healing, but she was removed from the Council and is a majus again. She is confident and determined, and also skilled in mental changes in the House of Healing, though has trouble healing physical wounds.

Enos: Thought to be a Methiemum, she and her twin brother Inas were the only survivors of a void which destroyed their family's merchant caravan. Enos and her brother are really Aridori, a species thought to be a thousand cycles extinct. She is also an apprentice in the House of Healing to Rilan.

Inas: Where Enos, his sister, is a bit cold and distant, Inas is warm and friendly. Inas belongs to the House of Strength, which deals with the music of constitution, plants, and resistance. He is apprentice to Caroom. Inas makes friends easily, and both he and Enos are enamored with Sam. Inas has been captured by the Life Coalition and his whereabouts are unknown.

Nara Reyhorer, "Rey": Rey is one of the Sureriaj, a xenophobic and isolationist species. Rey often cracks jokes and tells stories in his thick brogue, but doesn't always agree with the other apprentices. Rey did not experience much of what Sam, Enos, and Inas did. He trains with his mentor, Majus Kheena.

Caroom: One of the few long-lived Benish in the Nether, Caroom is a genderless creature with both plant and animal characteristics. They have a veterinary clinic, but also belong to the House of Strength. They are logical, intelligent, and straightforward, and act as mentor for Inas.

Hand Dancer: A gender-fluid Lobhl, the newest species to find the Nether. Lobhl have no vocal chords, and instead use their large, seven-fingered hands to communicate. Hand Dancer is an accomplished majus of the House of Power, and adept at discovering connections between seemingly unrelated happenings. Hand Dancer is also a well-regarded musician, using the Lobhl music of colors and shapes, performed on the instrument which is also called the Hand Dancer.

Supporting characters:

The Effature, Bolas Palmoran: an elderly Methiemum who is the de facto leader of the Nether, though he governs with a light hand unless there is a problem. He wears a diadem of Nether crystal, and presides over the Assembly of Species. He also runs the administration of the Nether's capital city of the Imperium.

The Council of the Maji:

> **Scintien Nectiset:** head of the House of Strength, a weak-willed but talented Kirian.

> **Freshtanatipieletournale "Freshta":** head of the House of Communication, an aggressive and impulsive Pixie.

> **Bofan A'Tof:** the previous head of the House of Power, a very old Lobath. He was murdered by Aridori.

> **Hathssas:** the new head of the House of Power. She is a young Sathssn.

Jhina Moerna Oscana: the Head of the House of Communication and the Speaker for the Council of the Maji. She is the point of contact between the community of maji and the larger Assembly. She is a proud and overbearing Etanela, and often butts heads with Rilan and Origon.

Fernand Vethis: replacement head of the House of Healing once Rilan was deposed, but secretly cooperating with the Life Coalition. He is now in Gloomlight prison.

Mandamon Feldo: an old Methiemum who has been the head of the House of Potential for many cycles. Only a handful of people remember he is able to hear the Symphony of Healing as well as Potential, and was once a member of the Society of Two Houses.

The Life Coalition: an organization that can create Drains in some way. Their objective is unknown, save that they want to "bring peace and promote life."

Nakan: a Sathssn and a member of the Life Coalition. He is possibly even better at hand-to-hand combat than Rilan, aided by his ability to hear the Symphony of Grace.

Zsaana: a very old Sathssn, and the head of the House of Healing before Rilan. He is now a member of the Life Coalition. He was responsible for some of Rilan's training in the Fading Hands style of martial arts.

Dunarn: another Sathssn member of the Life Coalition, she was responsible for capturing Sam and Enos. She can hear the Symphony of Strength.

For a complete list of the ten species of the Assembly and the Houses of the Maji, see the appendices.

CHAPTER ONE

Flight of Memory

- The appearance of a new house of the maji is not to be as surprising as its origin. My apprentice, who firmly appeared to be of the House of Communication, is the one who is showing me these new things, at my age. Truly, the Nether is changing.

Journal of Origon Cyrysi, Kirian majus of the Houses of Communication and Power

A chime erupted through the Imperium, as if all the crystal plates in the world rang and shattered at once. Samuel van Oen held his ears and, through the window of his mentor's apartment, watched a flight of alien birds split and scatter at the noise.

"What was that?" Sam dropped his hands from his ears as the sound stabilized into a deep, clear tone he felt in his gut. It was loud, but not as unbearable as it had been. Deep in the back of his mind, the Grand Symphony responded to the noise like a tuning fork against a plate of metal. The different rhythms fractured and multiplied at the chime, like the whole world was vibrating.

No one answered his question, as Majus Cyrysi was out again. The Kirian had spent more time in the libraries of the Spire than in teaching Sam, not that he was ever particularly good at teaching.

The tower of the House of Communication vibrated beneath Sam's feet as the sound lessened to a background hum. The music normally playing in its halls had ceased during the explosion of sound, but now picked up fitfully, warring with the chime's resonance. The flock of birds—with crests of orange, and three scaly wings down each side of their body—swooped in an irregular pattern, disrupted by the noise.

Sam went to the window and looked down. To one side, dust fell from the strange stone bridge that ran from the middle of the House of Communication to the immense wall of the Nether. He'd been out on it before, as it was a curiosity of this House, and maji occasionally used it to take in the view. There were a few maji on it now—a tall Etanela and two Methiemum—looking up at the immense wall of the Nether, bathed in blues and purples like a titanic sheet of ice.

On the ground far below, people milled around in confusion. Sam guessed the bell-like sound wasn't normal, but he'd only been in this place a little under two months. Before that, things became blurred and hazy in his mind. The presence that had rooted through his head took many of his memories. He remembered Earth, and that he had stayed with his aunt after something happened to his parents. Their faces refused to come to mind. Thinking about what happened at the Dome of the Assembly made him seek the silence of Majus Cyrysi's apartment, and he couldn't stop. He was obsessing about what he could have—should have—done differently. He was slowly spiraling down to a place of solitude and loneliness, and his body wouldn't obey his deeper wish to break the cycle.

Sam jumped back from the window as someone banged on the door. A spike like an icicle in his gut went through him. Sweat pricked his forehead.

Don't be someone new.

It could only be one of a few people, but his throat threatened to close at the thought of explaining why he was sitting here alone, staring out a window. How long ago had Majus Cyrysi left?

Sam put one eye to the peephole in the door, then sagged in relief. It was Enos. He could ask her about the sound digging its way into his head.

He opened the door and let his friend in, looking her over. There were bags under her eyes and she hadn't combed her long black hair.

"You haven't slept either, have you?" said Enos.

Sam let out a burst of air. It wasn't quite a laugh. "That's what I was going to say." He pulled her into the room by her hand, quickly closing the door. The hall should be familiar, but it didn't feel like the right day to go outside. Again.

"You hear that too, right? Do you know what—"

Enos shook her head. "No idea. I was about to ask you. People are running around like mad. I don't think anyone knows."

Then why would she think I knew? He stared at the closed door.

Enos followed his gaze, then took his other hand. "It's been a ten-day since you left Majus Cyrysi's apartment." She winced as if she had a headache. Probably that irritating chime. It was like a dull drill, pressing against the back of his head.

Sam frowned. Now wasn't the time to talk about going out. Couldn't Enos see he had other things on his mind?

"Before this noise started I was trying to remember...remember—" He bit his lip and focused over her shoulder. It was something about Earth. He'd almost had it.

"Remember what?" Enos asked, bringing his focus back. "Is it connected with the attack on the Assembly? Or about the new themes you hear in the Symphony? Can they help us find Inas?"

Sam shook his head. He was letting Enos down.

She won't want to be with me anymore.

He knew it wasn't true, but the fact beat against the inside of his head. Inas had been the other side of a scale, balancing him. Without him, everything was harder.

Ever since he'd changed an arrow from wood to iron, Majus Cyrysi, Majus Ayama, and Enos had known he wasn't of the House of Communication. He was a different house than Majus Cyrysi, his own mentor. Maji could only teach one who heard the same music. Maybe that's why the majus spent so much time in the library.

Majus Ayama's questions about him had increased in intensity since then, driving him to seek solitude. At least she didn't think he was Aridori any longer.

The heat of embarrassment filled him as his hands clenched around Enos'. He didn't want anyone else to see the golden glow when he changed the Symphony. Gold, not yellow.

Why am I always different?

"Has Majus Ayama found any more of the Life Coalition's hideouts?" Sam tried to turn the subject away from himself. The majus had been eliminating pockets of the Coalition's army for the last month and a half—the same length of time Inas had been missing. He hadn't been with any of the remnants, which meant the Coalition leaders likely held him close.

"Not since yesterday when you asked," Enos said. "I've been working with her to see if my connection with my brother might help locate him. Nothing yet." She winced again. "Today was rough."

He should have been there, helping. Enos checked on him every day. He wanted to go with her, but there was so much he'd done wrong.

If he concentrated, Sam could remember Inas' skin under his hands, Inas' breath against his cheek, his lips on Sam's neck. They were incomplete, only two out of three.

If only I had been faster, done more.

But he'd cowered behind a crate, when the Life Coalition attacked them outside the bazaar. Could he have stopped them from taking Inas if he'd known he was different? Sweat trickled down his spine, and he swallowed.

"Sam!" Enos said. He started and looked at her. Had she been talking? Had he missed things again? That infernal chiming sound was like a hammer to the brain, making him lose his concentration.

"I know what it's like to lose people," she said, and it snapped him upright. She knew him too well. "You either have to move on, or take action."

Sam looked away from the conviction in her eyes. Her family had died in a Drain, in front of her and Inas. He couldn't even picture the faces of his parents, nor of the person who raised him, on Earth. He couldn't remember what happened to his aunt, in the cold. The details slipped away like trying to hold melting ice.

Under the Drain in Dalhni, Sam had changed the music defining his being. He'd muted the strains of panic and frenzy that made him so anxious. It had helped, until the being in the Assembly stripped memories from him. Ever since, he'd been missing an important piece of himself. Experimentation with Majus Cyrysi showed he could hear another, deeper, part of the Symphony, but he couldn't reach that musical phrasing again, no matter how deep he dug.

It was as if the melody of his anxiety was unrecognizable—he didn't know himself any longer. He had been the one to move the Drain from inside the Nether to another place—a place he could no longer remember. If he could just change the music of his being again, he'd be able to go out, to help the others find Inas.

"It won't help to stay in here brooding on it." Enos pulled him toward the door. "Come help us. Majus Ayama says we're getting closer to Inas with each hideout she finds."

The last two members of the Aridori species. My closest friends. Linked, two instances of the same life. I have to find him.

But he resisted, keeping her in the room. It still thrummed with the strange, deep vibration. "Just talk to me for a while."

He was being selfish. How could she stand to be with him? He was always thinking only of himself.

Enos frowned, but came back to wrap her arms around his shoulders so she could look up into his face. "What is this, Sam? You've barely spoken with anyone beside Majus Cyrysi. You haven't helped look for Inas. You avoid the outdoors more than when I first met you. Why won't you tell me?"

Sam leaned into her, but kept his face to the window. The Symphony came to him easier now, and he hummed along with the trills and glissandos defining the flight of the flock of birds, swirling outside like a feathery whirlwind. The notes he heard were primal to the universe—sound and rhythm underlying reality. They were scattered, as if whoever conducted the music was distracted. As if the vibration was throwing off the Grand Symphony itself.

"I can't face everyone else, out there," he said into Enos' hair. "I did something terrible when I moved the Drain, but I can't remember what."

Abruptly, the sound faded, and the building stopped vibrating.

"That's better," Enos said, with a sigh. She pulled away and caught his eyes when he turned back. "Now tell me. You can tell me anything. We don't have secrets. Not anymore."

She had bared everything to him when she revealed her species—an underground remnant of a genocidal war, hidden for a thousand cycles. Why couldn't he tell her?

"What I hear is...different," he said. "Majus Cyrysi thinks I may be part of a new house of the maji."

"That's obvious from the gold aura," Enos said. "You need not be embarrassed about it. Majus Caroom asks about you. They have been depressed, I think, after losing Inas." She raised her chin, and he knew she was trying not to show her own pain.

"That's not all," Sam said. "I think the new parts of the Symphony I hear are linked to the way I moved the Drain." He was hedging, and he could tell Enos knew it by the look in her eye.

"Yes, that follows, even if I don't understand how it works."

There was plenty he didn't understand either.

"I'm getting to it." His stomach cramped. He'd kept this from her, when he was supposed to share. It had been almost four ten-days since the fight in the Dome of the Assembly. He'd had so many chances to tell her. He swallowed and tried not to throw up.

"I don't know how this new Symphony works. I could only move the Drain because...because someone told me how." There it was. The part he hadn't shared with anyone. He watched for her reaction.

Her brows drew down over dark eyes. "Told you? How? Who?"

"It's...strange." He flung his hands out to his sides. "There was a voice. I thought I was crazy—that I was hearing things. Then it told me it could control the Drains, that it *was* the Symphony. And...and it took some of my memories away. I sent the Drain somewhere terrible, but I'm not sure where. I hurt someone, but I can't remember how. Then the voice disappeared." His knees crumpled as the defeat welled up in him.

What did I lose? Part of me is missing.

He fumbled in a pocket of his vest for the pocketwatch. It was from his grandfather. He remembered that much. He held it up to his ear, closed his eyes, and let the regular ticking time his heartbeat until it slowed.

Arms wrapped around his back. "Sam, I didn't know."

"You couldn't have," he mumbled. "I didn't tell you."

While Enos held him, he let the music fill him, driving away the anxiety. The Symphony had that effect, at least. Even if he was useless, he could coddle himself with the fundamentals of the universe. He let it play in the back of his mind. The Symphony was a rich, full expression of the environment, each note linked to a physical representation, depending on the house the majus belonged to.

The alien birds swooped by the window in a "V," probably looking for bugs. The morning light from the titanic walls of the Nether washed out the colors, and lent a legato theme to the Symphony.

A majus of the House of Communication—which Sam was supposed to be—might hear trills in the melody that was the speech of the birds, but that majus would not hear the low thrum of the elements making up the flying creatures' bones, muscles, and scales. That rhythm was deep and solid, as if the rest of the music depended on its beat.

Sam found himself nodding in time, mentally reaching for the notes to adjust them to a different tempo. The golden glow began around his hands, but he pulled back sharply. Enos grunted at his movement.

What am I doing?

If he changed the key of the notes that defined the bird's bones, they might become wood, or iron, or oxygen. Sam had experimented with the new music he heard, but was no closer to defining it, at least not to Majus Cyrysi's satisfaction. The changes he might make skittered around his mind, like a forgotten word on the tip of his tongue. It flitted away, just like everything else.

"What happened?" Enos asked. He only shook his head, then noticed she was squinting.

"Headache?" he asked. Did Aridori get headaches? Maybe it would divert her from what a failure he was.

"It's nothing." Enos brushed away the concern. "Probably just that chime. It went through everything. I couldn't block it out."

"Any other news?" he asked, to shift the topic away from him. Again. "Besides a giant gong hidden somewhere in the Imperium?"

Enos shook her head. "Majus Ayama wants everyone who's been helping track down the Life Coalition to meet. I've been working with her on ways to track down their last outpost. My connection with Inas—" she paused, whispering the next words even though they were alone, "—means I can get a...a feeling from him every once in a while. Majus Ayama and I have been working to hone that feeling."

Working while I've been in here, moping.

He knew she wasn't implying that, but it was so easy to see she'd been working while he'd been useless.

"How does it work? Your connection with Inas—your other instance?" Sam asked. She'd spoken a little about it, but he still didn't understand. He hadn't had enough time together with the two of them after discovering they were Aridori. And before the Life Coalition took Inas.

"It's strange," Enos told him, gently tugging on his hand. She headed for the door, but Sam dug his feet into Majus Cyrysi's plush Festuour-made rug. Couldn't they talk just a little longer? "I've never been away from Inas for this long, so we'd never explored the connection. It's like...it's like a feeling someone else is in the room, but stronger." She rubbed her temple with her other hand. "It's almost not there at such a distance. Almost. I've been helping Majus Ayama reconstruct the location for the Life Coalition's headquarters with what I feel of him."

Then they might have a chance of finding Inas.

"You can go on without me," Sam said. "I won't be any help."

Enos pulled harder. "You aren't being helpful now, Sam. You know how long it takes to climb up the stairs to this apartment. I come by every day. You've waited until today to tell me you heard a voice connected to the Drain. Every day you say you can't leave. I—"

Enos clamped her lips shut, and spikes of icy certainty pulsed though Sam's stomach.

She'll say I'm not worth it. She won't come up here anymore.

Then he took in her messy hair again, the bags under her eyes, felt her chewed nails in their joined hands. She was dealing with the same things he was. And taking care of him. He was being an ass. Like always.

Sam opened his mouth. "Enos, I'm sor—"

Enos' head jerked back, her dark hair spilling over her shoulders.

She fell backwards, and Sam leaned forward to catch her before she hit the floor. She was limp, but her hands shook.

"Enos!" Sam called. "Can you hear me? What's wrong?" She didn't answer. Icy claws climbed up Sam's spine. He checked her pulse, but it was still strong.

Then what's wrong with her? Is it related to the Aridori?

He told himself he was comfortable with that part of Enos and Inas, but some part of him always looked for anything...strange.

Then I'll know if something is wrong between us. If they decide I'm more bother than I'm worth.

Enos shook once more, then opened her eyes. "I saw—felt—him," she said. "They pushed him into a box like the one in Gloomlight. They were hurting him! We have to get him out."

Enos had finally made a connection?

"We don't know where he is—that's the whole problem," Sam said, trying to push away the clinging terror at his Inas being hurt.

I have to do something.

He helped pull her to her feet.

"I...I might know more now." Enos looked up into his eyes. "I experienced snatches of sensation. What Majus Ayama and I did must have prompted it. Finally. It has to be enough. We need to find him *now*." She bit her lip, shaking. Sam's hands trembled. Inas was more important than anything else. They needed to be together again. Their trio was bigger than just he and Enos, and the two of them couldn't hold everything between them. Had the Life Coalition hurt him before? Was this simply the first time Enos felt it?

Have to get him out.

Sam turned to look out the apartment's window. He could see the top of the Spire of the Maji. The higher rooftops of the Imperium stretched out behind it.

"You have to leave the apartment, Sam," Enos said. "Inas is in pain. You've had your rest, but you need to come back to us. Tell Majus Ayama and Majus Cyrysi about the voice. We need to find him."

He looked down at her, then leaned forward and rested his forehead on hers. "I know," he whispered. Even just thinking about Inas in pain made his heart pound. He'd been hiding, after what happened in the Assembly, what happened to his friend. It was time to stop hiding. He reached for his pocketwatch, to feel the smooth metal casing.

"For Inas." For the three of them.

Enos gently pushed him away, then brushed her warm hand down his cheek. "I know what you've been going through, Sam, but Inas may not have a lot of time."

Sam closed his eyes, but Enos tugged at his arms. "Come on."

He gave in to her tugging and took a step forward. "You're right. You're always right. Just stay near me."

Together, they opened the door to Majus Cyrysi's apartment. For Inas.

CHAPTER TWO

Hunting Notes

- The physical building of the House of Communication is a source of pride to those who belong to the house. It is the tallest of the Houses, only second in height to the Spire itself, and that building rests against one of the endless columns of the Nether. Why was the structure built so tall? It generates complaints from many who do not wish to climb the stairs, but the original intent is forgotten, as it was built before the Aridori War and all records have been lost. Some argue the bridge connecting the tower to the wall of the Nether is a reason for the height, but as far as my research shows, it has no actual purpose.

A section of a report on the Houses of the Maji, filed in the Spire archives, 458 A.A.W., Author unknown

Rilan stomped along next to Ori, down a corridor in the Spire of the Maji. The more space she put between her and the Council's chambers, the better. She kept pace with her good friend for once, which showed how angry she was.

"So that meeting was not to be as bad as it could have been," Ori offered.

Rilan growled at him. When she looked over, his crest was flattened in submission. She sighed.

"I'm not angry at you, Ori," she said. "It's just...Shiv's eyes! I can't believe they have the *gall* to offer me a position as adjunct to the Council. As if they aren't sure I can handle the job!"

"They should not have been giving your old position to Szaler in the first place," Ori said.

Rilan waved a hand. She wasn't angry at Szaler either, though he had looked down at her from *her* old seat. He was a highly skilled surgeon, and deserved the position. He was competent in the Symphony, and ran the medical ward attached to the House of Healing.

"I refused it the first time they offered," she said, stepping around a pair of Lobath maji, deep in discussion. The Spire wafted in music from one of the newer quartets in High Imperium. They must have captured a live recording of a performance. "Truth be told, I don't want the position back. I'm too busy hunting down the Life Coalition and trying to find Inas. But I never realized without it, I'd have to beg for resources to track down the organization responsible for almost *killing the entire Assembly!*" She threw her hands up. "Bleagh."

"They are to be watching our progress," Ori offered. "We are close to finding the last concentration of their forces."

"It would be easier if Councilor Feldo was with the rest of the Council, but no one's seen him lately. The others are incompetent. We've been 'close' for a month," Rilan said, "and all that time, Enos' brother has been in their power. Who knows what they're doing to him? The Assembly Speakers think the Life Coalition is on the run, but they're consolidating their strength as fast as we find their hiding places." They exited into a vaulted hallway, populated by statues of previous members of the Council. Rilan's eyes were drawn to the stout plinth representing Ribothari Tan, Knower, one of the best known historic Council leaders. Every apprentice could quote his treatise on the House of Healing. They passed along the atrium, nodding to other maji.

"The girl says she can connect with her brother, creepy as that is, but we're going too slow," Rilan said as they got to the other end and turned left into one of the perimeter corridors. "I'm certain Inas is the key to creating a stable portal, but we need more information to provide the correct location vectors."

"Then you are not to be against using the Aridori's abilities when it suits your purpose." Ori's crest was carefully neutral.

Rilan barely kept from making the old superstitious gesture—two fingers across the eyes—when talking about the Aridori. She should be past that, since one was her *apprentice.*

"The adage says 'never trust what an Aridori says or does,'" she grumbled, "not 'don't take advantage of an Aridori.'"

"Are you really believing that?" Ori asked, and Rilan sighed.

"No, I don't." Enos was a good apprentice, and a staggeringly smart person. She was trustworthy and she'd go high in the House of Healing, one day. Rilan needed to stop acting like a bigot. "I'm frustrated at our slow progress. We're so *close* to finding the Life Coalition's main headquarters."

"What is to be the reason for such speed, Rilan?" Ori asked. His crest was spiky in anticipation. He was picking up on her nervousness, and he was right. Something *was* driving her to go faster, and it wasn't just Inas, though that was important.

She clenched her teeth, thinking, then veered into a side passage and stopped. She took his large hand, stroking her fingers down his until she could feel the points of his fingernails. She remembered the electric shiver of them running down her back last night. Their time together was keeping her sane. Chasing after a genocidal coalition who said they wanted peace, while trying to rescue an Aridori from them—the perpetrators of the *last* genocide, a thousand cycles ago—was enough to drive anyone bonkers.

"The Life Coalition's waiting, I know it," she finally said. She could feel it in her bones, and even in the Symphony. "Otherwise they'd make their play and wouldn't keep pulling back. I've got to find out what they want before they do...whatever it is. And we have to get Inas back."

"And you will be doing this how?" Ori asked. "How can I be helping you be at peace?"

She frowned. That wasn't what she thought he would ask. She didn't need to be at peace. She needed to root out the Life Coalition and get the Aridori back. If he wanted to do more...

"You have voids to study, or you could focus on your apprentice for once—see if you can drag him out of his room,"

"I am having much to do," Ori agreed, and his large purple eyes drilled into her. "But none of it is to be as important as you." Now he was the one holding her hand. His fingers swallowed hers, massaging them. "Tell me."

Rilan felt her chin lift, though she knew Ori could read the signs of her lie before she even said anything. "Tell you what?" She ignored the tightness in her throat.

His crest was spreading flat, curled at the tips in disappointment. "You have been drawing away from *us*," he said, then abruptly looked up and behind her, waiting until someone passed by. Rilan forced herself not to look around, to show she wasn't distracted.

"We've been busy rooting out the Life Coalition," she said, once he looked back. "And anyway, just last night we—"

"Stop," he said, and her eyes flicked away from his, unable to hold them any longer. They'd been together too long for secrets to stay secret, but still she resisted. She wasn't *ready*.

"Why is this search consuming you? Inas is not to be the reason, though he is important."

"But once we find him—"

"No," he broke in again, and Rilan pursed her lips. The obvious reply was to accuse him of interrupting her, keeping her from telling the truth.

Another lie. They had fought beside each other, interdependent, taking each other's every word as absolute truth. She knew what he would do next, as much as he knew what she would do.

Then why couldn't she tell him what scared her?

Her mouth was dry, but Ori only stared back. His crest flicked up, then out, moving as he saw emotion, lies, and truth flit across her face. It was like looking in a mirror,

"I can't—" she began, tried again. "I can't..."

No, that was all there was.

Ori, Brahm bless him, was nodding. "I am to be having trouble too, after the Life Coalition attacked the Nether—the one place we thought was impenetrable."

She clutched his thick, gnarled hands, brought them up to her face to kiss them. There was water on her cheeks. She hadn't realized she was crying.

"I had the power to direct a thousand maji," she said, and it came out as a whisper. "I could change the direction of homeworlds, or so I thought. The others kept me in the dark, laughing behind my back." She tried to stop, but couldn't, not pressed against Ori in a side corridor on the sixteenth floor of the Spire.

"Then they *removed* me, Ori. They took all that away as easily as if I was still an apprentice." Her voice dropped to a whisper, but the words were pulled from her. "They removed me right after the Life Coalition destroyed my city and killed..."

Killed my father. That strong, hardworking, stubborn, destitute man.

Ori enfolded her in his sturdy arms. His leathery, musky scent comforted her. "And you are wanting to take all this out on them." He leaned in closer, his lips on her ear. "Yet they do not matter. Can you not simply be satisfied with me for once?"

Rilan pulled back to look at Ori and saw her surprise reflected in the heft of his crest. She'd not only hurt herself by folding inward. They'd promised to give their old arrangement another try. She was pulling away before they'd even had a chance.

"We will be finding the Life Coalition and Inas together," Ori said. "With our other friends. You are not needing to be on the Council to have power. I was telling you this before you joined."

"You said it was a mistake," she said. It wasn't quite an accusation.

"I did, and I am still believing it. Your fire cannot be restrained."

Rilan pushed him away, not hard, but with enough force to let him know she had herself back together. "You're right." She was strong. She would continue, no matter what. Her father would have wanted her to do that.

She laughed, and the tightness inside loosened for the first time since the void appeared over her hometown of Dalhni. "Right as always."

"I will be requesting you repeat that the next time you disagree with—"

His words were cut off by an ear-shattering ringing, like Brahm himself had thrown all the kitchen crystal down the stairs.

"What by all the gods is that?" she shouted, one hand going to her ear, the other to her belt knife.

Ori's crest was going in all directions. "I do not know, but I am knowing that you are also correct. Too many strange things are happening, and I have voids to be studying."

As one, they started for the sky bridge.

* * *

Sam looked down the spiral stairs in the House of Communication, making sure he didn't step wrong and end up tumbling down the steps. Enos tugged at his shirt. Majus Cyrysi and Majus Ayama were charging up toward them. The old Kirian stopped dead, one hand on the banister, a boot poised to take the next step, his crest spiky.

"Ah. Sam. You are to be out of the apartment." He was trying to hide his astonishment, not that Sam could blame him, but the crest gave him away.

"Enos finally convinced me," Sam said. "Along with that weird ringing." And now the explaining and excuses would begin. Sam could feel the heat building in his face.

"Then this is to be growth. Good," Majus Cyrysi said. He fiddled with the sleeves of his robe a moment. "Speaking of that odd sound, now that it is thankfully to be gone, Rilan and I are needing to speak with you about your new abilities with the Symphony."

Sam bit back the apology on the tip of his tongue. Majus Cyrysi seemed...relieved. Well, if he didn't want to talk about Sam's self-imposed exile, then Sam wouldn't either. He could practically feel Enos ready to jump in.

"Ori and I gathered some of his research from a library in the Spire on the way here," Majus Ayama said. "The harmonics in the Symphony from that cacophony are like a few of the ones he recorded when you changed notes for him." She paused. "Good to see you out."

Majus Ayama was too much of a psychologist not to make some comment. He should really have a session with her again. They helped.

"We also were collecting some of my recent research," Majus Cyrysi said. "There is an aspect of the chime that triggers some memory, though I am not remembering from where. Something I have read. However, the sound was also giving me a novel idea how you may give us more clues to the Life Coalition's location. Rilan and I were discussing the urgency." The Kirian waved his claw-tipped fingers through the air, as if that would explain it. "By attuning your realization of the frequencies of matter around the areas where the portals were opened between the Nether and the places the Life Coalition were hiding, I am believing we may be able to—"

Sam let the Symphony theory wash over his head. He was terrible at it, no matter how much the majus tried to teach him. If the Kirian wanted to ask him about the ethics of a rogue group of maji trying to overthrow the Assembly of Species, he could have come up with an answer. He vaguely remembered taking classes on law.

I wanted to be a teacher, back on Earth, didn't I?

Instead, he heard deeper tones in the Symphony than Majus Cyrysi. And 'deeper' was not quite the right term—the majus had some five-syllable word for it Sam couldn't remember. There were notes hidden under the principal themes of the Grand Symphony, like the ones he'd changed when they fought with the Coalitioners in the Bazaar and disrupted the Nether's translation between his assailants. The notes were fundamental to the Symphony—something others couldn't hear.

"Does that mean the notes in common between the portals and the chime could be linked to Sam's house?" Enos said, and Sam stared at her. She had understood all that?

"I've been working with Majus Ayama and Majus Cyrysi while you were..."

"Hiding," Sam offered. He should feel more, saying that. He should have been sad, or panicky, or even guilty. There was a void in him, like the inside of a Drain. The voice that spoke to him had taken memories when it disappeared. Ever since, Sam had seen his surroundings as if through a lens of water. Everything was slightly closer to him than he thought it was.

"Er, yes," Enos said, giving him an apologetic look. "In any case, portals have intrigued me since Majus Ayama and I are working on creating one to reach Inas. Every majus can create them. Why? And you hear different frequencies than those of the other six houses." She leaned against the banister.

"Exactly what I am to be saying," Majus Cyrysi said. He looked back to Sam, his crest rising in anticipation. "Now you are out of the apartment, we can be going to some of the chambers in the Spire which have newer aural equipment. If you can be transcribing the tones you hear, we can correlate their frequencies with the exit points of the portals."

"Maybe they *are* all connected," Majus Ayama offered. "Could the sound be another attack by the Life Coalition? Though it only rattled my teeth."

"Ineffectual if it was," Enos said. "Are they building a new kind of Drain?"

"Not a Drain," Majus Cyrysi said. "The chime was part of the Grand Symphony. A Drain is to be an absence of it."

"I don't believe in coincidences, not after the last few months," Majus Ayama said.

"Neither do I," Sam agreed. He was starting to feel like he had before the attack at the Dome. He pushed his shoulders back.

Enos was right to push me out of the apartment.

He would make his own choices. He wouldn't be held down by a phantom he wasn't even sure was real. It would be good to see Majus Caroom and Majus Hand Dancer again. The only one missing out of their group was Inas.

And that thought sent his mood spiraling away. Had he really hidden in his room rather than looking for one of two people who truly understood him? He reached for Enos' hand, and she looked up, concerned when he touched her.

"Let's get downstairs, and then I promise I'll help you find the Life Coalition," he said. The knuckles on his other hand were white where they gripped the banister.

Majus Ayama nodded, but Majus Cyrysi looked down the spiral staircase as if he had forgotten they were standing on it. "Yes, yes. You two may be assisting me. I believe Rilan has some other preparation."

"How is the portal coming?" asked Enos as they trudged down the stairs.

"Slow," Majus Ayama answered. "I'm at a loss for where to get more information. You've been very helpful, but at this point I'm not sure you'll be able to contribute anything concrete."

Sam traded a look with Enos. Perhaps they could help.

"About that," Enos said, and both maji perked up. "Sam and I discovered something."

Majus Ayama stopped again and looked up the stairs to them. "What is this? Information about the Life Coalition? Did you connect with Inas?" Majus Ayama's whisper was like a blade of air. Her braid hung over one shoulder of her padded jacket, and her belt knife clinked against the banister as she leaned in.

"Enos had a seizure when she came to visit me," Sam said, then darted a look to his friend, and up and down the stairs. They were alone, and safe to talk. She was frowning, but it wasn't the 'we'll speak later' frown, just the one that said she was concerned. Then she wasn't planning to keep this from her mentor.

"What happened? Are you well?" White and olive spiraled up Majus Ayama's arm, but Enos waved her off.

"I am well. I think it was an effect of the experiments we have performed." Her eyes lit up. "I felt him—I could sense Inas!"

They spent the next few minutes filling the maji in on what happened. Sam saw the uncertainty in Majus Ayama's face as they spoke of the connection between two Aridori.

She still isn't comfortable with Enos.

But the majus didn't let her emotions interfere. Sam wished he had her control.

"Can you give me specific markers?" the majus asked. "Sights? Sounds? Tastes?"

"I...I think so," Enos said. She groped in the air with both hands. "There are textures, and a few sounds. How do I...?"

"Transfer them? Best to have someone from the House of Communication," Majus Ayama rolled her eyes toward Majus Cyrysi.

Sam's mentor had his crest fluffed, enough for the Nether to translate that the new ability also disconcerted him. Sam gripped Enos' hand.

She needs support just as much as I do. She's lost her brother, and has a secret people would literally kill her over. I've been terrible to her.

"I'll be there with you," he said, and Enos gave him a small smile.

"We'll get the details when we get down," Majus Ayama said, her eyes still locked on Enos. "Or Ori will."

They continued down the stairs, but Enos kept her hand in his.

"You don't mind that I told them?" he whispered.

"Anything to help Inas," she answered.

CHAPTER THREE

Impossible Portals

*- Yes, portals are strange. When you learn to open them—and you
will learn—you'll find your friends can too. It's shared by all six houses
of the maji, and no one knows why, so don't ask me. There are a lot of
theories floating around, but I've never read one that convinced me of
some secret part of the Symphony everyone has been missing. I think
it's just a part of the music that doesn't depend on which house you can
hear.*

*Part of a lecture by Rilan Ayama, then head of House of Healing,
speaking to apprentice maji*

Enos fiddled as she sat in the uncomfortable chair, a notepad in her
lap. It had been a busy two days since she'd gotten Sam to leave his
room. Most of it involved first working with Majus Cyrysi to dig out and
transfer the nuggets of sensation she'd experienced through Inas, and
then with Majus Ayama to add to the composition the majus was
creating to get her brother back from the Life Coalition. The whorls of
music her mentor composed were faster than she could process—more
complex than she'd ever heard. The usual structure for creating a portal
was a child banging on instruments in comparison.

During those days, Sam had been good to his word, staying with her,
even when he had to use his watch as a focus. Ever since the Life
Coalition attacked the Assembly, his anxiety had bloomed. Enos
thought over what he'd said of the voice in the Drain. It was almost like
her connection with Inas, but so much more invasive. She and her
brother co-existed and required each other. What Sam described was a
violation.

Enos looked over to him, sitting on her right. His hands were
clenched tight, knuckles white. They both needed Inas back. The time
while her brother had been captured—her other instance, the other
path she could have trod in life—was like missing a piece of her soul.
She'd never been away from him for so long.

Majus Cyrysi was wandering the spare chamber, situated on the sixteenth floor of the Spire of the Maji. A few high windows illuminated the space, but by the dust, it hadn't been used in some time. His feet made trails of footprints on the tiled floor, his robe sweeping circles around him and his crest flaring and swooping as if he were thinking deep thoughts. He didn't wait well, and Majus Ayama had called this meeting of everyone working with them to find the Life Coalition, after she had a breakthrough in the last few lightenings. A small fire of hope kindled in Enos' chest that the sensations from Inas had helped.

She'd felt him trapped in a box. Why was he there? Was it meant to make him reach out to her? Had the Life Coalition broken Inas and was now trying to capture her? She realized she was grinding her teeth and forced her jaw to relax.

Nara Reyhorer was the only other one in the room. Rey had surprised them all by ambling in soon after they arrived, and plopping down next to her and Sam. She hadn't seen the Sureri often since Inas had been captured. He'd been close to Inas, and Enos wondered what might have happened between them had Sam not arrived. But Rey hadn't shared in their fight with the Life Coalition. He was watching the Kirian pace, and she wondered why Majus Ayama had called him in.

Sam reached over and squeezed her hand, and Enos tensed. She hadn't been expecting the gesture, but he must have seen the worry on her face. Her control was slipping. There were only a few who knew of her true species. Her familiarity with the maji made her complacent. She grasped for the mask she'd shown Majus Ayama when she first became her apprentice.

"It'll be fine," Sam said. "Majus Ayama has a plan."

Enos sighed. Sometimes Sam assumed she thought the same way he did. She wondered, again, what it would be like if he had a connection to her as Inas did. The last month had brought them closer, and she felt she had an unfair advantage over Inas in their relationship. How many long talks would Sam need with Inas, once they found him, before they were all truly together again? Instead, the Life Coalition was baiting her with her other instance's suffering.

Enos' heart sped at the thought, and she squeezed Sam's hand back, then smoothed her pant leg. She remembered the texture of the dirt under her—Inas'—feet. The surge of emotion from him had been stronger than anything experienced in close proximity. What did it mean, being this far apart, with that strong an emotion? Had the Life Coalition learned from the other Aridori they'd captured—the unstable mess they'd found in Gloomlight prison? Were they doing the same with Inas?

Rey leaned over. "Eyah, so the majus is wantin' to finish off the Life Coalition? Won't they kill Inas for doin' that? Better to talk with 'em, I think. Some o' the representatives from my world even think the Snakey's aren't all bad. They say they're about peace, and lookin' fer a better life. Then again, some of 'em also think the Drain in the Assembly were a hoax."

The statement was so foreign, it stunned Enos out of a response. People were arguing in *favor* of the terrorist organization? They dismissed the Drains that killed so many people? But then, no Drain had occurred on Rey's homeworld, at least not where anyone had observed it. People were stubborn, when they couldn't see the evidence with their own eyes, and sometimes when they could.

"The Life Coalition *took* Inas from us," Sam hissed across her, and Rey held up both hands in surrender. A beam of afternoon light from the wall highlighted his hair, cut short to match the fuzz that covered the rest of his skin. She'd thought Rey's family, the Nara, were one of the less xenophobic families, but not if they thought the Life Coalition was a viable organization.

"Aye, they did, but yer also were goin' after them and tryin' to fight rather than speakin' to an agreement," Rey argued. "I want Inas back as much as yer do, and I'm thinkin' they'll give him back if we just ask nice. We've got 'em on the edge. It's time to bargain."

"She had a vision of Inas," Sam said, and Enos stiffened. Her tongue stuck to the roof of her mouth. He'd spoken before she could stop him. She specifically *hadn't* told Rey. He didn't know about her species. "The Life Coalition was hurting him."

Rey's hairy face scrunched into a grimace, making him even uglier. "Vision? How's that? Some majus thing I know naught about? House of Healing, eyah? Me house can't do that."

Play dumb, Enos thought furiously toward Sam. She tried to think of anything she could say that wouldn't sound suspicious, but her mind was blank, her tongue immovable. She stared at the others, useful as a dead fish, her mouth open. Her hands shook at the risk of revelation, drilled into her by her parents. If it had been Inas beside her, he might have understood her intent by the link between Aridori instances. But Inas wasn't here.

Instead, Sam's face changed to an expression of horror.

"Uh...yes, it's from the House of Healing, isn't it Enos?" he said, trying to cover his slip. Enos closed her mouth only to clench her teeth. They'd lasted a month without revealing her and Inas's species. It had taken days of pleading with Majus Ayama, though Maji Cyrysi, Caroom, and Hand Dancer backed her up. She loved Sam dearly, but how could he be so good at blurting out exactly the *wrong* thing?

Think of something.

Enos smiled at Rey. She wasn't certain what Inas saw in the Sureri. He was brash and loudmouthed, and only a little less bigoted than other Sureriaj she'd met. But then, Inas made friends a lot easier than she did.

Change the subject. Get away from the Aridori.

"Don't you think the Life Coalition should be destroyed? After what they did to the Dome of the Assembly?" The Drain the Coalition started there badly damaged the building. The attack demonstrated even the impenetrable substance of the Nether was not immune to a Drain's space-warping effects.

"Oh, aye," Rey answered, "but yee've got to look at the reputation the maji and the Council have bodged together for themselves. They're not greatly liked at the moment. What with the fears o' the Aridori, people are upset. Yee've got to admit the Life Coalition has some effective propaganda, callin' for peace for everyone."

Enos stiffened at the mention of her species. Sam did the same. She'd not done enough to derail Rey.

"Surely you can't put the Assembly and the maji on the same scale as the Aridori?" She thought her voice stayed quite calm while asking the question. Their parents had trained them to stay aware of people's response to the "extinct" race.

"Enos," Sam said, but she put her hand on his without even looking. She knew where they would be, clasped and wringing against each other in his lap. His pulse was fast. She didn't think he would have an anxiety attack, but he was not calm and neither was she. He fell silent at her touch.

"What?" Rey asked, jutting his receding chin forward. "Wha's he gonna say, ey? Are yer to claim the maji don't have nasty spots?"

"That's not it," Sam said. "All organizations have problems when they get too big, or powerful. I just...I don't think you can equate what the Life Coalition's done with anything the maji have done."

"And how long've yer been here again?" Rey asked.

Lately, any mention of Sam's homeworld sent him into a panic. When there was time, she needed to dig into what the voice said to him, without making him retreat into his anxiety. It wasn't always easy to tell Sam's panic states apart.

"I've...I've been here long enough," Sam stuttered. Enos could see him breathing too fast, and her belly clenched in agreement. "I've studied."

"Eyah, but yer did no see it," Rey pressed. "Me homeworld's not rich, but we work hard. There were rumors a few cycles back of the maji interfering in inter-family politics—changin' the way we govern things. What's to say the Life Coalition don't have the right idea, shakin' things up?"

"Attempting to *assassinate* the entire Great Assembly is not the same as 'shaking things up,'" Enos snapped at Rey, and his eyes opened wide. She took in a long breath. The vision of Inas made her itchy, like she was coming down from the heightened sensation of changing her form.

But Rey wasn't done. "Aye, it's no the same, but yer hafta admit the Life Coalition has some good points. They say they want us to be at peace, that together, we can work ter havin' more resources fer everyone. How is that bad?"

"They put us in a *cell*, Rey," Sam said. His voice was gaining heat, and Enos felt his pulse even out, under her hand. He'd told her anger blunted the effects of a panic attack.

"They did say they weren't trying to harm us," she reminded Sam.

"Weren't try—" Sam broke off, his mouth hanging open, staring at her. Enos had to look away from that glare.

She had been the one who forced their escape from the cell. Revealed herself to him, in a moment of terror for her life. He was right—the Life Coalition *hadn't* planned to hurt them, but when they figured out she was an Aridori, she was as good as dead.

Except they've kept Inas alive. For what purpose?

"Eyah," Rey sat back with a smug smile. "I'm not saying the Life Coalition is so great, o' course. Just some of what they say makes some sense. Just talk to 'em and we can get Inas back."

Enos pressed down on Sam's hand as he attempted to rise to his feet.

"Quiet!" barked another voice, and they froze and looked toward Majus Ayama. As they'd been arguing, other maji had drifted in, and were staring at the three of them. Enos sunk down in her seat. How much had they heard? She risked a glance to Majus Hand Dancer, seated nearby. The slender Lobhl flipped a complicated hand gesture toward her. The Nether translated it as contrite, shared embarrassment.

Majus Caroom, to their other side, humphed and leaned back against a pillar. Their species didn't sit.

"If you apprentices are quite finished," Majus Ayama snapped at them, "I'd like to share my progress on creating a portal to the Life Coalition's main forces." She scowled at Enos. "We are trying to save your brother, last I checked."

* * *

Rilan glared around the room. Everyone who had been helping her track the Life Coalition was here. Ori, of course, had insisted on standing near her, as if he was also in charge. She'd hoped he'd caught the hint she'd prefer to give this speech alone. She held back the sigh and looked from Sam to Enos to Rey, heads bowed like ducklings unsure where the crocodile was. They'd almost ruined the atmosphere of the room, and her announcement was one that required attention.

Here it goes.

She smoothed her hands down her sides to keep them from shaking. This was the reason she'd called everyone together. It was time to finally corner the rogue organization.

"After a month of research, I have an answer for you." She leaned forward, almost coming up on the toes of her boots. She could practically taste the anticipation in the room. As much as she distrusted—no, truthfully she *feared*—Enos' abilities as an Aridori, they had been invaluable in creating the complex composition she held even now in the back of her mind. The music tugged at her, urging her to express it. They'd only get one chance for surprise.

All eyes were on her, and she reveled in the tension for a couple seconds. She could almost smell it.

"The Life Coalition's main headquarters is on—no, *inside*—a moon of Sath Home," Rilan revealed. She wanted to bounce up and down. She hadn't even told Ori. The calculations—double and triple checked—had taken her an hour. Little wonder she hadn't been able to find them. "They must have had a majus from the House of Communication create breathable air."

The exclamations of surprise were worth the suspense. Hand Dancer gestured wildly, and Ori's crest looked like he'd just stepped into a blast of wind.

<This location is highly unlikely,> Hand Dancer—who was male, at the moment—signed. The Lobhl rarely held expression in their faces, but Hand Dancer's eyes were even wider than usual. His fingers popped and danced in the air with alarm. <Have you verified this data with any Sathssn? I am unaware of further programs to venture into the space around homeworlds.>

Rilan paused to see if the Lobhl was making a joke, but it seemed he wasn't. The mute, genderfluid species had a strange sense of humor, and of honor.

"This Sathssn, you can check with *me*," Kheena—Rey's mentor—protested. "This, it is more than 'highly unlikely.' It is completely impossible." He took a step forward from his place near the door and pushed his cowl back to reveal a face covered in light green scales, set around bright red eyes. Kheena was a newcomer to their group, but Rilan had invited him because of his proficiency in the House of Potential, and with portals, and because he was already connected to Rey. He was nowhere near as religious as the Life Coalition or the Most Traditional Servants. He was more also representative of the quick minds and scholarly bent of the Sathssn, instead of the small organization tarnishing the species' reputation.

"The Methiemum's space program, it was the only one of its kind, and that failed, as Majus Cyrysi can tell you."

Ori shot the Sathssn a sour look and Rilan raised a hand half toward him. Ori stepped back, sulking, his crest flat. The crash landing hadn't totally been his fault.

"Well they got there *somehow*," Rilan told him. "You may want to ask higher-ranking members of your government, Majus Kheena. The Most Traditional Servants have access to a surprising amount of information."

<I feel I must investigate this question more, if it does not cause offense.> Hand Dancer's flashing fingers conveyed his disbelief, and it rang in Rilan's head like a just-remembered sequence of words, courtesy of the Nether's translation of languages and intent. <How were Sathssn able to travel off their planet to a place no one has ever visited?>

"Me, I have no idea," Kheena said. "The dioceses hierarchs would certainly make a new revelation available to my people, were they able to travel through space without a majus."

"More important, is this one absolutely certain the calculations are, hmm, correct?" Caroom rumbled the question, their bright green eyes flashing with interest. "What information backs up this, hmm, claim?" It was the most involved she'd seen the Benish in a month. Benish didn't show depression in the same way as Methiemum, but Caroom was hurting and frustrated with their inability to rescue Inas. "Further, even with facts pointing to this, hmm, novel location, it does not matter without a way for *this* group to reach the same location using, hmm, a portal." Caroom rumbled. As usual, they cut to the heart of the matter.

"Excellent question," Rilan said, choosing to ignore Hand Dancer's part of the puzzle. She'd thought about it, but there was no simple answer. "It leads me to the second part of my announcement: I can make a portal to this moon." More mutterings from the group before their last member asked the obvious question.

"You can make a portal to a location unknown to the maji?" Panen asked. Rilan had known the wari—the third gender of the Lobath— socially for many cycles. Timpomitnob Gompt, Watcher, an old friend, had vouched for hir when they'd had lunch a few ten-days ago. Rilan had asked for a recommendation of a trusted member of the House of Grace, since Gompt was busy with some project or other. Rilan hadn't seen the old Festuour in a while.

As with an orchestra, it was important to have all the instruments. With adding Panen, Kheena, and Rey, the maji and their apprentices in this room covered all six houses of the maji—and whatever Sam was.

The most powerful changes to the Symphony always required the music of the six houses in tandem. Sam, however, was an enigma. She'd seen him change materials into another element altogether. Ori, in a moment of weakness, had revealed how jealous he was of his apprentice.

Panen had hir head-tentacles tied up in a mass on top of hir head, and hir continually surprised eyes held Rilan in place. Panen was sharp enough to know when she wasn't being completely truthful. It also helped zie was of the House of Grace. That house was almost as good with interpersonal interactions as the House of Healing. "I trust no Life Coalition members have given you the coordinates."

"Correct," Rilan said. This was the tricky part—revealing how she'd created the calculation for the portal's musical signature without revealing she'd been mentoring an *Aridori*, for Brahm's sake. She tapped her fingers together in front of her. "I was fortunate to gather several specific identifiers—scents, textures, and visuals—about the Life Coalition's location, enabling me to construct a composition. It *should* allow me to recreate a portal to this moon."

"Should?" Caroom repeated. "This one has not, hmm, tested the portal?"

"Of course not!" Rilan drew in a breath and lowered her voice when she next spoke. She shouldn't have snapped. "The only advantage we have over the Life Coalition is surprise. They have their hooks in some of the dioceses, and they have supplies hidden all over the ten homeworlds. We'll only get one chance at this."

Surprisingly, Rey was the next to speak. He glanced around at the maji, as if he was waiting for someone to ask the same thing.

"I know a smidge about portals—not near as much as yerself or me mentor, o'course—but ain't it one o' the hardest compositions to create a portal from scratch? Yer'd need—what—enough identifiers to define the melody of a place yer'd never experienced? It's nigh impossible to do such a thing!"

Rilan gave him her best piercing glare. "Yes. I *am* that good."

Rey slunk down in his chair. She gave the Sureri credit, though. Kheena must be an excellent teacher. She'd never created such a complex musical structure without hearing the original piece in the Symphony, or having it transferred to her from another majus.

Hand Dancer gestured with his overlarge hands. <Have you asked the Council about this? Such an aggressive move would require their approval, would it not?>

Rilan shook her head.

"The Council was to be giving us their permission to investigate the Life Coalition," Ori said. "We are still to be operating under that assumption."

It was a weak argument. Feldo had *implied* to Ori—when he visited the Council alone—that their group should look into the strange coincidences concerning the Drains, the secession of a sect of the Sathssn, and several attacks on the maji. They'd been operating under that directive since before they knew the Life Coalition existed. Rilan hastily cut off any other arguments.

"The Council—or what remains of it, now Councilor Feldo has disappeared—never rescinded their directive to track down the Life Coalition," she hedged. "We must keep them from creating any more voids. The threat to the homeworlds is too great."

The Coalition had made no more voids since the one at the Assembly, and Rilan hoped they no longer could, but Ori's studies had revealed nothing new about the aberrations that disobeyed the laws of the universe. She scanned the gathered maji. The Life Coalition used all six houses to create the voids, and Ori insisted they needed all six to stop them.

"Then you are asking this group to, hmm, directly engage a rogue group of maji and soldiers?" Caroom asked.

"I believe it is the only way we will get your apprentice back," Rilan answered. Caroom knew Inas was an Aridori, though Panen, Kheena, and Rey did not.

Caroom grunted, a deep thump like a felled tree hitting the ground. "Then shall this group open the portal now?"

Rilan tried to contain her shock. "What, here? Now?"

"This one has the melody," Caroom said, extending their hand with a creak. "One's apprentice is a month missing. Is there a better, hmm, time?"

There was silence. When a Benish—a slow and contemplative species—was pushing for quick and decisive action, it paid to listen.

"We could find Inas now?" Sam asked, popping to his feet as if his pants had caught fire. Rilan's apprentice was only a moment after him. Enos' eyes were wide, her hands clenched by her sides.

"In addition, we may be able to be capturing some portion of their leaders, or perhaps learning the method by which they were creating the Drains." Ori's crest was high with excitement.

"This, it is a perilous method of travel, majus," Kheena cautioned. "Are you certain it will work?"

Rilan clamped her teeth together to keep from making a snarky remark. She nearly succeeded.

"There's one way to find out." The music tugged at the back of her head, begging to be made into reality.

"I must make one more observation," Panen put in. "We are not at a registered portal ground, so technically this is illegal."

No one said anything.

Then, "This group is aware of, hmm, the risks," Caroom said. "Yet one wishes greatly to see one's apprentice. If others of this group are not satisfied, those ones could leave before, hmmm, being a party to this illegality."

No one moved.

Rilan could feel the rhythms she'd built up rising from her center. They could surprise those murderers right now. Stop the Assembly from falling apart.

"I'm going to try the portal," she called out, already taking notes from her core. She placed them in the sequences she'd grown to know well in the last month. Feet in dirt, darkness around, rough walls, musty air, echoes of speech from the close walls...

Someone might have called out for her to wait, but Rilan closed her eyes and placed the last notes in the musical sequence. A portal was a bridge between the melody of the place one was in and the place one wanted to go.

Rilan could *feel* the portal trying to connect. Just a little more. Change one more note. One more adjustment.

Now someone *did* cry out.

That was Enos.

She swallowed and opened her eyes. The others were staring at her. Panen had one foot forward, as if zie would stop her, but there was no oval of black rotating into existence. The resistance in the Symphony weighed against her like a lump of lead. The composition wasn't yet complete enough to open the portal.

"It was not opening," Ori said, always willing to state the obvious.

"I can *tell* that," she snarled, then ran a hand through her hair and down the braid that trailed down her back. She stared up at the vaulted ceiling of the little meeting room. "Shiv rot my teeth!" she cursed, then looked back at the assembled maji.

"Well, this was a waste of time. A secret one person holds is still secret. But now you all know how close we are, we need to strike before the Life Coalition gets word, through whatever means, that we have found their base of operations."

That was when she saw Enos, fingers curved and grasping her head. Sam bent over her like a hen poised over her eggs.

"What happened?" Rilan called. Several of the others were watching Enos silently gasping and writhing. Rilan was two steps closer before she realized what she was doing, one hand extended with olive and white swirls forming around it. The music of the portal faded into the background, replaced by the strains of the House of Healing. Now it would be doubly hard to open the portal any time soon. The Symphony would resist her.

"Let me help—" she began, but a frantic Methiemum apprentice burst into the room, panting.

"Maji and apprentices," she gasped, "you are all required immediately at the Dome of the Assembly. The leaders of the Life Coalition have appeared, and demanded a place in the Great Assembly."

CHAPTER FOUR

Becoming Anew

- In the four ten-days since the attack on the Assembly, we have discovered eight locations where the Life Coalition has hidden supplies. We also determined they had an army of at least eight thousand troops before the attack. Not all were trained, but the Coalition co-opted several well-known commanders of military divisions from all over the ten homeworlds. The troops they committed to the push in the Dome of the Assembly were their least trained, and, I think, expected to fail. Only because Sam redirected the void of energy—I still don't know how he managed it—were we able to cut their takeover off at the knees.

From the notes of Rilan Ayama, majus of the House of Healing.

Sam followed the others, half supporting Enos. She waved off her mentor's help, saying she was well. Sam wasn't convinced, but with the flood of maji leaving the Spire and heading for the Dome of the Assembly, there wasn't time to stop and investigate.

"Did you see him again?" he asked Enos. She had been silent since they left the chamber. Sam had been busy negotiating the twisting halls and stairs without having a panic attack. He'd been holed up in Majus Cyrysi's apartment too long.

He marked features of the landscape as their group headed to the tram connecting the Spire and the Dome. It kept him calm and made the Imperium more familiar. Sam squinted against the bright midday light from the walls of the Nether, which towered above and passed out of view far overhead.

"I did not *see* anything," Enos whispered. "But I experienced Inas' presence again. My skin was cold, as if pressed against metal."

They walked a few more steps.

"Fear." Enos raised her head, though she still leaned on him. "He was afraid. Sam, I have no idea what the Life Coalition is doing to him, but it must be terrifying for me to feel so much from him."

"And we can't do anything. I thought Majus Ayama's portal would work. Everything she does is successful," Sam said.

Not like me. I'm useless. Can't even walk across the Spire grounds without getting anxious.

Ever since the presence forced its way into his head, his thoughts had been scattered. Though the voice had vanished with the Drain and hadn't returned, he struggled with daily fear as he had when new to the Nether. Now, instead of fretting he wouldn't find a way back to Earth, he simply couldn't *remember* Earth.

"While what she did obviously didn't work," Enos said, "it created a bridge between me and my other instance." That sounded more like her regular self, though the last two words were so quiet Sam almost couldn't hear them. "I think the portal may have *almost* opened—enough to give me the impression of being near my brother."

"Then she's close to opening the portal and finding Inas." Hope rose in him. Sam rubbed his free fingers against each other, imagining it was Inas' hand and that he was here with them. "You felt all that from him?"

"Our connection is stronger than it was," Enos said. "Though I am uncertain why."

Rey dropped back from the rest of the group and Sam shot a wary glance at the Sureri.

How can he defend the Life Coalition, even a little?

When they'd first met, Sam thought Rey was a carefree joker, like some boys he'd known in school when he was young. Now he thought Rey might be the kind of person who hid pain and loss under their humor.

"Hopefully the tram won't be too crowded," he said to Enos, trying to gesture with his eyebrows that he wanted to get away from Rey.

Enos looked up at him, then frowned. "Yes. What are you doing with your face?"

Sam stopped twitching and whispered. "We need to talk with Majus Ayama about why...you know..."

Enos thumped his arm with one hand, darting a look to Rey, who was watching them curiously. She spoke in a normal tone. "Yes, I think Majus Ayama might open the portal on a second try." There was the barest pause, then Enos went on. "The impressions that make up portals are vague, after all. Maybe a memory added *in a different way* will work."

Rey shrugged. "Might do. Me, I've been studying portals too. It's sommat Majus Kheena likes. Bit of a hobby. Strange things, portals."

He's so calm, as if he wasn't recently defending a genocidal cult.

Rey could never know about Enos and Inas. Sam wished he wasn't so dumb around people. At least Enos hadn't asked him about the voice, ever since the chime rang at the apartment.

Doesn't fit in, hears a different Symphony from the other maji, has strange panic attacks, and has a voice is his head? If I tell anyone else, they'll think I'm even more disconnected from reality.

They caught the tram passing between the Spire and the Dome. There was a special carriage waiting for the maji, and their group filed on, between representatives of all ten species.

In their car, Majus Caroom and Majus Cyrysi spoke in hushed tones. Sam sat next to Enos, and Rey across the aisle. Sam made himself look up and take in the city, though his heart was climbing up into his throat. The columns rose on either side like massive translucent redwoods among underbrush.

Enos sat completely straight, her hands in her lap. Sam followed her gaze to Majus Ayama, deep in discussion with the Lobath Majus Panen I'Fon and Majus Hand Dancer.

"Come on," he said, reaching for her hand. "I'm sure she won't mind if we interrupt her to tell her about—"

He jumped as a deep pealing sound shimmered through the Imperium. It was the same noise, as if a giant had rung a bell the size of a house. The tram vibrated on its tracks and Sam clutched the back of the seat in front of him. The noise from the others on the train jumped a level, everyone talking at once.

"Again?" He peered out a window. Outside, the sound was more resonant than what he heard in his room two days ago. It filled the Nether with a thunderous call.

"Where is it comin' from?" Rey asked. Enos' hands clenched on Sam's.

"This is to be the second time this has happened," Majus Cyrysi said, breaking off his conversation with Majus Caroom. "I was attempting to research it, but there is to be nothing in the archives with similar occurrences. Only a few references I am not yet understanding." He peered back toward the House of Communication and Sam turned with him.

The tower-like House was just visible. Dust sifted from the strange bridge that arced from it to the wall of the Nether, catching the light.

Majus Hand Dancer had his many-fingered hands pressed to the wall of the tram. Lobhl did not hear as well as the other species.

<I feel it as thunder, but more musical, like the Symphony contained in one chord, or a crystal struck and vibrating.>

The noise was already starting to fade.

Majus Ayama shot the Lobhl a look. "Indeed. I wonder if it has anything to do with the Nether? Maybe it is a byproduct of the damage to the Dome of the Assembly? Or could it be a remnant from the Drain?"

"Then why would it start now?" Majus I'Fon asked. "Far after when the damage was done?"

Majus Ayama turned to Sam, and he shrank into the seat, trying to be unnoticeable.

"Was there something you did when you...caused the Drain to disappear? Might it link to this?"

Sam shook his head, and Enos put a reassuring hand on his leg. He wished Inas was on his other side to balance him. The spike of loss passed through him like a bolt of electricity and he swallowed a lump. "It's not what I did," he said, once he could breathe again. "I have no idea what it is."

Don't throw up.

"Are you sure?" pressed the majus. "We've seen you do—" she broke off, as if realizing how many people were around them. They had kept Sam's abilities quiet, and he hadn't changed the Symphony where others could see his color. He'd been hiding in his mentor's apartment. Only Majus Ayama and Majus Cyrysi had been there when he'd showed what he could do.

"—do strange things with the House of Communication," Rilan finished. "We may need to test you to see if there is a connection."

"I was conducting research yesterday," Majus Cyrysi added. "Though I was not thinking to examine this connection as well. If we are having Sam describe what he hears in the Symphony when the sound happens again—if it does—it would shed more light on this phenomenon." His mentor was staring at him, his head cocked to one side. The crest of feathery hair Kirians used to display emotion was up and spread wide. The Nether translated it to Sam as intent curiosity.

"I...I don't know about it," Sam said. "I can't hear anything special in the Symphony." He tried to touch the notes flying through his head, but they were slippery, sliding away. If he could only get a grip on them and dig into the core of his being, he would stop being so anxious. He'd done that before, in Dalhni, the city the Drain had destroyed. But it had been four ten-days since the attack on the Dome, and he hadn't done so a second time.

The peal of sound finally faded, though Majus Ayama still studied him. Sweat broke out on Sam's neck.

He spent the rest of the trip to the Dome in silence, watching the maji discuss what the chime might mean. Sam caught Rey staring at him too, a pensive look on his uneven and craggy face.

* * *

Rey trailed the others out of the tram, next to Majus Kheena. His mentor was watching the walls of the Nether as if they might show cracks after the recent deluge of sound.

"So the Life Coalition's finally slouched up and shown their faces in the Assembly. Reckon yer know aught of their leaders?" he asked his mentor.

Majus Kheena made an annoyed sound, then pushed his cowl back to better see Rey. "Possible, but not likely. Me, I know many of my fellow species. Though I try not to become enmeshed in political machinations."

"Sam and Enos say the leaders're maji, like us," Rey said. Majus Ayama had been sneaking around just as much as the Coalition. If she and the others were so holy and right, shouldn't they be in the open, revealing what the Life Coalition's aim was, instead of skulking? They'd lost Inas by going behind the backs of the Council. What was to say they wouldn't lose other maji?

Now the Life Coalition was coming clean, ready to talk like civilized beings. Yes, they were Snakeys, but so was Majus Kheena. Rey'd learned not all prejudices common on his homeworld were valid. Some were, but each species had their good and their bad. The Coalition definitely fell in that latter category, but by how much? They'd hurt some people, true, but the Methiemum had also fought the Sathssn over trading rights, some thirty cycles ago. More people had died then than all the ones injured in the Drains.

His mentor hadn't answered. The Dome of the Assembly rose above them, with the new hole in its top from the Drain. The one the Coalition had caused. Rey let his head incline, following the architecture of the massive stadium-like building. Back on Sureri, all the buildings were flat and boring, made to house as many family members as possible. Efficient family hierarchy was more important than beauty—at least outside, where anyone could get an impression of your wealth and standing. In the Nether, people put everything they had on show, from their names, to jewelry, to buildings, to fancy contraptions. He glanced back to his mentor. The majus' scaly brows were drawn down, shading his slitted eyes. He was also looking at the place where the supposedly impenetrable Nether crystal was missing, pondering heavy thoughts.

"There're only so many Sathssn maji," Rey pressed. "Could be yer know some of them. Maybe-like all of them."

They crossed the street in front of the Dome, waiting for one of the new-fangled steam cars to go by. It drowned out the music one of the tall and skinny Etanela was belting out on his set of longpipes, standing on a corner.

Majus Kheena took another moment to answer as they huffed up the steps of the Assembly. They arrived at the set of entrances leading into the lower section, where the maji sat. "About these maji, I may have heard rumors, passed through the elders of my diocese. But it only confirms statistical fact to admit that. There are only so many maji of my species, as you say. The Council, they have been asking Sathssn maji for their affiliation lately. It is not wise to advertise any wavering."

That wasn't good. Rey could see the start of sommat he didn't like, growing in the Assembly. All this fighting over Aridori, and the Life Coalition, and over who was better than who meant tensions were running high. His species and his mentor's were suspected whenever sommat went wrong, just because they liked to stay to themselves and call the other species on their gaffes. Rey had seen plenty of suspicious behavior from the other species. The Methiemum were one of the trickiest. They'd steal your valuables off you and sell them back at a profit. Inas was one of the only ones he didn't doubt. Inas was warm and likeable and...just a good friend. He shook the thought away. That was why he and his mentor were helping—to get him back.

"Our group's slidin' around like we're just as guilty," Rey argued. "Mebbe Majus Ayama has the Council's approval. Mebbe not. She's lied to us before." He turned to his mentor, making both of them stop as the rest of their group continued into the Assembly. "Don't yer wonder what this Life Coalition has to say? What possible reason do they have for settin' these great Drains into motion? For this?" he gestured upward. "Seems like, to me, there must be sommat behind their efforts. Why do they go to so much trouble? If we were just to listen to 'em for a moment, might be we'd learn what it is."

Majus Kheena regarded him for a moment, his eyes roaming over Rey's face. Rey resisted the urge to rub his nose. Finally, the majus reached up to stroke the little wisps of hair which grew between the scales on his chin. "About this, you speak logically," the majus said. "I too, think Majus Ayama and Majus Cyrysi, they may be hasty in hunting down the Life Coalition. And this, it is not because my own species leads them."

"Then we two will listen to what the Life Coalition says, in there, eyah?" Rey wagged his head toward the Assembly.

"Potentially," the majus allowed. They began walking again. "At least to see what the Life Coalition means to do, in claiming this legitimacy to the Great Assembly of Species."

Inside, the Assembly was in an uproar, everyone talking about what they would learn today. But that was like every time Rey had been to a session. The various representatives, speakers, and maji were always upset about this or that. Could be the Life Coalition, or mebbe the weird noise that thrummed through the Nether on the way here. He didn't think it was a big deal. The Nether did strange things all the time. Who knew what a semi-sentient giant crystal got up to? Mebbe it was bored—hadn't dug into enough people's heads lately, or whatnot. Rey admitted the translation it offered was helpful, but that didn't mean it wasn't creepy. He suppressed a shudder.

No, the uproar today was likely all about the Life Coalition. He looked down, over the tiers of seating reserved for maji from House of Potential. There were black-cloaked figures, far below, like shadows against the gentle glow from the crystal floor. A line of the Effature's guard stood not far from them. No weapons were in sight, but Rey saw a guard's hand twitch to her sheathed sword.

The Dome of the Assembly was big enough that the bottom of it rested on the true floor of the Nether, not the dirt and stone built up over however many cycles beings had lived here. Another freaky thing about the giant crystal—it was impenetrable. Once yer got to the crystal, that was it—yer couldn't go any farther. And if yer looked into the crystal, granddames preserve yer. It was like looking through miles of ice, and a mirror, at the same time. There was no end to it.

Yet his mentor had hinted that maji—and only maji—*could* pass through the crystal. It was some part of the test to go from apprentice to majus.

Rey found a seat near his mentor—apprentices were not usually invited to the Assembly, but there was a special allowance today. They really wanted everyone to be here. He looked up, to where a vast net supported many oiled tarps, draped over the hole in the Dome's roof. It let in less light than it used to, but the glow from the floor was enough to see by.

After a small eternity, the Effature—the old man what was in charge of the Nether, waved for things to actually start, and Speaker Oscana— the leader of the Council of Maji, and the head of the House of Communication—gave some speech about seeing what these Life Coalitioners were all about and how dare they come here. Rey twiddled his fingers through it, waiting for them to get to the point.

Rey sat forward when the black-cloaked figure in the middle of the small group stepped forward. Majus Kheena did the same, and Rey traded a look with his mentor. They would finally let the Life Coalition speak.

"Gathered representatives of the ten species," a high, clear voice rang out. None of the Life Coalitioners had pushed their cowls back, and it was impossible to see anything about their shapes, but they all looked to be the right size for Sathssn. That meant they probably all belonged to the more conservative factions of his mentor's species—the ones who covered their whole bodies so not a hint of skin poked out. All well and good, but Rey wondered how hot they got in all that fabric.

"Today, we have come before you to speak as equals." There was some murmuring running along the seats at that. "Though us, we have kept hidden for the many cycles our organization has existed, now, we have determined it is time to share our goal with the inhabitants of the Nether, and of the homeworlds."

The figure continued to make generic remarks about how great the Life Coalition was, without quite saying anything at all. Rey rolled his eyes. Why did important folk always want to talk so much? Just get to the point. Majus Kheena shifted, next to him. "Me, I could be back in my study, researching information transfer," he grumbled.

"I'm sure they'll say sommat useful at some point," Rey answered. "They came here for a reason." He narrowed his eyes, trying to see the figure better. There were five others with her. It was a female—the Nether had informed him of that much, in the creepy way it provided helpful clues. It was like he was remembering a bit of information he'd never learned.

"—and to show our sincerity in coming before you, me, I give you my name."

"Ah, here's sommat," Rey said. The revelation of names among his species was a time-honored tradition. It happened when things started getting serious.

"Me, I am Janas, leader of the Life Coalition," the figure said. She gestured two others forward, and one took a place on each side of Janas. "This, is Iano—" she gestured to her right with a gloved hand. "—who was at one time a majus in the House of Power. He has renounced his claim to the title of 'majus.'" Muttering and conversations began in the seated section of maji belonging to the House of Power.

"This, on my other side, is Zsaana, a majus who once belonged to the House of Healing, and even held its highest position at one—" The rest of her statement was drowned out by a rise of noise from the maji in the House of Healing, as well as from the floor of the Assembly. Speaker Oscana had risen to her feet, as had the Pixie who was the head of the House of Communication. Rey looked to the seats for the House of Healing, where Majus Ayama sat, unperturbed. He found Majus Cyrysi, in the section for the House of Communication. His crest was flat. If he'd been surprised, his feathery hair would look like he'd gotten struck by lightning. Kirians could never hide what they felt. That could only mean they'd known about the leaders of the Life Coalition. Which they'd also neglected to tell the rest of the people supposed to be working with them.

"Majus Zsaana," his mentor murmured. "This, it is a surprise. He was highly regarded among maji until he disappeared twelve cycles ago."

So it wasn't just apprentices the maji were keepin' secrets from.

"If such a prestigious majus is keepin' up with the Coalition, what does that say about its members?" Rey asked Majus Kheena.

The majus waggled a gloved hand back and forth. His slitted eyes were thoughtful. "This, it lends credence to the Life Coalition's claim they are attempting to bring peace, no matter those they have felled. Zsaana was well respected, even if him, he was a bit—" the majus paused, groping for a word. "—well, specist."

Rey shrugged. "Lots o' beings have a reason or two to dislike some aught species." He couldn't say too much. The Sureriaj knew well they were the pinnacle of evolutionary biology among the ten species. That the others called them out for their unattractive faces only proved their point. They were just jealous.

But Janas was continuing to speak. She hadn't introduced any of the other figures, so maybe they weren't as important, or they weren't as trusting to make themselves targets for several billion beings.

"The voids we created, had they not been stopped, would have already achieved the peace I speak of, with the loss of little life, comparatively." More muttering and even a few shouts for Janas to give up the floor. That one, Rey couldn't agree with. He'd seen reports of the desolation in the Methiemum city of Dalhni, and was sitting directly under the damage they'd done to the Dome. Janas ignored the jeers.

"You all, you say we have killed. Me, I say the Life Coalition has saved many more lives from destruction. Now, we must work the slow path to bring organization and order. Like everyone else here, we only wish to have enough time and energy to care for our loved ones." She lifted a gloved finger, as if to make an important point. "The Life Coalition, we have found a way to bring boundless energy to all the species in this Assembly. Such resources, they would halt the end of all things. This, would it not be an acceptable trade for a few sacrifices?"

"I would not call Dalhni 'a few sacrifices,'" Speaker Oscana said. Since she was one of the Etanela, her words slurred together, making it hard for Rey to catch them all. Why couldn't everyone just speak normal, as the Sureri did? "Nor would I discount those who died in this very room, from your actions. You have yet to tell us what this power source is or where it comes from."

The Life Coalition leader bowed her cloaked head, accepting the censure. "This, it is regrettable. For the time given us to develop the technology to create the great seeds, there was little occasion to make you see the path we walked. To alert you would mean you would stop us."

"And you were stopped!" called one of the Pixie speakers. A round of nervous laughter wavered across the Assembly, but quickly died.

Janas spread her hands, the black absorbing the light reflected from the Nether floor. "This, it is why we change our tactics and come before you now, in humbleness. You hear the pleading chimes of the Nether itself. What else would you call these cries that have occurred twice already? The Dissolution is nearing." There was muttering at that, but Rey got the feeling no one else believed those ravings either. He traded a skeptical look with Majus Kheena. "We see your power," Janas continued. "We know your might, and us, we are willing to share with everyone our divine plan to bring the great power to us, which will fix the problems of the Assembly and push back the Dissolution." She raised her arms wide, encompassing the Dome and its new hole.

"This is a strong claim you make, with little proof, but much suffering," Speaker Oscana said from her seat in the middle of the Councilors of the maji. "What if we do not accept this 'plan'? Your army has been decimated, many of your hideaways destroyed. Do you now come in peace only because there is no alternative? If we eradicate the rest of the Life Coalition, will we not have the same peace you speak of?"

Janas didn't flinch. She must've been bodged together from powerful stuff, to stand up to the stern Speaker and the glowers of the other sixty-six speakers who surrounded the figures. She didn't even acknowledge the guards looming behind her.

"The Life Coalition, we are not defenseless," she said, and her voice carried throughout the Dome. "Us, we come in peace, but also in strength. We make an offer in goodwill, but if we are attacked, know we and our allies will respond in kind. Us, we will also use the other powerful weapon in our arsenal—our Aridori assassins."

CHAPTER FIVE

The Viciousness of Tales

- The passage of time does many things, but its most pernicious of abilities is to dull the memory. What is not written or passed down orally is easily forgotten. What is communicated can be changed, either intentionally or not. I have lived a long time, and seen much. Yet there are things even I do not remember correctly, or do not trust in written accounts. Some important items I never did record for fear of discovery by the wrong person. I may regret some of those decisions in the coming cycles, based on rumors and actions coming to light.

From the Journal of Bolas Palmoran, Effature of the Nether, 995 A.A.W.

Enos sat bolt upright at Janas' proclamation. No one could get in a question through the multitude of representatives shouting over each other. She saw the ancient ward against Aridori—two fingers, passed in front of the eyes—repeated all over the Assembly.

Surely the Life Coalition wouldn't admit they held Inas? She glanced to Majus Ayama in the seat to her left. Enos' mentor was glaring as if she could spear the speaker with her eyes. Enos was almost surprised there was no aura of white and olive around the majus.

The Effature finally rose from his seat next to the Council of the Maji and made a gesture. The noise in the Assembly cut to a whisper.

"I am thankful for recent upgrades made to the speech System in this chamber," the Effature said in his low, warm voice. Something always drew Enos to him, the few times she had glimpsed or spoken to him. It was like he was a long-forgotten benevolent uncle, trying to please an unruly family. Enos' eyes went to the circlet of crystal perched on his head. Was it connected to the Nether?

Her parents had told stories of strange things the Nether could do, but when Enos arrived with Inas, they were surprised by how much the gigantic crystal interacted with those inside it. It had taken more than a ten-day to be certain the Nether would not give their species away, but it seemed content to classify them as Methiemum—the shapes their family took.

"When I reset the speech amplification System," the Effature continued, drawing Enos from her thoughts, "Speaker Oscana will ask the first question of Janas and the Life Coalition."

The colors of all six houses of the maji sprang into being as the Effature switched a set of levers and brass buttons attached to his chair, and she could hear muttering around her again. The seats were close, to pack in the multitude of diplomats and several thousand maji.

"I still think the Aridori are all dead."

"—heard one was attacking my neighbor's cousin. They were changing shape right in front of her and were to be taking her jewelry."

"—All a myth. It's some of the other maji, playing tricks on the rest of us."

"Janas," called Speaker Oscana, "you say you control Aridori. It has been a concern of this Assembly that there may be members of that ancient race still in existence. Can you offer proof for what you claim?"

Councilor Feldo had captured the Aridori Enos and Inas talked to in Gloomlight prison. Enos glanced at his empty chair. Speaker Oscana carefully hadn't said the Council already had proof of their existence.

Zsaana, the cloaked Sathssn next to Janas, took a step forward. Enos shivered at the memory of his glove on her hand, in the tunnels where the Life Coalition had held her and Sam. He was of the House of Healing, like her. He knew she was Aridori. He'd probably been the one to specify Inas be captured. Was her other instance with them? Would they dare bring a known majus apprentice before the entire Assembly?

"Proof, this we have," said Zsaana. He gestured to the other three members of the Life Coalition, clumped together while their leader spoke. They separated, and Enos saw they'd been hiding a small metal cube between them, the outside carved into twisting designs. It only came to their knees, and Sathssn were not a tall species. They must have cleared it with the Effature's guard, somehow, to get it in here. Several of the guards standing close behind them edged closer, but the Effature made a tiny motion with one hand and the guards retreated, hands at the weapons on their hips.

"The Aridori, it is in here," Zsaana said.

"It can't be," Majus Ayama murmured. Enos traded a look with her. Her hands were white, clasping the arms of her seat. Enos swallowed down a surge of fear and her nostrils flared as she tried to suck in enough air to keep the room from spinning.

"Do you feel anything from it?" her mentor whispered, casting a glance at those seated around them. "Is it—?"

No one was paying them any attention, and Enos reached out as she did when Inas was next to her, but there was no response.

She shook her head and whispered back. "It can't be. I...I think I would know it if it were him." She remembered the waves of emotion from her latest seizure.

Fear. Cold metal. It cannot be him, can it?

Enos leaned close to Majus Ayama's ear, hoping no one near could overhear. The Methiemum to her right was leaning half out of her seat, and one behind them was conversing with his neighbor.

"I felt him again, when you almost opened the portal. It was like you paved a pathway to my brother."

Majus Ayama clenched one hand at the news, but showed no other sign of surprise. She opened the hand again, as if to ask, 'well?'

Enos shook her head. "I felt cold metal through him, but...I do not think he is here."

The other three Coalitioners scraped the box forward as if it was very heavy, and the screech was headache-inducing in the silence of the Assembly.

Even after working with Majus Ayama, she had no idea how to connect with Inas intentionally. If that was a skill of the Aridori, their parents had not shared it. She knew little about connecting with her other instance, if they were not in the same room.

Could they have him in there? Forced to abandon his shape? Who would do that?

Yet Councilor Feldo had done so to the Aridori they captured. It might be a retained technique, like the hand gesture or knowing the Aridori changed form. It made a sick sense—how better to keep a shape changer from escaping than to confine them with only enough space for them to exist?

Majus Ayama raised her lips to Enos' ear, her breath ticklish as she whispered. "If he is not *there*, that means they have more Aridori. More than Inas, and more than the one that attacked Feldo."

Enos' heart climbed into her throat at the revelation.

There are more of my species. But Nakan had told her they had trouble handling one Aridori, when he took Inas. She assumed he referred to the one in Gloomlight prison, but even that Aridori was made of multiple instances. The Life Coalition had not been truthful.

"Deep breaths, apprentice," Majus Ayama said, and Enos nodded. It was what Enos said to Sam, when he got too anxious. She looked across the seats to where her friend sat next to Majus Cyrysi. He was wringing his hands, his eyes wide. As if he felt her gaze, he locked eyes with her.

The rotting conglomeration of Aridori in Gloomlight prison had been forced together with no solid form. They had spoken nonsense, lilting and multi-phrased. Just the thought of it made her shudder. There was so much she didn't know about her species.

"You all, you wish proof?" Zsaana asked into the stillness of the Assembly. His question was met with tense silence. He held one hand over the box and the white of the House of Healing spiraled down his arm. Enos could just hear the music he changed above the background noise of all the biological chords surrounding her.

Majus Ayama grunted. "Old bigot. He nearly cost me my first attempt at majus, back when I was an apprentice. He's latched onto something else bigger than him, looking for power."

What kind of power was that? Janas' protestations of peace and boundless resources in the face of the Dissolution hit too close to what Sam had learned from the voice. Trying to control the Symphony.

Zsaana slid several latches back, turned a dial, then raised the lid. A hush hung over the gathered representatives, and Enos shivered.

Don't be him. Don't be Inas in that tiny box.

Surely she would feel a connection if it was him. She reached to her other instance again, but felt nothing.

"I've never heard the Assembly this quiet," Majus Ayama whispered to her. Enos nodded absently.

A tendril grasped the edge of the box from the inside. The head that rose from the knee-high box was dark and iridescent, but unformed.

One hundred thousand beings inhaled.

Enos stared down, but the floor of the Nether was too far away. She risked a glance left and right. She *had* to see who was in the box. Could she change her eyes to those of eagles, in the middle of so many, while an Aridori—another Aridori—showed its face for the first time in a thousand cycles?

Enos shook herself. What was she thinking? She was an apprentice to Majus Ayama, the best head of the House of Healing for two hundred cycles, to hear her tell the tale. Had Enos been listening and learning for the past few months, or hiding like a scared child?

Both.

Enos let the Symphony of Healing rise up in her mind, like a concerto played on a thousand bells, by a hundred different performers. She blocked out the strains belonging to other people, narrowed it down to music of her own body, then of her head, and then her eyes. She used the notes from the core of her being—those that defined her—and adjusted the music, bringing the beat up, changing the key to a higher, tighter register.

When Enos looked at the box again she could see it clearly, though anything closer than the edge of the seats looking over the Assembly floor was a blur.

Their parents had never shared with Enos and Inas the true form of their species. She wasn't certain they knew. Their people had been in hiding so long that the women who had children—the few who did— gave birth by the regular Methiemum way, to Methiemum children. Their society did not allow changing form, except in the greatest need, and maybe not even then. To see an Aridori—a true, ancient, Aridori— was something she never thought she'd encounter.

The head had form now, shining black, with a pronounced snout. The body was bare, with scales that transmuted in the light from the walls, shifting from green to purple, to green. Long arms grasped the sides of the box and pulled the form up, as if rising from a shaft beneath the box. That tiny volume could never hold the being that came from it, but it rested on the faintly glowing—and impenetrable—floor of the Nether. The body had been compressed into a tiny cube.

"This, it is an Aridori," Zsaana said. "A form not seen in a thousand cycles."

He clasped a glowing white collar around the being's neck. The white would be invisible to a non-majus. It must be a way to control the Aridori. Zsaana was probably listening to any change in the Symphony around the being.

Her stomach roiled. At Zsaana's curt motion, the being lifted one foot from the box to stand on the floor of the Nether. It wore no clothes—none would have fit in that box with it—but Enos could find no sign of genitalia, hidden or otherwise. Even she did not know how her species reproduced, back when they lived in the open.

If not constrained, would the Aridori have sprung forward and started killing? That's what the tales from the Aridori War said, when her species was supposed to have massacred thousands, maybe millions of beings.

"Are you sure this isn't Inas?" Majus Ayama's breath in her ear made Enos jump and put a hand to her chest. "Do you really look like that? I've not seen that shape in even the oldest books of the maji. It's like all the records have been purged."

The Aridori made no other move, save to step fully from the box, their iridescent scales vibrating as if in a breeze. Their long fingers, black or deep blue like the snout, were clasped in front of their belly. They looked at peace. Their head swiveled to take in the multitude of people sitting above them, fleshy ears surrounded by curls of hair and twisting and turning like a cat's. The wide nostrils at the end of their snout flared.

Enos shook her head, then put her lips to her mentor's ear. "It can't be Inas. I would feel something. We didn't know about this shape. Our entire family was Methiemum." She leaned back, then glared up at her mentor, challenging her to say that Enos was less than that. She took back the change she'd made to her eyes, reveling in the energy granted from regaining her notes. But the majus' gaze was turned inward.

"We have a much larger problem," Majus Ayama said.

Enos looked up at her, heat growing in her belly. She didn't bother to whisper—everyone was talking over each other, enamored by the being below. "A larger problem? Larger than my brother being taken? Larger than the Life Coalition weaseling their way into the Assembly?"

"Yes," Majus Ayama stared directly at her. "Don't you see? The Life Coalition has more than one Aridori. Maybe a whole army. The soldiers they sent to attack the Assembly were just a distraction." She bounced one fist off the railing in front of them. "I don't know what Janas was talking about with their source of unlimited power, but it has to be related to the voids. We *must* open that portal and find where they're hiding."

Enos stared back at the Aridori, holding one hand in front of her to compare her warm copper skin with the black scales of the being who had risen from the box. Was that what she really looked like? Had Inas taken that form, imprisoned by the Life Coalition?

She watched the Aridori as they made a polite bow to the Effature, determined to remember every nuance of their movement. It was more important than ever that she find Inas. Whatever it took.

* * *

"Sit down, Enos," Sam said for the third time. He made a grab for her hand as she passed his seat in Majus Cyrysi's living room, but only caught a finger. It slowed her pacing, and Enos turned to him.

"They have Inas. He may be in a box just like the one we saw today. How can I relax? How can *you* be so calm?"

Sam gave a strangled laugh. It shouldn't have been funny, but it was. He was acting like the centered one, in control, while Enos was anxious and pacing. He should have been curled in a ball over the Aridori the Life Coalition had shown earlier that day. He was terrified.

Is it the lack of memories? Am I missing what I should know? At least for once I'm not taking all the attention.

"I don't know how," he said, "but I am. Can I help you?"

He recalled the sleek, handsome form that had risen from the box. Dark snout, iridescent scales, bright eyes, and mobile ears—like a cross between a bipedal lizard and a cat.

Or a miniature dragon.

The Aridori had bared their teeth, but Sam had seen the ring of white on the metal collar Zsaana clasped around their neck. The being was a prisoner of the Life Coalition, just as he and Enos had been.

Enos plopped down beside him on Majus Cyrysi's mint green couch, and buried her head in his shoulder. "It could have been Inas. I felt that cold surface through him. He might be trapped in another box, just like that."

"I knew that Aridori wasn't Inas as soon as they stepped out of the box," Sam murmured into her hair. It smelled of flowers, not ones he could name, but definitely flowers. Light and sweet.

Enos nestled closer. "How?"

"By the way they moved. Couldn't you tell? That wasn't my Inas," Sam said. He missed Inas' firm hand on his shoulder, his steady voice next to his ear, telling him things would turn out right in the end. Inas was nervous in closed spaces, just as Sam feared spaces that were too wide open, and filled with crowds.

"That means the Life Coalition still holds him, in another box," Enos said.

Sam's mind went back to the little box, far too tiny to hold the majestic Aridori who had stepped from it. "It doesn't have to be a box," Sam said. He could think of plenty things that were cold and hard. "Maybe he was only touching metal."

"Like those collars?" Enos asked, and Sam hesitated.

"Well, yes. Better than a tiny box isn't it?"

Zsaana had explained the restraint System in the collar. He said it was all that was keeping the Aridori from tearing into the nearest person. Sam didn't believe that. The Aridori he knew wouldn't do anything like that.

"We still must rescue him," Enos said. Her face was still in his shoulder. It was comfortable. That was him. Comfortable when he should have been acting. Saving his Inas.

"We can learn from this," he tried. "The Aridori changed much faster than you." Enos flinched against him. He didn't mind her changing form, but she seemed to think it would drive him away.

The Aridori had lifted one dark scaled hand, then transformed it to a long-fingered Lobath hand, then a scaly Sathssn one, then a wing, then a wicked looking scythed blade, all in the span of a few moments. It was an effective threat.

You can't drive me away from you.

"I do not know how," Enos answered. "Inas and I have no memory of the form that Aridori took. Our parents taught us we *could* change, but not how. It was forbidden. What they taught us was fragmented. I don't think my family knew much about the war." She raised her head and looked Sam in the eyes. "And now they're gone. They were so scared of being found out, but despite that, my people are in the open again. All our efforts at hiding were useless."

Sam held her for a time while she cried. He would have cried too, but without Inas' warmth holding them together, he had to be strong for her. They needed Inas.

And I need to figure out how to center myself again. I must find my own melody, where the anxiety sits.

Sam frowned down at Enos, and wiped a tear from her cheek. "You're working with Majus Ayama on the portal again tomorrow?"

Enos nodded, swallowed, and sniffed. "She still doesn't have it right. If I can connect with Inas again, that might give enough information. I wish I knew how it happened."

"How—" now Sam paused. "Can I ask how that works? Your other instance? Inas?" He didn't even have the words to make the question.

Enos sniffed again. "All Aridori are born in two, but not just twins. We're closer than that, linked mentally, and even physically, when we are born. In our family, both babies shared one umbilical cord. I do not know how it works with..." She waved a hand, encompassing the events of the day. "Our family was Methiemum, in all ways."

"But you are linked to Inas," Sam prodded.

I can pry without her getting angry at me. She won't push me away, just because of this.

"It's a feeling, when we're close," Enos said, oblivious to the thoughts tumbling around in his head. "Like I could finish his sentences. He would know when I was hungry. I knew when he got a good sale on our wares. When one instance dies, the other may live on, or sometimes choose to die, or may go through a significant emotional change, as my uncle did. Our parents didn't teach us about that either, not really. I suppose there could be more to it."

"Like how fast they changed."

Enos nodded into his shoulder. "I know so little. The Life Coalition must understand more about my people than I do." She scrunched up her face. "I hate them for that."

* * *

It was four days later and Sam was working with Majus Cyrysi when the summons came. The Imperium had still not calmed down from learning Aridori existed. The Assembly had been in session every day, arguing about what they would do. Sam hadn't ventured out into the crowded streets. He'd heard there was a spontaneous protest in front of the Dome. Even the music in the House of Communication seemed more martial.

Sam shook his head to clear it as Majus Cyrysi spoke.

"If the sequence is to be holding," his mentor said, "the chime will be coming in a few moments. Open yourself to the Symphony. See if you are able to determine the resonances this time." He twisted a dial on a contraption built of metal and cogs, and bellows pumped as a little hand began drawing a line on a sheet of vellum. Sam had no idea what it was supposed to do.

Sam also hadn't been able to divine what his mentor wanted from the great, resonant, bell-like sound. With the larger threat of the Aridori, everyone had settled on calling it a 'chime,' even though it was as like to a chime as a church organ was to a doorbell. The only similarity was that it rang.

The chime rang every day now, at the same time. People were getting used to it, and even incorporating it into advertisements: 'Get a bowl of Kirian maggots half off—today when the chime sounds!' Some of the street musicians were trying to harmonize with it, making it a backbeat to their compositions, though others sang of marching against the returned Aridori.

Sam pulled his pocketwatch out. Hours on Earth didn't line up with lightenings in the Nether, but he reset his watch every morning, and had figured out how they reconciled. It should be in three...two...one...

The little laboratory Majus Cyrysi had co-opted vibrated with the rest of Spire. If anything, the Spire vibrated more than the House of Communication, perhaps because it rested against one of the immense columns.

"Now! Tell me what you are to be hearing in the Symphony!"

Sam closed his eyes to block out the chugging equipment the majus hovered over and listened to the Symphony. The chime was giving all the chords a strange vibrato, like a struck gong.

But that was it. There was nothing *to* the music of the chime. He couldn't find its source. It seemed to be everywhere. He opened his eyes.

"Anything?" Majus Cyrysi's crest was spiking and waving with excitement. Sam shook his head, and his mentor deflated.

Unless...

Sam went deeper into the melody, swimming through layers that defined the stone of the Spire, the metal of the machine, and the flesh of their bodies. There *was* something solid beneath it all—a mass of roiling notes which at first had no rhythm. Then he realized it instead had an incredibly complex rhythm.

"I can hear..."

"What? What is it boy?" Majus Cyrysi must have been worked up. He hadn't called Sam that in a while.

"I'm not sure." Sam reached out, trying to grasp even one of the complex jumble of notes. His focus bounced off them, and he gritted his teeth at a sudden spike of pain and an instant headache. Sam grunted, and pressed fingers to his temples.

"I lost it," he said, and that was when the chime stopped.

"Not completely," Majus Cyrysi said, and pointed to the graph the machine had made. The needle was drawing a straight line again, as it had before the chime, but the intervening space was filled with a spiraling, fluting, sequence of whorls. One small section at the end went wild, the peaks of the graph stretching to edges of the page. Sam squinted at it, then looked at his watch, counting seconds to get the time of the graph.

"I think that last section is where I almost touched the music of the chime," he said.

Majus Cyrysi was hovering over him in an instant. Sam tried not to draw back from his faintly fishy breath. "You touched it? You are to be getting better at this. What was it like? What were the tempos of the music? The phrasing?"

"I...I..." Apprentices were taught musical theory, but he had hadn't gotten very far. A lot of the concepts were more difficult than when he'd tried to learn the piano one time.

Hey—I remember that. Playing the piano.

"Out with it! What were you hearing? Do not keep me in suspense—"

There was a knock at the door of the chamber.

Majus Cyrysi grumbled over and jerked the door open. "What are you to be wanting—oh. I see. Yes, I suppose he could come. Not as if I were conducting an important experiment with my apprentice."

Sam frowned at his mentor's scowl and spiky crest.

"The Effature is to be requesting your presence. Alone. Immediately. You had best be going. Just be thinking how to write down what you were to be experiencing. We are to be getting very close to an answer. I can feel it in my feathers."

***

Sam kept his head down, though he glanced up often enough to follow the Lobath attendant in front of him. This place was a maze of corridors. He flexed one hand, closing and opening.

He pressed his right forefinger into his left wrist, timing his heartbeat. Too fast. He fumbled into the pocket of his vest—the green one, which he thought would make the best impression. He'd at least had enough time to spruce up before he saw the Effature. The steady ticking of his grandfather's pocketwatch calmed him, and he brought it to his ear.

I have a grandfather, though I never met him. That means I have parents too. Why can't I remember them?

The question nagged at him, even with everything else happening. If he could key into the music he heard in Dalhni, then maybe he could get his memories back.

Sam turned a corner into another corridor, keeping the Lobath's braided head-tentacles in view. This hallway's walls were festooned with paintings, probably gathered from all ten homeworlds. Sam was learning to tell the difference between the species' favored expressions of art. His heart rose into his throat at the newness of the place. He'd never been in the Effature's palace before.

"This way, sir," the Lobath called, and Sam started. He looked up and found his guide standing in front a set of wide doors formed of purple heartwood from an unfamiliar tree species. He squinted at the wood, trying to place it. His father had...woodworked as a hobby? Was that correct? It was another detail the being in the Drain had missed scrubbing from his memory.

He shook his head and looked to the Lobath, forcing himself to meet the large, silvery, surprised-looking eyes. Sam glanced back down at the plush carpet. It was an expensive Festuour product. Strange that he could come to that conclusion, but couldn't remember what his father did in his spare time.

"He's in there?" he said, to put off going in the room.

The Lobath gave a curt nod, and placed a hand on the wood, ready to push the door open. "And quite busy."

"Oh. Ok," Sam said. "I'm ready."

The Lobath bowed him in, and Sam entered a comfy study, with bookshelves lining all four walls, even above the door frame. There was a little ladder in the corner, the fading light from the walls illuminating it. A System Beast in the shape of a large cat licked a paw, sitting on an end table. The mannerism was just a front. The creature could fetch and carry, vocalize reminders, and deliver messages.

The Effature's palace was set with its back to one of the great walls that towered over the city, and they must be at the rear of the building. One giant facet of Nether crystal took up the entire view from the window. Sam pulled his eyes away from it so he wouldn't have to stare into those endless depths.

That meant he turned to look at the Effature, who was sitting in a padded chair, a book held open in his lap by one long-nailed hand. He was wearing the same clothes he wore in the Assembly—a long robe with ornamentation of green and purple scales, and long sleeves draping around his hands. In fact, Sam had never seen him wear anything else. It reminded him of...he couldn't bring what it reminded him of to mind.

The ever-present circlet of Nether glass on the Effature's brow reflected Sam's face back at him. Did he always look so worried?

"Welcome, Sam," the Effature said, and gestured to a nearby seat. Sam numbly went to it and sat.

What is all this about? Why has the person in charge of the Nether called me for a private audience?

His hands shook and he pressed them firmly into his lap. "Um. Thank you, sir. Effature." Sam fumbled for the right word, sweat springing up on his neck. He didn't know how to speak, and he was probably giving offense with every motion.

"Call me Palmoran," the Effature said. His voice was low, and soothing, like a hot cup of tea, or a line of liquid chocolate dripping across a plate of fruit. Sam's heart slowed, his breathing stilled.

What is he doing? How can he make me so calm?

He had encountered the feeling the last time he met the Effature—Palmoran—in a little alcove while the Life Coalition were about to attack the Assembly.

"What did you want to talk about? Palmoran?" Sam asked. He blinked rapidly, swallowed.

The Effature's lips lifted at the edges, making his wispy white beard lift from his chest. His eyes crinkled at the corners. He was obviously very old, but still had a handsome vitality to him. "It's just a name—Bolas Palmoran—but I've had senior Speakers stumble over it more than you."

Sam was silent. *I have no idea how to respond to that. Thank him? Ask a question? He'll take back his words just as quickly.*

Palmoran sat forward, putting his book to one side. "I'm certain you are wondering why I called you here."

"Ah, the thought had crossed my mind." Sam winced as soon as he said it. That was the way he talked to his friends, not the leader of the Nether. But the Effature only smiled again.

"I don't invite many here—mainly senior representatives and maji—but there are many things coming to a head among the ten species. You are at the center of them." Palmoran's eyes focused on Sam, who leaned back, pressing into the soft back of the chair.

"What things, sir? Palmoran." A drop of sweat ran down Sam's side.

The Effature held up a finger. "The voids." Two more fingers. "Your arrival from a previously unknown homeworld, yet with a biology identical to a Methiemum." Another finger. "The re-emergence of the Life Coalition with the Aridori and their claims of a source of power." A thumb. "And now this unknown bell, or tone, rings daily throughout the entire Imperium." He pulled his fingers into a fist. "It is coming more frequently, as if building to an ending." The Effature looked away, then back. "I have come across several facts in my research which seem to point to this chime as a focus of sorts."

"You think those are all connected—" Sam began, then broke off as one of the conditions the Effature listed made its way through his brain. "Wait, the *re-emergence* of the Life Coalition? They've done this before?"

The Effature shook his head. "Not at all. Previously, they were a small organization championing peace between the species. They disappeared into obscurity some fifty cycles ago. I should have paid more attention then, but had other matters to attend to." He reached up with one finger and stroked the crystal circlet he wore, looking like he was listening to it.

Sam wondered if the Effature could hear the Symphony, but that would be...silly, wouldn't it? He wasn't a majus. He hadn't looked at the colors when they appeared in the Assembly.

"But others will handle the Life Coalition, either in the Assembly, or through the group of maji led by Majus Ayama," Palmoran continued. "Out of all of those items I listed, I brought you here specifically to talk about the ringing bell." Sam frowned, twisting his fingers one way, then the other.

Not about the Drains? Or why or how I came here from Earth?

"I don't know anything about them," he said.

The Effature nodded. "I realize that. How could you? Yet I have...call it a feeling...the sound is important." He rubbed a finger across the circlet again and looked distinctly worried.

Sam's breathing sped up again. What could worry this man? "You said you'd recalled something about it?"

"I have been the caretaker of the Nether for quite a long time," Palmoran said. "Long enough that old details fade after time. This circlet helps me keep important memories, yet I must know what a memory references in order to look for it. I fear the chime is one of them, lost until recently. There are, in fact, many occurrences which have been buried until lately." He frowned, his eyes staring far away.

How old do you have to be not to remember those chimes? They must fill the entire Nether with sound.

"What can I do?" Sam asked.

"There is one other change I did not mention, and which I think may be related." Palmoran speared Sam with his gaze again, and it was all Sam could do not to look away. "Your recent discovery of a different house of the maji."

Sam jerked up with a guilty start. "Um. Where did you hear about that?" He'd only shown Majus Cyrysi, Majus Ayama, and Enos.

The Effature smiled, then tapped the circlet. "A long time. This is another of those events which jogs a memory. There is a central reason these odd occurrences are happening now, and I want you to find out why. It is no accident you have been apprenticed into the House of Communication, though that is not your true House."

Sam put a hand on his green vest. "Me, sir? I'm just an apprentice. I can't even get back home."

"There is a word I wonder if you have heard recently," Palmoran said, leaning forward to catch Sam's every move. "The Life Coalition leader mentioned it today, which gave me pause. *Dissolution.*"

Sam felt like his blood was turning to dust. The being that stole his memory had mentioned the Dissolution. "I've heard of it," he said, his voice quiet.

"I would appreciate if you paid attention to any more changes connected to these three things," Palmoran said. "The bell-like sound, your house affiliation, and signs of the Dissolution." He cocked his head, his eyes narrowing as if remembering. "Perhaps...take a walk on the bridge connected to the House of Communication."

"The bridge? I've been on it, but what does it have to do with anything?" Sam was losing track of this strange conversation.

"It connects to the wall of the Nether, and I judge this is important, though at the moment I cannot say why."

"I...I'll keep it in mind," Sam said, and tried not to wince.

Could I have found anything more stupid to say? And why doesn't he know more about this bridge? He couldn't have just forgotten it.

"Please do so—" the Effature began, when a low note sounded from a crystal globe on a table farther in the room. The cat System Beast hissed, and jumped down, prancing to a bookcase.

Sam had thought the crystal was just a decoration, but the Symphony pushed into his head, chords swirling together. It almost sounded like a portal, formed when a majus opened a doorway between the melodies of two places. But this was different—slower, and lacking full coordination with the music of this room.

The Effature looked at the crystal, which was swirling with colors, then looked back, a line of worry between his eyebrows. "Ah, I believe I will have to cut this meeting short, Sam," he said. "There is other business I must attend to."

"That's...um...fine, sir," Sam said.

What do the chimes have to do with the part of the Symphony I can hear? And with the Dissolution? That sounds bad any way I think about it. I should get more information before I leave.

"Should I shut the door on the way out?" was all he said.

"If you don't mind, Sam," the Effature said. He already seemed drawn into the crystal, looking into its depths, hands reaching out.

Sam closed the heavy wooden door behind him with a click.

Restarting

- I have kept watch on whether people speak of the Society of Two Houses. Eventually, it will fade from the memory of the Great Assembly of Species, helped by little nudges in history books and lectures. Very few understand the latest developments in technology, and only maji can fully visualize how the Symphony accentuates the most detailed fabrications.

With the loss of the Society so many cycles ago, our societal advancement has languished. The achievements of this organization were great in scope, but also troubling in their moral direction. Yet who can truly say how many should be sacrificed so a greater number may live better lives?

Now, when I pass maji in conversation, I hear no discussion of second houses. Those maji who have that rare ability, as I do, are merely interesting phenomena, not individuals to be feared and reviled. I feel I am very close to my goal. We will achieve those heights again.

Personal journal of Mandamon Feldo, Councilor for the House of Potential, 992 A.A.W.

Mandamon Feldo, Councilor for the House of Potential, knocked at the door of a moderately well-to-do house in Poler. It was near his childhood home, though that place had been transformed some twenty cycles back into a series of small shops. Mandamon pursed his lips, and kept his eyes forward. On the future. He rocked to his toes and back, though his knees complained at the motion. He wasn't as young as the last time he'd been here.

A rhythmic *squeak-tap* of a mechanical joint came through the closed door. Getting louder, repeating. Mandamon ran a gnarled hand down his extensive beard, now more white than black, or even than gray. Meetings like this brought the passage of time to the forefront of his mind. His other hand brushed an old paper, carefully folded in the inside pocket of his longcoat.

Finally, the door opened with a cry for oil, and Mandamon lifted an eyebrow at the lack of maintenance.

"Hard to reach up that high anymore," said an elderly voice. Familiar, but with a subtly different timbre than he remembered. More resonant.

"I've got another design to work on," Mandamon told his old friend Timpomitnob Gompt, Watcher. He took in the contraption she was seated on—obviously some version of a System Beast, but with no discernible head. It was a bit like a giant arachnid, made of metal and wood, with a seat where the thorax should be.

"It's about time," Gompt said, with as little pre-amble as Mandamon. Her still-bright blue eyes glared at him from behind glasses set on her furry snout. Her fur was grayer and sparser than it had been the last time he'd been here, and she was thicker too. Well, so was he.

In all, she looked good for a Festuour of her age. If she'd been standing, she'd have been of a height with him. She still wore her bandolier of tools across her chest—most custom made—but little else, in the way of her species. "Me and Krat have been waiting for you. Come on in." The System Beast clattered around in a complicated dance, conveying Gompt's bulk deeper into her house.

"I've been out of touch for a while," Mandamon said, for something to fill the silence. They walked down a front hall lined with certificates of invention and pictures of Gompt's friend group. He watched her wide ears twitch as he spoke. There were several faces Mandamon didn't recognize in the pictures. Recent members. He was normally the one to put others on edge, but now the situation was reversed. Gompt was a dear friend—one he'd not seen in far too long.

"Yeah, dealing with the Council is like lying in a bed filled with scrub fleas," Gompt remarked, sweeping one hairy, three-fingered paw out to the side. "It's only a matter of time until they bite you."

"I've missed your quips," Mandamon admitted. "It's been...a while."

"It's been over twenty cycles, you great oaf," Gompt said over her shoulder. Mandamon was about to retort when another voice cut in.

"Twenty cycles, two months, and four days." It was mechanical, stitched together from words spoken by a living being. In fact—

"Kratitha?" Mandamon said. His voice shook, and it wasn't from his age.

"Krat," came the disembodied voice. "My namesake worked with big lug here. No help from you."

Mandamon only realized he had stopped when Gompt and her conveyance did the same, then did another dance to position the furry Festuour facing Mandamon.

"She made all the recordings before she passed on," Gompt said. "Helped me put Krat here together. She calibrated the personality herself. Wouldn't let me touch it." Gompt patted the metal and wood of an armrest.

"I'm...I'm sorry," Mandamon said. He swallowed. "I've been too absorbed with other matters."

"Scrub fleas," Gompt humphed at him. "Never answered my letters, never came by to visit." She gestured at the System Beast she rode—a System Beast imprinted with a name and a personality, of all things. "I don't get around as well as I used to, and your silence made me afraid to reach out lest I disturb some part of your intricate plans."

Mandamon looked away from her blue-eyed gaze. Truthfully, though he'd at first kept away from any majus once associated with the organization he'd belonged to in his youth, his term on the Council lately occupied all of his time. He'd seen no friends in cycles, not really. He'd never taken a lover either. That sort of thing just wasn't interesting to him. He'd been starved of interactions with genuine friends, for the last several cycles. The Council didn't count.

"I should have come," he mumbled.

"Oh, I see Rilan Ayama every now and then," Gompt continued. "She keeps me apprised of your exploits," Gompt's tongue protruded in a Festuour grin. "I don't think even she realized you belong to both the House of Potential *and* the House of Healing. Bet you could have shown her a thing or two about the Symphony, if you wanted."

She turned and Krat lumbered into the next room. Mandamon followed them. His fingers twitched to figure out what his old friends had done with the System Beast architecture. The commercial ones were just dumb beasts—nowhere near the true capacity of the design. Was it possible to preserve enough of a personality to encode it into the music underlying the contraption? He'd done his own work with System Beasts over the cycles, but ever since the Society of Two Houses had been dissolved, fifty cycles ago, he'd kept the more advanced aspects secret, as had Gompt and Kratitha. With the Council looking over his shoulder, he'd ceased regular contact with his old friends, for fear of letting their association take up a presence in the minds of other maji. Or that's what he told himself. He should have come out here to see Gompt.

He'd worked hard over the cycles to keep the status of two-house maji relegated to a curiosity. The Society, and those maji with access to two aspects of the Grand Symphony, had pressed too far and used less than ethical means. That incarnation was best forgotten, and through his diligent work, now it was.

"You aren't here to reminisce, are you, Mandamon?" Gompt snapped him from his line of thought. "What is this all about?"

Mandamon shook away the memories and took in the Festuour. He'd known she had problems walking, even twenty cycles ago, but had done nothing. Kratitha had been alive then, able to help—to take the burden off him. He'd missed the old Pixie's death, wrapped up in a mission for the Council. Gompt herself was... Mandamon cocked his head. He was familiar enough with Festuour anatomy to see the signs.

"Something is changing in the Grand Symphony itself. There are too many new factors where nothing has changed before," Mandamon said. "Though perhaps I should first ask how to address you."

"Finally noticed, did you," Gompt chuckled, brushing a paw absently down her smooth belly. "Shows how long you've been out of touch. I transitioned before Kratitha passed on. She helped me through the toughest times." Mandamon detected some bitterness there, certainly directed at him. Well deserved.

"Yes. I apologize." The words were stiff, not said regularly. "I should have kept in contact. Over time, my duties in the Council have grown quite hefty." He watched Gompt. She—no, *he* seemed only partially satisfied by the excuse. That was reasonable. It was time to renew this relationship for real.

Mandamon bent forward in a deep bow, ignoring the creaking in his spine. "I am here for your genius, Gompt, and your friendship, if I may have it again. There are momentous changes afoot, which require, shall we say, a higher level of competence in the maji? I have a new design to implement, and it will require the finest manipulation of the Grand Symphony." He straightened, and looked at his partner in design of the System Beasts.

Gompt stared back for a while, his furry snout closed over his teeth, glasses pinched between hairy drawn brows. Mandamon nearly said something else, just to fill the silence. Was this the reaction others had to him, in his capacity on the Council?

Gompt's frown broke and his mouth opened, tongue lolling out. "Oh, Mandamon," he said. "So serious all the time. Never change." He clapped his paws once, and Krat rose up, bringing her jointed legs together until Gompt's face was level with his. Mandamon stiffened with a wince, smelling the Festuour's hot breath, slightly sweet and spicy.

"What do we do first?"

"Our first task," Mandamon said, "is to restart the Society of Two Houses."

* * *

Mandamon focused on the Symphony, listening to the melody around him. He strained to remember the image of the swamp on Loba.

"Time's wasting." Gompt poked him in the back with one hairy paw.

"I know, I know," Mandamon said. "It's been a while. Give me a moment."

"Be easier if we had someone from the House of Communication," Gompt said. He had his arms crossed, leaning back in the saddle on which he sat. Krat danced from leg to leg, shifting Gompt's bulk. They'd spent the last several days going over Mandamon's list of two-house maji, and putting out subtle queries.

Mandamon dropped his attention from the Symphony for a moment, lowering his hands. "Yes, just the Houses of Potential, Healing, and Power between us. Only half the Symphony. What a shame." He'd forgotten how easily Gompt could flip his switches. It was a pleasant change from the incompetence in the Council.

The scent of woody pulp filled his nostrils as a memory surged of him and Gompt on Loba, mere months after the Society of Two Houses was closed. "Ah, that's the right sensory cue."

The Symphony surged again, and he clamped onto a sequence of notes defining the melody of the garden behind Gompt's home. They weren't using a portal ground, which was technically illegal, but then, so was the Society they were attempting to resurrect. Mandamon had a specific goal, and telling the rest of the Council would only make it harder to achieve. Besides, they were busy with the aftermath of the Life Coalition's attack on the Dome of the Assembly. He'd been stupid not to realize how the organization had grown, hidden for so many cycles.

He placed a slightly different sequence of notes from the core of his being into the music. Switched this section with that, and made the swell of the music turn from a listless ballet to a waltz. He raised his hands and an oval of black spread in front of him, rising until it was his height, ringed in an aura of brown and white.

"Got it," he said.

Gompt tapped on Krat's controls and the multi-legged System Beast scuttled past Mandamon. "Hope it is correct," Krat said, before Gompt's furry head passed through the portal.

Mandamon emerged behind the Festuour and the portal spiraled shut behind him. His notes returned as the Symphony modulated to this place's usual theme. He pushed his shoulders back, taking in a deep breath of humid air. Soggy ground gave beneath his boots, and large, fleshy fungoid stalks cast patches of shade.

"Zie lives over in that direction, if I remember correctly," Gompt said, pointing a paw off to his left. There was a path through the fungal trees, which shaded the mud and patches of moss littering the ground. His other paw was pulling at the bandolier he wore so it sat better over his paunch. "But it's been a long time. Zie could have left, or died, or—"

"Zie's still here," Mandamon said. He took an old piece of paper from his suit pocket, and unfolded it. "I've been monitoring all the two-house maji. Sitting on the Council has its benefits, after all."

"Some benefit," Krat's mechanical voice croaked. "Couldn't even come visit."

"Well I knew where you were..." Mandamon stumbled over the last word. "Where one of you was, at least."

"Past is past," Krat muttered. The System Beast's metal-tipped toes made indentations in the moss as she shifted from leg to leg.

Mandamon sighed and began stumping over the marshy ground to a small collection of huts made from resinous brown tissue. They rested in the center of a patch cleared of the tall fungal spires, and seeded with lush blue moss to keep the mud away. Loba wasn't his favorite place to visit, but it was familiar. All the ten homeworlds were. He'd traveled across each one in the cycles since he was a young man in the Society.

"This marsh is terrible for Krat," Gompt said as he was bumped over little ponds, and stems, and fallen mushroom caps.

"Will have to do routine maintenance after return," the mechanical voice said. "Detecting high level of moisture between metal and wood interface in several leg joints. Swelling will occur."

"We'll be there shortly. Stop your complaining," Mandamon said. "Laryn I'Hon is of the Houses of Strength and Communication. We used to call that a 'Negotiator.' It's an interesting combination in any case, and Laryn should be helpful to convey information about the Society to other two-house maji. We need to let the right people know what we are doing."

"Great," said Gompt. "Zie will be a good addition then, since everyone knows you're a terrible communicator." Mandamon looked back to see Gompt's blue eyes staring at him over the top of his glasses.

"Not going to let that go, are you," he said.

"Not for long while yet," Krat rumbled.

"What is this new device you have anyway?" Gompt pressed. "Will you let the thrycovolar out of the cage when we get to Laryn's residence?"

"Better to tell you all at the same time. Have patience." Mandamon turned away so he couldn't see Gompt showing his teeth in exasperation. The mystery would draw the Festuour on, and the System Beast for that matter, if Krat was anything like her progenitor.

Mandamon headed for the tiny village. That way neither of them could see the small smile threatening through his beard. It was good to be with his friends again.

* * *

"It's been an age since I've seen you, Touching Digits," Gompt said. Mandamon shifted on the sideways cylinder where he sat. It wanted to roll this way and that, and it took an effort to keep from falling off the side. Though the style was popular among the Lobhl, this was not a chair for an old man like him. He eyed Krat's shiny metal and wood legs, supporting Gompt's bulk. Maybe he would build his own System

Beast conveyance, when they were done tracking down prospective members of the new Society.

<It is a p-pleasure and honor for you to arrive on Lobhl,> Touching Digits signed. The Lobhl's speech echoed in their heads with something like a stutter, marked when their middle fingers tapped together while they signed. Their large hands, each with five fingers and two thumbs, made a quick turn in the air, marking a question. <We have few visitors to our homeworld. May I ask how you find our planet? Are the inhabitants pleasant? The colors acceptable?>

"We did have a little trouble finding your home," Mandamon said. "Neither Gompt nor I are familiar with any dialects of your hand sign, which made it hard to ask for directions. However, your people are very conscientious. They continued asking questions until they solved our problem and we arrived here." In fact, several had followed them all the way to Touching Digits' color post, which marked what the Lobhl called their "claim of individuality."

As maji, Mandamon and Gompt were affected differently by the Nether, able to understand other species even when on one of the ten homeworlds. Non-maji did not have the same reaction to the Nether, and so Mandamon and Gompt's vague gestures were not translated back for the Lobhl. Fortunately, Touching Digits, a majus of the Houses of Communication and Potential, did not have that problem.

<And the colors?> Touching Digits accompanied the question with a complex intertwining of their fingers, translated as a description of several colors Mandamon had no name for.

"Right pleasing," Gompt said, while Mandamon was still thinking of an answer.

"Ratio of green sequence and magenta contrast forms informative bivariate color scale," Krat's mechanical voice broke in.

<Excellent.> A double flip of the fingers. Touching Digits had no trouble addressing Krat as another participant in the conversation. <What was your t-task today? You are both still male, yes?> Gompt nodded at that, with a sly smile on his long snout.

"We've come about the Society of Two Houses," Mandamon said. He hoped he wasn't breaking any social norms by getting straight to the point, but the Lobhl had asked. The mute species had a strange concept of honor and politeness.

<This gathering was d-disbanded fifty cycles ago, shortly after I joined,> Touching Digits signed, and Gompt nodded.

"We're getting the players back together," the Festuour said. "Got a new design that needs the old crowd, so the boss says." He threw a furry thumb at Mandamon.

<Boss?> The thumb waggle indicated polite confusion.

"A figure of speech...or language," Mandamon said.

"He is on the Council of the Maji," Gompt said. "Got to afford the bigwigs their respect."

<Yes. T-this is indeed important,> Touching Digits signed. <Without hierarchical constraints, how would the Assembly function?> They sounded completely serious. Mandamon threw a sideways glare at Gompt, while Touching Digits adjusted the scarf they wore around the lower portion of their head. It draped down into a shawl covering the Lobhl's shoulders and chest. The species did not have the same concept of gender as most of the others in the Assembly, and so it was considered polite to ask which gender the individual had assumed, as it tended to change with the task at hand. Touching Digits had made it clear they were agender, as they did not currently have a gendered responsibility.

"At any rate," Mandamon said, pulling the yellowed paper from his inside pocket, "I have it marked you are of the Houses of Communication and Potential? What we used to call an 'Innervator' in the Society?"

<That is accurate,> Touching Digits signed. Their eyes followed Mandamon's hands as he unfolded the paper, and Mandamon, as he often did when speaking to a Lobhl, wondered how his speech was translated to one who spoke only in gestures.

<I had only just made the acquaintance of the m-members of the Society before it was shut down. I had not even completed my rituals of new connection with the other members. Moortlin had t-tasked me with research on new energy production, though that project unfortunately was canceled at the closure of our organization. I have spent many cycles since w-working on the growing number of electric lights that grace the Nether and the homeworlds.>

Mandamon blinked after the Lobhl finished, letting his brain process the information coming to it. It was as if he had the memory of hearing Touching Digits make the speech.

"We could've used you on the System Beast project," Gompt put in. "Always had trouble with the power conduction."

"Would have put too many of House of Potential on the project," Krat's mechanical voice cut in. "Kratitha complained of you two already."

"You remember that?" Mandamon asked the System Beast. He didn't want to derail their conversation, but if Krat had memories of Kratitha's life, then...

"Select memory transcriptions stored, along with picked recordings from Kratitha," Krat said. "Enough to interpolate for data."

<I have f-followed the System Beasts ever since their creation,> Touching Digits said. <I did not forget my brief stint in the Society, though we were t-told by Moortlin themself to stay quiet.>

"And well you did," Mandamon said. He took in the Lobhl. Their head was bald, and nearly featureless, and Mandamon's attention naturally went to their hands. There were signs of maturity present there, with scars on several fingers, and thick skin around the fingertips. Mandamon guessed the Lobhl was of an age with him and Gompt, though he wasn't certain how long their species lived.

"The point Mandamon is dancing around," Gompt said, "is that we're wondering if you would like to rejoin the Society. We need the members to build this confounded device he wants to make, but he's staying silent on what exactly it is until we get more maji."

Touching Digits' hand folded in and out, showing consideration. <I am most p-pleased with the fact of your invitation,> they said. <I am honored you come within the range of my claimed space on your own volition.>

"Meaning you...are willing to join?" Mandamon asked. The Lobhl occasionally had issues in communication with the other species.

<I...believe I would.> Their hands paused a moment before the nimble fingers began another dance. <Yes. I have contributed to several new inhabitants of my homeworld, but have no strong t-ties to any of them. I have lately been...adrift, I think. It will be a pleasant change to work on a project with aliens again.>

Mandamon gripped the paper in both hands, keeping them still. "Excellent," he said. "So far is it us, and a Lobath named Laryn I'Hon. Zie is younger than us, and was not around when the Society disbanded. But zie is willing to help our search for the edges of knowledge of the Symphony."

"Zie's also in the House of Communication," Gompt said. "We thought it would be good if you two were to spread word to some other two-house maji we've found. That way it won't take us an age and half to gather everyone up."

<Will not others hear about this g-gathering?> Touching Digits signed, their fingers showing the question. <Shall we not tell them?>

Mandamon nodded. "That was the biggest failing of the Society in the past—its secrecy. I will not fall into that same trap again. This time word will get out. But by that point I mean to be ready."

<Ready? Forgive me, but ready for what?> Touching Digits asked.

"For the Dissolution," Mandamon replied.

CHAPTER SIX

Providing the Peace

- The Aridori are a constant thorn in the archivist's side. So many records were destroyed in the Aridori War it is as if our history begins merely a thousand cycles ago, though that is ridiculous. However, it is exceedingly hard to find surviving records of substance. There are many small things—financial statements, inventory lists, and personal letters—that let us know the Assembly of Species existed. We also know there was a great fire in the records room of the Palace of the Effature.

The Aridori, when they launched their attack (if that was what actually happened), destroyed all records they could find, whether or not it mentioned them. We must depend almost exclusively on oral records to recreate the events.

Excerpt from "A Dissertation on the Ten Species, Book XII: The Aridori"

Rey skulked up the massive stair leading to the Great Assembly. It was not in session today, but that did not mean it was empty.

It had taken six days of persuasion to get Majus Kheena to admit they might be able to talk to the Life Coalition leaders on their own. The Snakey's claims of some great source of power, and that they all had to work together now instead of murderin' each other, were not enough to overcome the Assembly's reticence. Perfectly understandable, and coupled with a healthy fear of the Aridori meant they were being interviewed—or interrogated—by the Council of the Maji and the Speakers nigh constantly to find out the right of things.

Instead of Rey's idea to approach the Coalition directly, his mentor surprised him by suggesting they slip in before the Coalition next parleyed with the Speakers and the Council.

"It's clear," he called back, and his mentor's dark robe hurried up the steps behind him. There were a few of the Effature's guards around the curve of the building, not looking in this direction.

"Us, we must be careful. This, it is not necessarily condoned," Majus Kheena hissed. "Simply because me, I share their species, that does not mean I wish to be accused of collaboration with them."

"Eyah, and yer would rather be workin' sums back in yer hidey-hole, I know. But I want to get Inas back as much as the rest of the group, and they're comin' up with nothin' useful."

Did that mean he wanted Inas back *more* since he was sneaking inside the Assembly? He would have thought Enos at least would be itching to find her brother.

"Agreed. Direct negotiation, it has uses. But listening to Majus Ayama, it seems the Council, it is not doing the job it was meant to."

"Aye," Rey returned. "'Specially now Councilor Feldo's skived off the last month or so."

"This, I have noticed," his mentor mumbled as they hurried up the stair.

Inside, Rey searched the empty seats of the Assembly. It looked very different, standing on the floor. The Council and Speakers must be used to looking up the nostrils of several thousand maji and ten times that number of delegates. They shimmied around, close to the wall. The Speakers and more guards would be here soon.

"Me, I must wonder why the Coalition did not deploy such a weapon as an Aridori openly before now." Rey's mentor scowled. "One of those beasts, if the tales are true, might have flipped the tide of the attack right here, not so long ago. The entirety of the maji, they could not stop the void the Life Coalition summoned. There is more going on and us, we must find out."

"I was right beside yer," Rey said. "Good we got out when we did." He'd seen Majus Ayama and the others running around the floor, coordinating the counter attack to the Life Coalition's intrusion into the Dome of the Assembly. They'd popped in from nowhere at the last moment, as usual. Didn't tell him and his mentor what was goin' on 'till later.

Majus Kheena grunted in agreement, then pointed. "The Life Coalition members, they should be in one of those alcoves." He pointed to several hanging curtains spaced around the floor of the Assembly. Behind them were cubbies dug into the stone forming the first story between the glowing floor and the lowest set of seats for the maji.

They kept to the wall, quickly tracing the circumference of the floor until Majus Kheena brushed aside the curtain of the nearest alcove. "Not this one."

Rey got to the next one before him and tugged it open. "Eyah, they're in here."

He stared at the leaders of the Life Coalition, seated in chairs. Four cowls turned in his direction. No one else was here yet, thank the Greatmother.

"You, you are not Speakers," one of the Snakeys said—the female who'd led the discussion in the Assembly.

Rey made a show of gesturing his mentor in, who, he noticed, had pulled his cowl forward. "Yer right, we are not. Instead, I give you Majus Kheena of the House of Potential. We're a mite pressed fer time, yer understand." That probably wasn't the best way to say it, but those dark hoods staring at him made all his hair stand on end. Creepy Snakeys.

"And you, what is it you want?" another said. Rey thought it was the one introduced as Zsaana. The voice was old and dry, even if Rey couldn't see anything under all that cloth.

"Us, we wish to talk," Majus Kheena said and Rey tilted his head in agreement.

"Mor'n that, we want my friend back," he said.

His mentor shot him a look, but he didn't care. The Life Coalition had held Inas for over a month. Rey was willing to entertain listening to their side of things, but they'd have to give him up first.

The Methiemum was one of the only ones Rey could truly call a friend here in the Nether. He listened when Rey spoke, and was fun to chum around with. If he'd been Sureri, Rey would have thought about making a pair with him, being brother-husbands while looking for a suitable wife. His people weren't normally too accepting of outsiders, but he'd seen at least one trio here in the Nether where a husband had been a Festuour. Could he do that?

Zsaana sat forward, then tilted his head to one side, inside his cowl. A Snakey who'd given up the power of the Council itself for this new life. "Your friend, he is a member of the Life Coalition?"

"No, yer took him!" Rey said. "Yer all are wantin' to join the Assembly now? I dunno why, and I don't really care. But yer can't be kidnapping people and negotiatin' in good faith. Give him back!"

"In the Life Coalition, there are many who wish to give up their old life," the female—Janas—said. "We are accepting of all."

"He. Is. Not. There. Willingly." Rey emphasized every word.

Majus Kheena cleared his throat. "This, it is a good time to mention that this would be a gesture of goodwill, which I am certain would help your bid to rejoin the Assembly, whatever your true reason is."

"All our members, they are able to leave us at any time," Janas insisted. "They believe in the work we do."

"The Aridori, they are not," Majus Kheena mumbled.

Rey waggled his head. "A point, but we aren't talkin' about the Aridori, now are we?" He wasn't interested in ancient scare-tales. So they wouldn't just give Inas back, would they?

"We also wish to learn more about your positions and the timing of your bid to join the Assembly, especially after the, ah—hostilities." Kheena waved a hand out the curtain, at the larger Assembly, which was still missing part of its dome. It was the other reason his mentor had suggested sneaking in to see this group—to find out why they'd been willing to negotiate suddenly. Perhaps Rey had come on too strong in the beginning, asking about Inas.

"Yer've got another reason for being here," he broke in. He faltered when the others stared at him, but swallowed, and continued on. He wanted to understand what drove these Snakeys, if not as much as learning where his friend was.

"We think yer want peace. We understand yer have some message, along with this talk of power. Why aught would yer come back here? Yer need the force of ten species to help yer out. Why?"

Zsaana was still watching them, or at least the opening of his cowl pointed at Rey. He seemed to be the principal speaker for the group, probably from his time on the Council. "The Life Coalition, it strives for a new age for the ten species. Our prophesied source of energy will make this possible. You do not follow the traditional ways, do you?" The last was directed at Rey's mentor, and Kheena reluctantly shook his head. "Ah, but if you did, you would know of what we preach."

"Me, I've heard plenty of fundamentalist tales," Majus Kheena said. Rey looked back and forth. His mentor was not overly religious, a rarity for a Sathssn.

"This, it is no tale," Zsaana said. "Even you should remember Slithen the Dreamer."

Majus Kheena scoffed. "Him, he is an old littermate's story."

"It is true," Janas broke in. "Me, I am Slithen's descendant. My brother Essra and I learned his tales from my parents when we were young."

"But Slithen's line, they were already supposed to have access to great influence in the stories," Kheena protested. "Something so strong, they could have taken over the dioceses. Why does the Life Coalition then grovel at the edges of Sathssn society?"

"Great influence, like the control of Aridori prisoners?" another of the cloaked figures said. Janas lifted a glove, as if to strike the individual, or take the words back.

Rey had had enough of all this mystery and skirting around the truth. The Life Coalition obviously wasn't going to spill their hand.

"I donna really care if yer think yer are more powerful than the Assembly or not, or if yer want some magical peace ray," he said, and all the Snakeys turned to look at him. "If yer are so high and mighty, then yer can give Inas back, whether yer think he's a willing participant or no."

"The one you spoke of before, then he is called Inas?" Zsaana hunched forward, as if waiting for the perfect moment to strike.

Rey frowned. "That's right. He's a close friend." He drew his brows down. The other species called Sureriaj ugly, so maybe he could use that to intimidate these Snakeys. "Give him back."

"Hmm. A dangerous request," Janas said. "Any friend of an Aridori, we must regard them as suspect as well."

Rey blinked, taking a moment to process Janas' words. They couldn't mean they thought—

"What? What do yer mean by that?" He just wanted his friend back. "I'm speakin' of a Methiemum man. Good buddy o' mine. I'm fine yer all into peace, but takin' hostages crosses the line. The Assembly won't treat with yer if that gets out." It would only take a word to Majus Ayama to spread it everywhere.

"Not so much of a friend, is he, if he did not trust you with his true species?" Zsaana asked.

A pit of ice was growing in Rey's belly, but he refused to be drawn in by the Snakey's lies. "What are yer talking of? Yer saying Inas is

Aridori?" He looked to his mentor, but Majus Kheena had his head cocked, staring at Rey.

"Us, we are saying just this," said Janas. "We have sequestered him with the others of the ancient enemy."

"But he's..." Rey paused, trying to take in what they were saying. It couldn't be true. Inas was a *friend*. He wasn't one of the murderous Aridori. He couldn't be. They were all dead.

Except the Life Coalition had one—or more than one. "The one in the box—" he began, but Zsaana was shaking his cowl.

"That, it was not him. The Aridori you knew as Inas, he has not yet been trained."

"Trained?" Rey was adrift, as if floating in a sea of sand. What were they doing to Inas? But if he really was an Aridori... No. That was stupid. "Where are yer keepin' him? Give him back to me!" He realized he was standing, breath coming hot from his nose. When had he done that?

"Peace, apprentice," Zsaana said. "Inas, he will not be released. We will not let another Aridori War begin."

"But he's not...Inas isn't..." Rey couldn't concentrate. None of this made sense. Inas was his *friend*—he'd even had thoughts of making an offer of brother-husbands to him.

"Perhaps, our arrival here, it was not the best of times," Majus Kheena said, rising to his feet. "The Speakers, they will surely be on their way."

"Indeed," Zsaana replied. "But you, now you have some idea of the capacity and power we offer to the Assembly, in our search for true peace. Tell them that."

Never trust an Aridori.

The air in Rey's lungs was lead. Could he trust the words of the Coalitioners over his friends? But what reason did they have to lie? They hadn't told him Inas was Aridori until he named his friend. Before that, they'd seemed willing to let him go. It was impossible. Could it be true?

His friends. Hah. So he thought. *She lied. Both of them had. This whole time.* Of course Enos had to be one too. Which meant Sam had to know. Those two were inseparable. Rey's hands clenched into fists. What other secrets did they hide?

"Come Rey, let us leave," Majus Kheena said. He sounded shaken. Rey followed him without a backward glance at the Snakeys.

* * *

Enos forced down the spike of anger.

"Try it again," Majus Ayama said.

She'd *been* trying, for most of a lightening. Just because that Kirian couldn't get the information from her, didn't mean—

"Be thinking of the sounds and sights again. Any description of the interior will place more markers," Majus Cyrysi said. His long fingers, each tipped with a wicked-looking hooked nail, stretched toward her forehead. This hadn't worked any of the other times they tried it.

Now Enos' anger was once more replaced with fear. Fear of discovery, though these two already knew she was Aridori. What was she scared of? She swallowed, and wished Sam was here, but Majus Cyrysi had given him practice work on the theory of the Symphony. He was stuck in the majus' apartment, which was perfect for Sam.

She let Majus Cyrysi's cool fingertips touch her brow, and suppressed a shiver. *Be calm. He's helping to save Inas.*

"We are needing more markers to make the portal. Anything will be helping," the majus repeated, "but especially sounds—no! No, concentrate!"

Enos felt herself slipping away. It had been such a tentative connection to Inas each time. It hadn't happened again, and now she only felt nauseous.

She ducked away from the Kirian's hand, closing her eyes to force the feelings away. They *had* to find Inas. The vision of the sleek form rising from that little box haunted her dreams. Was Inas in one of those right now? How much did the Life Coalition know of him? Of their family? She should know more about her own species, but the Life Coalition had stolen that knowledge from its prisoners.

She'd never been away from him this long. Her parents had told tales of Aridori separated from their other instance so long they could no longer form a connection. Alone. Adrift. Without another half.

"Are you sure there's enough information to collect from her, Ori?" Majus Ayama asked. "We know little about how Ari—"

"I can be doing it." Majus Cyrysi cut her off. "We have a resource, if you are but to be letting me use it." He ran a hand down Majus Ayama's arm, but she only frowned at him.

"It's been over a month and we still haven't chased down the Life Coalition. I feel like I'm running into a wall, repeatedly, headfirst, while trying to create this portal."

Enos let the fear of losing her other instance climb up into her throat, focusing her on the task. "Try it again. I have to help my brother and I'll try as many times as it takes. Just let me get into the right frame of mind—"

Someone pounded at the door to Majus Ayama's apartment.

"Oh, what now?" her mentor said, and stomped to the door.

"Rey—what's wrong?" Enos asked, as soon as the Sureri pushed the door open. He looked like he might be sick. Or throw something.

"Yer didn't tell me. Yer and Sam. When did he find out? After they took Inas away? When was it, eyah?" He'd crossed the floor before she had time to react, and Enos saw the aura of brown around him only belatedly—the House of Potential. He put a hand to the front of her vest and she found herself flying across the room, until she smacked into Majus Ayama's couch, falling over it in a heap.

The Symphony flooded her, white rings coming to life around her hands and cadenzas tumbling through her mind. What had gotten into Rey? Enos struggled to get up, but her mentor and Majus Cyrysi were in front of her, one ringed in olive and white, the other in orange and yellow. Both held hands out in front of them.

"What is going on?" Majus Ayama yelled at Rey.

"Is Kheena knowing where you are?" Majus Cyrysi asked.

Rey ignored them both, his eyes fixed on Enos. "Yer didn't tell me yer are *Aridori!*"

The maji's hands drooped, and Enos felt the fight go out of her, like water poured from a bucket.

He knows. How does he know?

Sam. Was he still studying in Majus Cyrysi's apartment? He wouldn't have gone out by himself, would he? No, Rey said Sam didn't tell him.

She was right to be scared. This is exactly what would happen if the Assembly found out about her and Inas. They'd be dead before the day was out.

There was a soft click and Enos looked over Rey's head. Majus Ayama was locking the door.

"We should talk," her mentor said, her voice quiet and dangerous. Majus Cyrysi stood with his arms crossed, crest as spiky as if lightning had struck it. His face was calm, but Enos thought he was anything but.

Just like me.

"Rey—we didn't...I didn't tell you because—" She was babbling.

"Because yerrer an Aridori!" Rey yelled. "And so is Inas. An' now the Life Coalition is goin' ter 'train' him, or torture him, or sommat else horrible." He clenched his eyes and teeth together, groaning. "Eyah, I donna even know if I'm supposed to like him any longer. He's an Aridori. Yer can't trust 'em, eyah." He looked up, his face a mask of pain. "How can I ever trust either of yer again?"

"The Coalition is doing what to him?" Enos asked, ignoring Rey's pained expression. Was that what she'd felt? Did her seizures come because her other instance was being tortured while she connected to him? She hadn't even known she could feel him, from halfway across the universe. If Majus Ayama was correct, he was trapped inside a moon of Sath Home.

"And more importantly, where?" Majus Ayama said. The white of the House of Healing still glowed around her, as if she would force the information from Rey if he didn't volunteer it.

"Them Snakeys—the Life Coalition. Me and Majus Kheena sneaked in to sit a bit with 'em, on account o' he's a Snakey too, yer know."

"I am aware Majus Kheena is a *Sathssn*," Majus Ayama said. She could have frozen water with her voice. Rey's eyes widened.

"Er, Sathssn, eyah. In any case, they started blabberin' on about their secret weapon, like they've been hidin' Aridori away all these long cycles, but only this special sect, or whatnot." Rey seemed to be losing steam. "Save they sound like they really do want to join forces again for this peace they're bringin'."

"They *do* have more than one of my species," Enos said to her mentor. Majus Ayama nodded, as did Majus Cyrysi.

"They are potentially to be having many more, if they are to be possessing the remnants of what the Sathssn squads captured at the end of the Aridori War," the Kirian said. His crest rippled and his eyes roved somewhere far away, lost in thought. "It is recorded that the prisoners were destroyed, but I am wondering at the life spans of Aridori. With no fixed biological structure to age—"

Enos cleared her throat, trying to get the conversation back on track. She wasn't that old, and her parents had never shared their age.

"But they confirmed they have Inas, and they...they know what he is?" She asked Rey, who sneered.

"Aye, they know he's a filthy Aridori, just like yer are. To think, back when we were runnin' from mobs in the Imperium, when people were suspectin' Sureriaj of bein' Aridori in hidin'. Yer were there beside me the whole time. Liar." His face was no longer comically ugly. It was twisted into anger.

Enos stepped back, as if struck. "We couldn't tell you, or anyone. They would have—"

"They'd have chased yer two, rather than us," Rey finished for her.

"But...you still want to get Inas back?" she asked the Sureri.

Rey's face cleared, now confused more than angry. As if he had just realized what he was saying. "I do. More'n anythin'. Granddames save me from myself, I donna know why, but I do."

"Then no matter what you are to be feeling about Enos," Majus Cyrysi said, "our objectives align. We must find a way to meet again with the Life Coalition leaders."

"I...could probably talk with 'em again," Rey said. He looked between the three of them, his face screwing up in one of his rubbery Sureriaj expressions. "But Majus Kheena would have to agree to sneak us in."

Enos stared at him. He had a way to contact those who held her other instance prisoner.

I'm worth as much to them as Inas.

Before the maji could say anything else, she stepped in front of them, close to Rey. "Take me. Tell them I can heal Inas, if they bring him to meet me." The old Aridori in Gloomlight prison had messed with his mind. She had no idea how to help him, but they must have seen his hand, melted into a rigid claw. Perhaps that was why he was in a box. They were getting rid of that infection.

"Shiv's knobbly knees! Not a chance," Majus Ayama said, though Majus Cyrysi stroked his moustaches in thought.

Enos spun to her mentor. "It is the only way to get him back. They will not willingly let him go."

"No," Majus Ayama said again. "We will force our way into their headquarters,"

"With what?" Enos retorted. "You said yourself, you've been building the portal for a month. It's not working." She gestured to Rey, who was watching wide-eyed. "He has another way."

"And you are thinking you will simply dance away from the Life Coalition with your brother?" Majus Cyrysi asked. "I am certain they will be suspecting a trick of this nature."

"Then think of what I could find out about the Life Coalition, if they captured me!" Enos would say anything to convince the maji. She *had* to have Inas back. "I could even talk with the other Ari—"

"No!" Majus Ayama said. She swiped both hands in front of her, as if pushing away the suggestion. "I will not lose you to the Life Coalition again. That is final."

"But—" Enos didn't finish the sentence, as she saw the storm in her mentor's face.

"I am to be agreeing with Rilan on this point," Majus Cyrysi said. "Yes, there is a chance of rescuing your brother, and as much information as you could gather, the risk to your well-being is not to be worth it. You are knowing what the Life Coalition did to the Aridori we saw in Gloomlight. No, we must be developing this portal. It is to be the only way."

Despite herself, Enos shivered, thinking of the mass of senseless Aridori mashed into one body. Its gibbering ran through her mind: *free us to slash, to tear, to bite and squeeze and pull and rip and taste and—*

She made herself exhale, releasing tension with the breath. The maji were right. It was a stupid idea to risk herself, and Inas. Without her, Sam would... Well, she didn't know what he would do, but it likely wasn't healthy.

"I...you're right. I wasn't thinking," she told her mentor. Majus Ayama gave her a sharp nod in response. Enos turned back to Rey. "But if you talk with them again..." Something else struck her. "Was Zsaana there?"

Rey blinked in surprise. "I...eyah, he was. What of it?"

"Tell him to look at Inas with the Symphony," she said. "He hasn't been right, since the Gloomlight prison. Tell him—" It was a risk, but maybe, just maybe, the Life Coalition would give him back—a broken Aridori. "Tell him Inas isn't yet worthy of the form, and must be returned to us. We can fix him." The image of Inas' hand sprang up in her mind, half-melted, stuck in one position. It was the hand that had touched the insane prisoner.

"I...can do that," Rey said. He sounded completely lost. At least he wasn't screaming any longer.

"Also tell them if they harm him *at all*, the Life Coalition will lose any bargaining chips they have with the Assembly. I swear they will." Majus Ayama's face was almost white with fury. "And now, Reyhorer, I think you have somewhere else to be. Breathe a word of this to anyone and by Brahm's majestic balls, all the punishments your granddames heaped upon you will be as nothing!"

Rey turned, fumbled with the lock on the door until it turned, and practically ran from the room.

"That might have been overkill," Majus Cyrysi remarked to Majus Ayama's frown.

CHAPTER SEVEN

Plans of Overture

- The first scientific team to investigate the Grumv Vugm Mugv, or Avians, found their bodies had responded to pressures of living inside the Nether for an extended period. Here the changes are represented by shallower lungs, as there is no air pressure differential at the top of the Nether, and tougher claws, which act as a replacement for metal tools they lacked. However, their species is not native to the Nether. This means the group colonizing several large cities spread out across the top of the Nether's volume must have arrived from a homeworld at some point in the past, and then been unable to return.

Notes from committee meeting on scientific results from study of the Grumv biology.

"Look at this thing!"

Sam peered around Majus Ayama's shoulder at the giant mechanical beetle. To get them in to see the machine, Majus Cyrysi had pulled strings with scientists he knew at the House of Power and with Matthiawi Burris, Reader, the Effature's legal minister. Sam was still reeling from being at the strange and eventful first meeting with the Grumv that morning. A new species in the Nether—one which lived above the clouds, at the very top of the enclosed crystal. Counting the Aridori, that was twelve species, not ten. They reminded him of a cross between peacocks and pterodactyls, and the members of the species he'd talked to were all very pleasant.

Due to Majus Cyrysi's connections, and Burris' good graces, they had been allowed a quarter of a lightening to investigate the contraption before a bevy of maji and scientists would descend on it.

"I am to be thinking Councilor Feldo would be quite interested in this," Majus Cyrysi said. "A shame he is missing. As I recall, he had quite a lot to do with the original creation of System Beasts. While this is not to be exactly the same thing, it is very near. I wonder if—"

"Later, Ori," Majus Ayama said. "Let's take the chance while we're here to look this marvel over. It's a welcome break from chasing the Life Coalition and trying to unravel those shiv-cursed chimes."

"I can't imagine climbing up the wall to the top of the Nether," Sam said. Just thinking of the sheer, translucent cliff face made his hands clammy. And an Etanela *girl* had made the journey with her mother on this beetle. "What do you think, Enos?" he asked. She had been quiet, the past few days. He attributed it to being tired from helping Majus Ayama create a portal from scratch. From the majus' sharp replies when he asked, it wasn't going well.

Not that he was getting anywhere in studying the chimes with Majus Cyrysi. No one else was either. Several maji had studied it, with little progress, though the Council hadn't issued an official statement. To take a break, his mentor had promised some test to clarify his abilities in the Symphony. The Effature's request rang through his head. He felt like he was failing the old man already.

"Hm? Yes, very brave," Enos answered. "I cannot believe that Kirian with them, though."

"Kirian scum is to be what he is," Majus Cyrysi huffed. His crest looked like the sea after a storm. "I shall be notifying all of my connections on Kiria not to trust Wailimani with any other grants. First contact must be handled delicately, not by coercion! Why, if this had been done when the Lobhl joined the Assembly, I doubt we would have even incorporated them into—"

Sam let his mentor's speech wash over him as he poked at the metallic legs. The contraption really was a marvel. It looked like a giant stag beetle from Earth, shiny black and several times larger than him. Large enough to ride on, as the Etanela had. It was mechanical, and there were little doors all over it, opening to display complex arrangements of gears and levers. Another hatch on the top was big enough for a person to climb inside.

He went around the front. The horns looked as if they were made of Nether glass. He squinted, listening. The music surrounding the horns was incredibly complex, just like the music around any piece of the crystal.

"Look at this, Enos," he said, then turned when she didn't answer. She had one hand on the beetle's carapace, but was looking far away. He snaked a hand into hers and she started.

"Did you think about what I told you, about Rey?" she asked quietly. The maji were still arguing about what would happen now the new avian species had met the Effature and been offered entry into the Assembly.

"I did," Sam said. His heartbeat spiked at her question. He'd tried not to think about such violence, from Rey, of all people. He hadn't been there to protect Enos.

What would I have done? Punched Rey? I'm pretty sure he could wipe the floor with me. I might have hurt him if I used the Symphony. The Sureri was wiry and stronger than he looked.

Sam cradled his pocketwatch in his vest pocket with his other hand, letting the ticking be a regulating force. "At least he's working to get Inas back, since we can't seem to do it."

"But by what method?" Enos asked. Now her attention was all on him. "He talked directly with the Life Coalition leaders. They *told* him Inas is Aridori!"

"Yeah, and that they won't give him back. What are they *doing* to him?"

"Torture." Enos face was stony. "I am certain. It is why I felt such powerful emotion from him. It must be. I am certain they are doing horrible things to him."

"But you haven't felt anything else from him, have you? Not since those two times. It's been a ten-day," Sam whispered. He eyed the maji. They had a limited time with the beetle, but this was more important. Enos was contemplating some idea, but he couldn't figure out what it was. "Is he...do you think he's still..."

"He is alive. They wouldn't do that to him, and besides, I would know." Enos absently ran a hand down a segmented leg. "Rey will talk with them again. Do you think he can convince them to give Inas back?"

Sam shook his head. "Convince a militant group of Sathssn religious fanatics to give up an ancient enemy—sorry—like ones they've been holding on to for a thousand cycles? Even Rey's not that good." Their vibrant friend had talked himself out of almost every situation he'd gotten into.

"The alternative is to invade the Life Coalition's stronghold, and they might kill him if we do that. Don't you want Inas back?" Enos' face was tight, her eyebrows drawn down, her lips pursed.

That's a low blow.

"Of course I do," he said. He let go of the pocketwatch and took her hands in his. "More than anything. But the Life Coalition is up to something else with their talk of a power source. I just can't see it." He squeezed her hands. "Everyone is acting like they did nothing wrong—like killing, and destroying part of the Assembly, and keeping Aridori are a fair trade for what they can offer."

"Would you rather have him than me?" It took a moment for Sam to realize what Enos meant. She wasn't thinking along the same lines he was.

"What? No! Why would you say that?" He'd spoken too loud. The maji looked up from their investigation of the beetle and his heart raced at the thought of losing her. He took in a deep breath. "It's fine," he told them. "I'm fine."

Majus Cyrysi's crest said he didn't agree, but the maji turned back to the shiny black metal, whispering.

"I want *both* of you here," he whispered to Enos. "I can't choose one of you over the other. That's the whole reason we work together."

Enos fell silent, but she squeezed his hand again.

"It's just that—" Sam broke off when the chime sounded.

It had gone off that morning, rather than in the afternoon as was usual. It had rung every other day, then at the same time every day, for a total of eleven days. Now it was changing once more.

"Again? That's the second time today. It hasn't done that before."

Enos stumbled as the reverberation shook the building.

"I think that's our cue to leave," Majus Ayama said. "Come on Ori, they'll kick us out, once the maji stop running around because of that chime. Maybe this will force the Council to finally issue a declaration that it's dangerous. Or that it's not. Who even knows?" She threw her hands up.

Sam followed the maji out of the room where the beetle was held for research. The ever-present music playing in the corridors of the Spire was shaky and skipping from the effects of the chime. It seemed to disrupt many of the Systems in place around the Imperium. He'd seen a

System Beast come to a full stop and fall over in the middle of the street the day before.

In the corridor there was a group of people milling around. Sam drew close to Enos as they passed, feeling the familiar heat of panic at too many people, too close.

I need Inas too. We have to get him back.

He reached for that calm pool underneath the Symphony—the one he'd been able to access in Dalhni. It was still out of his reach.

When he looked over to thank her, he found Enos watching him. She picked up his hand and squeezed it.

Sam made himself smile down at her, as if everything was fine. What was she going through, if he was torn to pieces over Inas being gone? She shared not just a sibling's connection, not just a twin's connection, but even more. He was her other instance, connected across the universe. It was a powerful thing, and Sam's gut twisted in a spike of jealousy. He wanted to share that with them, to be even closer. He would give anything to know how Inas was doing.

Enos pulled him back until the maji disappeared around the next corner, then rose to her toes and kissed him. Sam almost reared back in surprise, but managed to stop his first, stupid reaction. He melted into the kiss.

"What was that for?" he asked when they separated. "Not that I'm complaining, just that—"

"Remember I care for you," Enos broke in. "And Inas and I will always be around for you. Even if only one of us is here, our two instances are linked."

Sam gave her an uncertain look, but nodded. "I'll remember," he said.

* * *

The day after the Grumv were introduced to the Assembly, Sam found himself staring around Majus Ayama's apartment. The majus had been forced to move when she lost her position on the Council, and he still wasn't used to the new apartment. It didn't help he hadn't been here in several ten-days. He swiped a speck of dust from the top of a chair.

He'd come with his mentor to find Enos, but she wasn't here. The kiss kept going through his head, as did her behavior. He tried to pretend it was just her concern over Inas, but there was more than that. Rey had set her off on a new thread and he didn't know what it was.

I should find her and talk to her again. I don't know what she's going through, but I know what it is to go through anxiety. I can help her this time.

He'd made up his mind and was walking to the door when his mentor called him.

"Sam, come here," Majus Cyrysi said. "We are to be finding answers, not cleaning the furniture."

"Wouldn't mind a good cleaning," Majus Ayama muttered. She positioned four rods in front of her on a desk. One was wood, another stone, a third iron, and the last was Nether crystal.

Sam frowned. He'd finally made a decision, and now they wanted him.

He approached the desk. "Where did you get that?" he asked, pointing to the core of crystal. It reflected the light from several lamps, though he could see through it. "I thought the Nether couldn't be cut."

"Until now, that has been the case," Majus Cyrysi said. "The beetle-like contraption we saw is dating perhaps even from before the Aridori War. It can be drilling through the crystal, in some manner unknown to maji. It has been providing several cores from the wall. This is the test I was to be telling you about."

"Even so, it took some work to secure this sample," Majus Ayama said. "The folks researching it in the Spire weren't happy when I requested it, but I still have some clout with the Council. Since they're finally investigating the chimes—now they're ringing twice a day—we can work on this instead."

"Now, be listening to the Symphony," Sam's mentor said. "This is a test I have been wanting to perform with your unknown connection to the Grand Symphony, but until now I have not been having the required resources."

Sam sighed, tried to push thoughts of Enos and Inas away, to let the music run through his mind. Each breath fell into a rhythm with the Symphony, and it dragged him farther in, to deeper melodies. With enough time, he might find that place of peace, hidden within him.

Lips pushing against his, warm and sweet. Small hands in his, tightening.

In the silence, his mind frantically replayed Enos' kiss, trying to figure out why he fixated on it. They'd shared lots of kisses. This one felt...different.

"Close your eyes," Majus Ayama said. Sam shook himself, then did as he was told. There was a sound of objects rattling.

"Be telling me where the one made of Nether crystal is," his mentor said, but Sam's hand was already rising, pointing to the rod second from the left, the one that had a vastly more complex progression of chords than the others.

"Not surprising. Anyone can hear that," Majus Ayama said, and there was more rattling as she moved them around again. "Which one is stone?"

Sam pointed again, to the place where the steady, lumbering beat resided. More rattling. Really, what were they trying to prove? He could tell which was which easily from the music.

"The wood?" Majus Cyrysi asked. Again Sam pointed, and again there were scraping sounds.

"And the iron?" Majus Ayama asked. He pointed.

He waited a moment, and when nothing else was forthcoming, opened his eyes. The maji were both frowning at him.

"I can hear the wooden one and a bit of the Nether crystal," Majus Ayama said, "but the others don't have a component in the Symphony of Healing."

"You can't hear the music in all of them?" Sam asked. He clasped his hands together. Was he the odd one out again? He could hear music in everything. It was just a matter of what notes he could touch.

"One who is to be of the House of Strength might be able to access some notes from each, from what I know," Majus Cyrysi said. "But you are seeming to overlap houses."

"Which ones do you hear?" he asked his mentor.

"In Communication, only the one of wood, because of the living channels that were once to be flowing through it. I am also to be hearing some of the Nether crystal piece, both with Communication and Power. The House of Power can access the iron rod."

Then why could he hear all four? "But I can't do things those Houses can do," Sam protested.

"Can you hear them?" Majus Ayama asked.

Sam blinked. "The houses? I...should I be able to?"

"You heard the Symphony of Communication when I was to be teaching you," Sam's mentor said. "You were even changing it, yet I am increasingly certain you are not to be a member."

"I don't—" Sam started, but Majus Ayama waved a hand at him.

"Listen." She picked up the rod of wood—oak, it looked like. How did Sam know that? Had his father taught him? He couldn't remember....

"Listen!" the majus repeated, and Sam's head jerked up. An aura of white surrounded her hand, and the wood twisted, as if it wanted to grow toward a light source. The House of Healing could do that sort of thing, with organic objects.

But he couldn't hear anything. That was silly. He wasn't the House of Healing.

Yet he *had* heard the House of Communication.

Sam concentrated, sorting through the melodies that drifted through his head, from the ones in the building's floor, to ones above their head. And then...

There was a high, chiming sound, a repeating trio of notes sounding as if they were played in another room. Sam focused on it. They belonged to the wood, but they were changing, the notes braiding into a different rhythm. He reached out and tugged one note away from the sequence.

The wood snapped straight, and Majus Ayama inhaled sharply, then shook her head.

"Well, that was unpleasant," she said. "Like someone jerking a chair out from under you while you're sitting in it."

Majus Cyrysi's crest was splayed in surprise, his eyes wide. "Were you changing the Symphony of Healing? I heard nothing."

"He did," Majus Ayama said, while Sam opened and closed his mouth. He wasn't sure *what* he had done. "Or at least he took a note away from the change I made. That's not to say he could make the original change." She cocked her head. "In fact..."

Sam backed up as the dark-haired woman came toward him like a shark swimming toward a minnow. The bell at the end of her braid chimed as she walked.

"Shiv's teeth, I'm not going to eat you," she said, then sighed. "We've been through this before, Sam."

"Yes. Sorry." Sam rubbed at an arm. Between Inas missing, and Enos acting funny, and his jumbled and missing memories, he was a mess. If he could fix even one of those things he would be making progress. Instead he was adding questions to those he hadn't answered.

He stood straight as the majus put her small hand out, which blossomed with a white and olive aura.

"Tell me if you can hear any of these changes," she said.

Sam swallowed, going slightly cross-eyed at the palm in front of his face, but listened. There was the music from the rods of material, and music from the desk and chairs in the room. He could even make out an occasional high-pitched note, like when the majus had changed the wood. But around him, nothing.

"Well?" Majus Ayama asked. Sam shook his head and she lowered her arm, the auras fading away.

"So you can't hear all of the House of Healing."

"I wonder if there are parts of the House of Communication you are also not to be hearing?" Majus Cyrysi mused. "Yet you have been changing the nature of components I cannot hear. Each house has overlap with others, in areas where the Symphonies are similar. The House of Strength and the House of Healing are both to be having some capacity to work with plants, for instance."

"We'll work on that part later, Ori," Majus Ayama said, going back to the table with the rods on it. She picked up the one of Nether crystal. "This one has to go back to the maji researching it, so I want to focus on it." She held it out to Sam.

He bit his lip, but stepped forward, reaching out to take it. "What do you want me to do with it?"

"Anything," Majus Cyrysi said, and Majus Ayama nodded.

"It is the one substance the houses of the maji can hear, but cannot touch. Can you?"

Sam frowned, then looked down. There was music there, intricate chords and arpeggios so fast and tightly interwoven it was nearly impossible to comprehend, much less grasp the notes. He'd tried it before, but the song of the Nether crystal was too strong.

That had been when he thought he was of the House of Communication.

Sam listened to the ream of notes, like the most complex concerto, played by a master violinist, at double speed, and backwards. He reached for a note, only to have his mental grip slide away from it.

He clenched his teeth and pitched into the stream of music. It buffeted his consciousness, too much information to understand. The Nether crystal was like...like a computer. A memory came to him, of working for technical support to pay for college. Computers like the ones on Earth were probably an alternate path from the sophistication of the ten species. However the Nether crystal... He closed his eyes, letting his focus fall completely into the object in his palm. Normally there was repetition in the Symphony. Listen to what defined a simple object for long enough and eventually its music would repeat. Here, however, the music was so fast and complex he couldn't hear an overall theme.

He let the room, the Nether, and his fears fall away, living in the stream of music defining the small rod of crystal. There *was* a theme to it, but it was evolving from moment to moment as if the song was being written, and re-written. If he could just get in advance of the music, and change where it was going...he grasped at notes, and held them for an instant, but the music slipped away.

Sam let out a long breath, and his eyes popped open. The maji were staring at him, wide-eyed. Majus Cyrysi's crest was sticking straight up. "What?" he asked.

"The Nether crystal was to be changing color, just briefly," Majus Cyrysi breathed.

"The whole rod glowed," Majus Ayama added, "but then it stopped. What did you do?"

"I couldn't change it," Sam said, eyeing the rod. "But I held a few notes until they slipped away." He looked back to the maji. "It's alive, and constantly adapting. That's why maji can't touch it. The Nether changes its own music, directing what it will do." He searched for words to describe what he'd felt. "It's as if there are streams of information in the music, processed and going to different places. It's thinking. The Nether is alive."

That wasn't the best explanation, but for someone who had never seen a computer, it might serve.

"We were knowing the Nether acted like an immense living being, but we were never thinking it is to be rewriting its music," Majus Cyrysi mused, fingering his moustaches. "It is to be changing the state of matter in which it exists."

"Is that why maji can pass through columns?" Majus Ayama asked.

"Wait—pass *through* the crystal?" Sam looked between the two. Majus Cyrysi's crest was splayed flat—a sign of derision.

"It is to be a parlor trick the maji use to make themselves feel special when graduating from apprentices to majus," he said. "The test is to be held within the column the Spire is built against. I remember Rilan's test well."

"You missed my test," Majus Ayama said.

Sam's mentor raised a finger. "Yet I am to be remembering the circumstances around it very well."

Majus Ayama frowned, but said nothing to that. Sam hadn't seen Majus Cyrysi stymie her like that often.

"Then could you just walk through the wall of the Nether?" he asked.

Both maji shook their heads. "It is to be much too thick," his mentor said. "The Nether sustains one while passing through the relatively thin wall of the column—"

"But it still feels like running the length of the Imperium afterward," Majus Ayama finished. She waved the topic away with a hand. "But this is a tangent. What you discovered about the Nether crystal here, today, none of the six houses have been able to discover. This is new."

Oh no. I'm the different one again. Why can't I just be normal?

"New, yes," his mentor said, one finger tapping his moustache thoughtfully. He switched topics. "But not unknowable. In fact, I am thinking I may be guessing what your house is, Sam."

Majus Ayama's eyes were alight. "We have limited data, but I see where you're going. He can affect the Nether. We know there have been ways in the past to manipulate it. He can change the parts of the Symphony dealing directly with the substance of things."

"That part is occurring in all the Houses," Majus Cyrysi said.

"But there are none fully devoted to it. I think you're right, Ori." Majus Ayama paced back and forth across the little room.

Sam looked back and forth between the maji, his stomach tying in knots. He didn't like the unknown. He liked old and comfy things. Still, their description *felt* right. He had changed the shaft of the arrow he'd found after the battle at the Dome. Since then, anything he'd changed was physical in nature.

"What would you call it?" he asked. "My house?"

"I believe we should be calling it the House of Matter," said Majus Cyrysi.

CHAPTER EIGHT

Changing Places

- The electrification of the Nether is a slow process. Because of the many different technologies already in place—the resin glowstones of the Lobath, the water-light storage of the Etanela, as well as many different light-giving Systems created and maintained by the maji— the need for pure electric lights was less than anticipated. I believe eventually, electric conduits will replace many Systems created by maji, thus relieving our order of the burden of maintaining them. Electric lights will brighten the dark corners of the Imperium and illuminate those who use them for nefarious purposes.

From a written account by Touching Digits, Lobhl majus of the Houses of Communication and Potential

Enos had told Majus Ayama she was going out, but not where. Her mentor had some test for Sam, and though it would help him if she were there, this was more important. She *had* to do this. He'd forgive her, she hoped, when Inas was back. She gripped her pants leg with one hand, bunching it up to keep her nails from digging into her palm. She paused outside the door, trying to steady her breathing. Was this what Sam went through all the time?

She swallowed, and knocked.

Rey opened the door to the apartment he shared with Majus Kheena in the House of Potential. Enos had waited until she saw the Sathssn stride away on some errand, to corner Rey. His face curled up in a sneer upon seeing her.

"I've made up my mind," Enos said.

"Yer...yer have?" Rey took a step back, and Enos barged past him while he held the door open. She couldn't be certain he would have let her in otherwise.

"I have," she said, once inside. She crossed her arms and waited until Rey pushed the door shut, frowning. "No Aridori tricks," she added.

"Ah, well, if yer put it that way, how can I refuse yer, eyah?" Rey screwed up his face, but Enos didn't miss the little light of humor in his dark eyes.

"Have you scheduled another meeting with the Life Coalition?" she asked.

"Oy! A little louder, mebbe?" Rey said, stepping toward her. "The neighbors two down might not have heard yer!"

Enos resisted the urge to step back, clenching her fists where they were each hidden under the other arm. Rey was—had been—their friend. If Sam hadn't arrived, he and Inas might have—anyway, it didn't matter now. He wouldn't do anything to her. Would he?

"Well?" she said, though a little quieter. "Have you?"

"I put a crawler in Majus Kheena's ear about it, eyah," Rey said. "Sommat official this time, no sneakin' about." He held up hands as she opened her mouth. "He's workin' on it. It's what he was off about before yer arrived. Best guess is a few days, though." Rey shook his head. "Never seen anyone so eager to crawl in with them Snakeys before."

"Tricky Aridori, remember," Enos said, and Rey rolled his eyes. She let the silence grow for a moment. "You want Inas back. So do I. Sam *needs* him back. He isn't doing well with just me. He's still not recovered from what he did at the Dome of the Assembly."

She stared at Rey, then licked her lips. It was now, or she would lose her nerve, and they'd never get Inas back.

"Use me as bait. We know they want...Aridori," she faltered as she named herself, seeing the mixture of disgust and hatred that flitted across Rey's face. "Tell them I can heal him. If I'm quick enough, we can take him back. My brother must get real help."

"Heal him? Wha's bodged up?"

Rey knew about them. Might as well tell the rest. "We spoke to one of the Aridori the Life Coalition had captured, when we visited Gloomlight Prison. The Aridori, they...infected Inas somehow. His hand was paralyzed, before the Coalition took him, in the warehouse."

Rey stared at her, his face contorting in one expression, then another. He lifted his chin, stretching his neck out as if it hurt. "I donna like Inas bein' harmed. An', well, yer've never led me wrong in the past, have yer? Lied, yeah, but I...I can see why." He pressed his thin lips together. "Sorry about using the Symphony on yer."

Enos took in a deep breath, then let it out. To have to excuse her very existence was so tiring. "I accept," she said. "I can see why you did it. We've all heard the stories about the Aridori. Even my family didn't know whether they were true."

"I'll grant yer some of the worst may not have been truthful-like," Rey said, "but so many tales, hauntin' kids for a thousand cycles, can't all be wrong. Yer'll have to excuse me if I don't leap into yer arms."

"And what about Inas?" Enos felt her shoulders straighten as she said the words. "You want him back."

"Aye, I do," Rey said. "Greatmother help me, but I have no clue why. Mebbe he can tell me why. Fella's just so blasted likeable."

Enos wanted to throw the nearest object at the Sureri, to make him see she and her brother were the same. Even with different personalities, they were two instances of the same origin. The Aridori might have committed crimes in the distant past, but that was history. She would never do anything like that, and neither would Inas.

"Now, I'll let yer know as soon as I hear sommat," Rey said. He stepped sideways, letting her see the door. He might have accepted her, but that didn't mean he wanted to be near her.

Enos clenched her jaw, but walked toward the door. With one hand on the knob, she turned back. "Don't tell Sam, please," she said.

"Not a word," Rey answered.

* * *

Enos' heart pounded as she and Rey approached the abandoned building on the outskirts of Low Imperium. It had taken three days to set up the meeting, as Rey had to signal the Life Coalition representative without his mentor knowing. The walls of the Nether glowed softly on their way to the darkness of midnight.

"Eyah, not a great place methinks," Rey said, and Enos had to agree.

"Whatever gets Inas back," she said, reaching for the old doorknob. It looked like it might fall off on its own if she wasn't careful.

"Aye, whatever," Rey agreed. He'd been skittish of her, eyeing her when he thought she wasn't looking and keeping several arm lengths distance between them. Sam had been overprotective, when he was around.

Enos was almost temped to spin around and shout 'Boo!' but the feeling of tumbling into the couch under Rey's change to the Symphony kept her from doing so. She paused before entering the old building. "You do not regret your decision to speak with the Life Coalition, do you?" she asked.

"Not a bit," Rey said, a little too fast. "If we'd just tracked 'em down and talked to 'em, we could have avoided all this. I'm sure of it."

Enos opened her mouth to argue, but then shook her head. Did Rey even know when the Life Coalition first made a move? By that point it had been too late for her and Inas' family, for Sam's home, and for Majus Ayama's birthplace. What was talking to them going to do? The Coalition had made up their minds long ago to race after their fabled limitless resources, no matter whether they professed peace or war, killing whoever got in their way. They were only talking with the Assembly now because the ten homeworlds were on guard against the Coalition creating any more Drains. Their plans had been revealed, and failed.

Enos wished Sam was here. She was stronger with him. But he couldn't know about this until it was done. He'd try to stop her.

"Hello?" Enos pushed open the door and stepped into the dim interior of the building. If they were early and the Life Coalition contact brought Inas by way of portal, she might be able to hear some of the music defining the other end. If she was lucky, she could take that information *and* Inas back to the others.

Don't get sloppy.

She hoped Sam would forgive her for doing this without him. He was not good at subterfuge. But when it was over, he would have Inas back, and her brother's natural geniality would pull Sam from the funk he'd been in for the last several ten-days. She hoped.

"You two, you are early," came a voice Enos recognized. She looked into the darkness. She could change her eyes to adjust to the dim...

No.

Changing was what brought this on in the beginning. Their parents had instilled the instinct never to change shape in Enos and Inas. She had forgotten that instinct in the panic of the Drains and her capture by the Life Coalition. It had gotten easier every time. That downhill slide had all started with the cloaked figure opposite her.

"Dunarn," Enos called out. She let her hatred of the Life Coalition slide into the word. They knew more about her species than she did. While her family had been hiding, they had been torturing her people. "Making it your business to guard the Life Coalition's prisoners?"

"For this, I asked to come," the voice said. Enos could just make out movement, though the Sathssn's hood blended in with the shadows.

"Yer, er, know this one, do yer?" Rey said. His voice quavered.

"She captured Sam and me when we were separated from the rest of the group on Methiem," Enos told him. "Imprisoned us with no explanation. No time for us to *talk* with them. And that was when they didn't know about my species." Enos realized her voice was gaining in volume and tried to tamp it down.

"Yer—yer really goin' to play this to the hilt, Enos?" Rey said. It was the most contrite she'd heard the Sureri. "I'm thinkin' mebbe I didn't noodle all this through as much as I'd like." There was scuffling behind her, as if Rey was backing away.

She ignored him. "Where is he?" Enos called to Dunarn. Her eyes hadn't fully adjusted. "I'm ready, assuming you kept your word. Did Zsaana see what I said about his injury? I can heal him. He's my other instance." She just needed an instant with Dunarn off guard, and they could escape.

"Me, I always keep my word," Dunarn said. "The other Aridori is here, as promised. Though him, he is not the one who needs healing."

"What does that mean?" Enos strained to see. Was there a shape on the ground? What had they done to him? "Inas, can you hear me?" She closed her eyes and tried to sense the connection between the two of them.

Like an itch on the back of her neck, or a hair tickling her arm, it was there. It was weak and *wrong* somehow. There was a difference in him and it coiled back along their connection, reaching for her. Her head twinged, but she shook the discomfort away.

He's in pain. I can feel it.

"Come closer, little one," Dunarn crooned. "To reach your other instance, you must be closer. Near me." It was a challenge. The pain she felt—it was not all aimed at Inas. Some was purposeful, to draw her in. They knew of the connection between instances, after all.

But she was powerless to resist. Inas was so *close*. One leg moved forward, to the bunched, unconscious shape.

"Yes. You, too, can be trained by the Life Coalition. A capable, complete Aridori trained for our arsenal. With you, unlimited energy is within our reach."

"Trained? Complete? What do you mean?" Her voice wavered, but still, she took a step forward. She let the Symphony of Healing cascade through her head, listening to strains of music, trying to decide what to change. She had gone against Dunarn and the House of Strength before, with poor results.

"Nothin' good, Enos," Rey called. He sounded far away. "I think I was mebbe wrong. Come back with me!"

Enos lifted her chin to stare down her nose at Dunarn. The Sathssn were a short species. "Where's your resolve now, Rey? No. I'm going to check him, to make certain he's well." The Sureri wasn't as committed to Inas as she thought, not when it really mattered.

She took another step, next to Inas' body, then squatted down, still trying to keep an eye on Dunarn. The Coalitioner did nothing, but Enos held the music of Healing ready. Something was wrong with this whole situation, but she couldn't understand what. Why *had* the Coalition agreed to meet her?

"Inas. Can you hear me?" she whispered to the shape on the ground. She put out a hand, touching warm skin. Too warm. Inas was feverish, his face almost scaly. He didn't move under her touch, but he groaned. She quickly ran her hands across his body, checking for anything out of place. Her other instance. That path which could have been hers, under different circumstances.

Inas' body was not in its usual shape. His arms quivered under her fingers, as if he was starting a shift. His face felt too rough, and he had the beginnings of a beard. His legs were bent, and twisted. There was another toe, or claw, on the back of one calf.

"Oh, Inas," she whispered.

"Now, assassin," Dunarn called. "Take your due and accept your power!"

Under her, Inas's flesh, though he was still unconscious, molded around her hands. Enos jerked back, but his skin stuck to hers, trying to bring her into him. Trying to enfold her as the Aridori in Gloomlight had contained others. As it had infected Inas.

"No!" she cried. "What did you do to him?" She struggled, climbing through the song of Healing to disengage their bodies, but his song was so similar to hers, she couldn't differentiate. He was pulling her in!

"No! Inas—stop!" She shouted but the relentless creeping of his skin over hers continued. He moved as if asleep.

Tortured. Coerced. They had made him do this. She dove deeper into the music of Healing, searching his body.

There. The thread of corruption coursed through him, as if it polluted his very makeup. *That* was what was reaching for her, pulling him along with it. She snipped the notes that made it up, in a surgical application of her notes, and jerked her hands free.

"This, it will not do," Dunarn said, and an aura of green surrounded her. Enos' knees adhered to the floor, pinning her in place. "Me, I was sent to bring both of you aberrations back to Nakan and Zsaana. I will do so."

"Rey, help me!" she called. She felt his presence more than heard it, a wave of energy as the House of Potential bolstered her.

"Yer were supposed to bargain in good faith," Rey said, and now his voice was harsh, strained with changing the Symphony.

"There is no bargaining with the cursed ones who started the war. You, you may bargain, but not her." Dunarn laid gloved hands on Enos' shoulders, gripping hard. Enos struggled to throw off the grip, but it was like iron. Her body was compressing, held rigid by the House of Strength.

"Not acceptable," Rey said, and Enos' limbs loosened again as spirals of brown Potential combatted the green of Strength. He had both hands up, his eyes casting around for anything else he could use. The room was bare.

"I have to wake him up," she told Rey, and hunched against the hands trying to pull her away. "Keep her off me." She dove back into the Symphony of Healing, searching for how Inas' consciousness had been repressed. At a guess, it was Zsaana's work, and he had taught Majus Ayama. Could she ever hope to undo that?

Yes, she could. Inas was like her. She simply had to listen, to see the differences between them and make the music the same. As she changed notes, she felt Inas stirring, the connection between them sending feelings and emotions back and forth with intensity. They would be three against Dunarn's one.

"Stop this game. Both Aridori, they will come with me," Dunarn said and Enos rocked backward under the Sathssn's grip. She grasped at Inas, trying to hold them both to the ground.

"I...canna...hold both of yer against her!" Rey's brown warred with Dunarn's green, and the wiry Sureri slid forward across the floor. Whatever he was doing with the House of Potential wasn't strong enough to resist the House of Strength head on. None of the other houses were. Even if Enos changed their bodies with Healing, she had a feeling Dunarn would overcome them. She was too strong, a full majus versus two apprentices, with Inas still incapacitated. It was a simple equation, and one which did not fall in her favor. All three of them might wind up under the Life Coalition's control. Unless she changed the rules.

Whatever it takes to rescue Inas.

She bent down to her other instance, straining against the Sathssn's hands, whispering in his ear. She didn't know if he could understand the words, but it was worth a try.

"Go with Rey. Find Sam. Help him, and let him help you. Tell Majus Ayama why I had to do this." Then she called to Rey. "You can't hold both of us. Get Inas out of here."

They want an Aridori? They'll have one.

She stopped adjusting the music of Inas' body. He would wake soon. She turned on Dunarn, rising to her feet, fighting against the Symphony of Strength and forcing the Coalitioner to confront her not only physically, but with song. She dove into the melody of the Sathssn's body, trying to weaken bones, loosen tendons.

It was a losing battle, but she wasn't trying to win. The House of Strength was like green spears of song, striking her changes down as fast as she made them. The Sathssn growled as she pulled Enos forward, and Enos let her. Rey had his hands around Inas' legs, dragging him out of the warehouse. She had to keep the Sathssn occupied so her other instance would have a chance.

Behind Dunarn, a hole even darker than their surroundings spun into being, surrounded by green and burgundy rings.

Enos looked back to Rey, silhouetted in the door. "Take care of him," she said.

"I will," Rey answered, and Enos stopped resisting Dunarn. They tumbled through the portal.

* * *

Sam awoke to fevered knocking on the door of Majus Cyrysi's apartment. He swiped at his eyes, trying to breathe deep to calm the surge of adrenaline. Nothing happening at this time of night was good.

He made his way cautiously to the door, threading a path through a few items he had stored on the floor when he ran out of space on the shelves. He knew where each of them lay. There was more light in the hallway, and Sam found a window with the barest glimmer from the great wall of the Nether.

It must be, what, first lightening? Just after midnight.

The knocking continued, and as his mentor was not getting up—or more likely, he was spending the night at Majus Ayama's apartment again—Sam crept to the front door. He stopped there, staring at it.

It's just a door. Open it.

The knocking was turning into banging.

Sam gulped, reached out, and pulled the door open.

Rey nearly fell on him, supporting someone who was groaning, their head of dark shaggy hair covering their face.

"Were yer gonna take all night about it? Leave us out there on the landing? Took me ages to get him up all the steps." Rey was babbling. "I would nae have come, but I didn't know where else to go. Any majus would have me skewered. Speaking of which..." Rey looked around Sam.

"Uh, he's out," Sam said, assuming Rey was looking for Majus Cyrysi.

Rey slumped a little, bringing the other person forward a few steps. "Oh thank the Greatmother. I'd hoped he were visitin' Majus Ayama tonight."

"Why?" Sam asked. "Did you want me? Who is this—" He broke off as the figure raised their head.

"Oh my God." Sam rushed to Rey's side, taking Inas' head in his hands. He ducked under Inas' arm and helped the two of them into the room. "Where did you find him? How? We have to tell the others. We have to tell Enos!" He struggled with the two to Majus Cyrysi's couch.

Inas looked bad. He had a beard, and dark circles under his staring eyes. His body didn't feel the same shape as Sam remembered. There were odd misshapen lumps on his torso and his legs were bent.

"It's ah, not that simple, yer understand," Rey said, once Sam had run out of words.

"S...Sam?" Inas mumbled. Sam laid his friend down on the couch, moving around to his face. Whatever Rey said dissolved into the background.

"I'm here." Sam laid his hand on Inas' chest, his forehead. He was even warmer than normal. His hair was uncombed, and the clothes he wore stank. They were torn and ripped, and as he watched, they twitched on their own.

Those aren't real clothes. Inas made them.

"Enos," Inas said, and Sam nodded, brushing Inas' hair back.

"I know, we'll tell her," he said.

"She said to take care of you," Inas said.

Sam frowned, running fingers down Inas' cheek. "You're not thinking straight." Inas' skin was burning up. It almost felt like it was moving under his fingers.

"Er...he's right," Rey said from behind them. Sam whirled around, but kept one hand in contact with Inas, as if he would disappear again.

"What do you know? Where is she?" he asked.

"Enos saved Inas, though I had me some doubts," Rey said, his face screwing up into a grimace.

"But she's safe? What happened?" Sam's stomach was churning.

Don't throw up. Have to help Inas. And Enos.

"Fought her off. Saved me," Inas croaked out.

Sam leaned back over him. Why wouldn't anyone tell him what happened?

"Fought off who? How? How did they get you here?" He wanted to shake Inas, and also to kiss him. He'd been asleep moments ago, and now everything was falling down around him.

"Life Coalition," Inas said. One hand waved toward Rey. It was the same one that had been melted into a fixed shape after Inas spoke with the captured Aridori in Gloomlight Prison. But that hand was back to normal now. No, not normal. One finger lengthened, then another shortened. Inas was changing shape uncontrollably. Just like they said the trapped Aridori had.

"You found the Life Coalition?" Sam asked Rey, who shook his head.

"More like they found us. Majus Kheena set up a meetin' with 'em, but they were...amenable to Enos seein' her brother to fix him up." He must have seen something in Sam's face because he held up his hands. "Eyah, it was a stupid idea, now I'm thinkin' straight-like. It was a trap. Of course them Snakeys wanted both of them."

Now Sam's hand left Inas. He was across the room before he could think, pushing Rey back into a wall. The thin Sureri wasn't as strong as Sam was. That was a surprise. Rey's eyes widened.

"You gave Enos to the Life Coalition? Do you know what they'll do to her? Didn't you see him?" Sam threw a hand back toward Inas, but its movement was halted. Sam turned.

Inas was on his feet, and held his arm, his other hand reaching toward him. His eyes were dark. "They want us, Sam," he said. "They'll stop at nothing to control the Aridori."

When Sam glanced at Rey, he saw from the Sureri's grimace that he knew, and wasn't happy about it. Rey and Inas had been friends before Sam met either of them.

Inas tugged on Sam's arm, bringing him closer. "Thank you for trying, but she...she did this to save me. I sensed her resolution to bring me back when she fought Dunarn. She's so much stronger than I am. She'll hold on until we rescue her. Not like I did."

That sentence would need explanation, but Sam let himself relax into Inas' embrace, pulling the other man closer, his coarse beard rubbing against Sam's cheek. "I missed you," he said into Inas' neck.

"I missed you too." Any further words were cut off as Inas pulled him into a kiss, hard and needy. Several ten-days of tension drained from his shoulders. Even with Enos gone, even with the Life Coalition trying to coerce a place in the Assembly, he felt more whole than since before he moved the portal in the Dome of the Assembly.

Rey cleared his throat, and Sam moved back from Inas, running a finger down the other man's face. The shifting had stopped with the kiss, though Inas' eyes were locked on his. He looked...hungry.

"We should, er, probably let Majus Caroom know Inas is back. The Benish has been right gloomy."

"Let's get you cleaned up first," Sam told Inas. "You can use my stuff. You'll feel better with a shower and shave. That beard is itchy."

Inas gave a shaky smile, but Sam caught the flash of teeth behind his lips. Just for a moment, the light made them look pointed.

CHAPTER NINE

Halls, Doors, Locks, and Collars

- For the last thousand cycles, no one's been certain of what an Aridori looked like. There were more stories than you could shake a stick at, but nothing more definite than what your third best friend heard from their next door neighbor, who heard from their optometrist. Now, we have an eyewitness of over sixty thousand people at the same time, who all saw that creature rise from the box in the Assembly. I was representing my province of Blarth at the time, and I can back up what everyone else says. I've seen one of the fabled nightmare beasts with my own two blue eyes. They're not as scary looking as I thought they would be.

Report by Floripartaren Fult, Speaker, to her head of state.

Enos pulled against Dunarn's iron grip as the portal collapsed behind them.

"Let go of me!" Her notes were constricted by Dunarn's emerald green aura surrounding her. Her hands trembled by her sides, like they were moving through concrete. Majus Ayama always told her not to go head-to-head with a member of the House of Strength. Now that horrible wall of music pushed against her skin, keeping her from moving faster than a crawl.

"Inas and Rey will go straight to the Assembly. They'll know what you've done. Your negotiations are doomed if you're kidnaping apprentices." At least Inas was free. Enos stretched away, trying to pull Dunarn off balance, but the cloaked Sathssn was rooted to the floor by her music. In contrast, Enos felt much lighter than in the Nether. She tried to turn the quarter notes of Dunarn's grip to loose sixteenths, but when she attempted to insert her notes into the music, she met with a wall of force she couldn't hear.

Dunarn chuckled—an unpleasant sound. "None of that, apprentice. Your mentor, she must have told you the advantages of the House of

Strength. As to the Assembly, them, I do not think they will hear much, unless your other instance is willing to share his species as well."

Enos gritted her teeth and dug her feet into the packed dirt of the floor. The Sathssn was right, unfortunately. "I will not be one of your trained assassins." She took the chance to gauge her surroundings. They were in a small room, the walls of unfinished gray rock. They could be anywhere, but from Majus Ayama's guess, this was a cave in a moon around Sath Home. The air was breathable. The Life Coalition must have used maji from the House of Communication.

"Your brother, he said much the same when we first brought him here. Yet it only took a few days to persuade him to our thinking. You too, you will serve the Form." Enos didn't like the sound of that.

Dunarn jerked her arms, and she rose from the floor in a bouncing arc as if she were only a fraction of her weight, twirling around the Sathssn, who shoved her down in front of a tunnel.

"You wear at my notes," Dunarn said, and beckoned. Two cloaked figures who'd been standing in the hall came closer, iron manacles held between them. An aura of colors swirled around the restraints.

No. Escape. Must change.

Changing her form was the last thing she should do, but what else was there? She was effectively cut off from the Symphony by Dunarn's music.

Enos stiffened, her hands in fists. She focused on her wrists thinning, to slip from the manacles, but she was too slow. It would take several minutes for her body to react. Dunarn held her arms in a grip as tight as those manacles would be.

"You are too cowardly to have me unbound?" she taunted. It was her only remaining weapon, but the tightness in her stomach was a counterpoint to her bravado. Her eyes roamed the dim room. Plain rough stone and floors scuffed from the passage of many boots. If she had a few minutes, she'd understand the melody of this place, and once she did, she could push against the Sathssn's control to make a portal away.

"Too smart," Dunarn countered, forcing Enos' arms closer to the shackles. The other figures were on either side of her. "I wish not to waste notes making you comply. This, it will be faster until you understand as your brother did."

Enos gave one last desperate tug, but though the Sathssn was smaller, her grip was unbreakable. Panic rose like shards of ice in her belly as the attendants clamped the metal restraints tight around her wrists.

She gasped at the sudden quiet. The Symphony faded to a buzz in the background, its notes no longer within Enos' grasp.

No. I can't lose the Symphony. Her eyes darted back and forth, searching for anything that might help. *Even without the Symphony, I can still slip away given time...* Her wrists were still thinning, and her thumbs moved inward. She'd be able to slip out of the manacles soon.

"That is not all," Dunarn said. "For you and your other instance, you require not only the wrist-cuffs."

A shock of cold metal against her neck made Enos shiver violently, and Dunarn pushed her face-first to a rough wall, clicking something tight around her throat.

A shock coated her spine like liquid lightning and Enos collapsed, gasping. Her arms returned to their normal shape. She raised her manacled hands, feeling the unbroken surface around her neck.

Like the one they brought to the Assembly. To control the Aridori.

"Changing your form, this is inadvisable," Dunarn chided. "This blasphemy, it will hurt greatly without permission from one of your guards."

Escape slid away and Enos' gut clenched. *Should have told Majus Ayama where I was going.*

"Follow close," Dunarn said, as she threaded a smaller chain through a link in the front of the collar to matching links on the manacles. Enos wouldn't even be able to stretch her arms out to full extension. "Us, we have not yet bound your legs. But we will drag you if we need to."

The two guards entered the tunnel and Dunarn gave Enos another shove so she stumbled into the corridor. She tried to stop, but her gait had turned into a sort of bouncing skip. There was even less pull from the ground than the one time she had been to Etan with her family's merchant caravan.

Dunarn shoved her forward and the guard's robes drifted up in the air with each bounce. Their boots were high enough that none of their scaly skin showed. Enos was familiar with that skin. She had changed herself into a Sathssn when they visited the Aridori in Gloomlight

Prison. She'd unwittingly worn the skin of those who'd subjugated the remainder of her species.

She was trapped, but still not without options. Eventually, the Life Coalition would slip up. *I'll gather what information I can, and then I will free myself.*

She cataloged the tunnel they passed through, but it was simple stone, with occasional torches for light.

Inas had been injured and shaking off the effects of the Aridori in the Gloomlight Prison when he was captured. Enos was, if not prepared, then at least well rested and free from sickness. She would do better. Well, they hadn't stopped her from speaking, had they?

"Is this a moon of Sath Home?" she asked.

She looked back in time to see Dunarn's cowl twitch in surprise. "You Aridori, you are a prisoner. You need not know where we are."

So Majus Ayama had been right.

"We are coming for you. You can't hide here forever." She tried to make the threat sound realistic. Dunarn only grunted.

They were far above Sath Home. How had the Sathssn opened a portal here? Maji had to have been to both ends of a portal before making one, or have another majus communicate the music at the other end. It wasn't as if they could fly through space. Enos recalled the failed attempt by the Methiemum several cycles back to build a majus-powered rocket. It had crashed. Had the Sathssn somehow duplicated the design in such a brief time? But to dig these tunnels, through rock, would have taken a long time.

They turned off the main corridor and passed into a larger area, the rock walls looming overhead until the shadows hid them from torchlight. Dunarn pushed a rusty iron door shut behind them. They must keep the portal room separated from the rest of the area. Another layer of secrecy?

There were other figures in black cloaks here, though Enos couldn't be certain they were all Sathssn. The Life Coalition army that attacked the Dome of the Assembly had consisted of all ten species. She soaked up all the details: signs of construction in that corner, a Methiemum with his cowl back there, carrying a load of rocks, no Systems in evidence, all inside one giant cavern.

The Life Coalition were still expanding, with no help from the Assembly. They were confident in what they were trying to do.

How far can I get if I run?

Not very far, and she'd rather have the use of her legs. Dunarn's casual threat about dragging her hadn't been made with hatred in her voice—merely certainty.

Cloaked figures stopped their work as they passed. Several took steps toward her, but Dunarn waved them away.

Enos raked in sensations as they walked. Stone walls and rough floors, the stale smell of air too long in one place, mixed with the tang of broken rock. It was like a mine, but it couldn't be open to space, could it? Those who built the shuttle on Methiem said there was no air to breathe in space. So they were trapped in a floating rock, likely with no exit save by portal.

She heard indistinct voices, discussing her as she passed. Clangs and crashes sounded in the distance where the Coalitioner had come from with the load of rocks. Probably digging a new tunnel.

If I gather enough memories, even if I cannot access the Symphony, I may be able to tell Majus Ayama of it, if I get back. When I get back.

The tension raised her shoulders and tightened her back. At least Inas was no longer here. She would survive, and he would recover. Perhaps her mentor would work with him to forge another connection between the two of them.

Or will I open one when they shove me into one of those boxes, formless and terrified?

She had told no one where she was going, except for Rey. She silently pleaded he would see through his disgust long enough to tell the others. He would take Inas to Sam. He had to.

Dunarn halted and Enos stopped her bouncing stride with a hand against the rough wall, leaving scrapes on her palm. The guards took up stations to either side of a crude door.

"This, it is where you will stay," Dunarn said, gesturing with one glove to the slab of rock. "Once we know the other beasts, they will not immediately kill you, you will join them. We must start your training as soon as possible."

Enos realized Dunarn was talking about other Aridori prisoners— multiple prisoners. Her heart thumped at the prospect of seeing them, for good or ill.

* * *

After Dunarn closed the slab of a door, no one touched Enos or even paid her any attention. The room they locked her in was tiny, with a bed hewn from stone, and a roll of some animal's fur spread over it. The manacles and collar constrained her every move, but did nothing to actively harm her. If only the Symphony was not so far away. Investigation of the manacles showed the House of Healing had a part in the System. It must be a smaller version of what had kept her and Sam trapped in the cell. But there, they'd been able to hear the Symphony. This must be a refinement of the technology.

That night—or what she assumed was night—she settled on the hard bed. The animal fur did little to cushion it, and the guards had removed neither her collar nor her manacles. She would have been able to open a portal if they had.

The second day, Enos tested the locked door to her room on a schedule. Three hundred breaths, bang on the slab. It brought no one, and by the middle of the day, she paced, clenching and unclenching her hands. She longed to stretch her arms, but that was impossible.

The Symphony was a tiny voice, rather than the usual raging crash of music. Enos managed some sleep, but after a full day, the manacles and collar chafed her wrists and neck. She'd even tried—once—to change the shape of her hands, to escape the manacles. It had taken five minutes for her to stop screaming and the burning feeling to leave her. The collar left a ring of reddened skin around her neck.

By the third day, Enos sat huddled on the bed, her stomach rumbling, her mind roving in ever darker circles. She'd given up banging on the door when it finally opened and a cloaked figure slipped through, as quick as thought.

"These accommodations, are they to your liking?"

Enos recognized the silky voice. She'd heard it, alongside Dunarn's, when they'd taken Inas. This was the Sathssn that even Majus Ayama could not beat in a fight. Nakan.

She tilted her chin up, but said nothing. She felt nothing.

Inas is safe.

"I see. You, you will learn to answer when spoken to. We must train you like the other blasphemers to the Form." Enos couldn't see anything of the Sathssn's face beneath his dark cowl, but his words sounded like he was smiling. "My people, we are the ideal choice to restrain the remnant of the Aridori. No one else wanted the task and so, it fell to us."

Enos couldn't keep from speaking. "Yet you never told the other species, for a thousand cycles?" Her family could have taken in the other prisoners, if they'd known.

"No one else would have rehabilitated the last of your miserable species as we have," Nakan said. "Now, you come with me. Us, we have work to do."

"What about food?" Enos asked. At least when she and Sam had been caged, they'd been provided regular meals. That had been before the Life Coalition knew she was Aridori.

An aura of blue and dark purple formed around Nakan's gloved hands, and he reached out toward her collar. A shock like a knife cutting into her belly doubled Enos over.

"Food, it comes as a reward for our pets," Nakan told her. "Now come."

Enos gasped, levering up from the bed and straining to put one foot in front of the other. The aura came back as Nakan raised his hands, and Enos tried to move faster, to obey.

"I'm coming," she said. "I'm coming."

"Good. A benefit of seeing the colors, it seems," the Sathssn mused. "For me, there is less need to discipline."

They went back into the maze of tunnels, passing other figures draped in the dark fabric the Sathssn wore, but Enos kept her eyes on Nakan's back. Sometimes she saw a member of another species, their cloak thrown back as they carried a load, or chipped away at the stone to build a new tunnel. Was this the same way she had come before? All the tunnels looked the same, poorly lit by torches.

She tried to pay attention to detail, but her mind wandered in her hunger and pain. The collar sent shivers of agony down her neck.

I will escape this place, and I will bring back any of my people I can.

Then they stopped, and Enos leaned against the wall in relief.

"This, it is our training room." Nakan extended a hand toward a door like all of the others. He unlocked it with a complicated-looking key and pushed it open.

Inside, the room was bare but for two small iron boxes, at the opposite edge of the room. The little cubes captured Enos' eyes. They were only about knee-height.

Nakan's laugh was rough and grating as he shut the door behind them. "This, it is where our disobedient pets go. These two, they never learn. Not even after a thousand cycles."

The confirmation was enough to jolt Enos from staring. "You have Aridori still alive from the war?" She assumed the original ones had reproduced since then. She was expecting to see children of those Aridori, not the ones who started the confrontation.

Nakan turned to her, and light from the torch that illuminated the room caught his slitted eyes beneath his cowl. "You know little of your own species, do you? Your kind, they can live for very long times, if properly encouraged."

"What's that supposed to mean?" asked Enos. She strained to gather her strength. The walk here had given her a second wind.

Can I escape through the door?

Nakan could set off the collar from a distance, and if the Sathssn knew more about her people than she did, that reduced her odds. Enos wondered how much Inas had learned. Would he have even been able to tell her, in his state?

"Let us see, shall we?" Nakan hissed, and strolled toward the two cubes. Enos followed as if a leash tied them together.

On both boxes, Nakan punched hidden buttons, and the auras of the Symphony sprang up around them, though Enos could hear nothing. The top unfolded, and beneath were undulating masses of flesh. Sickness crept up her throat. Enos couldn't tell if the substance was skin, or muscle, or in between.

Then the flesh roiled, bunching up in both boxes. Enos' mind went to the box in Gloomlight Prison, with the tendril of substance rising from it. These shapes, however rose into identifiable creatures in a few seconds and Enos' eyes widened at the speed of their change.

Both had iridescent scales of green and purple down their chest, turning to almost silky black on their arms and legs. Their heads were dark, with long snouts and tendrils under their chins. Large eyes under black-scaled ridges looked down on Enos, one set purple and the other blue.

"Meet your fellows," Nakan said. "We call this one Zhaddi," he pointed to the one with blue eyes, "and the other one is Putra."

Enos looked between them. This must be what her species looked like. It was the second time she'd seen this form. Her parents had never shown her, and she wasn't certain they'd known.

Enos swallowed. Even with the collar and manacles, a sense of awe rose in her at seeing these ancient Aridori close up.

"I am Enos."

Putra—the one with the purple eyes—snorted. "That is not a true Aridori name." Their voice was rough and low. "No doubt you come from one of the pathetic tribes who tried to hide amongst these insects." Putra flicked a finger at Nakan.

"Look—she knows nothing of her people. I can tell just from the way she stands," said Zhaddi, the one with blue eyes. Their voice was higher than the other one.

"Now pets," Nakan said. "Be nice to Enos. Us, we will choose a new name for her soon, and you must teach her proper respect for her betters."

"Respect?" Putra sneered. "For you, you degenerate cockroach? I would rather spend another cycle inside my box, without form."

"That can be arranged, *slave*," Nakan said, a whipcrack in his voice, and Putra shook their head like a horse refusing direction. Nakan turned to Enos. "Them, they are both quite unhinged, unfortunately. As you will certainly be, after a few cycles of our training. It is unavoidable, to train obedient assassins."

"Never insane. We are royalty of our kind!" Zhaddi flung one hand out, and now it had claws, sharp as needles, lengthening as Enos watched. Nakan dodged quicker than Enos could follow, the blue of the House of Grace springing up around him. Then Zhaddi shook and collapsed, the tiny scales melting into each other until the Aridori's form was indistinct, drooping over the side of the container that still held both creatures' feet trapped.

Nakan raised a hand from a device he wore on his wrist, which glowed with colors of several Houses. Enos closed her mouth. What could make an Aridori lose their shape like sand dissolving in water?

"Even without the collars, we still have control," Nakan told her, centering his cowl over his head again. "You, come with me. We will go back to your room. Prepare yourself. Tomorrow, you will meet the others. Them, they will want to show you how to change as fast as these two. A blasphemous thing, but necessary."

Enos followed in Nakan's wake, as helpless as a fly caught in a swift stream's current. She remembered the lash of emotions the last time she changed her shape. It interfered with every little task, trying to pull her to feel more, seek out another satisfying thrill.

The Life Coalition would make her change her shape constantly. She ground her teeth.

More information is my only way out. I'll gather as much as I can, and then I'll take Putra and Zhaddi with me.

CHAPTER TEN

The Wall

- The walls of the Nether are curious things: thought to be impenetrable, looming far above civilization, made of some strange crystal substance that responds to both thought and touch. I have long been interested in further research, but without a sample, detailed analysis was impossible. How to study a substance that cannot be cut? This Nether crystal not only forms walls, but the basin which holds earth, stone, and civilization. It also presumably creates a ceiling, far overhead. I am surprised more people do not think of the crystal which encloses the Nether.

Morvu Francita Januti, Etanela explorer and big game hunter

Rilan came around the side of the table, laying a hand on Ori's shoulder as she looked over the pile of papers and parchment in front of him. Some looked quite old. Soft music resonated through the halls of the House of Healing and despite the fabric she'd attached to her new apartment's door, she could still hear it.

"How long have you been up?" she asked. She'd only awoken with the morning's chill and realized Ori wasn't with her.

"I have been researching the sound that keeps ringing through the Nether," he said absently, his crest still slicked back in concentration. "It appears to be restricted to the city of the Imperium, from reports I am to be hearing. The committee the Assembly has detailed to investigate has been less than useful, as usual. There must be an explanation, but I am not to be finding it, and neither are they."

Rilan pointed at a parchment. "The bridge connected to the House of Communication? The one that arcs to the nearest wall? What does that have to do with anything?"

"Possibly much," Ori said. "I believe Sam has mentioned it, and I long wondered about its use. It continues to come up in my research, though Tuulan is deriding my belief in it. They have always been recalcitrant concerning legend—one reason the committee they lead is not to be getting anywhere. In two ancient accounts, I have found it to be linked to 'calls for conference,' whatever that is to be. It has been the only lead I can find on the chimes." He sat up straight, looking to a timepiece on one wall. "In fact, if the sequence is to be continuing the way it has, it should be starting right—."

The whole apartment shook as the bass chime sounded, resonating like a bell the size of a building, and Rilan clutched at Ori's shoulder. The music from the hallway splintered and halted, as a porcelain vase her father had purchased on Etan rocked and pitched to the floor, too quickly for her to catch it.

"Shiv's nosehairs!" she swore. She had little enough to remember him by.

Rilan had encountered one earthquake in her childhood in Dalhni, with a similar effect. "The shaking gets worse each time!" she shouted over the noise. "So you think the bridge has something to do with it?"

Ori nodded, his crest ruffling. He stared at the shards of pottery. "It is likely to be the place where the call is answered, if this parchment is correct." He jabbed a finger downward, his curved, clawlike fingernail spearing one passage. "I am believing this document was translated from another source just after the Aridori War, though the rest is to be lost. The author may have been intending to save information that would otherwise have been destroyed."

"So this has happened before?" Rilan yelled. There were several historic buildings in High Imperium that sustained damage after the last ten-day of shaking. If it kept up much longer, the historic district would need serious renovations.

"There are also to be two mentions of movement." Ori screwed up his face and his crest came to a point in frustrated confusion. "I cannot be telling if this movement is *in* the Nether, or *part* of the Nether, or whether the chimes are an alarm connected to it, though that is what I suspect."

"Do we know who started the chime? Who's the one making the call?" Rilan asked, and Ori's crest rose.

"I had not been thinking of that." That was true Ori form, leaping toward the answer without thinking about the causes.

The chimes died away, though echoes rang between buildings in the Imperium. Music in the hall outside the apartment began again, jerking and discordant.

"The bridge is the only structure touching the wall, if I remember correctly," Rilan said. "Everyone else keeps away from it not to block the light. If the chimes are involved with the workings of the Nether, then perhaps that's why the bridge was built in such an odd manner."

"It is a strange construction, of that there is to be no doubt," Ori said, tapping his cheek with a fingernail. He rose to pace, thinking. "It has been there so long, none of the maji in the House of Communication question it, save to be taking walks along its length."

"Then it must not have been used for its intended purpose in many cycles," Rilan said. "Why was it built?"

Ori looked down at her, his eyes narrowed, his crest rippling. "An excellent question. The answer may be helping us immensely." He took a step forward so he could run a hand up the side of her face, his long fingernails trailing shivers in their wake. His fingers brushed up into her hair and Rilan leaned into the motion, taking in a deep breath. "You do know you were being wasted on the Council."

She had taken offense at him saying that in the past, but no sense of injured pride rose this time. "I don't miss it," she said into his hand, and realized she meant it. There had been days where she wanted to stab everyone in the council chambers. She hadn't been nearly as stressed since they removed her. It might have been for the best.

She purred as Ori trailed his hand through her hair and down her long braid, making the bell at the end ring.

"An adventure then," she said, once she caught her breath. "We should take the whole group to the bridge. Maybe we can discover why—" she jumped as someone pounded at her front door. She ran a hand down Ori's robe, but gently pushed him away with the promise of more to come later. "Who is that?"

Was it Enos, back at last? The girl had been out for a day or so. Rilan hoped she was with Sam. If she was missing much longer, Rilan would go looking for her.

She went to the door and pulled it open. Sam and Rey spilled in, but the third person wasn't Enos.

"Inas!" Ori took two longs strides forward at her exclamation. She was about to close the door when a wide figure stumped into view around a corner. "And Caroom!"

A few minutes later, they were settled in her apartment, Caroom leaning against a wall. The Benish's dour look from the past several days was lifting, their eyes glowing a cheerful green again. But while their apprentice had returned, now Enos was missing.

She kept her cool, barely, while listening to their story. Afterward, Rilan glowered at Rey, keeping her seat only with an effort. Her jaw flexed, and if she had her way, she would be out the door this instant, but they needed more information.

"You let Enos be captured by the Life Coalition? *Again*?" Every word was a low growl. "I've only just gotten her back." Yes, she was an Aridori, but Rilan, Brahm bless her, was actually getting used to that part. "Do you know what *happened* to her the last time I lost my apprentice?" She clenched her fists to keep from throttling the Sureri. She was standing now, too annoyed to stay in the chair.

"Why does aught all keep blamin' me?" Rey whined. He slouched as far back in his chair as he could, head ducked away from Rilan's ire. "It was the lass' idea, and no effort on my own part would have stopped her. I just wanted to talk with the Coalitioner blokes. She was the one with the plan to save Inas, and it nearly worked perfectly."

"Nearly. Yes, we have Inas, but you could have tried harder to stop the Coalitioner. That means you let her be captured," Rilan insisted. Maybe it wasn't fair, but she didn't want be fair.

"So I was supposed to fight away a full majus of the Life Coalition?" Rey shot back. "And House o' Strength at that? She'd have flitted us all away, eyah, and I'd not be tellin' you what transpired."

"Those Coalitioners are not, hmm, maji," Caroom rumbled. Their eyes were dark pinpricks of anger.

"And the answer is yes, you should've fought them to keep my apprentice from unknown torture at the Coalition's hands," Rilan said.

"They would not have released me," Inas said. He held up both hands, one toward Rey and the other toward her. They were shaking, and Rilan hardly kept the disgust off her face as something rippled beneath the surface of his skin. "Please stop. It won't fix anything. They already have her, and as Rey says, she sacrificed herself to bring me back, though she tried to save all of us. I have her and Rey to thank." Sam was half holding him, making soothing sounds. Rilan wasn't sure Inas could stand up on his own without Sam's help. He was a mess.

Rilan stared at Rey until he grimaced and looked away. He wasn't telling her all of it. How had he gotten so close to the Life Coalition? She wondered if she should report this to the Council, despite her current relationship with them. But admitting she'd lost her apprentice *again* was likely to get her demoted back to an apprentice herself. She didn't even know if that was possible, but she didn't want to chance it. They had kept Inas' disappearance relatively quiet, mainly because of his species. If the Assembly as a whole knew the Coalition was keeping an apprentice, the negotiations with them might take a far different tack. She shuddered to think of the Aridori assassins loosed with no warning on the unsuspecting Assembly. No, better for the Life Coalition to want to negotiate. For now.

"Why did you want to talk with the Coalitioners?" she asked the Sureri. "How did you get in contact with them?"

Rey looked back, his hairy face crumpled into a grimace. "I bothered Majus Kheena to set up a back and forth with 'em. We both thought they had more to what they were on about. Sommat they wouldn't say to the Assembly, but might to one o' their kin."

Rilan crossed her arms, but let Rey get away with his answer, such as it was. Coming at the Coalition from multiple sides wasn't far different from what she had been thinking. Though his mentor wasn't here, she noticed.

"Does Kheena know about all this?" she asked. Rey hung his head.

"Not all, no. I will be tellin' him, short-like."

"You do that," Rilan said. It wasn't her place to punish another majus' apprentice, though she wanted to.

"What about the one who was taking her?" Ori asked.

"Dunarn took her," Sam said, and Rilan's attention snapped to him. "She was the one who captured Enos and me the first time."

"She worked with the...Aridori prisoners, though not as much as Nakan." Inas shivered as he spoke, his words broken and soft. He looked rough, even after the obvious cleaning Sam had administered.

"Just rest," Sam told him. "You can tell us later."

"No." Inas pushed him away with a weak hand. "They had barely started on my 'training,' even after almost two months. I resisted as long as I could." He gave a shudder, and Sam held him close.

Rilan looked between the young men. At least they had each other for comfort. What about Enos? Furthermore, what about Rey? He'd gone to great lengths to get Inas back. How reckless was he, to bargain with the Life Coalition on his own? Even if he told his mentor, she had to talk with Kheena about him.

"What 'training' is this?" Rilan asked. She crossed to Inas. "May I take a look?" She directed the question to Caroom as well, who gave a creaky nod. The Benish was hovering like a mother hen.

Inas moved in Sam's grip, and for a moment, he seemed to pull away from her, his face lengthening and shifting. He opened his mouth, and Rilan swore she saw fangs instead of teeth. Then he was the same as always. "You already know, as does everyone here, so I suppose it will not matter," he whispered.

The twins had shied away from her hearing their biological signatures in the Symphony of Healing. Once, it would have revealed them as Aridori.

Rilan closed her eyes and let the music rise in her mind. The Symphony of Healing around Inas had holes, with measures where the music skipped a beat, or a note was out of place. She thought even Sam didn't know how much effort the Aridori was putting forth to appear normal. Panic and the urge to flee echoed through the music of his mental state. His body was another matter. The song was fluid, changing key and notes. She could see little ripples in his flesh. What had the Life Coalition done to him? But Sam wasn't even flinching away from the undulating motion passing through Inas' body.

Physical healing was not her forte, and even if it had been, the Aridori body was strange, with its ability to change shape. But she could treat his mental torment—that *was* her specialty. Rilan took a few notes from her core and placed them in spots where the chords skipped in Inas' psyche, smoothing rough edges caused by sleeplessness and captivity. Inas sat straighter as she did, leaning into Sam. It was a permanent use of her notes—she would have to regrow more from future experiences, but in this case it was worth the cost to see Inas breathe easier. It would not erase the scars of his suffering by any means, but it would help. Now they just had to rescue his sister. Again.

"Oh. Thank you," Inas breathed. His eyes were still hollow, but brighter. He flexed one hand as if it ached. "I did not realize—"

"Often we do not feel a burden we've held for a long time," Rilan told him.

"How is one's, hmm, apprentice?" Caroom said. "One would have brought Inas sooner to a medical practitioner, but as that one says, the risk of others discovering that one's biology, hmm, outweighs many other factors."

"I am well," Inas said before Rilan could reveal what she thought. Sam shot a concerned look at Rilan for confirmation. She hesitated, then nodded back to him.

"I think he will recover, with your help. He needs rest," she said. "We won't know all of what he went through until he tells us," at this she shot Inas a look, but he had his head down again. "From what I heard in the Symphony, it will take time to adjust back to this life." She looked around the room. "It's up to all of us to help him."

"I will," Sam said immediately.

"One is hesitant to suggest, but, hmm, would Inas be able to add to the markers for the portal to the Life Coalition's headquarters? Then this group may be able to rescue that one's sister." Caroom brought their wide hands to grasp each other with a creak like branches snapping. Their eyes were dim. Rilan knew they were worried about their apprentice.

"They...they have a field which damped my access to the Symphony," Inas said. He wasn't looking up, and burrowed into Sam's arms. "I could not create a portal back to the Nether. My impressions of the Life Coalition's headquarters are very limited. I saw only two rooms."

"We may still be attempting," Ori said, his voice soft, "if you are to be up to the task."

"I can try," Inas mumbled into Sam's shoulder. Sam patted his back.

Rey pushed to his feet, looked once to Sam and Inas, then away. His shoulders slumped and Rilan wondered what the Sureri thought of Sam and Inas together. "If we're all happy here, mind if I pop on?" he asked. "Got some things to tell the majus, yer know."

"I suppose," Rilan said. She stared at Rey until he ducked his head again and scampered for the door. He might not be committed to bringing down the Life Coalition, but she didn't think he would actively work against them. He *had* gotten Inas back, when the rest of them couldn't. She stared after him until the door closed.

Enos was just as complicit in her abduction. Rilan couldn't fully blame Rey, but he had his own secrets, and she hadn't been watching him as closely as the twins and Sam. She wouldn't continue that mistake.

The next several lightenings were concerned with Ori trying to coax location markers from Inas' memory, while Caroom and Sam paced and got in the way. Inas grew more haggard throughout, his hands shaking, and strange changes rippling through his figure. Rilan was about to suggest they give in for the day when a rumble interrupted them, shaking the building.

"Again?" Ori said. "This is not to be the time the chimes should ring. The pattern has changed again."

"It's rung three times today instead of two," Sam said.

"And it's getting more insistent," Rilan added. The plates on her shelves rattled and she watched, ready to catch any that dropped like the vase had.

She turned to Ori. "We have plenty of problems between the Life Coalition, Inas's return, and now Enos going missing, but I think you should keep looking for old records to tell us what's going on. We won't be able to do anything if these chimes vibrate the Nether to pieces around us. I'll work on the portal. It's the only way we have to reach Enos."

* * *

In the days after Inas' return, the chimes grew more unrelenting every day. Sam worried over Enos missing. None of them had a way to get her back. If Majus Ayama's portal had worked, they would know how to reach the Life Coalition, but now they had little choice but to wait until the organization made another move.

He thought of the Effature's direction to learn more about the coincidences. He'd learned more about his house, hadn't he? But nothing about the chimes or the Dissolution. What else did the Effature know that he hadn't told? Sam would ask Majus Cyrysi if there was a way to contact the Effature, soon. Now wasn't the time. Only the routine of taking care of Inas kept Sam from having anxiety attacks.

"Just a little more," Sam said to Inas that morning. He'd had a poor appetite since he got back. Inas pushed the bowl away and Sam frowned at him.

"You're acting like me, Inas," Sam said. His friend had gotten scared at unusual things, stayed inside, and pulled away from others.

"Just give me a few days," Inas said.

"You haven't even talked to Rey." The fact sent an unfortunate sliver of satisfaction through Sam, though he chastised himself for not being bigger than that. But with Enos missing, he wanted Inas all to himself. Rey's connection to Enos' disappearance, however much he protested they were both at fault, did not endear him to either Sam or Inas, even though the Sureri had also been a factor in freeing Inas. He'd been missing the last few days from meetings with the maji. Sam suspected Majus Kheena had him working through some punishment.

"I'm getting better, Sam," Inas replied. Sam sighed and cleaned up the table. He'd have to urge Inas to take a shower later. He turned for the little kitchen.

"Wait," Inas said. "Come here."

Sam put the bowl down and went to him. Inas raised a hand but the fingers were changing, lengthening and shortening. Sam took his hand and smoothed the ripples in Inas's flesh.

"You're still having trouble with that?" Sam said. "Maybe if we—"

"I said it will take time, Sam," Inas growled and jerked his hand back. His face showed sudden anger, eyebrows shadowing his eyes.

Sam stopped himself from backing up. Why had Inas called him over, then? He held his ground against Inas's change and stood silent, waiting until Inas looked away.

"I'm sorry," Inas took Sam's hand again, this time gently. "It *will* take time, though."

"I know that, Inas," Sam said. "We'll get there."

* * *

Three days later, Sam's anger at Rey, worry for Enos, and frustration with Inas was drowned out in the throbbing thrum of the chime. It drove everything from his mind. It was even hard to hear the Symphony, much less the sounds and music of the House of Communication.

When he could hear it, the chords wobbled like a violinist with too much vibrato. Majus Cyrysi's penthouse apartment shook like a tree in a hurricane, but all the Imperium's tallest buildings trembled in the sustained vibration.

"It's gone off four times already this morning!" Sam shouted to Majus Cyrysi as he exited his room. He had to hold on to the doorjamb so he wasn't shaken off his feet. "Have you found anything else?"

Majus Cyrysi came from his room, his crest waggling in all directions. "The bridge must be the key! I am thinking this is the culmination of the signal—likely today. Be finding Rilan and Caroom. I am to be going up to the bridge now. It is still the only lead, but I am certain something will be happening soon." Majus Cyrysi practically flew out of the apartment, heading down the stairs, his multicolored robe whipping out behind every long stride.

Sam sighed, but watched him go. Inas was on the couch—he'd been living in the majus' apartment, which Sam wasn't going to argue with, especially with the nightmares that woke him. He dreamed about what had happened to him, or what he suspected was happening to Enos, but wouldn't give Sam specifics. Majus Caroom wasn't happy about Inas getting even further behind on his lessons, but they also would do whatever they could to help their apprentice recover.

Inas was still having trouble with his form shifting, and Sam didn't know what to do about it. They had held hands, and even kissed, but there was always a reticence underneath. Sam could feel the flinch of Inas shying away when they touched. What had the Life Coalition done to him? He wouldn't say.

"Come on. Let's find the others and catch up," Sam shouted over the noise. Inas levered to his feet, but said nothing, ready to follow him out of the apartment. Butterflies rose in his stomach at the prospect of leaving the apartment of his own volition, rather than with someone else.

No, that's not right. Hiding *behind someone else.*

Did Sam need someone more wretched than him to drive away his anxiety?

What does that say about me?

Once he caught up with Majus Ayama, on her way to the offices of the Spire, she directed him to gather everyone else. Only Majus Hand Dancer was at a concert in High Imperium and could not attend, though Sam guessed such activities wouldn't go on much longer with the ringing of the chime.

"Up to the bridge," Majus Ayama directed them, pointing around the circumference of the House of Communication, the tallest of the houses. "I can't concentrate on refining the music for the portal with this thing going on." Sam saw her hands clench. He was not the only one sick with worry for Enos.

The chime hadn't stopped, and people were milling around the Spire grounds. No one would accomplish anything while the noise and shaking continued. Sam imagined the rest of the Imperium was in as much unrest. He jumped as one of the moving sculptures in the Spire grounds crashed to the ground. That was the third one to fall in the last two days.

"Why the bridge?" Majus I'Fon asked.

"Ori has been doing research on this Shiv-cursed chime," Majus Ayama said over the noise. "The bridge has some connection in the old texts he's found. There are notes about the Nether shifting, like this is a warning bell, or things are moving. He feels something is coming, so up the bridge it is."

The bridge was only midway up the height of the tower, and Sam breathed a sigh of relief at not having to climb the whole stairway, though he'd gotten a lot fitter since arriving in the Nether. Multiple flights of stairs were the norm here.

He had peered at the bridge a few times from the doorway that connected it to the rest of the tower, but only while passing its floor. It was constructed of polished and fitted stone, with rails that came to his waist. The stone was like that of the House of Communication, white with variegated stripes that caught the light of the walls. They could see Majus Cyrysi on the bridge when their group arrived, but he wasn't alone.

"Sir!" Majus I'Fon called out to the Effature. Hir tentacles were unbound, and they hung around hir head. The old man was standing next to Majus Cyrysi, one finger stroking the edge of the diadem that graced his head. "How did you get here?"

The Effature turned back, his robe swishing around his feet. He cast an eye over the assembled maji, nodding to himself. "The usual way—by foot."

Sam stifled a snort of laughter, and even Inas gave a shy smile, though he didn't look up. Sam watched his hands to make sure they weren't changing in front of the old man. Inas was stable, for now.

"The Effature was to be meeting me up here," Majus Cyrysi said, his crest wild. "He was listening to my conclusion that this artifact of the House of Communication might be a meeting place of sorts."

I guess I won't have to make an appointment with him, then.

Sam wondered whether the Effature had spoken to his mentor about their discussion. How did the old man know these things were so important? The Effature rubbed his diadem again, and Sam's eye was drawn the crystal. Was it connected to the Nether? Had it told him why the chime was ringing?

Palmoran passed his gaze over the collected maji, stopping on him and Inas for a beat longer. "I have dredged up ancient records lately from the storage rooms beneath the palace. Our civilization lost much when the Aridori War occurred, but the worst was the loss of information, from what I can tell. Yet a few documents mentioned a 'great sound' in the Nether. They hearken to a meeting, and pointed me toward this bridge."

"And you did this all yourself?" Majus I'Fon asked. The Effature nodded. What other resources did he have?

"But if this is a call to dialogue, hmm, who will this group meet?" Caroom asked. The Benish looked side to side with a creak, barely heard over the ringing chime. It seemed louder, this close to the wall. They gestured to the other end of the bridge. "There is only the wall of the, hmm, Nether. This bridge has never had, hmm, a purpose."

It was true. The bridge arced out from the House of Communication—the closest of the six houses of the maji to the tremendous wall. But it was a dead end. Why would anyone make a bridge where there was no entrance?

Sam looked down its length. It not only ended at the wall, it looked like it vanished *into* the wall. By mutual assent, their group walked down the bridge's length, probably a hundred paces. Sam stopped close to the massive wall, trying not to look too closely. Its crystal depths went on forever, and it was disorienting to look into the translucent material for more than a few moments.

"When was this built?" Sam pointed down to the bridge, but Majus Cyrysi shrugged, his crest flaring.

"Unknown. The Houses of the Maji have been here since before the Aridori War, and this bridge was to be here since the house's construction, if I am to be correct."

"I believe you are," the Effature added in his deep voice. It carried through the chimes. "Sam, will you look at the very end of the bridge?"

Sam did so, and ran a finger around the intersection of the stone bridge's railing and the crystalline wall. It wasn't a reflection. He could see the bridge passing *into* the crystal. Colors trailed his finger, in green and blue and brown—in fact, all of the colors of the Symphony.

"How can the bridge be inside the wall?" he asked.

Majus Ayama came forward, Majus Cyrysi and Caroom following her. "As we told you a few days ago, maji enter the crystal of the Nether on their testing, though that usually happens in the columns, not in the wall. It would be pointless to go into the wall, but the builders must have used that ability to fasten the end of the bridge so it wouldn't fall. Maji could go a short distance inside before running out of air."

So it's not a bridge to nothing. Just not something anyone can access.

"No one knows what's on the other side?" Sam looked between the maji. Majus I'Fon was staring up the height of the wall, hir large silvery eyes reflecting blues and purples from the crystal. Rey just shook his head, and Inas was staring at a spot of lichen on the bridge, not paying attention. Sam ached to put a hand under his chin and bring him back into the world, but there wasn't time.

"I have been saying before," Majus Cyrysi said, "The Nether is not exactly inside the universe. I am not to be knowing if there is even anything at all on the other side."

"Yet, hmm, there is a bridge," Majus Caroom rumbled.

Majus Kheena stepped up beside his apprentice. He'd been silent, watching everyone. He differed from most Sathssn Sam had met, almost never wearing his cowl. Today he didn't even have gloves on.

"The Nether, it sustains us, but there are limits to what even it can do," Majus Kheena said. The other maji turned to him. "The walls of the columns, they are thin, relative to this wall." Majus Kheena gestured with one scaly hand back toward the Spire of the Maji, towering above them, slumped against the column in the middle of the circle of Houses. Then he swung the hand back to the wall. "This, it is extremely thick. The Nether, it can only sustain the oxygen and nitrogen required for continued breath for a brief time. The column wall is thin enough that this, it doesn't matter."

Sam placed his hand on the crystal. "Then why are we here? Does the Nether want us to walk into the wall?" Colors played around his hand, and he could feel the chime reverberating through the crystal, as if it was being generated, or something was moving deep in the limitless facets of the Nether. He would be alone, confined, inside the wall. It was the opposite of what made him panic.

"You could," Majus Cyrysi said, and when Sam looked back, he had his head cocked, as if he wanted to see Sam try. "But only maji can do such a thing, and you would have to be returning to us within seconds, or you would be asphyxiating."

Sam pressed his hand harder against the blue and purple surface, and just for a moment, he thought it shifted beneath his hand. He stepped back, looking at where the ends of the bridge disappeared into the wall. Rey stepped up beside him, frowning at the crystal expanse.

"Though non-maji may be brought along," the Effature said. Everyone turned to look at him at the pronouncement.

"Brought along? I've never heard that," Majus Ayama said. "You seem to know more than even the Council, and they have records of the maji going back to the war."

The Effature shook his head. "The Council does not know everything. It has been quite a while since it was done." His eyes fell on Inas, and some expression Sam couldn't place crossed the old man's face. "I suspect a connection between the chime, the shaking in the Imperium, and this bridge. I am very close to remembering what that is."

Both Majus Ayama and Majus I'Fon were staring at the Effature as if he held many more secrets. Sam suspected he did.

"Were you also finding the mentions of movement within the Nether?" Majus Cyrysi asked the Effature. "If so, your information is to be as good as the best offered in the Spire of the Maji. We must only be decoding such knowledge."

Sam sidled to Inas while the others talked and reached for his friend's arm, wanting the comfort of his presence. Inas tensed as he did, looking up from the rail of the bridge. He let Sam take his arm, and Sam could tell he was trying to relax. Maybe he would, with time.

The Effature gave a slight nod to Majus Cyrysi's words. "I saw the same information. As some of you doubtless suspect, I have been reticent with information in the past, and perhaps held too much back. The most recent cycles are teaching me this."

It was a strange semi-apology, and Sam searched the other's faces, trying to figure out what was going on. Even he could tell the Nether's caretaker was acting out of the ordinary. Majus Ayama was squinting like she did when she was almost at the solution to a puzzle.

"Would you mind telling us exactly how long you have been holding on to this information?" she began. Her tone held nothing but respect, yet it was firm.

"I believe I am having the same question," Majus Cyrysi added. His crest flattened, and the Nether translated it as embarrassment to Sam. "I have been making discreet inquiries, but few know anything more."

The Effature sighed, and pulled a hand down his long white beard and moustache. "Yes, it is about time for that question again, isn't it? You are wondering how long I have been in charge of the Nether."

Hints of their conversation ran through Sam's mind. *I have been the caretaker of the Nether for quite a long time—long enough that old details tend to fade after time.* He remembered the Effature touching the diadem he wore several times, as if it were giving him information.

"Me, I think the question has crossed every majus' mind at some point," Majus Kheena said. "Especially when we hear stories from those much older than us."

"And when the maji request, hmm, material from the palace archives," Majus Caroom added.

"Not that they often honor the queries," Majus I'Fon huffed. Sam wondered what information the Lobath had requested. How often did the Effature interact with maji outside the Assembly?

"I have discovered further details past what we discussed at our meeting, Sam," Bolas Palmoran addressed him, and Sam's chest seized as everyone looked at him. "You did not take that walk on the bridge I suggested, did you? What about other connections between the strange occurrences since you arrived in the Nether?"

"I...I...haven't made much progress," Sam whispered. He tried to keep his gaze on the Effature's face, so he wouldn't have to see Majus Ayama's eyes boring into him.

"I feel we may discover more quite soon," the old man said. Sam realized he had avoided answering the maji's questions about his age.

"Aye, that's a fact," Rey said. Sam looked around. The Sureri was still at the wall, staring into the disconcerting depths, one hand cupped around the edge of his face. "Yer all should better get over here. I think someone's comin' through."

That was when the incessant chime finally stopped.

CHAPTER ELEVEN

Emissary

- Lately, my mind has conjured ancient memories to the surface—likely as aspect of the diadem I wear, and its connection to the Nether. It has access to far more than I can comprehend at one time.

I begin to remember the crystal of the wall is not all it seems, nor is that which we know as the Nether. The Nether is said to exist outside the universe, yet what we know of it is far smaller than what it encompasses.

From the Journal of Bolas Palmoran, Effature of the Nether, 1003 A.A.W.

Sam worked his jaw in the sudden silence. The lack of sound was a heavy pressure in his ears. He'd gotten so used to the chime over the last several lightenings he'd begun to ignore it.

"Someone is to be coming through the wall?" Majus Cyrysi was the first to realize what Rey said. "How is this to be possible? Is this what the chime was for?"

"Eyah, right there." Rey pointed one long finger at where the bridge would sit, if it continued through the wall. Sam squinted, trying to ignore the distracting facets of the Nether crystal. Their group came forward to huddle at the end of the bridge. The wall was not quite transparent, and Sam could see some way through it, but it was impossible to determine distance.

There was a figure, growing larger, the shape unlike any of the ten species. It seemed distorted, shorter than a Lobath and taller than a Pixie, but the proportions were wrong, like the figure wore a flaring dress or robe.

"This, it is impossible," Majus Kheena said. "The Nether would not sustain a person long enough to travel from..." The Sathssn paused.

"From whatever is to be on the other side." Majus Cyrysi finished. His crest was wild, shifting shape every few moments. "This cannot be!

The Nether is to be existing outside space and time. There *is* no 'outside.'"

"True to a point," Bolas Palmoran said from behind. There was a collective shuffle as they turned to him. In the wall, the figure made slow progress, and Sam was loathe to tear his gaze away, as its approach drew him. "Perhaps I found more than Majus Cyrysi in my research. The exterior of the Nether links to no place in the known universe, but an interior wall like this one may lead to..." The Effature squinted, and stroked the diadem on his head. "To other facets?"

Majus Ayama cocked her head. Sam was glad to see everyone looked as confused as he felt. Even Inas had looked up, his eyebrows drawn as he frowned. What did the diadem do?

"What do you mean...other *facets*?" Majus Ayama said, very slowly.

"There is more than this?" Majus I'Fon spread hir long fingers out to encompass the Imperium, Gloomlight, and further. "Yet we have never seen it."

"Yes." The Effature seemed animated, his hands moving faster, his eyes brighter than Sam had ever seen. "The Nether communicates such wonders as I have...forgotten?" He sounded confused, unheard of for the Effature, and looked up. His diadem caught light from the wall, throwing it back in a rainbow of color. The Nether's caretaker reached up both hands, whether caressing the crystal or trying to hold his head, Sam wasn't sure. Something new was happening—another of those events the Effature warned him of.

"The diadem tells me ever more. The chimes—they warn of facets of the Nether in transit. It has been many centuries since we were so close to..." The corners of his mouth drew up. "I remember. Those memories have been gone so long. Oh my. My. Yes. However could I have forgotten *her*?" Palmoran took one unsteady step toward the railing, delicately placing one long-nailed hand on the polished stone, as if he would fall over without its support. "You must understand, the diadem I wear both aids me and constrains me. There was no need to remember such information—" he broke off and winced, the wrinkles on his face seeming to deepen, "—for so long. So many centuries."

"Forgotten *who*?" Majus I'Fon asked. The end of hir head-tentacles wriggled in exasperation. Majus Kheena gestured at Majus Caroom, both of them talking in indistinct voices.

Majus Cyrysi whirled in a circle, looking at the walls. "You are saying this *facet* of the Nether is to be encircled by these walls?" He was animated, his crest spiking. "The Nether is to be large enough that maji can be opening portals from the Imperium to Gloomlight, and from Gloomlight to Poler. It is to be nearly as large as one of the homeworlds. Yet you are to be telling us this is not the only section of the Nether?" His crest stuck almost straight out, and he pulled at his moustaches with thumb and forefinger. Majus Cyrysi stopped his twirl, his eyes fixed on the diadem. It was a miniature mirror of the wall, crystal reflecting crystal.

The Effature gave a slight bow. "Indeed. A fact I had forgotten until moments ago." He looked up at the wall. "I am as surprised as you."

"What else have you kept from us? Have you endangered the Assembly or the Council by your omissions?" Majus Ayama asked. She was next to Bolas Palmoran, one hand ringed in white and olive, as if she would take the information from him. The Effature waved her away and stood straight.

"Much, I am afraid, but I do not think I have put you in danger. There is no time to explain further. After the coming events, I must reveal several secrets I have kept for a long while." He put one thin hand to the green and purple variegation on the front of his robe of office. Sam peered at the hand. Some of the liverspots were gone, the joints smaller. It looked like the hand of a man much younger than the Effature. His pale cheeks had sparks of color in them, as if his body reflected a memory of an earlier time. Was all this an effect of the diadem?

"Until then, it will be a delight to see Crominu Vaevicta after all this time. There is so much I have forgotten."

"This person is, hmm, who?" Caroom asked. Their eyes flashed with curiosity and their body creaked like an oak in the wind as they shifted back and forth.

"Why, the Effature of the next facet of the Nether," Palmoran said. "My...a good friend of mine from long ago." Sam caught the hesitation. That was not what the Effature was going to say. Closer than friend, then? "This must be her representative. Yes, the diadem speaks to me— an ancient ritual I had no need to know for long cycles. Their side must have also recognized the changes that are coming."

"Changes? What changes?" Majus Ayama squawked, but there was a knocking sound behind them and a yelp from Rey. The figure was still indistinct on the other side, one limb raised to tap on the crystal again.

"The changes that accompany the Dissolution," the Effature said. He turned to Sam, his hands ushering him to the crystal. "The sequence is coming back to me. The Nether wishes a connection made. Please, come forward."

Sam looked around. "What, just me?" Why him? He'd never even seen this place before a few months ago.

The Effature nodded. "The diadem suggests you are the one. I believe you are connected, though I do not know why."

Shaking, Sam stepped to the wall, raising one hand. The figure on the other side mirrored his movement, their hands overlaying.

The chime sounded one more time. A single, low, *thrum*, and all the colors of the Symphony bloomed around his hand, including a ring of gold and of silver.

Sam gasped, and stepped back. His fingers had touched not the cool crystal of the wall, but something made of flesh.

As he skipped away from the wall, a figure emerged. Their three, pointed, stalk-like legs clacked on the stone of the bridge. As Sam reached the rest of the group, everyone else took a collective step back.

The figure was surrounded by a halo of silver, dissipating as they stepped from the wall. The colors of the Symphony—all the colors, Sam realized—flowed away from the being in a rainbow, washing outward and over the crystal from where the figure had emerged.

His mind went to the Dome of the Assembly, nearly two months ago, when he created a portal so large a Drain fit through. The presence there had taken many of his memories, but not this one. The portal had been ringed with gold, the color associated with his new house. But there had been another color. Silver. Just like the halo around this creature.

"You are the representative from Vaevicta?" the Effature asked into the silence.

The creature—the person—tapped the ends of their legs, encased in pointed wooden shoes, in a rhythm on the stone. They were squat and gray, wearing a tunic of white shiny fabric, which covered the three legs from above the second joint. The body was low to the ground, and two of the legs emerged from the front of the torso, while the third came from the back. Their arms ended not in hands, but in three-fingered pincers. Sam caught sight of a third arm, barely visible around the back.

As he watched the figure, the Nether offered identifiers to Sam on their—no, *xyr*—body movements.

The head—which was round with a strange strip across the forehead instead of eyes—nodded, then waggled side to side. Underneath the head was a flat hard surface that must have been the person's jaw. It unhinged strangely, in four sections that grated against each other. Sequences of color flashed across the band on xyr head. The Nether translated the combination of the two as language.

"I am come at the urging of the Symphony and the insistence of my Effature. The synchronization bell has rung," xy said. "The pathway has been opened by your prophet." It sounded like a ritual speech. As when talking with a Lobhl, the words appeared in Sam's head like a memory of someone who spoke moments before. The voice was low and gravely.

"We welcome you to our facet of the Nether," the Effature answered. "Though you have come at a trying time."

"Yes. There is a discord in the Grand Symphony. The Dissolution comes too soon. Can you not hear it?" Large flaps unfurled in three even sections around the head, waving as if they sensed something. The Nether translated this as a questioning tone. The flaps cradled what Sam had originally mistaken for part of the person's head, but now he saw xy was wearing a flat hat, like a cross between a mortarboard and a wimple.

Majus Ayama twitched her head side to side when no one spoke, then took a small step forward. "We have not heard the discord in the Grand Symphony, but then, our facet has been undergoing conflict, as the Effature says."

Xyr head flaps centered on the majus. "Yes. Friction in the physical universe reflects the discord in the Symphony. The Dissolution should still be many cycles away, yet it looms closer. It is why the Nether has moved our facets together. Do you sense this as well?" The figure lacked eyes. Maybe the large ear-like flaps served the same purpose. They shifted among the stunned group, focusing on each person individually.

"The Dissolution, this is a child's tale," Majus Kheena said.

"It is not," the person said. The flaps fixed on the Sathssn.

"How do you know this?" Sam was surprised to hear the question from his own lips. It had just popped out.

The being at the Dome mentioned the Dissolution, and so did the Effature. I've heard that word too many times.

"It is my business to know of the Dissolution," came the reply. The Nether offered more details on body language and gender, though slower than before when Sam had met a new species. The ear-like flaps aimed toward him and he hunched under the notice. Xy must know he was the one who touched xyr claw through the wall. He didn't want to be called out—to be different. He turned to Inas, clutching the bridge's rail. Rey was standing behind him, looking worried. Sam turned back. He had to be strong.

"How may we address you?" The Effature asked. "Do you have a name? A title?" One elegant hand fingered his diadem, as if he searched for more information.

"I forget my manners," the person said. "I am Prophet Wor Wobniar. My species is the Nostelrahn. Do you not have your own line of oracles? One must have been here to open the way."

"I have never heard of a true oracle," Majus Cyrysi said. His head was cocked to one side, his eyes roaming over Wor Wobniar. Sam remembered that inquisitive stare all too well.

"Would you like to come with us?" Majus Ayama asked. "We have rooms where you can be comfortable, and talk to various representatives. We have only recently met another new species, so negotiations about the Assembly are going on currently."

"We can take you to meet our Council of Maji," Majus I'Fon offered.

"I would instead speak with the one who opened my way to this facet. The tradition is for the prophets to meet first," grated Wor Wobniar. Xyr mouth pieces slid against each other, lights in purples and oranges flashing on the strip above. The flaps whipped side to side, then centered on him. Xy knew. "They are here, in this group." The legs made a tattoo on the bridge as they scuttled forward, faster than Sam would have thought possible. Their group collectively reared back as Wor Wobniar came closer.

Majus Ayama's gaze fell on Sam. He swallowed, feeling his heart speed, the familiar nausea rising, and he grabbed for Inas, who was frowning at Wor Wobniar. He looked up at Sam and a shaky smile slid across his face.

"You can do this, Sam," he said.

Enos would have told me that. I need to be strong for Inas.

Something about their exchange must have alerted Wor Wobniar, and all three of xyr head flaps centered on Sam.

"You are the one then? Will you change the Symphony? Any small adjustment will do."

Sam froze. Everyone was looking at him. He had spent the last month hiding his gold aura from other maji. Now they would know he was different. His hand on Inas' back gripped and Sam took it back before he grabbed a handful of Inas' shirt. He stuffed it in his pocket instead, feeling the smooth lines of his pocketwatch, feeling the *tick* of time beneath his fingers.

Majus Cyrysi had dubbed the changes he made as of the House of Matter. His breath came hard through his nose, but he forced himself to listen to the music. There was no going back. He closed his eyes.

The rhythms of the Symphony described the people and objects around him. The wall itself was a monumental edifice, as resonant and mighty in song as in reality. It loomed over the rest of the melody, impossible to ignore, but separate and unchangeable; a monolith in the Symphony. The softer, gentler sections of music defined flesh and bone of those around him, the clothes that hung on them, and the air around them. His pocketwatch was a steady low march, reflecting the steel and brass cogs. Beneath them all, trading chords with the wall where it intersected, was the stone of the bridge they stood on. Its chords were even simpler than the watch.

That's easy to change.

Sam took a few notes from the core of his being, trying to ignore the glissandos and trills in the music as others moved and traded glances. He peeked down at one hand, saw it wreathed in a gold aura. There was an intake of breath from Majus Kheena that made his heart beat double-time.

Sam placed the notes between two measures, bridging a gap in the ponderous music that defined the stone as a solid, gray material. The beat was like the casing of his pocketwatch, with only a slight difference in the key.

He meant to change a small section, out of sight. However, as his notes incorporated into the music, they replicated with the beat, and a sheet of shining metal flowed from under his feet in all directions, surrounded by a golden glow.

I can't control it.

He scrambled to take his notes back, but the change pulled more from him, leaving him breathless. Sam hunched in as the others stared. The stone of the bridge transformed, becoming shiny burnished steel like the watch. It climbed up the railings, effortlessly recreating the intricate marble accents into whorls and flowers made of pure steel.

Despite the maji staring at him as if he was as strange and unknown as the Nostelrahn from the next facet, a tinge of pride stirred in his chest at the accomplishment.

"This! This is what I am looking for!" Wor Wobniar's head flaps centered on Sam and xy scuttled closer, legs echoing a drumbeat on the steel. "Not only a prophet, but at last, a new majus of the House of Matter. I have been searching for this occurrence in the *Vloeinkaal* for my entire life. Finally, I have found my new apprentice!"

"Your apprentice?" Majus Cyrysi squawked. "He is to be *my* apprentice!"

The House of Matter? Had Majus Cyrysi stumbled upon the actual name of his house, or had the Nether translated what Wor Wobniar said to a term they understood?

The flaps waved, and moved to Majus Cyrysi. "He must come with me, to my facet of the Nether, if there is to be any hope of keeping the Dissolution from crashing down upon us like a tsunami before the correct time."

"Eyah, debate yer apprentice all yer want, but what the bloody hell did Sam do?" Rey said. Sam didn't look at him, heat rising in his face.

"I feel *my* apprentice, he has a point," Majus Kheena put in. "Us, are we going to talk of what happened? Here, there is much at play, even disregarding a new facet of the Nether, which we will have to discuss thoroughly."

"Yes, is there now also a, hmm, new house of the maji?" Caroom asked. They shifted from one leg to the other with a creak of snapping wood.

"I think I heard part of his change," Majus I'Fon said, one finger at hir earhole.

"You're one for pronouncements, aren't you?" Majus Ayama directed at Wor Wobniar. "Why would we let you take him?"

"Ahem." The Effature made a slight noise, and the others turned to him. He looked at the Nostelrahn. "Were you sent here by Vaevicta because of the chime, or to look for a new apprentice? These are very different objectives."

Wor Wobniar's head flaps wavered in the air for a moment. After a pause, the Nether offered the translation as embarrassment. Then colors flashed across the strip on xyr head as xyr jaw grated together.

"I admit, my vision of what must come coincided with the Effature's call for a representative." Xy extended all three arms. "Yet the chimes called for a meeting between the facets *because* of the coming Dissolution. They are indistinguishable. This is fundamental to the House of Matter reclaiming its station among the other Houses." Wor Wobniar's flaps skipped among the group. "We have met, yes? So that aspect has been concluded."

"No. There are many who would be interested in another facet of the Nether," Majus I'Fon said. "And the Council of the Maji at the very least should be here to observe a practitioner of a new house." Zie turned wide eyes on Sam. "Or rather, two houses." Zie looked back to Wor Wobniar. "We saw the silver glow about you when you came through the wall. The House of Matter is not the only new Symphony we witnessed today."

They are arguing because of me.

"I'm not sure what happened," Sam said. He gestured vaguely at the shiny metal bridge. "I didn't mean to do this. It got away from me."

Wor Wobniar's head flaps centered on him again. "I can teach you," xy grated, purple and green flashing in the strip across xyr forehead. Xy poked a claw in Majus Cyrysi's direction. "He cannot. You must come with me. It is logical, anyway, for the prophets to pave a path between the two facets."

Sam shook his head before he registered what he was doing. Thoughts of Enos and Inas streamed through his head. Enos was still missing. They had to get her back from the Life Coalition. Instead, this person wanted him to go somewhere new and different.

"Wor Wobniar had a silver glow, didn't xy?" Rey said. "An' Sam here glowed all gold-like. Those ain't the same house." He looked to the prophet. "Yer can't teach one not of yer house. Yer don't hear the same Symphony."

"The Sureri, hmm, has a point," Majus Caroom rumbled.

"This is to be true," Majus Cyrysi said. "Are you also to be of the House of Matter, that you can be teaching him more fully?"

Wor Wobniar hesitated, xyr head flaps wavering again before settling on Sam. "You are of the House of Matter. I have seen that much with certainty. Have I not already said my affiliation?" Xy was hedging.

"You said you are a prophet, or an oracle," Inas said. At Sam's surprised look, he gave a small smile. A little of Inas' affability was still in there. "I was listening."

"Yes, and what is an oracle or prophet but one who sees that which is to come, and which has passed?" Wor Wobniar said. Xyr tone was patient, or at least the Nether translated it that way, like a teacher speaking to a rather slow student. "I see the *Vloeinkaal*— the ebb and flow of events. You would call it the House of Time."

Majus Ayama and Majus Kheena began speaking over each other while Majus Cyrysi gestured at Sam, but what he said was lost in the noise. Beside him, Inas whistled a low tone. "Xy sees time?" He looked to Sam. "That would have been handy to have a few months ago."

Sam found Inas' hand and squeezed. There was a deep pool of hurt in him, still full. Sam hadn't talked with him about what had happened during his imprisonment by the Life Coalition. He tried to signal a promise they would talk soon.

"Maji, please," called the Effature, and the maji sorted themselves out.

"Then there are two new houses here," Majus I'Fon said. "The House of Matter and the House of Time. And you can hear both?" Zie stared directly at Wor Wobniar until the Nostelrahn shuffled on xyr tripod legs.

"I perceive only the House of Time, not that of Matter. No one does, save this one. Another reason for him to come to my facet."

Sam inhaled deep, then let it go. Again, he was different. But this time, the feeling was freeing. He had finally showed what he could do. He was of the House of Matter. Hesitantly, he reached for the notes he'd placed in the bridge, trying to pull them back and reverse his change, but they slipped away. He grimaced. Could anyone teach him? The prophet at least knew what he was.

"Then why should you be taking my apprentice?" Majus Cyrysi's crest was straight up, as ferocious as Sam had ever seen him.

"Because he is also of the House of Time." Wor Wobniar stated, one claw held out toward Sam. "And I *can* teach him of that. Can you?"

Sam stared back. He had two houses. The certainty of the statement settled into him.

Wor Wobniar can show me what I am.

"I...that is, I am to be certain I can...I mean..." Majus Cyrysi's crest fell. Majus Ayama laid a hand on his arm, and Sam barely kept himself from going to the grumpy Kirian. He really was a terrible teacher.

A well of certainty was building in Sam. He looked to Inas, who he still needed near him, or he would have another panic attack. Inas would recover faster near him, too.

There was silence for several seconds, as Sam struggled with what he knew had to happen.

"But he can't just go with you," Majus Ayama said. "We've only just met you. We have no idea what's happening in your facet, what species are there, what the social or political situation is. Why should we even trust you?"

The Effature spoke, his hand on the diadem again, as if it spoke to him. "I have access to enough memories to know the next facet is peaceable, or was when I last had news of it. But that was long ago. Which means there must be a diplomatic channel created between our two cultures. If the Dissolution truly is the threat both I and Wor Wobniar suspect, then it would be beneficial for Sam to go through for a few days."

Majus Cyrysi gave an indignant harrumph—his crest was all over the place. It pained Sam to see his mentor so frazzled.

The Effature continued. "If Sam can learn the method to pass through the wall as the prophet has, he can then bring a delegation back to us."

"All respect to this one who speaks for the Assembly, yet this one does not speak for the, hmm, Council, yes?" Caroom folded their arms with a snapping noise.

The Effature acknowledged the point with a nod. "Yet Sam hears a part of the Symphony none of you can. Even the Council cannot teach a house not their own. Is this not correct?"

Caroom rumbled, but said nothing.

"Then since they are not here, perhaps this group may offer an opinion in their stead?"

More silence, while the maji all looked at each other.

"Maybe he could go with Wor Wobniar for a few days. See what this other facet is about, and if xy really can teach him. We might gain more allies," Majus Ayama said. Sam's mentor slumped, his crest falling flat.

Sam tried again to grasp the notes of the bridge, but they wouldn't budge. They had replicated too far, cementing with the original notes of the structure. He wouldn't be able to get them back until he learned more. To learn more he would have to go with the prophet.

He'd stayed in Majus Cyrysi's apartment for days. Enos had pulled him out of that funk, but she was gone. If he went back, Inas wouldn't be able to pull him out, not in his state. And what about his friend? Inas needed a familiar presence with him, to heal.

I have to go. I have to find out what I am. Why I'm here. And Inas has to be with me, for both our sakes.

"What do you say, Sam?" the Effature asked.

"I promise I'll come back soon," Sam told Majus Cyrysi.

Just like that, he'd decided. He'd developed an affection for the arrogant, grumpy, old Kirian over the last few months. He was loyal to those around him. But Sam needed more than he could teach.

Sam looked to Wor Wobniar. It was hard to find a place to focus, as xy didn't have eyes, so he fixed his gaze on the strip of light. "It will be for a few days, and then we'll come back? We have important things happening, and a person we must find. But you can teach me how to control this?" He gestured at the bridge again.

"I can teach you of the lost houses of maji," Wor Wobniar said, flashing xyr lights. "Even a day or two in my facet of the Nether will give you enough to practice for many days. I can take you through the prepared passage in the wall. Only one with our abilities can do this and I can show you how." Xy waved all three of xyr claw-like hands in the air. "I vow I will bring him back to you. But we must leave now. There is much to do." Xy scuttled a few steps back to the wall.

Sam looked to Inas, hunched over the steel railing. He stared back at Sam, the pain in his eyes clear. Something shifted under the skin of his face, then smoothed away. He had to have someone help him over what he was going through. Sam had experience with that mountain of anxiety pressing on his back. Inas had been living in his apartment instead of his mentor's. A few days for Inas might be too long.

Enos told him to look after me, but I think she meant for me to look after him, too. I need him and he needs me.

"Do you want to come?" he asked, holding out a hand to Inas.

Almost in slow motion, Inas' head came forward, then back up. A nod. "With you," was all he said.

Sam looked the question to Wor Wobniar, who paused, xyr stubby legs tapping the steel in thought. Xyr head flaps waved toward Sam, then shifted to the Aridori.

"He is not of the same house."

"That one is also one's apprentice," Majus Caroom said. "Which, hmm, one just got back, and has not seen nearly enough." Their voice had a snap Sam had never heard before. It made him want to find somewhere to hide. He swallowed and gathered his courage.

"Only for a day or two," he promised, holding up both hands. He wasn't sure whether he was addressing the Benish or the being who had come through the wall.

What am I doing and where did I get the courage to do this?

"He needs me, and I need him. Isn't that right, Inas?" Sam raised his voice at the last part.

Inas shook himself, his face haunted. One of his hands clenched. Only because Sam was watching did he see the ripples cascading up his arm, like worms wriggling through his skin. He didn't think the others had seen. Inas looked over the group of maji, as if just realizing they were watching. Then he opened the clenched hand and touched the steel railing of the bridge with a frown. Sam wondered whether it was for him or for the tremors that still shook his hand. "I would like to go. My sister told me to stay close to Sam."

"Which is another question we don't have a suitable answer to, I might add," Majus Ayama said. "We need to find her, quickly. The only reason we are here is, well—" she gestured to Wor Wobniar.

"There are to be many unanswered questions here," Majus Cyrysi said. His crest was drooping like he'd just dunked his head in water. Sam felt for his mentor, but without real training, he would never know what he could do.

"I believe much may be answered if Sam is to go with Wor Wobniar," the Effature said. "If Inas also wishes to go, then perhaps he may act as another ambassador to the next facet of the Nether. There are many unsettling coincidences lately, and I would like answers as much as the rest of you. Two will remember more than one." He turned to the Benish. "Will you accept your apprentice's departure for a few days?"

Majus Caroom harrumphed, and crossed their arms with a creak. "Hmmmmm," they rumbled. "Inas has been nearly absent from one's care since that one returned. If this journey will cause that one to recover from the pain experienced, then one will allow it." They stumped forward stiff-legged, stopping in front of Inas. "Does this one feel travel with Sam will aid?"

Inas locked eyes with his mentor. Sam hadn't seen them interact as mentor and pupil often, but Inas had been more proficient in changing the Symphony than Sam or Enos before he was captured. Majus Caroom had taught him well.

"I believe traveling with Sam will help me, Majus Caroom," Inas said. "I promise, when I return, I'll be ready for your lessons again."

Majus Caroom seemed to accept the answer, and Inas took an unsteady step forward, reaching for Sam's hand. The warmth of Inas' body engulfed Sam's fingers and he squeezed.

"And we may well have more resources and species to draw from afterward," Majus Ayama said. She looked thoughtful. "I look forward to the species from your facet traveling here."

"Then we'll go with Wor Wobniar?" Sam said, half as a question, and half as a statement.

Majus Cyrysi sighed. "If it is to be helping you Sam, you should be going."

Sam blinked. That was not the answer he expected, and from his mentor least of all.

"Make certain you are to be remembering everything you are learning on the other side of the wall. I want to be told when you return."

"One will, hmm, be interested as well how the other facet views those of the House of Strength," Majus Caroom rumbled.

Ah. That was more like it. His mentor was always one for learning, if there was a chance. Sam looked around, but the other maji appeared content to let the two speak for them. Majus Ayama was peering at Wor Wobniar, and Sam guessed she was listening to the Symphony of Healing, trying to get a bead on the Nostelrahn's anatomy or mental structure. Only Rey was scowling, off to one side. He divided his glare between Sam, the bridge, and Wor Wobniar. He did not look to Inas.

"Then I will prepare," Wor Wobniar grated, the words appearing in Sam's mind. Xyr head flaps folded back against xyr head, and the strip of lights faded to a dull gray.

An aura of silver grew around the alien, and xy gestured with one claw for Sam and Inas to come closer. As xy did, everything around them slowed, the movements of the group behind them languid. Someone was speaking, but it blurred into a low rumble.

"Into the wall," Wor Wobniar said, and the three of them stepped forward.

Old Hiding Places

- The Nether has a defined floor which cannot be altered. As the walls are impenetrable, so is its base. However, there is a larger accumulation of dirt than most people think. Many do not know of the elaborate tunnel structures existing below Gloomlight, nor of the caves, several hundred feet deep, below a certain estate near the outskirts of the Imperium.

From a report by Morvu Francita Januti, Etanela explorer and big game hunter.

"I remember this place, Mandamon," Gompt said. "It's right near where the old Society mansion used to stand." He was perched on Krat, as usual, squinting in the light from the walls. It was tenth lightening, when they were at maximum brightness. "Tell me that Sathssn couple doesn't still live here. They'd be, what, pushing ninety cycles? Sathssn rarely live that long."

"They are not here," Mandamon told his old friend, and raised his voice so the rest of the group could hear. It had grown large in the last few ten-days.

He, Gompt, Laryn I'Hon, and Touching Digits had been busy talking to old friends and using long-dormant connections to locate the others gathered here. Their little gathering now had twelve additional maji. Five of them were his age or older, remnants of the original Society: two more Methiemum, an Etanela, one Sureriaj female, and another Lobath.

The seven younger ones were the future. Barring the Etanela, Yutirei Janerea Retina, who might live another fifty cycles or more, the rest of them were getting on. It was important to pass on the good the Society had done, rather than focusing on its deficits. He'd start that today.

Over the last two days, he'd given the growing group of maji directions to an intersection of two streets in Poler. This afternoon they'd drifted here, in ones and twos.

"However, the couple's handiwork *is* here," he continued in a louder voice, so everyone could hear. "This house has seemingly been abandoned for cycles, though no one else bought the land, or even squatted on the property. Why?"

<This is a q-question you want an answer to?> Touching Digits flipped his fingers up in a query. He had said the adventure of searching out this place made him male today.

"I will give you the answer," Mandamon said, and pushed the door open. It wasn't locked.

Inside, Mandamon lowered himself down with a wince into one of the chairs he'd placed in a circle, surrounding a little table. He wasn't young, by any stretch of the imagination. Maybe not too old for this last project, though. If the troubling coincidences were really coming to a head, he had little time.

He looked around while the others settled themselves. The old house was unchanged from his last visit, and for many cycles before that. His first encounter had been when he was young, meeting the original occupants with Gompt. Later, he had come back to search for what he would soon show the group. The couple's son, Essra, had lived here for several cycles, or at least that was the front he put up. When Mandamon paid him a surprise visit, he had caught the Sathssn in the lie. The Life Coalition's resurgence had been...unanticipated. Harha and Slitho, the owners of this house, had told him and Gompt about their organization, but back then it was a small group, devoted to peace between species. It had transformed, or revealed its real purpose, in the cycles between then and now. If Majus Ayama had only known the name of the organization she'd been investigating when she first informed them of the voids, he would have paid more attention. Too late now, though he was very familiar with the Life Coalition. Another reason for him to act outside the purview of the Council.

"So we are in an abandoned house. If there is no one here, then why are we?" Laryn said, before zie sat. Zie trailed a long-fingered hand over hir dusty chair, though it was a stretch to call it that. It was a section of tree trunk, roughly sawn. All the furniture was the same—simply made with the least change possible to the original materials. Even the paneling on the walls was nothing more than planks cut from fallen trees.

"There is a very specific reason I've brought you here," Mandamon answered. "Every house of the maji is covered at least twice, and you come from all disciplines, new and old, from ones who work in technology and innovation, to ones concerned with social sciences and aid. I have sought out each of you individually."

"And we'll be wondering why until you stop yanking us around and tell us," said Gompt. Mandamon frowned. His old friend couldn't stand a solemn ceremony.

There was one more he would have liked to add to their group, a member of the Houses of Communication and Power. Origon Cyrysi was a good pick for the new Society—able and inquisitive, if a bit grating—but Mandamon had cautioned the others from contacting him. He'd long been watching the Kirian, but his involvement with Rilan Ayama would shed too much unwanted light on what he was doing here. Later, when it was public, he'd extend an invitation. Origon had been a child when the Society fell, and there had never been a good time to bring him in. Kratitha had worked with him once in defending her home hive, and vouched for his skills.

So. Sixteen maji and one sentient System Beast were an adequate start for two ten-days of work. There were others who might join later, but it was enough to start.

"Some of you know this already, but most have heard only hints. I consider this gathering to be the first of the new Society of Two Houses." Mandamon looked around for reactions. Confused looks from the young ones, knowing ones from those older. As it should be.

"The Society—the last iteration of it—was disbanded fifty cycles ago. My mentor Moortlin led it. They kept the Society's practices secret through their long life, though the inventions and discoveries benefitted the technological progression of the Assembly. Moortlin even instituted a geas, devised by a majus long dead, which kept members from even hinting at their affiliation."

"This, it seems excessive," said one of the new members—a Sathssn with her cowl back and hands ungloved, her inquisitive red eyes searching for answers in Mandamon's words.

He ducked his head. "It was. And it led to the downfall of the organization. I intend to make this version public, directly after we finish our first project. Its success will guarantee the Society's standing as an influential force." He paused a moment, looking around the group. "If anyone does not wish to be a part of this, now is the time to say so."

No one spoke.

"Very well," he said. "How many of you have heard of the Dissolution?"

A few of the younger maji chuckled. One Methiemum majus whose name he hadn't caught, hardly older than an apprentice, turned to his companion and whispered in her ear. She was named Emma something. She giggled. Well, he might have been flippant when he was their age, but then, at that age he had also been a member of the Society, putting together the proposal for development of the System Beasts.

<You have mentioned this word before. You are s-serious?> Touching Digits signed. His middle fingers trembled against each other. <Jokes from other species do not translate well into my speech.> His eyes were large and he gave a flip of his many-fingered hands to demonstrate he meant no offense.

"I am serious," Mandamon said. He'd anticipated this response. The Dissolution was not often spoken of.

"It's a night-tale," Gompt said. He'd complained about it whenever Mandamon brought it up, and Mandamon gave the old Festuour a glare. Undermining his credibility wasn't helping. He'd talk to Gompt about it later.

"Probability of truth is very low," Krat added. "Scant existing evidence."

"Oh, it is true," Mandamon continued. The giggling Methiemum were watching him now, their smiles replaced by frowns, as were the rest of the group. He'd led classes of people older than the average age in this group. "No one knows exactly what the Dissolution is, save a time of significant change." He waved a gnarled hand at the others watching him. "You may laugh at the thought, but don't tell me you haven't heard of it." A few heads nodded. "For a fiction, it is highly persistent, yet our culture has forgotten most facts about a war that consumed our very civilization. The Dissolution was many centuries before that. Why is it remembered?"

Now there were questioning faces. Laryn looked surprised, but then Lobath often did.

"I have put together scraps of parchments, rumors, and plain guesswork over the cycles. I have access to the collected information of the maji, on the Council of the Maji, and of the Society, through my mentor, yet traces are scarce."

He sat forward, rubbing his aching knees. He'd done too much walking today. "From what I can tell, in the Dissolution the entire universe is reconfigured. Is it destroyed? Is it recreated? That, I do not know. But it is changed in fundamental ways, and I will be prepared for it. That is why we are here."

Moortlin had passed on what research they had gathered, before they went back to Aben to plant themself. It was one of hundreds of files the paranoid old Benish kept on potential threats to the ten species.

<What will the D-Dissolution do, if it affects the entire universe?> Touching Digits signed. He made a sign of confusion, fingers interlacing. <Would we all be destroyed?>

"Uncertain," Mandamon answered the Lobhl, "though I think our species have a chance of living on. I believe the Dissolution will affect all creatures everywhere, though how, when, and where—" he spread his hands. "It has happened before, and I think there must have been maji then. There is evidence to support that they protected the rest of their people."

"You will do same thing?" Krat asked, her mechanical voice crackling monotonously. "Protect ten species?"

"*We* will." Mandamon waved one gnarled hand to indicate those in their little circle. "I have identified this place as conducive to create a shelter against the changes of the Dissolution, using the combined technological and Symphonic efforts of two-house maji. I intend this Society of Two Houses to protect against incursions that ordinary people, and even the majority of maji, cannot resist."

There was muttering in the group. The Sathssn darted glances around the room. She would be familiar with this type of construction. The two Methiemum had their heads together, and a Lobath and a Festuour next to them traded glances. He'd held himself aloof from the maji the others gathered, preparing for this meeting. He'd get to know all of them soon enough.

"This is a lofty goal, Mandamon," Gompt said. "Are you reaching for the stars when you can't yet reach the top shelf? The old Society—" the old Festuour paused and looked around, but the geas keeping them from speaking of it no longer functioned. "The old Society did nothing like this. We were just a bunch of outcasts trying to keep busy."

"Not completely true," Krat crackled. Gompt frowned down at the contraption that moved him around. Krat danced back and forth on metal and wood legs, clacking on the floor. If Mandamon had to guess, he would have said Krat was nervous.

"Her, what does she mean?" the Sathssn asked. The rest of the group wasn't as comfortable with Krat's sentience as Gompt and Mandamon, who had worked with System Beasts for over fifty cycles.

"You been keeping things from me, Krat?" Gompt growled.

"Perhaps not voicing things when there was no relevance," Mandamon suggested. "There are many secrets Moortlin kept from us. I know some, through cycles of research, but lately I found a new one. I had heard rumors of a source for nearly unending change to the Symphony, but had no proof." He gestured to the Sathssn majus. "Surely you have heard the legend of Slithen the Dreamer?"

The Sathssn frowned. "This, it is a local legend, particular to the Most Traditional Servants. No one with sense gives it credit."

Mandamon nodded. "Yes, many of logic and reasoning wouldn't. Yet it appears in Moortlin's notes, cross-linked to comments on the Dissolution."

"What's the story?" Emma asked, and Mandamon transferred his gaze to the young woman.

"In a few words, a seer of the Sathssn—a holy member of the diocese of the Most Traditional Servants—was sent a vision of beings the Assembly has never seen. There are no descriptions of who or what these beings are. I believe he thought they were divine in some way. They spoke to him of the coming Dissolution, and a power strong enough to stop it. These otherworldy beings might also be noted in Moortlin's files, though it is a connection I don't think they ever made."

"Stop the Dissolution?" Laryn asked. "What are you getting at, Mandamon?"

Mandamon creaked to his feet, and began pacing. He had patched together this theory from many sources, not all reliable. But the picture they told was unmistakable. He only had to lead the others step by step to the obvious answer, so he didn't scare them off and ruin his plans for a new Society.

"The real reason I brought you here was not dusty furniture unused for cycles." He swiped a finger through a line of dust on the top of the table in the middle of the circle of chairs. "What I have to show you is downstairs. Laryn, if you would help please."

Together they moved the table aside, the Lobath shooting suspicious glares at him. Once it was clear of the circle of seats, they could all see a trail free from the worst dust, outlining a square of floorboards. He reached down with a grunt and pulled on an iron ring. That would make his back hurt tomorrow. A section of the floor came with it, and he added a few notes to the chorus of the Symphony describing the rusty hinges, imparting a little of his momentum into them. The trap door swung up easily, surrounded by an aura of brown, and he took his notes back. He no longer had any to waste, at his age.

"They *were* hiding something, weren't they," Gompt said, Krat clicked forward so he could see down the hole. "I knew it. Always thought that couple was holier-than-thou, but I never would have known *this* was here."

As the others lit the lanterns Mandamon had instructed they bring, the darkness fled to reveal a ramp into a large section of tunnel, reaching down and away from the foundations of the house.

"Krat should be able to navigate this," Mandamon told Gompt, who nodded appreciatively, pushing his glasses back up his snout.

He led them below the house, into tunnels of rough, excavated dirt. There were few large stones in the Nether, since it had no mantle as a planet would. However, there was plenty of compacted earth between the house and the floor of the Nether. He suspected it had collected over thousands of cycles, as beings arrived through portals and brought detritus with them.

Mandamon gestured to the equipment and devices, collected from various hidden rooms and abandoned buildings where he had stashed them over the cycles. While Gompt, Krat, Touching Digits, and Laryn had contacted the others, he had brought the equipment here by many portals over a matter of days.

Touching Digits stroked a piece with scores of fluting cylinders extending from a central sphere. <A color melder. I thought the S-

Society was the only place that had one of these.> His hands indicated surprise.

"It was," Mandamon answered. He'd kept some of these pieces for over fifty cycles, knowing they were unique. "Please, explore. Some of these items may be familiar to the oldest of you, but all are valuable and, I believe, essential for the new Society."

He watched them, his beard covering his smile, while they made exclamations of surprise over pieces of technology thought lost in the original mansion's closure, or expressions of enjoyment over how they could use esoteric equipment in an experiment. The two young Methiemum huddled over a pneumatic hose-assembling fixture, wondering how they could use it increase the speed of new water line construction. Laryn and the other Lobath eyed a prototype radio transmitter, though this one had the ability to save messages passing through it—which the modern versions did not do.

After letting the others mill, Mandamon coughed to get things started.

"Let us imagine a scenario," he suggested, and waited until the others disengaged from their investigations and gave their attention to him. "Some of you remember the old Society. To put it bluntly, you must know that as a majus controls more aspects of the Symphony, they often exhibit what we might refer to as...instabilities."

<A bit harsh, but I will agree,> Touching Digits signed, his fingers twisting in hesitant acceptance. <Does this not invalidate your concept of a new g-gathering of two-house maji?>

"And what do you mean by 'more aspects?'" Yutirei, the Etanela asked, suspicious. "Maji can control either one aspect, or two."

"Not necessarily," Mandamon said. He raised one finger. "There have been isolated cases, never well documented."

"Cases of what?" Gompt asked. "It's not like there are maji who can hear three aspects of the Symphony."

"Untrue," Krat grated.

"Girl, we need to have a long talk when this is over," Gompt said. "You've been holding out on me all these cycles."

"Krat has the right of it, though I don't know how," Mandamon said. He'd only found Moortlin's notes on their encounter with the strange child about a cycle ago. It had been well hidden in the old Benish's notes, encrypted with a particularly difficult cipher. "Three-house maji do exist, though so rarely they are almost never observed in their brief existences. However, they are an almost unlimited font of power."

"Power, this is as in the legend of Slithen the Dreamer?" the Sathssn asked.

"Forgive me. Tell me your name again," Mandamon said. "My memory fails me as I age."

"Gretahn, Councilor," the Sathssn answered. Under his stare, she continued. "Of the houses of Power and Healing."

"You will make an excellent addition to the Society, Gretahn," he said. "And you are correct. The Life Coalition has designed their own method of contacting those who gave Slithen his dreams, and you have seen their results in the Dome of the Assembly." Several maji shivered, and Touching Digits made a sign to ward off ill intention. "I think I have a better way to contact those who made themselves known to Slithen, for I believe they were three-house maji, signaling from where they have secluded themselves outside our existence. The Sathssn would not understand their true potential."

<But you do, and you want to s-summon one of these maji, like a wira hunched over their bowl of herbs, making arcane signs to make a color-spirit appear?> Touching Digits twisted his hands in an unsure laugh.

"Perhaps not so fancifully," Mandamon said, "but yes."

"Then this, why hasn't it been done before?" Gretahn asked. Her slitted eyes watched the others, flicking every once in a while to him.

"Two house maji are often regarded as a bit...odd," Mandamon said, and there was a smattering of nervous laughter. Mandamon opened his hands. "I will be the first to accept that label. We are in like company here." He watched the exchanged glances, the subtle shift in body language. Those were the seeds of the camaraderie that built the previous Society—a shared bond of secrecy and acceptance.

"Use your imagination. You know how you regard the melodies around you. How would it feel to access a third aspect of the Grand Symphony, when it takes so much concentration to affect two? Can you imagine the stress on the individual? How much effort it would take to parse three Symphonies running through your mind?"

"But none of us have ever suspected three-house maji exist," Emma objected. "Surely we would see some sign, if they are so powerful."

Mandamon caught her eye. "But what if, by having access to a full half of the six houses of the Grand Symphony, they can perceive the coming Dissolution? Little wonder they secrete themselves in some other place to avoid it. Yet some seek to warn our reality through dreams. They may even be willing to help stop or slow what is coming."

"If they are so powerful, what need is there of our help?" The other young Methiemum asked, in a shaky voice.

"I hypothesize we must assist any who wish to cross back to our existence to aid against the Dissolution," Mandamon said. "My theory is that the sound of this universe is too great for the three-house maji to bear for long. Thus they move to a pocket universe, or another reality, where the Grand Symphony is lessened, as are the effects of the Dissolution. To help them return and thus harness the power they represent, we must create safe passage and protection from the effects of the Symphony."

"He has a point, though," Gompt said, pointing to the young majus. "These beings, if you're correct, contacted this Slithen fellow. Does the Life Coalition have designs on them?"

"Unknown," Mandamon said. "Though the house above is abandoned, these tunnels have only been empty since the maji recently chased the Life Coalition from them. It was one reason I chose them." That got their attention.

"Are you sure those suckers aren't coming back here?" Gompt asked.

<The Life Coalition is too busy hiding from Rilan Ayama and her group to d-deal with these old tunnels, I suspect,> Touching Digits said.

"This is the only place I know of where the Life Coalition made a headquarters in the Nether," Mandamon said. "So this shall be where we contact the three-house maji." He gestured to the equipment he had rescued. "These pieces can aid us, I believe. I have the basic idea for a design, but we will need time, dedication, and a source of energy to complete it."

"We put together plenty of projects with large power sources back in the old days." Gompt patted Krat's flank with a furry paw. "Krat here takes quite a bit of power, both from the Symphony and from more esoteric sources."

"Most of which I provide," Krat added.

Mandamon looked to the group. "Are you with me in bringing a three-house majus to our reality to aid us in holding back the Dissolution? Will you help me create a space to safely channel their energy?"

There was a beat of silence.

"I will do this," Krat said.

"You know I'm all in," Gompt added.

<As am I,> Touching Digits signed.

The rest followed quickly. This time Mandamon let his grin grow. The first task of the new Society of Two Houses.

"Let us begin," he said. It was time to get to work.

CHAPTER TWELVE

The Jaws that Bite

- My fellow Speaker Nara Jartharian had been feeling ill for a few days, and missed his first ever Assembly meeting. I went to his home in High Imperium to see if I could help, but Jarth would not let me in. We had been friends for many cycles, and had helped each other in many times of strife. Yet when he returned, he acted as if nothing happened. Our friendship has cooled in the past cycle, and by the Greatmother, I think he sometimes looks at me as if I were a meal of stewed desert jumper rather than his old friend. Power does strange things to some people.

From Accounts of the Assembly, 843 A.A.W.

After one more fitful night alone with instructions to conserve her mental and physical strength, Nakan brought Enos to where they kept the other Aridori—yet another room in the vast complex. Enos wondered how big this asteroid was. Big enough that the room where she met Putra and Zhaddi was only a place of confinement, for when the slaves of the Life Coalition misbehaved.

"The others, you will meet them in here. It is where all the vile Aridori live, sharpening their claws and their wits to be our assassins." He gave her a little shove through the open door. He did not come inside, and shut the door quickly behind her.

As the stone door closed, her manacles and collar dropped to the floor. There must have been a System installed in the two that cut off when Nakan willed it, outside the door. Enos instinctively reached for the Symphony, but slammed against another barrier keeping the music from her, as if she had struck a plate of glass. She nearly stumbled at the shock, but turned it into an exhale and a step forward. She guessed it wasn't a good idea to show weakness in front of these Aridori.

"Ah, finally, our new member arrives," said Zhaddi, the blue-eyed Aridori. They looked Sathssn today, though as tall as a tall Methiemum. They had kept their eyes the same blue color, though. Sathssn had yellow and red eyes. The disconcerting creation was obviously something the Aridori had created from different species. "I sensed you, in the Assembly, when Zsaana showed me off to all the lovely people there."

Enos shivered at the directness of the statement. They had known about her before she even knew they existed. What else did they know?

"We will introduce you," Putra said, blinking their purple eyes. They were still in the black, green, and purple scaled form Enos had seen them in yesterday, though their hands were large and furred, like a Festuour. Neither Aridori gave a hint of gender, and since they were no longer in the Nether, it could not say.

She frowned. She hadn't realized the day before, but without the Nether translating, the Aridori had understood her. The Nether gave those who could hear the Symphony the ability to understand any language, even when not in the Nether, but these Aridori were not maji. They must have understood her native dialect.

"Do you speak the Traders' Tongue?" she asked. It was the language she spoke most naturally.

"That, and many others," Zhaddi answered. "After the first ten languages or so, they become easier, especially when one can change the state of one's vocal chords."

Putra held up their hands, which now sported five fingers between a thumb on either side. <We have even learned three dialects of the Lobhl's communication,> they signed. Enos blinked at the memory of the words appearing in her head. <They are such an interesting species, but we had little time to study their culture and biology before we were recalled.>

"Let us introduce you," Zhaddi said. They gestured toward the four silent figures on the back wall of the room. Each was in a similar state, combining aspects from various species.

Like elsewhere in the compound, the room was a rectangular cave hewn from the rock. Ten smooth lights shone from around the upper extent of the walls—majus-made of some sort, perhaps to keep the Aridori from having any unnecessary implements. Aside from that, the room was featureless. One door, sealed shut, a ceiling just high enough not to feel claustrophobic, but with no extra space. There was a small grate in the door which provided airflow, but the aura of white, brown, and yellow showed it was protected so no Aridori could slip through.

Even in Enos' limited experience with changing form, she could tell the Sathssn knew how to effectively imprison Aridori.

"They are like us, though not as gregarious," Putra said, pointing to the four others. "Imprisonment takes its toll on different personalities in different ways."

The others stared sullenly at Enos, and the two talkative Aridori did not offer any names for them. Was it because the Sathssn hadn't given them nicknames? Zhaddi and Putra said Enos' name was not Aridori. Did they even remember their original names?

Finally the biggest of the four spoke. They had the face and crest of a Kirian, but the feathers were bright green. Below that, their body was like a Pixie, stretched to a Kirian's height, covered in interlocking plates of dull blue chitin. "You are here to replace the other? The Accretion? The new Aridori who tried to take their place was not fit for our group."

"You mean my brother?" Enos said. She found she had one foot forward already, ready to take on this ancient nightmare of her ancestors.

How dare they doubt Inas! What did they do to him?

The big one laughed. "You mean your other instance. Do not use the words of those bound to one form. We are better than they. Our instances are ourselves, given slightly altered conditions." The Aridori leaned forward, Kirian face opening into a slavering grin that stretched wider than their cheeks. There were sharp Kirian teeth inside the mouth, but they were multiplying, as the face grew black scales. "I would have absorbed him in another few days, had these shrinking Snakes not let him go. His form was weak from containment."

Putra made a tutting noise, and put one hand on the big one's chest. They snarled, but then Putra snarled back, the low rumbling growl putting the hairs on the back of Enos' neck on end. The big Aridori closed their mouth, but kept their eyes on Enos.

I am in danger here.

At least Zhaddi and Putra seemed to like her, for some reason.

The big Aridori's last words finally made their way into her mind. *Absorb?* What did the creature mean by that?

Then Enos remembered the thing in the box in Gloomlight, the formless Aridori, constrained to no solid shape for so long that they were completely insane. Councilor Feldo had captured them, but they were not just one Aridori. They were several, merged into one...Accretion.

"Absorbed—" Enos began. She looked at the six Aridori, all fluid in form, changing faster than she had thought possible. "Have you all..."

"They were the best of us," Zhaddi sighed. "There were many more with us, originally. We were the last left from the Sathssn's squads, rounding up our people. We absorbed our other instances and became our full selves, but the Accretion, they were the best at new shapes. They took the rest of our fellows into them, keeping only the finest parts. They were, of course, utterly without reason."

"And you?" Enos asked. The question popped out of her mouth while the rest of her furiously tried to find an escape route. The rough wall dug into her back. She had retreated without meaning to. It was only a matter of time before they tried to eat, or absorb, her. Without the Symphony...

"We are only moderately reasonless," said Putra, in all seriousness, taking one step forward.

Enos blinked again. She had been too focused on the big threatening one. Putra and Zhaddi weren't any less dangerous, for all their gregariousness. She was struggling to keep up. Her chest tightened as she processed another piece of information. "Your other instances? You...you absorbed them?" That was why she couldn't get a feel for the Aridori's gender, or even personality. It was as if different parts rose to the surface as they spoke. Each instance was a unique path of existence, but one could not take both paths at once. That was the whole point. One self, divided in two. No wonder these Aridori were confined.

The others shared knowing smiles, and then Putra's face shifted from black scales to green, their snout shortening, their eyes changing this time to yellow, with red slit pupils. Sathssn. "We've all absorbed our other instances, young one. It is part of becoming an assassin for the Sathssn. It is required."

"It is also the thing the Sathssn masters hate the most about us," Zhaddi continued. "The more effective we become, the more we are an offense to the Sathssn's Holy Form. We have another version of ourselves. What is worse than having two forms? Which is the ideal?" The Aridori sniffed. "That was why they sent your other instance to lure you here."

"Lure?" Enos said. "I had to fight to save him from Dunarn. So that's why they would meet with me. They wanted one of us to absorb the other." Her lip rolled up in a sneer at the thought, but she remembered Inas holding her, his skin trying to crawl into hers, to soak her in. He never would have done so if he had control of his faculties, would he?

No, she could not doubt Inas. Anyone, even Sam, but not Inas. He was her other instance. Her other self. She would not allow herself to think ill of him.

"What did you do to him, to make him try to absorb me?" She was shouting, but she didn't care.

But the Aridori didn't react, or at least not as she expected them to. One in the back nudged another, a knowing grin on their face.

"And here we thought his training was doomed," Putra said, their smile far too wide for their face. "Just goes to show if you keep one of us penned up with no shape for long enough, you can get us to do anything."

Zhaddi nodded along, but the big Aridori grumbled "I still wanted to take him. I would have if the Snakes hadn't stopped me."

"How...dare you!" Enos' teeth clenched, and she came forward from the wall, but Zhaddi only laughed in her face.

"And now you will have the thrill of the hunt!" they cried. Their eyes flashed—actually flashed, like an angry Benish.

"I will not *hunt* my brother!" Enos protested. She specifically did not call him an 'instance.' These Aridori *were* without sense.

"He was defective," the big Aridori said. They still had too many teeth, and smiled whenever Enos looked at them. "The Accretion infected him, and has started to devour your other instance from the inside out. His path was defective, and should make way for yours. I would have relieved his suffering, but better you take him if you do not want the Accretion to come for you once they have finished converting him."

Enos' chest felt as if iron bands bound it. Inas' hand had been stiff and cold when they carried him away from Gloomlight prison, and it had gotten no better before Nakan captured him. "Inas helped them— the Accretion—to die. They couldn't have done anything to him. They were too weak."

Putra scoffed. "Too weak? The Accretion? They were the strongest shifter in the past thousand cycles. They could assume another's shape in less than a minute, then kill them and dispose of the body so no one would know the difference. They did so, on several occasions, even in the upper ranks of the Great Assembly."

"Before they were quite so unstable, they successfully impersonated a Speaker for over three cycles, back in eight-forty-two," Zhaddi added. "They will take over your other instance, though it may take many cycles for them to convert enough mass. Best you strike before they have the chance."

Enos wanted to fight them over it, to defend her brother, but she knew why they were urging her on. She could *feel* they were correct. Inas was warm, generous, a solid presence able to hold up any other person. But though a stone was strong, it did not change events. She was the river to his rock. She won all their arguments as children.

I should have fought Dunarn harder. But how could I have known?

"How...what happened to him, while he was here? It was almost two months."

Zhaddi was by her side in an instant, reaching for her hands. She stepped back, but the other Aridori didn't press, simply stood with their hands out—tiny green and purple scales iridescent in the majus lights in the little room. Despite herself, she had to know. If Zhaddi meant to attack, they could have done so before now. Enos stepped forward and took their hands.

There was a tingle, as if she had shocked herself on metal, except the feeling went on, roaming up and down her arms.

"Your other instance became much better at the ancient ways while we had him here," Zhaddi said. "We all exercised with him, as we do with each other. It helps us keep in practice. It hones our killing instinct and lets us judge our standing with each other. The Snakes who imprison us are the ones who devised the torture of the formless box. Even we would not do that to one of our own." Zhaddi rolled their eyes at the big one. "Despite what that one says, if he hadn't improved, one of us would have absorbed him in days."

Zhaddi did nothing to exclude themself from that list, and stared hungrily into Enos' eyes as they held her hand. Enos wanted to pull back, but that would show weakness. That was death in this room.

Zhaddi's gaze was riveting, and Enos could feel an aspect unlocking inside her—a side she had never explored, a side her parents and other family had forbidden from conversation.

"You will learn, as he did, or you will be absorbed to fuel one of our bodies. We Aridori do not live forever on our own." Zhaddi smiled, and now they had too many teeth, just like the other one. It was infectious. The other Aridori were grinning at her like sea killers after a guppy.

"Tell her of the other part," Putra urged. "She will have to know, and if she refuses, then it will be easier to absorb her. I like her, but we can't be biased against the newest."

"What are they talking about?" Enos asked. She looked down at her hands. Zhaddi was still holding them—no, worse than that. Their hands were meshed together, fingers seeping into wrists, tiny scales becoming Methiemum skin. Enos' heart jumped into her throat.

Is Zhaddi trying to absorb me?

As if they could hear her, Zhaddi was nodding vigorously. Their teeth spiraled outward, forming lips of sharp incisors. Yet they spoke clearly.

"We will not hunt him—that will be your job. Your other instance will be the first you absorb, if you are strong enough."

"No," Enos whispered. She could feel Zhaddi's fingers creeping up her arm, lengthening, burrowing into her flesh. They nodded again.

"You will." Zhaddi said. "Your bond is powerful. I can feel snatches of him through you, so that connection is already open. Surprising when you know nothing else. This is good. Your combination will be even stronger. You will unlock your true potential."

The link between us. Majus Ayama helped me open it with her work on the portal.

"He refused, time and again to hunt for you," Putra added. "The Snakey masters were getting annoyed at him, so they put him in the box." Putra thought for a moment. "We argued for him—Aridori are not so easy to find. And better to keep his body around for parts than have our masters dispose of him." Putra came forward, hunched in as if they had a secret, and now Enos was pulling against Zhaddi's weight, every muscle tense, but she was connected firmly to the unhinged Aridori. Her breath rushed through her nose, but she didn't break eye contact. That would be fatal.

"They do not understand, the Sathssn," Putra continued, as if nothing was happening. "They are fleeting lives, and we are passed from master to master, told to go out in the world and create chaos. Their group's name has changed over the centuries, but never do they truly understand us. They merely contain us."

They will kill me, right now. The thought burned through Enos.

Or maybe not kill, but keep my mind nestled deep inside one of them, constantly crying to get out.

She remembered the chorus of voices that accompanied the Accretion's pronouncements. How many spoke through its mouth?

She had to keep them away.

Be better. Shift now. Make them see I am useful.

The feeling, the memory, welled up inside her. She could be another person, down to the very last piece hidden inside. She had done it before. All Aridori were capable of it. Every time she touched another, she took their imprint, saving it for later.

The last person she had become surfaced. The face had been Hathssas, the new Councilor for the House of Power, but that was a mask. The body came from a Sathssn merchant her family dealt with many cycles ago. She felt the pricking of scales pushing up and through her skin. Hair retracted, becoming wispy, finding its way out between scales on her scalp. Inside, organs were shifting, and several new ones grew like grapes on a vine, thrusting into opening spaces inside her. It would take time, but she could show them. She would stand here for a lightening or more—as long as it took to change.

Zhaddi laughed, and suddenly their hands were off her arms, and she was stumbling forward, free.

"Bold, isn't she?" they said. Putra nodded, as did the others, without names.

"But so slow," Putra added, cocking their head. "Were we that slow, in the beginning? It has been so long." They came close, running one hand down Enos' face. "I think I like you, young one. Your other instance took more than a ten-day before he committed to change for us. You take action. You lead, out of your two instances. It was the same for all of us." They spread a hand, taking in the rest of the room. "That is why we survive. We were the strong versions. We adapted."

"Come, learn from us," Zhaddi invited. "We are all hungry to know you better, to see your defenses." When Enos did not immediately come, Zhaddi laughed, their lips-of-teeth scratching against each other. "We all know each other's' defenses. It is how we know our rank. We are each proficient enough to keep another from absorbing us, yet none so strong we could stand against two at once."

"We would never do that, though," said one who had not yet spoken. They had taken the form of a Lobath while Enos was there, but they had too many head-tentacles, and their fingers writhed as if they had no bones. "Alliances are a thing of the Pillars, not of the Blessed."

Enos noted the emphasis on the words, as if they were names of clans, or factions, but did not ask. There was too much else she needed to pay attention to, mental and physical. She wished the Symphony was available, but it was faint and far away. Whatever the Life Coalition was using was even more powerful than the System that kept her and Sam from escaping last time.

* * *

The rest of the day passed in a flash. Enos learned from all six of the Aridori. Each would take a turn to show her a way to shift, or a fresh form to explore. Each time, Enos felt her heart race in anticipation. She *enjoyed* shifting. The emotion built in her until it was a roaring beast, ready to lash out. She became more observant, more focused, as the tide of feelings built in her. Enos could *feel* them vying against each other. There was a reason all six trained with her. She was learning from them, but they were also learning her strengths and weaknesses so they could absorb her. It was exhilarating. It was terrifying.

When she attacked the smallest of the six Aridori for getting too close, the others only laughed—including the one she had scythed with the claws she had instead of fingernails. The wound in the other Aridori's chest bubbled with pale blood, but as they changed from the form of a Pixie with stringy hair—which Pixies did not have—the wound closed, leaving only a thin scar parting the fur of a short, fat Festuour.

Enos stayed in the Aridori's room that night, or what the others decided was night. She could see the brown, orange, and blue auras around the glowing majus lights high on the walls, even if the Symphony was an indistinguishable buzzing. She glanced toward her collar and manacles, forgotten by the door, next to the pile of collars for the rest. Well, she had other tools than the Symphony.

Nakan never came back to check on her. Enos didn't know if he had forgotten her, or if this was where she was supposed to stay. She wasn't hungry, either. Was that an effect of shifting? Or maybe because her stomach hadn't stayed in the same shape or place all day and wasn't sending the right signals, even though she had resumed her normal Methiemum shape.

"You have done well today," Putra told her, putting an arm around her shoulder and squeezing her too close. Enos forced herself not to tense or show the anger building up at the fear of the more experienced Aridori's presence. But Putra inhaled as if she smelled bread rising in an oven. "Even Aridori need sleep. We do not go on forever, though you will find you have more stamina after you take your other instance into yourself. Less need for sustenance. Keep the best parts, eh?" Putra squeezed again, then released her, and patted her arm. "Now find a comfy spot on the floor. Sleep well, and don't let the others nibble on you while you rest." They winked one purple eye.

Enos shivered and found a corner far away from the others as the majus lights dimmed, casting the room into utter darkness. The room was stagnant, as the tiny grate in the door only let in a small amount of air, but the lack did not bother her as it normally would. Two of the nameless ones slept in a pile, limbs tangled. The others found patches of stony floor in the cavern.

Enos twisted and turned, trying to find a comfortable place, but she was too keyed up, her heart still beating like a System Beast at full speed. Her thoughts turned back to the Nether. Were Sam and Inas not looking for her? How many days had she been trapped? She hadn't thought about Sam all day, and Inas only in terms of how she might best him in strength or cunning. Had they even told Majus Ayama she was taken? She clenched a fist against the cold floor as the rage built up in her stomach.

Those ungrateful two, fixated on each other. Sam was probably nestled against Inas, sleeping. The thought made Enos' lip curl. She would rip them both to shreds when she got free and found them. She would pull chunks from Sam, and take her other, ungrateful, instance into herself to make a better version. Inas was useless without her anyway. He had always been weak—a silent figure behind her. Why she could...

Enos shook her head so violently it smacked on the rock of the floor.

What am I thinking?

This had happened the last time she shifted, but this time was much worse. The anger surged up in her, wanting to claw and rend. She balled her hands into fists to keep from growing razor-sharp talons.

Is this why we never shift? The uncontrollable emotions?

Her parents had mentioned it, but Enos had never believed there was an impulse so strong she couldn't control.

I would tear them apart for lying to me, if they were not already dead. I should...

No. She shouldn't. She must be at peace. She needed to sleep, or tomorrow she would be weak, and the others would see it and circle her like carrion birds until she collapsed. They were not her friends, even Putra and Zhaddi. The others—

The others were not all asleep. She could see the outline of one, by a faint residual glow from one of the majus lights, and a sliver of light through the grate in the door. If she changed the Symphony of Healing, she could tweak her biology without depending on the rage-inducing method of the Aridori. She grasped at the faint notes of the music, but pushing through the barrier the Life Coalition had installed was practically impossible.

Enos gave in to the urge to let her eyes adjust as she'd practiced earlier. The light grew from a hint to a warm glow.

The one creeping toward her was the big nameless one—the one who had first threatened her. They must hope for an easy kill, to disrupt the balance in their group. They would take the place of the Accretion if they had the chance. Enos waited, patiently. Her anger was a fire in her belly, making her reckless.

But the other Aridori had spent lifetimes honing their skills. Enos must have twitched, because the other sprang across the remaining distance too quick for her to follow. In a second, they had pinned her arms and legs and pressed her into the floor. The malleable flesh of the Aridori dug into her, trying to take her over.

She would have screamed, but another limb—she couldn't tell if it was an arm, leg, or tentacle—pushed across her face and into her mouth. It filled the opening, sealing it completely.

Enos desperately sucked in air through her nose, her anger lessening.

I really know nothing.

How stupid was she to think she could hold off another Aridori with centuries of practice, after one day?

She struggled, but the other held her fast, silently, curling around her like a tree snake, compressing and transforming. Her left hand suddenly went numb, as if it no longer belonged to her.

It didn't. The big Aridori was absorbing her into them. And she could do nothing.

No! Not nothing. Even if I have little experience with being an Aridori, I am an apprentice majus.

Enos made herself relax, to release the anger that vied for her attention. The other Aridori flowed over her and she only resisted enough to keep them from enveloping her whole. She should have done this to begin with. There was only one advantage she had over them. But to succeed, she needed almost all of her attention. There was no other choice.

Please, let this work.

If it didn't, she would forever be a small voice inside another being, slowly driving them mad. Madder.

Enos shut away all other sensory input—easy as the thing around her covered her eyes and ears. It encased her, and every part of her body was under the same pressure. She delved deep into her mind, struggling to find that place where the Symphony lived. It was only a faint echo, barely loud enough to hear individual notes.

Have to touch the music.

Her left foot went numb, and the feeling began climbing up her leg.

I am a majus!

She didn't even need control—merely to touch the music, to make one change. If this was anything like the System in the room where she and Sam had been held, she *could* overcome the barrier.

There. One sequence of music, louder than the rest. Her own body was clearest to her, even over the body of the other Aridori pressed around her. She was still distinct, and the music of the Symphony proved it. She was still a person.

Enos reached for a note, straining as if it was just out of her reach. The barrier was there, but it flexed, like a thick sheet of paper.

Her other foot went numb. There was no feeling up to her left thigh.

Just have to make one change.

Her mental fingertips scrabbled at the invisible wall, stretching it, pressing through a tiny hole. The music was so far away, but her will curled around one note, and she pulled with all her might, forcing the nonsensical change to the melody. One change was all she needed.

Enos remembered the effects of the Life Coalition's barrier all too well. She had been shocked into near unconsciousness when she and Sam were trapped. She was ready when the lightning surge passed through her body, and by extension, the body wrapped around hers. She went rigid as the spasms passed through her.

The other Aridori paused, and Enos got the feeling of a retreat. However the shock was nothing like what Enos had experienced after several attempts in the cell with Sam. The charge would only grow with repeated attempts. It was not enough to permanently stop the thing trying to absorb her body. She could feel them gathering again. It would take too long to build the charge up enough to halt their advance.

Then she realized the true advantage she had over this ancient creature—over all other Aridori she had met.

I cannot change the Symphony, but I can hear it change.

Enos shifted, listening to the notes change as her body transformed. They were far away, but audible. The Symphony of Healing defined their bodies. The big Aridori had partially meshed their music with hers, adjusting key and tempo so their music pulsed as one. Good. Enos made small adjustments to her form, listening to how it changed the song.

She couldn't change the notes, but she *could* spread her change to the lump of flesh attached to her, listening to the Symphonies of their entangled bodies. They had nearly the same musical structure.

What—what are you doing?

The voice was not hers. It was from the big Aridori, now they were so closely linked.

I am correcting your mistake, she replied.

The change flowed as her rage pushed for revenge. The other's music was complex, but not as complex as it should have been. The mind was stripped of specifics, burned away over cycles of captivity and deprivation. The body was even simpler, especially in this fluid form.

Enos followed the melody as it sped up, a rampaging crescendo of anger, letting her body change with it. Where there was only hunger and impulse in the other's mind, Enos replaced it with her ambition, her strength of will, her love for Inas and for Sam, her appreciation of Majus Ayama as her mentor. Where the other's body was unfounded, loose in structure and identity, Enos replaced it with her life as a Methiemum. She knew who her parents were, who her society was, and how she contributed by being Methiemum and a merchant. She shifted her body, and listened.

The other tried to hold her off, but with weaker and weaker surges, until the impressions she received from them were blatant, weepy, imprecations.

Don't take us. We can show you new things—many bodies and ways to change.

Enos gained traction, bringing feeling back to her hands and feet.

We have power, and experience. We are so old. Yes take our body, take control from us. No! You cannot! We must be in control. That has been the way for so many cycles—since the Great War.

There was more than one personality rising to the surface, each battling for dominance. It only weakened her prey.

Stop resisting. It is time for us to be absorbed, as we have absorbed others. That was all from one voice.

Do you not remember the path of the Pillars? This one does, even if the other is stock from the Blessed. This was another voice, calmer than the others.

Take us, child, and learn of your ancestors.

The big Aridori suddenly stopped fighting, and Enos flowed over them. There were...accommodations, and Enos could breathe, and feel, and hear, and then she could *see*.

Enos opened her eyes, and found Zhaddi and Putra standing over her. The ones with no names watched her from the corners of the room.

"I told you I liked her," Putra said. They were smiling. It was not at all pleasant, but Enos didn't care. She hadn't meant to go quite so far.

The other Aridori was gone and she felt...full.

Enos rose to her feet, peering in the darkness down—down?—at the two Aridori. She was big. Why?

"I can show you how to get rid of the unneeded parts," Zhaddi said. "You've more than proved you are capable." Enos looked down in revulsion. Her body was half Methiemum, half a conglomeration of other species. Two of her left arms ran hands down her side, feeling a mix of scales and feathers, fur and skin.

"Please, help," Enos said. "I don't want to look like this." Something buzzed at the back of her head, and it wasn't the Symphony.

"You still need to absorb your other instance," Putra warned. "The Sathssn are very strict. But this is an excellent, if unconventional, start."

"Now, watch carefully," Zhaddi said, and proffered an arm, a mass of flesh rippling down it as if it were sliding off. "Look inside for the parts that are no longer needed, or do not work as well. Make yourself more efficient—faster at changing, better at breathing, more useful for our masters."

Enos followed the other Aridori's lead, and for a time the room they were in became messy. Blood was not an issue, but organs kept their images of what they had been for the longest time. There were several from the big Aridori which added new and exciting abilities Enos never imagined she could have. Yet there was only so much space. She would not change the overall shape of the form she had lived with so long. Or not much. She had to make hard decisions.

The others drifted over as she worked, some accepting parts she discarded, as they were better than ones they owned. Zhaddi and Putra even took a few for themselves. The big Aridori had been powerful.

Enos found parts had been damaged in the struggle, and she hadn't even noticed. One of her eyes was punctured, though she was no longer certain who it belonged to. When she finished, she was back down to two, but they were different colors. She wondered what Sam would think about that, and about her new height. She had always wanted to be a little taller—not the monstrosity she had been after the merger, but a little. It would be easier to reach Sam's mouth when they stood close.

Enos found herself lost in thought, while the others moved around her. The release of extra parts washed away the building rage, replacing it with familiar emotion from when she was close to Sam, but not one she would have thought to encounter here. He was always so sweet, and with the new changes, she could be so much more with him—to him. There were positions she'd show him, especially if she adjusted, just a bit. So many possibilities.

Enos shook herself, and heard Putra chuckle, low and knowingly.

"I know what thoughts drift through your head. It is always the same, after one absorbs another, and the one you took was strong."

The buzzing rose in the back of Enos' head, and she made out muttered words like "feast" and "taste" and "stroke."

"Would you have let them take me instead of the other way around?" Enos asked Putra. Putra cocked their head, but the other Aridori didn't answer. None of them did.

Enos slept soundly for the rest of the night.

Nakan finally came back the next morning, and set to grumbling when he saw the state of the room.

"These Aridori, like snakefish from the lakes back home. Put a new one into an established habitat and you'll find only a single fat one left in the morning. Disgusting." His cowl panned around the room, settling on Enos. "Are you taller, or me, am I imagining things?"

Enos didn't answer. She was too busy looking over the Sathssn's robe with her new eyes. She could see the insignia all over his cloak. They were woven in, but the markings were not visible to the other species. None of them saw into the spectrum above the purple colors.

Nakan was festooned with weapons and equipment, as if he planned some operation. A nasty looking knife gleamed at his waist and its blade caught the light strangely, as if it was not reflecting solely into this place. He was going somewhere, but Enos didn't dare ask.

After more grumbling, Nakan went back to the door. "You, try not to eat any more of your group. The Life Coalition needs more than one assassin. There is still important business to be done, especially after I return today. My actions, they will change everything."

"Changing things again, captor?" Putra taunted. "Last time the leaders did not appreciate your initiative."

Nakan bristled, turning from the door. "Janas and the rest, they do not understand tactics as I do. You beasts, you wait until the end of today. The Effature will not run his assembly forever, will he?"

He slipped from the room, closing the door and locking it after him.

The Effature? What does that mean?

"Ha, I wondered how long Palmoran would run things," Zhaddi said. "That one was always too twisty for his own good. Always got the good roles."

Enos stared back at the Aridori.

And what does that *mean?*

CHAPTER THIRTEEN

A New Facet

- For hundreds of cycles, maji have asked where the Nether is placed physically in the universe. The answer is: nowhere. As far as we can ascertain, the Nether does not share physical reality with the galaxies the ten species inhabit. One could not fly across the stars and reach it. Yet maji arrived by portal, far in the past, and transmitted those coordinates to others. I interviewed the Lobhl majus who first contacted the Nether, and they said the experience was not one they could describe. It was completely by accident that they opened a portal here. They were attempting to travel across their homeworld and missed, badly. We still have no data on where the Nether exists, though some of us live our entire lives in it.

Transcript of a paper by Jarrol Maertn, Councilor for the House of Grace, 971 A.A.W.

The crystal bent around Sam. Wor Wobniar, close enough to hug, skittered forward, pushing through solid material, and Sam and Inas followed, arm in arm. All the colors of the Symphony surged around them, leaving trails through the translucent crystal. Some trails pinged off the shield of silver Wor Wobniar had erected as soon as xy pushed into the wall.

They had been walking for several minutes—walking both *on* and *through* the crystal. Or maybe it had been a full lightening of the wall. It was impossible to tell in here, as Sam slowly dragged one foot in front of the other. Inas did the same beside him, and that was the only thing that kept the panic deep inside Sam from exploding outward.

Am I breathing? Why am I not sinking?

His heart should be hammering, but Sam couldn't even feel it beating. Inas had his left arm captured in a death grip, and Sam had to use his right as a counterbalance to surge forward, like walking through water.

He should be panting with the effort of forcing his way through. He should at least feel the need to breathe. There was nothing, except his thoughts echoing through his head.

Is this in the Nether? Can it feel me moving through it? Majus Cyrysi said it supplies nutrients and air. Is it doing the same to me?

There was no answer from the Nether, of course.

Another step. Another step. Wor Wobniar's piston-like legs chugged forward mechanically, taking them further from the only home Sam had left. He knew Earth existed, or probably did, and that there were people who had raised him, but memories were scarce. The Nether was where he lived, at least for now.

Is the silver glow around Wor Wobniar pure Time? It was around xyr when xy came through the first time. I can hear it too. I can hear two houses.

The music was as if from chimes made of spiderwebs and glass, the sound so light in his head he could barely make out individual notes. It had been overwhelming to make the portal to remove the Drain in the Assembly. He'd put notes into that change and never gotten them back. It had been a permanent change to the Symphony. Was this one too? If so, how could Wor Wobniar hold it for this long?

It was a few minutes, or a few lightenings, or a few days later when the vague blur in front of them cleared.

There is crystal directly in front of my eyes. It's touching my eyeballs!

Best not to think about it.

Sam could see shapes, growing clearer as they came closer. How far away was—

Wor Wobniar lurched forward, and the dome of silver around xyr fizzled and disappeared. The need to breathe surged—the gulping, horrible pulsing of drowning—and Sam swung his head around looking for help. The pressure from his chest grew into a desperate need for fresh air. He couldn't move fast enough. He would die here.

Inas' grip on his arm tightened into a painful grip. He must feel the same need. Was this all a lie? Was Wor Wobniar going to leave them here, encased in the wall...

Another step forward and the crystal parted around him, turning into chilly air, and Sam sucked in great lungfuls, cooling him. Inas dropped his arm and gasped, hands on knees. Sam kept his footing with an effort and looked up to Wor Wobniar, who showed little sign of distress, save that xyr mouthparts were flexing open and closed, like a fish gasping in air.

They stood on a bridge that was the twin of the one on the other side. This one was of stone, as the other had been before Sam accidentally transformed it. He hadn't noticed when the structure disappeared inside the wall, though it didn't connect all the way through the crystal.

Stairs ran down from the bridge to a small hill of earth, butted up against the wall. At the bottom, buildings marched into a city that was definitely not the Imperium, yet had a similar feeling. Sam could see strange creatures passing between the buildings, the largest portion of which looked like Wor Wobniar.

Then Sam heard the memory of xyr voice in his head, and looked up to catch the end of a trail of colored lights across xyr brow. "The transition was not pleasant, even according to the accounts left by previous prophets. The chime announces the closest conjunction of our facets, though perhaps they were not as close as in eras past." Xy shook all three arms, as if getting rid of a feeling. "Nevertheless, we have arrived in my facet of the Nether. Be welcome. The transition would have been impossible had I not protected us."

Inas straightened, hand on his back, breathing in deeply. "The protection was the silver dome you made?" he asked. He appeared more attentive than he'd been in days. The air here was richer—a different mix than in their facet.

"Yes, of the House of Time. I can teach you this." Xy directed this at Sam.

"But I'm also of the House of Matter," he said.

Wor Wobniar's head flaps centered on Sam, with one of the three flicking toward Inas. "It is common practice for one who can hear two houses to have a primary teacher. The House of Matter will be harder for you to master, as there are no others who can hear that aspect, but it is your primary house. It is the one you attune to more naturally."

Sam snuck a glimpse at Inas, whom he was taking away from Majus Caroom and his training, no matter how much everyone agreed this might be better for him. He already seemed more awake. But Sam hadn't forgotten his promise to talk about his imprisonment. As soon as they had a few minutes free.

"If we are ready to continue?" The prophet tapped a foot impatiently. Inas pulled himself upright, and Sam saw the struggle it took him. He grasped his friend's hand, ready to help in any way he could.

Wor Wobniar's explanation that he was closer to the House of Matter made sense. Everything Sam sensed about the Symphony was tied to a physical characteristic, rather than the odd conglomerations the aspects appeared to be. Those of the House of Communication could control air, but also affect speech. The House of Grace could affect water, but also how people moved. He affected matter at its basic level. And he could also hear a house that affected time itself?

Wor Wobniar, oblivious to what was passing between him and Inas—or xy just didn't care—waggled one claw in the air in an indeterminate gesture. The lights on xyr brow blinked, then continued a progression as xyr mouthparts beneath grated together. "Seeing time is not as useful as one would think, to an intelligence which lives inside it. Compare it to a water bug swimming through a reservoir, yet able to see the currents. Does it help them steer? Maybe yes, maybe no."

Sam took in a quick breath as he understood. If you tried to change the course of currents as they swept by you, any effort you put into it would immediately be lost.

"Any change is a permanent use of your notes, isn't it?" he asked. Wor Wobniar's head flaps snapped toward him.

"What do you know of this?" xy asked. "You have adjusted the *Vloeinkaal*? This is not a practice a novice majus should attempt."

"I..." The words stuck in Sam's throat. He had told no one of the silver aura mixed with the gold when he made the immense portal. If that was even what Wor Wobniar meant by '*Vloeinkaal*.' "I don't know," he finished lamely.

"Sam, what did you do while I was away?" Inas asked. "Is this like what you did to the bridge? When did you discover you weren't of the House of Communication, like Majus Cyrysi?"

Sam smiled at Inas. He was speaking more, opening up. If only he had done it *before* they walked through crystal to a previously unknown facet of the Nether. There wasn't time now for the intimate talk Inas deserved. Sam had so much to tell him, about Enos, about the attack on the Dome, about the voice, and about what he could do.

"There have been a few changes," Sam told him. "I'll tell you the first chance I get. I promise."

"Why not start now? Why not when I got back?" Inas' grip on his hand turned hard, as did his words. The warm skin on Inas' hand writhed, as if it wanted to engulf his. Then the motion died away.

"You were in no shape to talk, Inas. I tried," Sam said. "I don't know what's changed since we passed through the wall, but this is the most alive I've seen you since you got back. I can't imagine what happened to you."

"Then ask." Inas leaned in close, and Sam's gaze traced the curve of his lips as he spoke. "I need to get this out of me, or I will never recover."

Sam was about to speak, but Wor Wobniar's tapping toes clicked against the stone of the bridge, echoing in the still air at the top of the hill. Despite himself, Sam turned to xyr as xyr head flaps oscillated between them.

"Are you ready?" The Nether translated the memory of xyr meaning as xyr mouthparts ground together.

Sam ground his teeth. "Can we have a few minutes? What are we here to see, anyway?"

"Who, not what," Wor Wobniar said. "We are to meet with the Effature, Crominu Vaevicta, and our time is short. Best to start now. The walk there will take a few minutes."

"But we—" Sam raised a hand to Inas, but Inas shook his head.

"You are right. It will wait, for now." Sam didn't like the way Inas' eyes pinched at the corners. Before he could object, Inas turned to Wor Wobniar. "What about the Assembly? Won't they want to know we are here as well?"

"Assembly?" Wor Wobniar's head flaps waved uncertainly. Sam was getting a feeling for xyr expressions.

"A place where representatives from the ten—where however many species live here—meet," Sam said. He didn't want to talk about the Assembly. He wanted to talk to Inas, but Inas wasn't looking at him.

"I see." Wor Wobniar adjusted xyr feet on the bridge to a trio of clicks. "It does not work like that here. The Effature has supreme authority. You and your Aridori will have to meet Vaevicta direc—what is it?" The Nether must have translated their surprise to Wor Wobniar.

"You know what I am?" Inas asked. His anger was gone, replaced with fear.

Sam stood perfectly straight, the tiredness from his passage through the wall forgotten. He put out a hand protectively, in front of Inas' chest. Maybe talking later was a good thing after all.

"Being Aridori—this is not a known thing in your facet?" Wor Wobniar asked.

"It is not," Inas said. "My sister and I have kept it secret our entire lives, until recently." He spared a glance toward Sam, who cringed inward at the memory of revealing that secret.

Don't hate me, Inas.

"Where *is* your other instance?" Wor Wobniar asked, and again, Inas looked shocked. It was a phrase Sam had heard Enos use, but he still didn't know its full meaning.

"You do know of our species," Inas said, but Wor Wobniar waved a claw dismissively. "She rescued me from those who held me, but they captured her in the process."

"The others are already looking, and we will get her back from the Life Coalition as soon as we can," Sam added. "That's one reason we can only stay a short time here."

Wor Wobniar made a strange click hiss—which the Nether translated as surprise. Sam turned back to xyr.

"This organization steals those of the Aridori species?" Wor Wobniar asked. "Despicable. Here they would be hunted down."

"How would—" Inas started, but the other being made a curt gesture.

"Later. We must get to the city, especially if your time is short. The Effature wants to see you." Without waiting for confirmation, xy scuttled away on xyr three spear-like feet. Sam traded a glance with Inas, and they hurried to catch up.

The bridge led to a set of stairs, winding down the hill and into the city. Sam looked around for buildings like the Houses of the Maji, but there was nothing familiar on this side of the wall. Even the city itself was strange, after the chaotic warren of the Imperium. This city was low, like a giant's hand had pressed it into the ground. No building was taller than four or five stories. There were more organic materials used, rather than the multi-colored stone and occasional metal ornamentation in the Imperium.

The first building they passed was fashioned from a single giant shell, the exterior a brilliant iridescent blue. Sharp protrusions grew like hooks from every edge, and places for the missing eyes and muscular connections were made into doorways and windows.

How did that thing get in here? Could they open a portal that big when it was full-grown, or did it grow that big here? If so, where are the others?

There were no building-sized creatures crawling through the city. He looked to Inas, who was gawking as much as he was.

"Have you seen anything like this before?" Sam asked. Inas shook his head, his hair swinging around his face. It was still unkempt from his captivity, and Sam's hand rose, almost of its own accord, to comb it back behind his ear. Inas leaned into the gesture. His anger seemed to have dissipated as quickly as it arrived.

"Even on Etan, where the cities float on the sea, they did not have creatures with shells like that," Inas said.

A block later, they goggled at a structure made from strands of webbing, stretched out like strings of a cello, each twisted with the strands next to it until the whole was a mass of fibrous ribbons, obscuring the inside. Next to that was an oppressive mass of stone and earth, as solid as the webbed building was light and airy.

They began to see the people who inhabited this facet, and the old panic rose up in Sam at the unintelligible sounds of crowds. The mesh of so many voices made it impossible to pick out one conversation, and the whole was far too much to bear. He reached for Inas' hand, and his friend put an arm around his shoulder, pulling him close.

"It's new for me too," Inas whispered. "But the fact that it *is* new is good."

"Is it?" Sam asked. His breathing was speeding up, even though he was trying not to hyperventilate. His stomach rose into his throat. The air was rich and heady, and Sam felt like he could have run a mile easily while breathing it.

"It is better than being trapped inside a small box," Inas answered, his voice unexpectedly hard. Sam forgot all about his breathing for a moment.

"We tried so hard to find you, Inas," he said. "I'm sorry. You know I would have done anything to rescue you, don't you?" Except he hadn't. He'd hidden in Majus Cyrysi's apartment.

They'd stopped, and Wor Wobniar clicked xyr feet ahead of them, swiveling to fix them with xyr head flaps. "Time is short."

"You're right. We'll talk later," Inas said. He tried out a weak smile and it made a spike of guilt race through Sam's gut. "I feel better just being with you. It's just going to take a while to get over all of it."

Sam embraced Inas, letting his lips rest against Inas' neck. There were little hairs there, invisible to view, and Sam wondered if they would still be there if Inas changed his shape. Then Inas pulled him after Wor Wobniar.

What are my stupid problems, compared to what Inas has been through? Yet he felt himself shutting down, ready to curl into a ball. He always made it about himself. *Not here. You've been picked as the first one to visit another facet of the Nether. Don't mess it up! Just be normal! Watch the crowds of people.*

Sam eyed the species passing. It was a mark of how long he'd been in the Nether that new aliens did not occupy all of his attention.

None of the beings were the same as the ones in his facet, and as he took in details about them, the tightness in his belly loosened. There was so much to see, even if there were crowds. Focusing on details helped push away the anxiety of too many people. And of abandoning Inas.

We'll clear everything up soon. He forced himself to look around. Once they got to their destination and met the Effature, then he'd have a long talk with Inas. Just holding his hand calmed him.

The beings here favored six appendages, rather than the four of the other facet. There were many others of Wor Wobniar's species, scuttling in and out of structures at high speed. They seemed to live in the organic creature-buildings. Sam could see flashes of color through openings, as if the insides were pearlescent.

The second most populous being was predominantly purple, though there were occasional dark blue ones, and they were shaped like two tripods stacked on each other, with a head in the middle. They moved on three legs, but the legs twisted and untwisted around each other on joints with large ranges of motion, as if they were trying to tie knots on the ground beneath them. Their heads were connected to the middle of their bodies, and often they bent over so the upper tripod could also be used for walking. These beings had eyes—three apiece, but again, no recognizable mouths. When Sam and Inas passed a group standing together, a buzz arose, like a horde of crickets chirping, and the Nether translated snatches of speech, snippets of wonder and excitement at the strange creatures among them.

"Much excitement. Very amaze. Beings so strange."

"New parts of Nether. Wild feelings."

"So wow."

"They rub their limbs together to communicate," Inas said, and Sam nodded. The Nether's translation of their speech was staccato, each sentence chopping off abruptly.

"They are called the Praveadi," Wor Wobniar offered. "Skilled engineers, even if they will not answer a direct question. Best to let them get on with whatever they want, sometimes."

Another group of the beings were constructing a new residence, rubbery white filaments winding around each other to make a funnel-shaped web. When complete, it would be like the one Sam had seen earlier.

Less populous were a lumbering species, with dull gray, brown, and green shaggy pelts. They weighed easily ten times as much as the next largest alien and moved fluidly, six short legs repeating in concert, like a caterpillar. Each one had two heads, one in the front and one in the back, though the rear head was smaller than the one in the front, and hairless.

"Are there other creatures riding them?" Inas asked.

"Not riding," Wor Wobniar called back over xyr shoulder. "The Caraakn are two creatures in symbiotic partnership. Makes them good bureaucrats. If one forgets something, the other will remember." Xy waved a claw to a passing behemoth. Smaller arms unfolded from around the rear head as it chittered in high-pitched speech. The arms were incredibly long and multi-jointed, and one fished in what looked like a saddle draped over the creature's back. It pulled out an ornamented cube, which the arm held before the front head. The front head turned to look at the cube, and its legs sped up, turning its lazy stride into a lumbering canter as it rumbled a string of low, interconnected syllables Sam couldn't make out. "Must be late for a shift."

"How many species are here?" Sam asked.

"There are five," Wor Wobniar answered. "My own are called the Nostelrahns. I have mentioned the Praveadi and the Caraakn," xy indicated the tripods and the lumbering beasts, "there are also the Lufvurn, and the Aridori."

Sam struggled to note the individual names, certain he'd forget them. He'd had the same trouble when first coming to the Nether, but now the ten species were easy to catalog.

"You recognize the Aridori as a species?" Inas asked at the same time as Sam said "Who are the Lufvurn?"

"We do, and look up," Wor Wobniar said.

Sam raised his head, careful to go slowly in case it triggered a panic attack. First he saw the columns, like in his facet. They rose into the sky, lost to sight overhead, but around them flew beautiful creatures with three rippling wings on each side of their body. They were sleek and long, with marbled colors.

Each Lufvurn had a different pattern, like someone had mashed an entire box of colored clay together and rolled the whole thing into a cylinder. The different hues spread out along the wings, ending in radiating spirals at the tips, which fluttered in the wind. "They're beautiful," Sam said.

"And arrogant about it," Wor Wobniar said. "A Lufvurn will talk you to death about the mystical significance of their pattern and how they are uniquely suited to sing the praises of their god." The Nostelrahn made an irritated clicking noise with xyr mouthparts. "They are bores, yet they are fantastically skilled at problem-solving and pattern recognition. Give one a problem to solve and they will come back a lightening later with three solutions you'd never have thought of and a dissertation on why you asked the wrong question in the first place."

"Like flying butterfly snakes," Sam said to Inas, who nodded, but frowned. Was he angry again? "What is it?"

"The Aridori. There are here as well as in our facet. How did they come here, and how long ago? Did the war affect them?"

Sam froze. Once again, he'd ignored Inas' pain. He pushed the feeling away. It was a very good question.

"They seem to be accepted. Maybe the war didn't happen, or maybe—"

"Ah here we are." Sam didn't have a chance to continue the thought, as Wor Wobniar halted. Inas and Sam stopped with xyr. They were at a solid wall of stone, a couple stories tall, embedded in a web of the white filaments with which the Praveadi had been building. The edifice went as far as Sam could see in either direction. Other buildings butted up to it, but there were no towers, or higher floors, or even any significant features.

"This is the Effature's compound," Wor Wobniar said. "She will explain everything to you."

CHAPTER FOURTEEN

Apprehension and Evasion

- The House of Grace is probably the least understood house of the six, even to those of us who can hear this aspect of the Grand Symphony. The House of Potential is reputed to be the most complex and unknowable, yet it also has the most research performed on it. Ask any majus who can hear the House of Grace what it can do and you will receive a different answer, from affecting balance, water, temperature, elegance, or speed. But the most interesting answers imply the House of Grace is the only one with the ability to interfere with other houses, even extending to untying other changes to the Symphony.

Ponderings on the Grand Symphony by Panen I'Fon, Lobath Majus of the House of Grace

Rey watched Sam and Inas fade into the wall of the Nether, accompanying the strange beasty from the next facet over. Even more aliens existed. He should have known, logically, but did they all have to be so bizarre? The Methiemum and the Kirians were roughly the same shape as a normal Sureri. The Lobhl had too many fingers, and the Etanela were just too tall. The rest—Rey shivered. Bunch of weirdos. And now this thing that looked like a three-legged desert scuttler mated with a flagpole. It wasn't just him—the others were staring too, breaking off into little groups to discuss. His mentor came to stand beside him. The Sathssn were pretty far up the eerie spectrum, but at least they had a healthy appreciation for how strange everyone else was.

Rey sighed. He'd worked so hard to get Inas back, and what does the ungrateful lump do, but waltz off with Sam the first opportunity he got. Rey could have nursed him back to health as well as Sam, and not made him hike up all those steps in the House of Communication, to boot. He'd been told his version of his greatfather's juicespine soup was quite good. Or at least edible. Sureri were not known for their food.

He shook his head. Made a guy regret the effort he put in, but there was nothing to be done now, at least until Sam dragged Inas back to this facet.

And what about these other houses? House of Matter? Of Time? No such thing. Except Rey had seen Sam change the bridge they stood on with his own two eyes. Rey hesitantly touched a banister. Solid, and cold—just how he felt.

"Majus Kheena," he asked, "could this be sommat else? Mayhaps a manifestation of one of the other houses—Grace or Potential? Not really a new house, eyah?" He eyed the Effature—the venerable sir was talking with Majus Ayama and Majus Cyrysi, busybodies that they were. Majus Caroom was near the back, staring out over the city like the last stump left before the desert took over. They might understand Rey's feelings. They had just lost Inas again, too, and Inas hadn't visited his mentor more than once since he'd been back.

Majus Kheena shook his head. "This new house, I know nothing of it." The Sathssn rapped a gloved hand on the metal railing. "Though this, it is certainly impressive. There seems to be another facet of the Nether we knew nothing about. And there are more species than our Assembly has ever encountered." He looked to Rey. "How hard is it to imagine there are more aspects of the Symphony? Perhaps the other maji, they will have different opinions."

"But it's just so...irregular," Rey complained. "I donna want to be the soggy-pants o' this crowd, but donna yer feel—"

A portal cut off his words as it swirled open between them and the Effature's group, who were standing near the wall. Another Sathssn stepped out, garbed fully in black, and sporting several weapons, including a strange looking knife at his belt. The portal snapped shut behind him, as if this new arrival had pulled it closed as quickly as possible.

"Who is—" Majus Kheena hissed, eyes narrowed, as if he could learn from the interloper's dark, featureless clothes. "Nakan. You are of the Most Traditional Servants. And the Life Coalition, yes? You, what do you hope to accomplish...?"

"You know where he—" Rey started, but Nakan ignored them both and sprang into movement.

An aura of blue—the House of Grace—and dark purple sprang up around the newcomer as he glided over the steel surface toward the maji and the Effature. Majus Ayama's aura of white and olive concentrated around her arms and legs. She sprang forward almost as quickly as the Sathssn, while Majus Cyrysi, behind her, glowed with yellow and orange. Rey winced, and waggled a finger in his ear. The air had just changed pressure.

Nakan flowed into the two maji, and Rey fell into the chords of Potential, listening to the changes Majus Kheena made. Nakan was moving so fast there was a great store of potential energy around him. Rey's mentor bled it off, attaching those notes to his own melody instead. Not fast enough. Rey followed his example, bleeding their attacker's energy in a different manner so the Symphony wouldn't stop his change. Instead of adding to his potential, Rey sped his melody up and the world slowed down around him.

There was a flash of blue and Majus Ayama spun, stumbling. She hit the railing of the bridge and nearly fell over, grabbing on to the cold slippery steel. Nakan was already moving past her, to where Majus Cyrysi stood in front of the Effature, hands outstretched, the air rippling in front of him. He'd made some sort of shield, and Nakan scrabbled at it.

"Get him while he is stopped!" hissed Majus Kheena. "Him, he is after the Effature. This Sathssn, he is very dangerous!" His voice sounded lower, drawn out and slurred.

So the Life Coalition had stopped even attempts at negotiation? Along with their abduction of Enos, it seemed they had no intention of talking. Maybe Majus Ayama had the right of it after all.

Rey moved faster than he thought possible, running down the length of metal, assisted by the stolen energy from Nakan. He chanced a look back to see Majus Caroom holding firm at the other end of the bridge, a cloud of green and tan around him. The Benish was doing something with the House of Strength, but it was impossible to say what.

Majus Ayama had not yet recovered. She was a skilled fighter, Rey knew, which meant Nakan had to be even better, though right now he appeared stymied by Majus Cyrysi's shield. Rey pushed his legs. He was the only other one close enough. He left his mentor halfway down the bridge.

But still too far away. Nakan, rather than being knocked back by the shield of air, somehow found his balance. He slid back and drew the strange knife at his belt. It caught light from the walls and Rey winced. It was as if some light was not reflected, and other bits were reflected from a different source.

Only a few strides away. Rey reached out a hand to catch the Sathssn's cloak, as Nakan's hand lifted, a blue aura passing between his gloved fingers and the rippling shield. A ring of frost spread out from his fingers, and behind the barrier, Majus Cyrysi's eyes went wide, his crest spiking out in surprise. The Effature seemed frozen behind him due to Rey's excess speed, his face almost comically surprised. Rey followed his gaze to Nakan's knife. The Effature looked like he recognized it.

The frost spread across the shield even as Rey clutched dark, rough material between his fingers. The air wobbled and slid. Excess water combined with the drop in temperature changed the air pressure too much for Majus Cyrysi's barrier to hold. It burst, flinging cold droplets at Rey's face, and between blinks, Nakan surged forward out of his grip.

"No!" Rey called, but a shape brushed by him—Majus Ayama, recovered. Her legs churned, a white glow around them, and she grappled the Sathssn, but Nakan slipped around her, the knife flashing between them. Majus Ayama grunted and avoided the blow, but the slash continued as Nakan spun, slicing across the Effature's belly.

Nakan finished his spin and ran at Rey, who gaped at the slash, opening in slow motion across the old man's torso, flesh peeling back like the skin of a fruit. Rey made another grab for Nakan's cloak. A ripple went through the Effature, as if he were a soap bubble on the edge of popping. Flesh shouldn't move like that.

Just like last time, the material of the attacker's cloak slipped through Rey's fingers, though it was rough, and should have been easy to catch. It was done with the House of Grace.

Rey turned to see Nakan make another complete spin, neatly avoiding Majus Kheena's hands, his robe flowing out in a spiral around his legs.

Behind him was Majus I'Fon. Though the Lobath was also of the House of Grace, Rey didn't think zie had been trained in any martial arts like Nakan or Majus Ayama. The short majus put hir hands out to either side as if zie would catch Nakan. Hir own aura of blue and off-white sprang up, reaching out to meet Nakan's. The two auras warred with each other as Nakan shifted left, then right. Majus I'Fon was always there just before him.

The auras mixed, and Rey heard Majus Ayama grunt behind him as Rey took a step. If Majus I'Fon could hold Nakan for just a few instants—

In one fluid motion, Nakan drew another of his knives—not the one that reflected light strangely—and plunged it toward Majus I'Fon's center. The Lobath's eyes couldn't open any farther, but zie twisted out of the path of the blade. Nakan followed his thrust like a fish on a line, zipping past Majus I'Fon even as the Lobath spun back to catch at empty air.

Nakan's last opponent was Majus Caroom, who had set themself at the other end of the bridge like a rock wall, taking up nearly the entire width. They'd had the length of Nakan's attack to prepare, and preparing was what the House of Strength was best at.

Rey looked back to where the portal Nakan arrived through had stood. Portals were all one-way, and the Symphony resisted if new ones were opened too close to each other. If Nakan was trying to escape, so shortly after closing his last portal, he'd need to be far enough away. Everything depended on where Caroom had positioned themself. Were they close enough to stop the Sathssn?

Rey couldn't hope to catch Nakan. He could only look on in frustration as the Sathssn skidded along the steel of the bridge, his blue aura glowing like a fire, trying to sneak past Majus Caroom. Instead, his movement stuttered and slowed, his knees bending beneath his robe. Majus Caroom had used the Symphony to affect the Sathssn's connection to the bridge—strengthening it beyond his ability to jump. Rey ran, now there might be enough time to catch up. Out of the corner of his eye, Majus Ayama was a blur, headed in the same direction.

Nakan's hand finished its motion, though it seemed weighted by chains to the bridge. A swirl of blue and purple developed right behind Majus Caroom's head, angled upward, turning into a portal. Nakan's other hand rose and the blue of the House of Grace snaked around and between the green of the House of Strength. Rey could hear Majus Caroom's grunt of surprise from across the bridge. There was a snapping as if a tree fell and the green fractured, splitting into several fading auras as Majus Caroom staggered.

Nakan leapt, his connection to the bridge broken, and his hands landed on the Benish's shoulder's, turning the upward motion into a somersault around the majus' bald head so Nakan's boots angled at his portal. He slid through like a desert scuttler slipping into its hole, and the portal closed behind him. Majus Caroom groaned forward like a stump bending to the last water source.

Rey took his notes back, letting the extra energy he'd stolen escape. Time sped up to normal. The others recovered, then rushed to the fallen Effature, so tightly packed Rey couldn't even see the man, though he was creating a puddle on the metal of the bridge—dark, viscous blood. Rey counted silently. All the Houses of the maji were covered. He pursed his lips, looking between the ends of the bridge. More than anything, he wanted to go to the lovable old man, but if the maji couldn't fix up the Effature without him, he wouldn't add much. And he had an idea that might help just as much.

Rey made an educated guess that both portals linked to wherever the Life Coalition was hiding. They'd been barely far enough apart, especially for the short time between Nakan opening them. Something like that set up a resonance in the Symphony. It was the reason maji couldn't make the same change twice.

He had a bit of a talent for portals. It was difficult to catch where a portal linked to once it closed, but he could still faintly hear the two Nakan opened. Rey closed his eyes, blocking out Majus Ayama's frantic attempts to stanch the old man's bleeding. He couldn't help—he had almost no medical knowledge.

There. That was the resonance—faint, but reflecting the rhythm of the other end of the portal. The House of Potential had an advantage in this area, and Rey had an affinity for it. He went where the bridge connected to the tower of the House of Communication.

The music of that other place was still here. It wasn't enough to craft a portal, but fortunately Rey had a second source of music. Nakan had made a mistake in creating both portals so close together.

He ran to the other end of the bridge, passing the others on the way there, in a tight circle around the leader of the Great Assembly. Patches of the old man's face were rippling, wavering between his normal skin color and iridescent black. Had the knife done that to him? If Rey thought about it too long, he'd lose his one chance to track down the Snakey who'd done this to the Effature.

Near the wall towering overhead, were traces from the other portal. Rey puffed. The bridge was long, and he'd run it twice now.

The music here was even fainter, though Nakan's attack had taken maybe a couple minutes from entrance to exit. Rey raised his hands to the spot where the portal had closed, drinking in the melody.

The Symphony of Potential was low and tranquil, with only the soaring arpeggios detailing the bridge's height from the ground. That was a big source of energy he could tap if needed, though he'd probably have to jump off the bridge to do it.

Behind those notes were complex rhythms, speaking of another place, far away, cold and more devoid of energy. There was height and speed in the chords, which he compared to the impressions from the other portal. Together, they painted a larger picture, though still not enough to create a portal.

Rey spun. Majus Ayama had spoken of the Life Coalition's home base, on a satellite of Sath Home. Height, speed, and the low energy of the firmament were all consistent. Nakan was a member of the Life Coalition. He had gone back to his hidey-hole.

"I need the rest of yer information on the Life Coalition's base!" He shouted to the group kneeling around the Effature.

Majus Kheena looked up to him, his red eyes bleary. "The Effature, he needs immediate aid. We must move him to the House of Healing. There will be many there who can help. No time for other distractions."

Rey ignored his mentor and turned to Majus Cyrysi. The arrogant old bird had his head screwed on right. "Yer have the markers Majus Ayama's bodged together on the Life Coalition, do yer? Well, there are more here, and we have exactly one chance." He spread his arms to the two ends of the bridge.

At that, Majus Cyrysi pushed to his feet, his crest spiking up in surprise. "You are having enough markers to be creating a portal to the Life Coalition?" Rey saw Majus Ayama on the edge of his vision, her eyes fixed on Rey even as her hands worked to compress the Effature's bleeding.

"I do—give me the rest," Rey said. He waggled his hands. "Come on! Do yer want revenge for what that Snakey did to the old man or not?"

"We do," Majus Ayama said, then pulled Majus Cyrysi back down to her with surprising strength for her small form.

She set to bossing the others around like only a former Council member could. "Ori, make a binding of air and heat. Replace the compression I have here—no, right here. Good. I'm taking my fingers away. Panen, can you keep the wound from slipping around Ori's flows of air? Yes, like that. Caroom, a little stren—I see, already on it. Perfect. Kheena, work with me to make this a System. We need to it to last until the Effature reaches the medical ward at the House of Healing, but so any member of that house can unravel it. On three. Do you feel where I'm changing the Symphony? There should be a chord transformation around this area—I know you can't hear it, but *feel*. Yes. There. Now make it permanent. All—you will lose a few notes because of this, but I think we can agree it's worth it."

There were nods from the other maji, and Rey heard Majus Kheena moving phrases in the energy surrounding the Effature. The air practically buzzed with extra energy, festooning the Symphony of Potential with grace notes, tremolos, and trills.

When Majus Kheena made one final change, the embellishments solidified with a rushing squeal into the structure of the music.

Majus Ayama sat back. "Well, he's not dead yet, but I have no idea what that rippling phenomenon is in his face. Palmoran—can you hear me?" The majus gently patted the Effature's cheek. "Nothing. We have to get him stable. Ori, go help the boy."

Majus Cyrysi pushed to his feet and stumped to Rey, while Majus Ayama bossed the others around, planning to transport the Effature.

"Give me the other markers," Rey demanded. "I've got the rest all muddled up in me head, and I can't lose 'em."

"Hm. This is to be highly irregular," Majus Cyrysi grumped. "Usually it is the majus of the House of Communication who is to be opening the portal."

"Well if yer want to lose this location, go right ahead," Rey told the Kirian, whose crest fluttered like a wounded bat. Rey stared defiantly up at the arrogant old bird.

"If that is what you are wishing, then so be it." Majus Cyrysi lifted one long, clawed finger and pressed it to Rey's forehead. Information cascaded to him in a jumble of sights, smells, and sounds, sounding as if the music had been collected from multiple instruments of an orchestra. Rey backed away as the flow of information finished, blinking and trying to parse it all.

"Yer could'o gone a bit slower," Rey said, then waved a hand as the majus opened his mouth. "I think I've got a handle on the mess, though." His musical theory classes finally came in handy. Old teacher Srat would be proud.

Rey closed his eyes, arranging twenty different instruments on the fly. He smoothed the transitions, then threw the whole mess into the Symphony. He used his notes to connect his construct with the air above the bridge, then opened his eyes to see the hole spiral into being, surrounded by an aura of brown. Majus Ayama and the others straightened up, hearing the change.

"This leads to the Life Coalition's main base on this space object yer were talkin' about," Rey said.

"It does?" Majus Ayama asked. Her face was stony enough to scare off a whole pride of sand chasers. "Of course it does, don't answer that." She turned back to the others. "The Effature must get to the medical ward or he'll die."

"I canna hold it open forever," Rey said. "And without soakin' up the music on the other side o' this portal, I donna think I can open it again. You want Nakan? You want yer apprentice back? Now is the time."

"Anyone staying behind?" Majus Ayama asked. She glanced around at the collected maji, every face as hard and determined as hers. "I didn't think so." She looked back to Rey. "Can you hold it for a few minutes while we get help?"

Rey considered, then nodded. "A few minutes, yes." He wasn't staying behind either. The Life Coalition had answers to everything going wrong the past several days, from Inas to this attack.

"I will find the nearest majus," Majus I'Fon yelled over hir shoulder as zie took off down the bridge. There'd be plenty in the House of Communication, though it would be impossible to keep gossip of the Effature's injuries hidden.

"Good. Kheena, see if you can find any of the Effature's guard while Panen is gone. I need to monitor the Effature," Majus Ayama said. Rey's mentor ran after the Lobath, his robe flapping. "Finally, we can take this to the Life Coalition's own turf."

"And make 'em tell us why they're so obsessed with this power source of theirs they're willin' to tear up our own Effature," Rey said. He squared his shoulders against the strain of keeping the portal open. "No one does that."

CHAPTER FIFTEEN

New Realities

- The Nostelrahns are fighting again with the Lufvurn. The proposal the Lufvurn Multitudinous Fractal Theocrate put forward to divide labor in the city has problems, yes, but the Nostelrahn Head Guardian is making an overcautious response in ree's answer. Ree's concerns do not take into account the other four genders of the Nostelrahns adequately, and hardly address the problems with the upcoming Caraakn breeding cycle. I will have to make the weight of my will known to keep the leaders of the species in line.

From notes of Crominu Vaevicta, Effature

Sam eyed the broad wall of the compound. It was only a few stories tall, but took up many city blocks. A massive Caraakn lumbered by, the front head turned to argue with the spindly-limbed symbiote in the back. Above them, a flock of Lufvurn, like a child's crayon drawing of butterflies, disappeared over the top of the Effature's compound.

The aliens in this section of the Nether bumped, twisted, and flew past, and Sam twitched whenever one did. They grated on him worse than the ones in his section of the Nether. He wasn't used to them yet.

"How are you doing?" he whispered to Inas. The hurt when Inas spoke of being trapped in a little box was an ache in Sam's belly. He wanted to remove everything that happened and make him whole again. But the hand Sam held was no longer waxy and stiff, like it had been when Inas was captured. He had gained control of it while in captivity, though things still moved under his skin. How much pain had they put him through?

Inas was silent, staring up and around, and at first Sam thought he hadn't heard the question. He was about to repeat it when Inas swung his head to Sam.

"I'm thankful to be with you, Sam," he said, but there was heat beneath his words. "But it will take time to trust again. I know you won't hurt me, but I don't know if I can promise the reverse. I'm different. What I see and hear has more effect on me—I have to control how I react, what I try to do. Be cautious around me."

He started to pull his hand from Sam's, but Sam held it tight. It stayed the same shape.

"You won't hurt me," he insisted. "I know you. I didn't rescue you, and I hate myself for that, but I'll do whatever I can to make it up to you. I hope you can tell me what happened, in time."

Inas looked like his face might crumple into grief, then it opened into a smile, and he leaned into Sam. His lips were warm on Sam's mouth and he pressed in, hard. Sam melted under the pressure.

Time to tell him what I told Enos. It would be the start to them sharing everything. For real, this time.

"I'll start," he said, once they broke, and Inas pulled back to stare at him, confused.

"Enos knows this, so you should know too. In the Assembly, I made a Drain—a large one—disappear." He shook his head to stop Inas' question. "That's not the strangest part. I did that with the Houses of Matter and Time. I know that now. But there was a voice, and it told me things. I think it's behind the Drains and the Life Coalition. It has control over the Symphony like I've never seen before. It took some of my memories of Earth away, and vanished with the Drain. I haven't heard it since."

Inas held him while Sam let out a long breath. It had been easier to say this time.

"Thank you for telling me," Inas said, his tone low and serious. "Have you told the maji?"

Sam shook his head. "The voice hasn't come back, but I'm not completely sure it was real. If so, it was tied to the Drain and the Life Coalition hasn't made more of them. If she knew, Majus Ayama would think I've finally lost whatever reason I have."

"Possibly. Then perhaps you should tell your new teacher." Inas slid a glance over his shoulder, and Sam watched the tendons in his neck move. "Except Wor Wobniar is tapping xyr feet again."

Sam gave a bark of laughter. Their guide's head flaps wavered between them and the broad building. Surely xy wondered how unsuitable they were as ambassadors of an entire facet. Sam reluctantly released Inas, though he wanted to talk.

The architecture here was unlike the Imperium. If anything, it was closer to Gloomlight, but better lit and with fewer mushrooms. Sam squeezed Inas' hand and they followed Wor Wobniar through a circular portal. The doors were held wide open at an angle like a pair of shears. As they passed through, Sam could see they were pinned in place at the top of the semi-circle, so if released, they would slice back, covering the circular opening. He swallowed.

Inside, the building was open, save for carved and ornamented stone columns that held up the ceiling. There was only one story, though the ceiling soared three or four times his height. He ducked as one of the winged aliens swooped past, tail feathers brushing the top of his head. The light touch was like an icicle down his back.

No! I've been doing so well.

His fingers tingled, and his vision narrowed dangerously. His heart raced, and he couldn't get enough air.

Why now? Was it Inas' words? Our talk?

He tried to concentrate on Wor Wobniar, but it was like listening with cotton in his ears. He reached a hand in his pocket, to feel the comforting ridges on his pocketwatch.

"The Caraakn built this as a tribute to our Effature," xy told them. "It is meant to be a microcosm of the Nether itself." The Nostelrahn gestured to the forest of columns. It wasn't the columns Sam saw.

Groups of aliens crowded the building, some holding sheaves of scrolls and tablets. Caraakn were draped in colorful and elaborate fabrics that looked like wall tapestries laid over their broad backs. The Nostelrahns wore largely grays and whites, but the materials were fine, the fit tailored. The stick-like Praveadi had coils of thin metals forming decorative bracelets, while the airy Lufvurn wore nothing but their brilliant colors.

Sam saw the ceiling of the building, high above, in one sweeping glance, then looked down. There was too much. Too many people. Too close. All the effort of keeping his anxiety at bay was undone by one touch of a tail feather. Yet he should have collapsed as soon as he left the wall.

He panted, and pulled Inas to the nearest column. Everyone was staring at him. He could feel the pressure of their attention. The noise of a hundred conversations conducted in squeaks, taps, and rumbles bored into his brain.

"Inas, help me!" Sam hissed at him. He couldn't have a panic attack here. Wor Wobniar had asked him here as a representative of his section of the Nether. He had to act like a regular person. He had to be strong.

Why am I so weak?

But Inas' hand slipped away, and the constant warmth he emitted cooled as he drew away from Sam.

"You are well?" Wor Wobniar asked, lights flashing across xyr head. The flag-like head flaps trained on him, then transferred away, pointing at Inas. Sam followed their path. Why wasn't xy asking him more questions, like how he could be so ill-equipped to do anything worthwhile?

Then Sam saw what xy saw. He'd been distracted, asking Inas to help him when it should be the other way around. Inas was going gray—literally. His skin was darkening, matching Wor Wobniar's coloring.

He's changing shape, in the open!

Enos told of having too much emotion, after she changed shape. Had their talk layered more stress on Inas? Had Sam caused this?

Inas backed away, swerving to avoid one of the massive lumbering Caraakn, and Sam saw a third limb sprout from Inas' back.

He can't control it. I have to help him. Stop being weak.

The cool stone on Sam's back was pulling him, urging him to hide from the watching eyes, to give up. But he would not leave Inas like that.

Inas' hands lengthened, fingers turning to claws like those of a Nostelrahn, but worse—longer and sharper. His jaw separated into serrated edges, razor sharp. He took a tapping step forward on his toes. Above his tailbone, another leg trailed, half size. Inas oriented on a nearby purple alien, his arms reaching. The claws opened like a display of knives.

He's not turning into a Nostelrahn. He's turning into an assassin, like those of the Life Coalition.

Sam clamped down on his breathing. His chest felt like it might explode, but he took one step away from the column, then another. His heart raced, but he ignored it.

"I will not let this go wrong," he growled.

There was an insistent tapping next to him, and he realized all three of Wor Wobniar's feet were lifting and banging the stone floor in a rhythm. The Nether supplied that it was a warning Nostelrahns made when nervous. Xy would take care of the matter if he didn't. A memory of flashing hands and feet went through his mind and he had his answer.

What would Majus Ayama do?

Sam surged forward, his heart in his throat, and caught one of Inas' arms. He dragged the claw away from the dignitary and closer to him.

"Inas—don't do this," he pleaded, and the flaps that had opened on Inas' head swerved to fixate on him. Sam barely kept the claw away from his eyes. Inas clacked his jaw in a threat.

"Inas. It's me. It's Sam. Remember how much I...I care for you." The claws hesitated. "Remember the way you kissed me. What did they do to you there?" Inas—his Inas—would never react this way.

"Come back to me," Sam said. He pulled the blade of the claw toward his neck. "You can't want to hurt me." He fought against Inas' strength. The sharp edge was a finger-width from his throat, and Sam kept pulling, lifting his head.

Change back. Hurt me, not them.

Sam was winning the battle, though Inas was stronger. He felt the rasp of the claw prick his skin like a razor. Sam tugged harder, stretching his neck to tighten the skin. There was a sting of pain and he closed his eyes.

Then warm fingers brushed his throat, trailing down to his collarbone, and Sam let out a shaky breath. When he opened his eyes, Inas' face was inches from his. The flaps were gone, his skin turning from slate gray to warm brown. Suddenly, Inas' lips surged against his, hot and fierce. A hand traced down his side.

Sam melted back toward the column until cold stone hit his back, then grasped Inas' upper arms as Inas' hands sent electric tingles down his spine.

It's the emotion, not Inas. Changing makes him want to feel more of everything. I have to stop.

Slowly, reluctantly, Sam pushed Inas away, looking into his eyes. "Are you better?" he asked.

Inas swallowed, and Sam could see the vein in his neck pulsing to his heartbeat, fast and heavy. His eyes were half lidded and for a moment, he only stared. Then he blinked and his breathing slowed.

"Sam, I am so sorry." His voice was low and hoarse. "It was like someone else inside me, controlling what I did. I wanted to stop, but I didn't. I—"

Sam shook his head. "You don't have to apologize. I know what it feels like to be locked out of your own body."

Inas' face showed his puzzlement, then it cleared. "Is that what your attacks feel like?" Sam nodded. "And you worked through one to help me?"

"I..." He had, hadn't he? He wasn't used to controlling his panic attacks. "What did they do to you?" he asked again, but Inas looked away, shuffling back so he was no longer within kissing distance.

"They were training me. I'll tell you later." His head swiveled from side to side, as if realizing their audience. "We shouldn't keep the Effature waiting."

Sam shuddered and hunched in. The hall was nearly silent. If any beings hadn't been staring at them before, they were now. The weight of their gaze came back, like a heavy blanket smothering him. Wor Wobniar's clicking feet felt like a pick, driving into his skull.

Inas squeezed his shoulders, and as he smiled, the blanket lifted, just a little.

"You helped me. How can I help you?" he whispered.

Sam closed his eyes and found the Symphony. The beat was unfamiliar in these strange surroundings, but the music was comforting. He let it wash away some of the anxiety.

"We both have more to tell each other, when there's time." he said, and Inas nodded back. Then to Wor Wobniar, "I'm ready. Sorry about all this. I'm not sure we're the best choices to meet your Effature."

"We will find out, won't we?" the Nostelrahn said. "I have business with you, even accounting for Aridori instability. That species has learned to control it, over the cycles."

Inas raised his head at that. "You say other Aridori can handle this— this *surge* after changing?" He swallowed, and there were tears in his eyes. "I can't hurt my friends again. I don't want this anymore!"

Wor Wobniar's head flaps waggled, then pointed farther into the cavernous building. "Let us walk and I will explain."

They moved between two massive Caraakn, their rear heads turning to watch them even as the front heads, watching the floor, lumbered forward. A flock of Lufvurn coasted soundlessly overhead, a riot of fractal color.

"I do not know the techniques," Wor Wobniar said as they walked, "but the Aridori community has ways to deal with their emotional overload. There are still fights, and their community watch is involved from time to time to keep errant individuals from causing trouble in the rest of the city."

"Are they separate from the rest of you?" Inas asked. "Like some second-rate people?" Sam could feel the tension in his body, a motor warming up too fast.

In my facet, they were almost all killed. Yet Enos and Inas's families were peaceful. Is there any chance for the other species to accept the Aridori again?

"No. They are accepted, but the Aridori largely stay to themselves, with their elders' approval, and those of the other species. None of us wish for another war." The Nostelrahn's arms made a negating gesture. "There has been quite enough of that." Xyr head flaps swiveled between Sam and Inas. "The Effature can give you a more complete answer."

They passed farther into the building, and Sam wondered at the empty space. Structures in the Imperium were used to capacity, with stores built on top of others, and residences mingling with places of business, in styles from all ten species. Here, the crowds were sparse and vast stretches of open stone floor extended out of sight.

Only a group of the tripod-like purple Praveadi tumbled by on an errand, followed by a trio of Nostelrahns scuttling past. After the bustle of the entrance, this area was almost devoid of people. Was the Effature sitting all alone at the end of the building? Where was the Assembly? How did the species agree on what to do?

Sam listened, wondering if the Symphony could tell him. He'd heard little bits of Majus Ayama's House of Healing, and what Majus Cyrysi did with the House of Communication. Could he speak for all the houses? To meet the Effature in an official capacity, he had to be the best representative of his facet of the Nether.

Inas was composed again, hands in front of him, though his shoulders were tense. Sam wondered what help he would receive from an entire community like him. If they lived among other species, the Aridori had to control the emotional surge. Or did they simply never change? Sam shook his head. He had to focus on meeting the Effature. If it was anything like meeting the leader of his facet, it would take all his attention.

How much could the House of Matter tap into the other aspects? Sam had heard a deep aspect of the Symphony when disrupting the Communication between members of the Life Coalition, at the fight in the warehouse. Maybe he could do the same here to figure out the power structure.

Sam relied on Inas' arm to guide him while he concentrated. Symphonies overlapped each other in a complex web, and tried to catch the interactions. It was as if he overlaid Beethoven with Mozart, then dropped a Chopin minuet on top. He squeezed Inas' arm and let his eyes drift shut—the columns were spaced widely, and there were few beings around. Notes called out to each other, singing of different phases and expressions of matter. The liveliest melodies were attached to living beings, but everything, even the air, had its own music.

A complex spiral of rhythm flew overhead, and Sam looked up to see another Lufvurn glide by. This species' genders were strange, not mapping onto anything Sam had encountered before. Each one was individual and infinite, self-contained. The music accompanying this one echoed in the brightly colored patterns of...aeir wings. The Nether supplied the unfamiliar pronoun. Sam could almost see the notes swirling around aem, settling into the complex branching paths.

No, there is a connection here.

He squinted, and, for a moment, a wave of lines traced from the Lufvurn to him and Inas, to Wor Wobniar, to the building, to all the other beings here.

Sam gasped, his feet fixed to the floor at the panorama of direction and effect. Wor Wobniar's rear head flap centered on him, and xy spun, in a chorus of tapping. A silver aura enveloped xyr, just like when xy had come through the wall. Xy scuttled to Sam, the line of colors around xyr head spiking in intensity, rotating through reds, oranges, and blues, faster than he could follow.

Xy will tell me to leave. I've been causing problems since I got here. It's the first contact between facets of the Nether in ages and I'm ruining it. Just like me...

Wor Wobniar grasped Sam's hand with one claw, pulling it closer to xyr head flaps. "What did you do?" xy asked. "Can you do it again?"

The Nether's translation of the light show and the clacking jaws felt like buzzing in his head. "I... I was trying to listen to the Symphony," Sam answered, "to hear why this place was built like it was."

"And?" Wor Wobniar's strip of lights blinked furiously. "Did you see the *Vloeinkaal*?"

"I don't know what that is," Sam said. A small piece of his mind hammered at him.

Too much, out in the open. Too many people. Too much attention. He clamped down against the feeling, remembering how he pushed past it just minutes before.

"Did you see anything?"

The fleeting glance of the lines had been so brief he could have imagined it. He thought he'd seen them before he moved the Drain in the Assembly, but his mind was probably making things up, like it always did. He hadn't even told Majus Cyrysi or Majus Ayama about it. Only Enos knew, and she wasn't here. He'd left her just like he'd left Inas. The others had to be trying to get her back.

It was probably nothing. It was nothing.

"No. I didn't see anything."

Wor Wobniar still held his hand up, studying it as if it was of the greatest importance. "I understand," xy said, dropping his hand. "We're almost there." The strip of lights was dim, translated as a whisper by the Nether, and xy clacked xyr jaws in what would be a grunt in a Methiemum.

They passed the last few blocks in silence, and the number of other beings increased again. These were dressed progressively in finer and finer clothes, or at least Sam guessed they were. Fashion for a butterfly/snake cross with psychedelic wings was beyond him.

Sam, Inas, and Wor Wobniar approached the central feature of the area—a giant construction of stone, shell, and web, painted in a riot of striated colors. It ended in a pedestal, and on top of it perched a Nostelrahn, her three toe-claws equally spaced around the perimeter. On her head was a diadem. She was dressed in opposition to the other

Nostelrahns Sam had seen, in a scaled green and purple suit. It bore a startling resemblance to what his Effature wore.

Inas bent his head close. "She's a she," he whispered, and Sam realized his friend was right. The Nether was clearly transmitting a female gender for the Effature, when he had no context for Wor Wobniar's gender. Would it be rude for him to ask?

As they came closer, the Effature rose to her three feet and clacked down the side of the throne, like a crab scuttling across the beach. When she got to the bottom, she started across the floor toward them. As she did, the circlet attached to the top of her head caught a stray bit of light. It was exactly like the one on Bolas Palmoran's head.

"You are the representatives from the other facet of the Nether," the Effature said, through the translation of the colors that passed across her forehead. It wasn't a question. Her head flaps fixated on Sam, seeming to rake through even his thoughts, then on Inas. "Such interesting forms."

A ripple passed through her body, then another. Sam traded looks with Inas. What was happening?

"I am Crominu Vaevicta, but Palmoran must have already told you this. Welcome to my facet of the Nether."

Another shiver went down her body, bringing a wash of color with it. Slowly, her claws shrank and separated into smaller fingers, while the strip of light on her head disappeared as a snout pushed out, darkening to black, and growing tiny scales. Dark and knowing eyes emerged from under ridged brows.

The green and purple suit stayed, but was now a part of her body. Only the diadem did not change, resting on the top of her head.

Before them was the same sort of sleek, black-scaled creature as had been presented in the Assembly as a servant of the Life Coalition. Her body was lithe, like a cat stretched up on its hind legs, but the face reminded him of pictures Sam had seen on Earth of Chinese dragons, long and sinuous, with mobile tufted ears.

"You're an Aridori," Inas shouted, then clapped a hand to his mouth. He was wound tight as the spring in Sam's pocketwatch, and Sam put one hand out to him, uncertain if it might trigger another attack.

Crominu Vaevicta took one more step toward Inas, and he leaned toward her, as if trying to breathe her in. "This I am," she said, and her words were physical sounds instead of the Nether's mental translation of a Nostelrahn. "Yet I have spent several cycles as the most populous species of this facet." The Effature raised a hand toward Wor Wobniar. "It serves as good relations to feel what the other species feel."

Sam looked at the well-dressed beings in attendance. Some seemed interested in the change, as far as he could tell from the Nether's translation, but no one called the Effature out. A pair of Lufvurn, their long bodies wrapped around a column, bent their smooth heads together to discuss in a high-pitched stream of clicks, the words too quiet for Sam to hear.

"The others know of my species," the Effature said, coming closer. "I spend time as each, in a rotation. I am out of schedule to change, but then, this is an unprecedented event." Her hand rose, long fingers extended for Sam to take. Hesitantly, he did, unsure what to do. Did they shake hands here? The Effature intertwined her fingers with his, gently squeezing, then released. "Please, tell me what you call yourselves."

Sam and Inas introduced themselves, and gave a little information about the species in their facet of the Nether. The Effature nodded along, her expressive snout indicating familiarity with a few of the species. She cocked her head at the Benish, Pixies, Sureriaj, and Lobhl. Sam recalled some piece of history Majus Cyrysi must have told him that those species were the more recent introductions to the Assembly.

"You may call me Vaevicta," she said after they finished. Then she looked from side to side at her attendants, and Sam marveled at the iridescent sheen on her scales. The Aridori were a handsome species, if this was how all of them looked. "You have seen individuals of the Nostelrahns, Praveadi, Caraakn, and Lufvurn while you have been here." Various members of those species made motions of respect as the Effature named them. There were at least twenty of each in attendance, interspersed—or in the Lufvurn's case, twisted around—the many stone columns that held up the roof. The Nostelrahn's wore universally drab clothing, perhaps to counter that they spoke with color. The Praveadi wore shiny bracelets, pendants and rings on their stick-like legs, reflecting the light from glowing rocks placed high on the columns. Most of the Caraakn had large tapestries draped over their broad backs, which turned into elaborate collars for their rear heads, each sheet of fabric richly detailed with representations of scenes Sam guessed were from their homeworld. They featured lots of open plains. The Lufvurn wore nothing save their bright colors, looking like kaleidoscopes whenever they moved.

The Effature continued after introducing several of her highest-ranking attendants. "The Aridori stay to themselves, and largely keep to the section of the city farthest from the center. Theirs—ours—has been a long road, working to improve the others' view of them while perfecting techniques to cope with the swell of emotion that accompanies change." Here she stopped and gave Inas a long look. "There are still some who choose the hard path that once led us to conflict, though they are few these days. I hope to see a generation of my people where none seek the heightened thrill that comes with change. Too much of it drove my kind to ignite war."

"Since you are Aridori, was that why we could tell you were female, rather than Wor Wobniar's gender?" Inas asked. His eyes were bright, almost feverish.

"The Effature is female whatever form she takes," Wor Wobniar told them. Xyr head flaps switched from Sam, to Inas, to Vaevicta. "My species does have a female gender, one of five major ones recognized. You might call me a...'pruner.'" Wor Wobniar took a moment to come to the correct word, the lights on xyr head flashing in patterns as xy thought. "One who regulates the growth and health of the species."

Sam worried how much his recent change affected Inas, though meeting another of his kind seemed energizing. Was it better than the funk he'd been in since returning from the Life Coalition? The Effature spoke as if the Aridori had bettered themselves since the war. Maybe she could undo what the Coalition had done to Inas.

Does she remember the war? How old is she?

"How is dear Palmoran?" Vaevicta asked. "I had hoped he would come himself. It has been far too long, though I suppose he has more trouble in your facet, with the oppression of Aridori there."

Sam squinted at the sheen of green and purple on the Effature's chest. So like Palmoran's robe. "Was the Effature's costume inspired by the Aridori?" he asked. "Is it left over from before the war?" He was missing something.

Crominu Vaevicta laughed, a deep hearty laugh, and several other beings made sounds of amusement, though Sam couldn't tell whether they understood the joke.

"Palmoran? Take after an Aridori?" Vaevicta's snout opened in a smile, taking in him and Inas. "You could say that. He is my other instance."

Sam gasped as memories flickered through his head, connecting little moments he'd thought odd, but not enough to comment on. How had Palmoran stayed hidden so long?

Inas brushed past him. "Why didn't I see that?" His voice was still louder than normal, his movements jerky. It was like his metabolism had gone into overdrive, or he'd drunk a pot of coffee. Sam's hand crept up to catch at Inas' sleeve, but he pulled it back. What if he had suddenly found a group of humans—true humans, not Methiemum— alive here?

"Are there more Aridori in positions of power? How have you stayed sane so long? I have so many questions for you." Inas was almost nose to nose with the Effature. She was of a similar height to him.

Vaevicta laughed again, and took Inas' hand, twining her fingers through his as she had done with Sam, but now the gesture looked more intimate, and Sam frowned.

I am not jealous of an alien monarch, who just happens to be Inas' same species.

How did Aridori reproduce, anyway?

"Such a curious mind! I hope most of your questions will be answered eventually," the Effature said, then grew serious. "I promise we will talk soon, but for now, we must discuss the actual reason you are here: the prophet's vision of the coming Dissolution." She dropped Inas' hand and her striking eyes—a deep, dark purple, Sam noticed— fastened him in place. "Xy foretold you would be of the House of Matter, though it was thought lost. Is this true?"

"I think so, and I think I can also hear the House of Time," Sam said. "It's new to me, but the more I learn about my aspect, the more I can tell it's not like the others."

"So, another prophet in addition. That is as much confirmation as I need for now," Vaevicta said. "My houses of the maji are in an uproar since Wor Wobniar told them the news. Poor dears. They wouldn't know what to do without me."

Sam saw Inas' eyebrows lift, mirroring his. They exchanged a glance. The maji were her 'dears?'

"Where are the other houses?" Sam said. "Shouldn't the heads be here? Don't they report as a Council?"

"So many questions." The Effature watched Sam, and he stared back, entranced. "Things work differently here, young majus. I am the ultimate law. The maji do my bidding, and though they have some agency, mine is the only edict here." She waved a hand at the expanse of her palace. "You will not find them in this place, save in rare circumstances. More likely, they are on the homeworlds, tending to problems they are better suited to fixing."

"You have no crime here?" Inas asked. "No events the maji can help with?" He folded his hands over each other, dry washing. Sam recognized that gesture.

The Effature shook her head, the furry tips of her long ears shaking. "We have those things, but I am the one to deal with them. Most problems have no need of maji, if one is inventive. Best to save their notes for truly difficult problems, on the four homeworlds."

"Four homeworlds?" Inas asked, and he drooped for the first time since seeing the Effature. "I was hoping..." But Vaevicta was already shaking her head.

"Just as in your facet, I suspect, the Aridori homeworld has been lost. There are no Aridori maji, something that has been consistent for many, many centuries."

"But, he *is* a majus," Sam blurted. "Or an apprentice at least."

For the first time, the Effature looked surprised, and she took a long look at Inas. "An Aridori majus? Truly?" Inas nodded. "Perhaps we do have more to speak of than Wor Wobniar's doom and gloom. What of your other instance?"

"She is held captive by a fundamentalist group in our facet," Inas answered, his face darkening. "This is why we can only stay briefly before returning."

"I see," Vaevicta said. "Then we shall not keep you. But she is also a majus?"

"She is. I always thought there must have been Aridori maji before the war," Inas said, "but in our facet, they would have been hunted down. I thought...here..."

"The war came here as well," Vaevicta said, her expression turning cold. "It was a terrible time, but the species in this facet did not commit genocide. They discovered ways to determine our species, and found the hidden assassins by process of elimination. It occupied every species for many cycles." She paused, then glanced at the others in her court. They were all paying attention.

"Walk with me. Wor Wobniar should also come. Xy will need to take you this way." The Effature indicated Sam, then led them deeper into the huge building, past her throne and into dark corridors lit by occasional shining stones embedded in the columns.

"Our species was rounded up after the war," Vaevicta told Inas, while columns marched past on either side. The building seemed endless. "The other species, and the maji, found ways to contain us."

"I know some of those," Inas muttered, and Sam pictured the box the Sathssn kept their assassin in. How long had they kept Inas in one?

"Here, those who did not fight to the death were put in areas with only one way out and guards trained in containment. There were many more battles, though this time within our species. The two communities—those of the Pillars and of the Blessed—have vastly different ways to control the emotion felt after changing. It has always been a topic with the capacity to split the Aridori into warring groups."

"That's terrible," Sam said. There were too many times in Earth's history when people were forced into segregation or suppression. The Effature was dancing around some descriptions, but he thought he could fill in the blanks.

"But some were left?" Inas asked.

"Enough," the Effature answered. "The ones who remained—the Pillars—were largely of one mind as to how to control the urge for emotional response. They took it upon themselves to craft their social programs to reflect only one style of control, even to the point of choosing their mates so their children would be less likely to search out violence."

"That's eugenics," Sam protested, horrified. "They couldn't have known that, not for certain." There was a lot Vaevicta wasn't saying.

"And you are an expert in Aridori reproduction?" Sam hunched in at the rebuke. But then the Effature sighed. "You are correct. There were many failed...experiments, but the remaining population was determined not to repeat the circumstances that brought them to that point. They made certain each generation followed the traditions they had set down."

They were silent for a while, columns looming as they walked, gray and still, as if in judgment. Sam marveled at the Effature's history lesson. In his facet, no one knew anything of the time of the Aridori War.

"Over the cycles, the population chose again to interact with the other species," Vaevicta said. "Their guards agreed to let them mingle if they chose."

"But they must have been looked down on," Inas said, and the Effature nodded. After so long separated, that would have been hard to avoid.

A certainty was creeping over Sam, from hints here and there about his Effature—Palmoran, and from the way Vaevicta spoke.

"You were there, weren't you?" he asked. "You lived through this time. Did you live through the war?"

Vaevicta was silent for a long time, and Sam thought she wouldn't answer.

Then: "Yes, I was. And you must know Palmoran did too, as he is my other instance."

"I've seen other Aridori who've been alive since the war," Inas volunteered, and Sam stared at him.

Was he going to share that with me at some point?

"They were completely insane, and forgive me, but you don't seem that way." Inas was breathing heavily, and his teeth clenched. "How can an Aridori live that long and stay sane?"

"You wish all my secrets today," Vaevicta said, her tone icy. Inas folded under the glare, looking down and away in a display of subservience. Sam had never seen him do that before.

"Forgive me," Inas said. "I'm being impertinent."

The Effature waved an elegant hand. Sam realized he couldn't hear her footsteps. Her feet were bare, each with four, long toes. She was completely silent as she walked.

Which makes a good assassin. The thought crept into Sam's consciousness.

"You are being impertinent," Vaevicta agreed, "but this is an uncertain time, and many changes are coming, if one listens to Wor Wobniar."

Sam looked back. The ever present click-click-click of the Nostelrahn's clawed feet was in sharp contrast to the Effature's silence. Xy had given them space to speak with Vaevicta, though xyr head flaps showed xy was paying close attention.

In answer, the Effature tapped a finger against the diadem—the same one Palmoran wore—embedded above her brow. It was the only thing not to change when the Effature became an Aridori in shape.

"This is the source of my continued sanity, even at my age. I believe you will find Palmoran the same, though without easy access to shifting his form, I doubt he remembers nearly as much as I do. I assume he has not shown his species."

"He has not," Sam confirmed. "I don't think he'd be the Effature if he revealed that. Some people in our facet aren't even convinced Aridori are real."

"They...we are the creatures of nightmares," Inas said. "I thought my family was the last of us, until I met the old ones. My parents, and their parents, have spent centuries hiding from everyone else, pretending we are Methiemum—like Sam," he added at a look from Vaevicta. "It's so deep in our bones that my other instance and I had never changed shape until two months ago."

Vaevicta peered down her snout at them. "Fortunate you came with your friend, then," she said, and her pace slowed as a wall loomed up in front of them, dark and wide. A little ways off, there was a round doorway, like the one into which they'd entered the building. "You and I will talk about our species and what can be done," she said to Inas. Then she nodded at Wor Wobniar.

"The discussion of Aridori is always difficult," the Nostelrahn prophet grated to Sam. "Therefore, while that happens, I can show you the House of Time."

CHAPTER SIXTEEN

Ancient Restraints

- Stories of the Aridori have been in our society ever since the war, beginning with fact and gradually descending into rumor and speculation. Every few cycles, they spring to life again, as if there is some motivator keeping these night fright tales in our social consciousness. Is this simply because people enjoy a good scare when they know it cannot be true, or are there real factors involved, generating these stories? Perhaps another faction or community is gaining legitimacy by propagating them.

Part of a philosophical treatise by Punala Traelfa Tinala, in service to the government of the Fiery Sea Archipelago

Enos roused from a deep and peaceful sleep, looking over the prone forms of the other Aridori with bleary eyes. The majus lights high on the walls brightened into morning, and someone was banging on the sealed door.

"Right now, it is time for you to show yourselves to the Coalition leaders," a voice called. Was that Dunarn? Enos stretched. She'd had such...vivid dreams about Sam. She couldn't stop the smile that stretched her mouth.

"Come on, come on," Zhaddi said, shuffling to the door. They were furred today, like a Festuour, though not nearly thick enough through the body. Their head was also wrong, closer to the sleek, scaly black of the Aridori. Enos saw the others were similarly up and moving toward the door. She followed them.

"Not going to resist?" she asked the others.

Putra shook their head. "With a chance to observe the leaders? We will behave for this. We rarely see them. Such delicious movement— new parts and gestures to copy. There will be others around, too."

"Strange that they call for all of us," said one of the three Aridori with no names. A dissenting opinion reached up from within Enos. Voices sounded on the edge of her comprehension, like the echoes of the Symphony behind the shield the Life Coalition controlled. Enos pushed them back down. They did not have a say in what she did.

Yet you use our substance.

Enos stopped while the others went through the door. The voice had been clear, but now was lost among mumbling rantings. Enos drew in a deep breath, listening for the Symphony, and to the other Aridori talking about new sights and smells. Anything to get that voice out of her head. Her heart thumped in her chest. Was it even her heart any longer, or had that been a piece she stole? She couldn't remember.

The Symphony roared in her mind as she stepped out of the Aridori's holding cell and Enos reached for it hungrily, her eyes falling closed. The metallic *clack* of metal brought her back, dimming the Symphony to a dull murmur.

She looked down to see Dunarn locking manacles around her wrists. Without thinking, Enos changed the way her eyes took in light, not with the Symphony of Healing, but the way her people did. She took in the pattern of stripes on the dark cloth. There were more on Dunarn than on Nakan. A sign of rank?

"You should not have spent so much effort," Putra said to Dunarn, and Enos looked the other way. An entire troop of Sathssn were behind them, twenty or more, some armed with loaded blunderbusses, others with pikes and halberds. The tunnel was not small, but even so, they would have to push a forest of weapons aside to pass them. Torchlight gleamed off the metal blades.

"Get the collars," Dunarn directed to one of the unnamed ones. "No tricks or it will be your last breath." Several of the guards trained their guns on the Aridori Dunarn selected. They hunched, spitting, their back curving and growing a ridge of spines, but another soldier prodded them with the end of a spear and they slunk back into the room. They emerged a moment later with six shiny metal collars.

"Take one and close it around your neck," Dunarn directed. Zhaddi took one from their fellow first, reaching up to clasp the collar around their neck. The others followed, and at a gesture from Putra, Enos took one too. As it closed with a *click*, she realized her eyes were still like Sathssn eyes. She tried to change them back, but it was like pushing on a string. There was no response from her body, and her lips raised in a snarl.

They have limited me.

The Aridori who got the collars must have had the same response, because they reared forward, snarling, their spines bristling.

They got to within arm's reach of Dunarn before sagging, as if melting in the sun. The Coalitioner had one hand to a device on her wrist, wreathed in brown, blue, green, and white, all involved with the construction of the System.

The offending Aridori struggled to stay upright, their form loose and liquid, though not enough to slide out of the collar. Enos felt the retreat in the others even as a wave of disgust flowed through her. The device had stopped the assassin's shifting in that plastic state between forms, useless for anything. Zhaddi growled at them and smacked their chest with one hand. It left an imprint, like a handprint in wet sand.

"Now, behave, and follow me," Dunarn said. "The rest of you, will you be good from here?" There was a chorus of agreement, which Enos joined in.

"Then you five, you may have a reward." Dunarn lifted a gloved finger and pressed a button. Something loosened in Enos, just slightly. She might change, if she struggled hard enough, but it would be slower than before she'd absorbed the other Aridori—sluggish and gradual. How had she ever thought that was enough? How had she ever *not* changed? It was her birthright. She'd learned much in her few days with the other Aridori and the thrill of it urged her to do more, stretch the limits of what she could achieve. Now these Snakes wanted to stop her.

She eyed the offending Aridori, whom Dunarn had left in its pitiable state. They glared back, shoulders slumped and deformed.

Somewhere deep in her, a little voice dissented.

"Me, I argued against bringing you out where you could cause trouble, but Janas insisted. She is worried about..." Dunarn's cowl waggled, as she shook her head. "Follow me."

Enos hadn't realized how much space the Life Coalition's tunnels took up. She had been led from a portal room to her first bedroom, and then the short distance to the Aridori's cell.

Now they wandered down long, unfinished stone halls, big enough for five Sathssn to walk side by side. Their steps bounded in the gentle pull from the tiny homeworld. They followed Dunarn, and the guards followed them. In one place, they passed through a high, dark cavern where the torchlight did not reach the ceiling. Later, they crossed a woven vine bridge spanning a crevice echoing their footsteps back to them, as if they walked over infinity.

Enos had little sense of time in the caverns, since the last day—days?—with the Aridori hadn't been broken up by meals. The tunnels the Life Coalition had hollowed out of this asteroid snaked this way and that, occasionally crossing other dark openings. Enos watched and listened as they walked, though the guards said nothing, only their weapons clanking. In contrast, the Aridori were completely silent, down to their footfalls.

Enos guessed it was the better part of a lightening from their prison to where the leaders lived. In that time, she could have crossed most of High Imperium. The Coalition did not want the Aridori anywhere near them, not that Enos could blame them.

As they got closer, the tunnels became brighter and more finished, and they saw more of the Life Coalition army. Many had been killed in the battle at the Dome of the Assembly, but from what Enos could see, it reduced their numbers little. Cloaked figures made way for their group of thirty or so, barely a drop in the sea of dark fabric.

Look for weak points. Anything I can use to escape.

How long had she been here? It felt like months, but she thought it had only been a few days. Less than a ten-day. Were the others looking for her, or was Sam snuggling with Inas, glad to have him back instead of her? Anger and desire mixed within her. She wanted to *feel* more, egged on by the unfamiliar voices trapped inside. The collar and manacles itched and she almost flung herself against a wall, simply to feel. Even if it was the pain of hitting that solid surface.

"More members here than usual," Zhaddi whispered, cutting into her struggle. Did they know how much she chafed to do more? "I have been this way a few times. The captors pulled back all their members, likely from every other secret place they infested."

With a struggle, Enos heaved her discomfort away to focus on the conversation. She wouldn't have had to concentrate so much before she got here. "None of you changed form," she whispered back. "Why not?" The ability writhed beneath her skin. The collar was like a tight glove, keeping her shape steady, but with an effort, she could have pushed through the feeling.

Zhaddi shrugged expansively. Their Festuour shoulders were good for that. "Curiosity. We have not all been called together in many cycles.

Besides, if we did rebel, where would we go? Our species is dead." They tapped the collar. "As we would be, soon afterward."

"Captors like these killed our species, to hear you tell it," Enos said, jerking her head back to the troop of dark-cloaked Coalitioners following them.

"We still have the capacity for revenge," Zhaddi remarked, and their pleasant grin became malicious. "Our patience is far greater than one with such a brief life span can comprehend." They reached over and placed a furry paw on Enos' manacles. She was the only one to wear them. The other Aridori were unrestrained, though guarded by the soldiers behind them.

"Our captors have not had the combination of a majus and an Aridori before," Zhaddi whispered.

"We have observed many of the maji's Systems, though the cycles," Putra said by Enos' other side. She nearly jumped. The Aridori was noiseless when they moved. Putra had adopted a form like a Kirian's today, but the feathery hair continued all over their body, like a large bird. "I would guess both of these use a component of the House of Grace and the House of Healing. Am I correct?"

Enos squinted at her manacles, then at the collars on the other Aridori's necks. There was a large aura of white, but underneath, a sheen of blue. She nodded.

"In our experience," Putra traded a glance with Zhaddi, "some of their Systems have a tendency to interact with each other. I would not be surprised if the maji did not properly think through their creations."

Zhaddi lifted their hands under their chin, right in front of the collar. Enos followed their motion, hesitantly, and the glove of restriction around her body loosened. The Symphony suddenly became clearer.

Enos' eyes widened. She dropped her hands and looked to the others. The glove tightened, the Symphony quieted. The two Systems interfered and weakened each other! The music must have been composed at cross purposes, likely many cycles apart.

Putra had a large, predatory grin on their face. "Not now," they whispered. "When, and if, the time becomes right."

Enos stared down at the manacles.

Oh. There will be a right time.

"There may be opportunity in this day. We will have to see what the current leaders propose, and whether we like their terms," Zhaddi said.

They fell silent for the rest of the way, through populated areas of the caverns. Enos strained to grasp her collar and pull it away, but she forced the feeling down. She wanted to do...something, anything.

The halls and rooms were regular in shape here, finished and often with a false ceiling in the larger caverns to dispel the sense of vastness. The area Enos had lived in was barely more than a rough hole in comparison. The Life Coalition had been here for a long time. Decades or more.

Finally, their group entered a larger-than-average cave with a false ceiling, four times her new height, and ornamented with knots cut from some species of tree. Vines hung from them, loaded with purple flowers and green fruit. The air was fresher here, with a light, sweet scent. It made Enos realize how stale the air had been in the Aridori's prison. They were given the worst areas of this little homeworld, but when had the Aridori ever been given anything good?

I will take my birthright back from these thieves—pull it directly from their hearts if needed.

Had that been her thought, or one of the other voices? She wasn't certain, and that realization shook the anger from her.

Dark-cloaked figures were in little groups around the room, two or three times the amount in their procession. A few had their cowls back. The Life Coalition members were not all Sathssn. In fact, nearly half were from other species.

In the middle of the room were six seats, four of them occupied. Dunarn left them to take the fifth seat, and the guards clustered around them, though not too close. With Enos' augmented eyes, the seated figures' cloaks shone with ornamentation, more than any others here. In fact—Enos took another quick look around—the non-Sathssn members only had one large stripe across their chest. It was simple to see who was who and where they belonged, for those with Sathssn eyes. She wondered how many non-Sathssn knew about that.

For the moment, they were ignored. Enos peeked back over her shoulder. No, the troop of soldiers still watched them warily. Perhaps the Coalitioners felt safe with that little protection. If they knew the battle Enos had been in the day before, they might rethink their tactics, but she guessed the Aridori hid their internal power struggles from the

Sathssn. The Snakes were fools, to let the Aridori grow in power right under their noses. Putra and Zhaddi were right to look for opportunity. The urge to act, to find some outlet, buzzed under Enos' skin, but she had a strong suspicion she'd get a chance today to satisfy the urge changing left within her.

Instead, she watched the others of her species. They were entranced, little pieces of their bodies shifting from one form to another, though at a much slower rate. Enos only kept her form with an effort. A mane of Etanela hair was blossoming from the feathers on Putra's head, while a Pixie's wings were unfolding from one of the three nameless Aridori's backs. This display was met with disgust by several Sathssn, but no one screamed and ran from old night terrors come to life. They were familiar with Aridori.

"Where is he?" the Sathssn on the end of the row of chairs said. Her voice was cutting and authoritative, and Enos recognized it. That timbre was unmistakable. It was the one who led, when the Coalition had spoken in the Assembly—Janas. She remembered suddenly that it was also the voice that spoke behind a door, in another cavern, where she and Sam had been trapped, months ago.

"Him, he is late as usual." That creaky old voice was Zsaana's, and Enos' lip curled. Imagine, trading the position of head of the House of Healing for hiding in these tunnels. Enos wondered what the others had promised him. Power? Salvation? Wealth?

"We can start without him. That one, he does nothing but shoot off on his own agenda." Enos didn't recognize this voice. "Me, I would not be surprised if—"

The quick tap of boots interrupted the Coalitioner's tirade as another figure entered, dark cloak flapping around him. Enos knew just by the arrogant gait that this was Nakan. Now she had adjusted her eyes, she could see the designs on his clothes. She hissed, the well of emotion rising, telling her to find a way to *show* him what he'd done by putting her in with the other Aridori—

"Us, we should all rejoice," Nakan announced, breaking into Enos' thoughts. He waved a dagger—a short sword, really—through the air in front of him. "Me, I achieved what none of you could in how many cycles?"

"What have you done, Nakan?" the first speaker said, her words cutting through the air.

"I freed us, Janas," Nakan answered. "Should we wish, the Imperium, or even the entire Nether, it is within our grasp!"

"What madness is this, Nakan?" Zsaana asked. He sounded tired and Enos wondered how often Nakan went against the rest of the Life Coalition. That was a point of weakness, and she looked to Putra to see if they had spotted it. Putra's toothy smile was wide in enjoyment of the argument.

Nakan straightened, showing off the dark stain on the dagger he held. "This, it is the blood of the Effature. Many times we tried for his life, only to fail. Today was different. I struck a fatal blow against the old Aridori. No longer will one of the formless hold sway over the Assembly of Species!"

Silence washed over the room, and then the leaders of the Life Coalition began shouting.

"Our assassins, they will need new targets," Janas said, at the same time Zsaana said, "You directly attacked the Effature? You threatened everything we worked toward for cycles upon cycles!"

Other Coalitioners were up and moving around the room, making little knots of conversation before they broke off and reformed elsewhere. A strange sense of sadness washed through Enos, but it was not coming from her. Her thoughts were merely confused.

The Effature was an Aridori? How is that possible?

He was in opposition to us, in the war, an inner voice said to her. *He found his own way to survive—was it better than ours?*

Enos didn't shove the voice away this time.

You knew?

She watched the other Aridori. Putra had a hand up to their chest, Kirian eyes wide. Zhaddi shook their head at the other three.

We all knew him, though he did not know us.

What did that mean?

"You knew about the Effature?" she asked Putra, and the Aridori nodded. That must be why Enos felt a connection when she saw the old man. He was like her and Inas. But he wasn't out of control like these Aridori, was he? How had he remained sane, over so many cycles?

She didn't have time to ask, as Janas pounded the arm of her chair. "Quiet!" she shouted. "This, it changes the time of our movement, but not our plan. It is clear our negotiations with the Assembly, they will be fruitless from now on, yet we must increase our representation in the Assembly. Us, we must gain access to the font of power my great-great-grandfather foretold, by any means. Me, I will not be the one to destroy the peace of his vision." She gestured in Enos' direction. "The assassins must be let loose to do their jobs. More voices must be in agreement with ours."

"And us, how will we do that with the panic that will certainly sweep through the Imperium?" Zsaana hissed. He pointed a gloved finger at Nakan. "You steal a weapon meant only to control that species long under our control. You upstart, you rejected our path again, to what end?"

"To the greater glory of the Form," Nakan answered. He still held the bloody knife, like a trophy. Enos cast a sidelong glance to see Zhaddi glowering. She guessed they had seen that knife, or others like it, long ago. "With the Assembly in disarray, us, we have breathing space to move all our pieces into position, to welcome those who would bestow power upon us. Where the voids failed last time, now the Life Coalition, we will be ready and can seize the means to bring harmony to our homeworld at last." He flung a hand out toward the Aridori. "Have them, the damned, do our work for us, rather than sap our resources as they have for a thousand cycles."

"What are they talking about?" Enos whispered to Putra.

Putra shook her head. "This power has been their aim for many cycles, but we do not know what it is. They hide that aspect from us. All we know is that they think it will bring an era of peace and harmony to the entire Assembly."

"Or at least to their homeworld, according to Nakan," Zhaddi grumped.

"They don't seem like they're trying to bring peace," Enos observed, while the leaders began arguing. She eyed the guards, but they still watched the Aridori while their leaders argued, ready to counter any move to escape.

"Yet they named their organization after it," Zhaddi said. "They call it the Life Coalition, though it has had different names over the centuries we've been forced to serve."

"They would have achieved their plans a few months ago," Putra said, "save some young man singlehandedly stopped the void they had carefully constructed over months."

"Sam," Enos said, and the others looked at her. "His name is Sam, and he is an amazing person. Both me and my other instance think so."

Zhaddi traded a significant glance with Putra. "And he is Aridori?"

"Of course not," Enos said. "Inas and I thought we were the only ones left until I met you."

Putra looked like they would say more, but Janas broke in to their conversation.

"You, the assassin there," her gloved finger was pointing toward Zhaddi. "You will target the elder speaker for the Etanela. She has been speaking out far too fervently against the Life Coalition."

"I know this person," Zhaddi said, their voice loud in the silence. "Rabata Liinero Humbano. She is of a well-respected lineage among the Etanela. You wish me to observe her, dispose of her, or replace her?"

Janas waved a hand. "Me, I care not. Only silence her voice against our peace with the Assembly. That is all that matters. We must make up for time lost."

"How long would it take for you to replace her?" Dunarn asked. The postures of the other leaders of the Life Coalition indicated disgust at the Aridori, but Dunarn sat forward. She seemed one of the least religious of the leaders, save perhaps for Nakan, who was still glowering, his arms crossed and the knife dangling from one hand. Enos clenched her hands as the urge to confront rose in her. She could do as well as the others. She could replace the speaker!

No. What are you thinking?

Zhaddi cocked their head, Festuour tongue licking their muzzle. "A true replacement would take several cycles of careful observation. I could do a hasty one in a few months, but her aides would soon penetrate my disguise."

"No time for that," Janas said. "Kill her."

"Kill Speaker Humbano?" Zsaana asked. "Janas, you are certain of this? She is most influential and any foul play, it would be reflected on us, especially if the assassin is discovered."

Putra purred and stepped forward. "Send me instead. I am better at observation. I will replace the lovely speaker. I have observed her before."

The leaders, even Dunarn, drew back from Putra. The Aridori changed, growing taller, though slowly. The mane of hair they sported turned from light brown to nearly white. Enos recognized the face of the stately speaker emerging. She had seen the Etanela several times when accompanying Majus Ayama.

You knew her too. You can take that assignment. Prove you are worthy.

The voice welled up in her, and with both her inner self and this voice coercing her, Enos could not resist it. Her arms lengthened, almost without her control. She had extra mass, and talent, latent. Yes, why not take the advantage?

A tiny part of her knew this was wrong, but pride and certainty swelled in her as she changed shape.

You defeated us, and we will serve you now.

The voice pulled memories to the front of Enos' mind, advising how she should change to best match the speaker.

Enos took a step forward, her leg lengthening as she did. "Pick me. I have more knowledge of the Assembly and current events." What was she saying?

Putra hissed, turning to confront. Zhaddi stepped close to her other side, surprising Enos by picking her over their long-term cohort.

"You will fail this fight," they said to Putra. "Especially with two of us to your one."

Thoughts of Sam, of Inas, of Majus Ayama flashed through Enos' mind, battling with the images and feelings the other Aridori in her dredged up. The two assassins gauged each other, and her, but then Enos remembered:

"We are each proficient enough to keep another from absorbing us, yet none so strong we could stand against two at once."

"We would never do that, though."

Why were Putra and Zhaddi flanking her? The desire to fight them rose like a wave, crowding out other thoughts.

Seize your birthright as an Aridori, the voice inside her whispered. *We are the true rulers of the other species. Work with the others.*

Work with them? When they were threatening her? Enos tried to think straight. She took another step toward Putra, felt Zhaddi tense beside her. The other three Aridori backed away, leaving this fight to the most powerful. But was it a fight?

Tricky Aridori.

"Them, what are they doing?" Janas shouted. "Stop them!"

Nakan growled, stalking forward with his knife outstretched. "Me, I've killed one Aridori today, and I can kill more."

Putra hissed again, their teeth lengthening into sabers. Their head swiveled between Zhaddi and Enos, and Nakan.

Zhaddi growled, and their fingers sharpened into blades. They hunched inward.

Enos' heartbeat sped.

You are the dominant one, majus. Stake your supremacy! The voice in her howled, but Enos beat it back. Then another rose to take its place.

Watch their moves. Coordinate with them.

Enos growled. Her head was throbbing and she just wanted to *stab* something.

"How could one Aridori lead the Nether for so long?" Nakan taunted. "These, they are pitiful excuses for their species."

Both Aridori swiveled to Nakan, spitting and hissing, and an aura of blue and purple rose around him.

"Manacles," hissed Zhaddi, so low Enos almost didn't hear them. The single word drilled into her consciousness and the dissenting voices in her died away, watching.

This was the right time.

So it was a feint, at least partly. Enos knew if she had engaged Putra or Zhaddi they would not hesitate to batter her down and absorb her. The two were opportunists. Instead, Enos focused on Nakan.

He killed the Effature.

Enos' arms were long, like an Etanela's. She bent the manacles toward her neck and heard two themes battle in the Symphony, each veering the other away from harmony. The manacles buzzed and fizzed, and relaxed around her wrists. The collar hummed and the glove loosened around her. Enos flung the cuffs into Nakan's hood but the Sathssn dodged it.

The Symphony roared in Enos' ears. The notes changed as she changed form. They were the same thing, and she took notes from her core at the same time she shifted shape, strengthening the martial tempo of her movements and making her skin dense. She could change at speed again.

She stepped forward just in time to receive the slash of Nakan's knife. Enos gasped as the strange blade parted skin and notes at the same time. It cut a melody loose from the larger Symphony, unraveling it into curls of single notes and chords. What was the knife made of?

Nakan pivoted around the two slashing Aridori, who were now more blades than not, even slowed by their collars. The guards behind them wavered between the three others, but the assassins separated, flanking the troop, and Enos thrilled at the coordination in her siblings. They were strong! Strong enough to take on all these Coalitioner jailers now they had made a mistake!

Enos shrunk her limbs to normal size, but strengthened muscles in her legs, augmenting the change her shifting caused in the Symphony with her notes. There was so much she could do!

She gathered, and sprung up and out of the group, intending to make her escape.

A hand like a vice grasped her ankle, and the changes in the House of Healing unraveled like her song when touched by the knife. Nakan was reversing her change without her consent. The blue of the House of Grace crept up her leg as he slammed her down to the ground, knocking the wind from her. He ducked a slash from Putra and swerved around Zhaddi's jaws, keeping his grasp of Enos' leg.

"You, new recruit, will not escape," he said. He wasn't even breathing hard. Nakan dodged around the other Aridori's attacks as he dragged Enos away from them by the ankle. Enos twisted, snarling though she knew how the expression must look: rabid. Out of control.

She fled back into the House of Healing, trying to make her skin slippery—a key and chord change—but the blue of the House of Grace swirled around her change, preventing it. How was Nakan doing that when he couldn't even hear her House?

"You, new recruit, you will not shame me more," Nakan said. He brought the strange knife again across Enos' belly in a swift sweep.

Light flared in Enos' mind, and the Symphony broke into jagged, discordant shards.

CHAPTER SEVENTEEN

Passage to Time

- The House of Time differs vastly from the other houses of the Maji. For one, the music of Time cannot be controlled as easily as Communication, Grace, or Potential. It is less discernable to those existing inside it and thus it requires vastly more notes to make changes. Further, as time passes, portions of a change become irreversible. The notes of a prophet are precious, and we must accord their utterances utmost importance.

From notes of Wor Wobniar, Prophet of the House of Time and pruner of the Nostelrahn species

As Sam left the Effature Vaevicta with Inas, she reached out for his friend—his *boyfriend's*—hand. Sam pushed away a surge of hot jealousy at anyone else touching Inas, then was immediately embarrassed by his reaction. They were both Aridori. Inas needed support Sam couldn't provide. The Effature surely had advice to help him control his shifting. Inas was no longer wildly changing, but it was as if there was something else inside, fighting to get out.

He watched the Effature's slender fingers intersperse with Inas', and his stomach roiled. He would not be jealous. The fingers of that hand were longer than those of Inas' other hand. He wasn't fully recovered, and the Effature could help him.

"This way," Wor Wobniar said. Xy scuttled toward the doorway leading from the enormous building, one of xyr head flaps pointing toward Sam and the other two toward the exit. Sam moved slowly, looking back as often as possible. The old fear rose, now Inas was not by his side. He felt in his vest for his pocketwatch. He'd only touched it once since coming to this facet—less than usual.

Have to stray strong. Inas needs time alone with one of his species.

The Effature cringed as she probed Inas' arm. Their hands were clasped so tightly their skin looked as if it was flowing together. The protectiveness flaring in him almost made Sam sick. He wanted to be there, holding Inas' hand, but he couldn't. His own problems tugged at him. Like the House of Time.

Focus on landmarks. Make a map. He hadn't had to do that in a while.

Wor Wobniar was tapping xyr feet impatiently. Sam was moving too slow. He leaned against a column, trying to absorb its solidity, then moved from pillar to pillar toward the exit. Wor Wobniar was already there and waiting. Two of xyr arms clacked their claws together in irritation.

"I'm sorry," Sam said when he reached her. One last look back at Inas, absorbed in what Vaevicta was telling him. "I get...uncomfortable in unfamiliar places when I don't have someone I know around." It seemed like he explained that to everyone he met, which meant he was meeting people and getting out. Someone had told him to do that. Was it his aunt?

The thought nagged at him as lights flashed across Wor Wobniar's head. "The House of Healing is good for this, yes? It can soothe away chemical problems in being."

Sam raised an eyebrow. Majus Ayama hadn't wanted to use that method on him. "I prefer to work through it. Chemical method works for some people, but I don't react well with medication. It makes it hard to think straight."

"And you *can* work through it?" Wor Wobniar asked.

Sam paused. Not at the moment. He straightened his shoulders. He'd do better. "Yes. I'm working through it."

Wor Wobniar waved xyr head flaps in a shrug. "Seems such a defect can be extracted from a species with enough genetic preparation. But then, you differ from a Nostelrahn. I assume you do not have the pruner gender as we do. It is very effective at propagating the species in an acceptable direction." Xy turned to the opening in the wall, leaving Sam shaking his head at the callous suggestion of eugenics.

Do Nostelrahns really do that?

But then, Wor Wobniar referred to xyrself as a 'pruner.' If the gender role was what the Nostelrahns did as naturally as humans had children, or Benish budded, or Lobhl did...whatever they did to have children, then perhaps he shouldn't judge.

Outside, the wall of the Nether loomed close to the edge of the building and Sam took in a deep breath. He stared at the ground instead of into the wall's infinite depths. He'd get vertigo from looking up.

"You hesitate," Wor Wobniar continued, lights flashing and changing on xyr head, xyr multiple jaws grinding together. "The only one to be of the House of Matter in countless centuries suffers from an affliction of anxiety. You will have difficult trials ahead of you even without this disadvantage."

That made Sam look up, and he welcomed the heat that blossomed in his face and chest, forcing the panic into the background. "It's not a disadvantage—not one I can't handle. Have you made a portal so big it can fit half of that building inside it?" He gestured back the way they had come. "I do just fine."

Wor Wobniar's head flaps twisted and curled—in thought, the Nether supplied. "I see. Persistence can be as essential as skill. Then perhaps you are ready to visit the House of Time."

Sam threw one hand out. "Lead on." He tried not to growl the words.

Just what I need. The only person who can teach me about this weird new House is condescending and narrow-minded.

Wor Wobniar scuttled forward, reaching xyr two forward arms to touch the crystalline surface of the wall. There wasn't much in the narrow strip of ground between the Effature's palace and the wall, only the two massive edifices and a line of spiky white succulents growing between.

Sam frowned. This wall was at a different angle than the one they traveled through from the bridge to the city. He looked to his left, along the crystal surface, and in the distance he could see the other wall's bulk. This facet's Palace of the Effature was also located at a corner made of two walls. It was a popular building location with the excess light.

"The House of Time is this way," Wor Wobniar said. "You saw how we passed through before, yes? Can you do this?"

"Through the wall?" Sam asked. "I have to change the Symphony of Time to go through?"

Wor Wobniar directed all three head flaps at him. "You have demonstrated your ability in the House of Matter on the bridge. Now, let us try your other house. Listen for the changes I make in the Symphony." He was being tested.

The melody of his surroundings was in his head all the time now, but Sam focused on the chiming music of the wall—overpowering this close, like standing in a church while the bells were ringing. He concentrated and heard a second theme with a more deliberate feel, as if created. It wove its way between the thunderous chimes, creating space between the notes, lengthening the moments between seconds. Wor Wobniar's body was suffused with a silver glow.

"I can hear what you're doing," Sam said. "But I don't know what you're making. How does this help us pass through the wall?" Majus Cyrysi prefaced everything he taught with a big speech about what it did.

"Pay attention," Wor Wobniar said, still weaving notes through the melody. "Follow this composition to its obvious conclusion, and try your own variation."

Sam closed his eyes and reached for the core of his being, taking notes from his twisting inner spiral of music to create a theme like the one Wor Wobniar made. It wasn't exactly the same, or the Grand Symphony would push back, resisting the change happening more than once.

How did he adjust the House of Time rather than Matter? How did Majus Cyrysi determine whether he affected Communication or Power?

It's all part of the Grand Symphony. We just hear different aspects.

He wasn't sure that helped, but he persisted, placing notes in a sequence similar, but not too similar, to Wor Wobniar's. Rather than weaving through the chiming chords, he waited deliberately for the spaces where the notes were not, and let his notes take root. His composition was strange, a thing with as much silence as music, played in brief bursts.

"Look at yourself," Wor Wobniar said. Sam didn't question how the Nether translated flashing colors into speech when his eyes were closed. His brain would hurt and he was spending too much effort on his composition.

He opened his eyes and gasped at the metallic glow around his arms and torso. Silver, not gold. He'd changed the notes in only the House of Time.

"How...?" he asked, but Wor Wobniar was already twisting xyr head flaps to cut him off.

"You adapt quickly. This is good. Follow me and all will be explained." Xy scuttled forward and the crystalline wall resisted only a moment before the Nostelrahn passed through like a wet finger through a soap bubble.

Sam pressed one silver-outlined hand against the wall—he could see Wor Wobniar inside—and the colors of the houses swirled away from his fingertips. He pressed and the cool crystal of the wall pushed back. It was solid, impossible to walk through. Then as with his composition of jerky silence, his fingers found spaces in the solid wall and melted into the crystal.

Sam stepped forward into the Nether wall. Before his head entered, he took in a long breath by instinct, holding it as his face submerged.

Inside the wall, all was quiet. In front of him Wor Wobniar floated. The crystal was more like water than a solid.

Panic crested like a wave as Sam looked forward, up, and down. Inas wasn't here, and the wall extended in all directions, putting him adrift in the middle of a sea of nothingness. Imperfections and facets of crystal reflected distorted images. There was another anomaly up ahead, breaking the featurelessness of the Nether wall. He had no idea how far away it was. As easy to judge the distance to an island when stuck in the middle of a stormy ocean. Sam couldn't breathe in the wall, but his body didn't feel the need.

If I can't breathe, I can't hyperventilate.

The Nether itself wicked away his panic, though his heart pounded, and he clasped his hands together.

How can I move my arms while inside a crystal? No, don't think about it.

Wor Wobniar was already—walking? scuttling? drifting?—along, getting farther away. Like a corona of multi-hued lightning, the colors of the houses struck and reflected along imperfections. Green, blue, and orange arced toward him. Yellow, white, and gold found paths reaching up and forward, while brown and silver buzzed around like trapped hornets.

Sam put a leg forward as if walking, and he moved forward.

As he got used to the lack of sensations—smell, sound, and touch— his ears registered deep, thumping beats. They might have been echoes of happenings outside the wall, but here they sounded like heartbeats. They mirrored Sam's, save larger, as if from a gigantic animal.

The Symphony was loud inside his head, with nothing to distract from it. It penetrated him, flowing around and through, part of him. And finally, finally, he heard the music he'd been searching for over the last couple months—those sounds defining his being—his impact in the Grand Symphony, like seeing the back of his head in a mirror. These were the notes he'd changed in the ruined city of Dalhni, forcing his panic away.

Sam reached for the dissonant percussion of his anxiety, keyed louder than it had any right to be. It would take a permanent change to bring the music into equilibrium, and he still hadn't completely recovered from what he'd done at the Dome of the Assembly. He shifted notes in his composition, bringing the volume down a fraction. His heart slowed. His legs moved quicker through the crystal. If he'd been able to breathe, he would have let out a sigh.

But there was a void where those notes had been.

How many more can I use? Can I dampen my anxiety permanently?

Just a few more.

He lowered the volume again, and suddenly there were more themes audible in his music, as if his anxiety drowned them out.

He reached for the music, wondering what it could be.

Flashes.

His Aunt Martha cooking cheese hominy for breakfast.

Aunt Martha showing him how to sew.

His father, working in his shop.

His mother, teaching him how to climb trees.

He could remember their faces.

The voice hadn't taken his memories away completely. It had hidden them. He had to find the rest, but had no more notes to spare. The void in his core ate at him. Later. He would find this place again later.

He followed the Nostelrahn for what seemed like hours, tears dripping down his cheeks. Maybe it was minutes? It was impossible to say. The Nether supplied everything his body required, but he couldn't ask Wor Wobniar where they were going or what they would do. He simply reveled in those few memories. He remembered his parents and Aunt Martha, though what had happened to them was still vague. They had all died, hadn't they? Was he to blame? He still couldn't remember enough of Earth to return, and he doubted he ever would. But there wasn't anything left for him there, while here...Enos and Inas were here.

The prophet's head flaps faced forward and xy moved through the wall gracefully, like a fish slipping through the water. They were getting closer to the anomaly, which took up more of his vision.

Finally, Wor Wobniar's form shimmered, xyr silver aura sliding around facets of the crystal, and xy stepped down and turned, xyr three pointed feet doing a complex dance. Sam splayed one hand out against the edge of the Nether wall, but from the inside. There was a void or bubble, but *inside* the wall, completely enveloped by crystal. It was filled with vines and green, blue, red plants, and there was some sort of structure. Sam pushed through and out of the wall, stumbling forward.

His lungs complained and he blew out the stale air he'd taken in before entering the wall, then sucked in a giant breath, leaning forward with his hands on his thighs. He straightened and wiped his eyes, catching the Nostelrahn's head flaps all focused on him.

"It is a strange experience the first few passages through the wall," Wor Wobniar said.

"I...yes, it is," Sam said, once he'd gotten his breath back. "Where are we?"

The Nostelrahn opened all three arms, scuttling around in a circle. "This is the House of Time—placed where only one *from* the House of Time has access. I have been the only member since my mentor became one with the web, seventy cycles past."

Sam pulled his composition to the core of his being, standing straighter, regaining most of his notes. Part of that change had been permanent. He'd lost more notes in the other change, but those were fully worth the cost. He could remember his family's faces.

His silver glow faded.

"Walk this way," Wor Wobniar said, and gestured toward the building—like an ancient stone temple, covered in vines and flowers. "It is comfortable inside."

Sam followed xyr, sorting through returned memories. The space inside the wall was not large, a sphere like a giant terrarium inside thick glass. Plants grew wild across the ground, and even hung from the curved ceiling. It was cozy, especially if Sam ignored the depthless emptiness of the translucent wall. He stepped over a vine as thick as his thigh as they approached the building. Inas would have loved it here. He had a small shelf of plants in Majus Caroom's apartment.

"The House of Time, like the other houses," Wor Wobniar said, "can affect more than what its name implies. The change I made—and which you copied—compressed our bodies' experience of travel through the wall. Any other majus trying to reach this spot must turn back or perish in the wall from lack of sustenance. The Nether will support a being as long as possible, but there are limits."

"The maji mentioned that," Sam said. "But they said maji can only pass through the columns."

"Correct." Wor Wobniar pulled back a curtain of hanging vines. "Many aspects of the House of Time are non-reversible. We must be careful how we use our notes. We can compress and extend our experience for a few minutes and recover our music. Any longer and we will lose it."

"Non-reversible. I see," Sam said. Then what he used to regain his memories would not return to him. How much could he risk? He'd try again later, when he had more time. Some of what the voice took away might be gone forever. Still, he felt more centered than in days. He could learn this.

At the entrance to the temple of the House of Time Wor Wobniar clacked in a circle to face him. "I am the prophet of the House of Time," xy said. "There is an unbroken line of prophets in our facet, reaching from the time of the last Dissolution, though information has been lost over the centuries. Your facet," xy gestured to him with one claw, "must have lost its prophets and the House of Time at some point, or your Effature would have known more of the Dissolution."

"The Aridori War," Sam said. From what he knew, it was the most calamitous event in his facet of the Nether.

My facet. As if I've lived there longer than about two months. But before that is still hazy.

Wor Wobniar nodded. "That is likely."

Sam waved his hands, palms out. "So why me? Why the Houses of Matter *and* Time?"

"One of the oldest pieces of information we have," Wor Wobniar said, the lights on xyr head flashing a complex pattern, "is a scrap of information on the House of Matter. No one knows the physical location, but there are fabled to be artifacts of exquisite power inside. Those of the House of Matter may once have been as numerous as the other aspects of the Grand Symphony."

Xy climbed two steps, then turned back. "I suspect many of those ancients of the House of Matter were also attuned to the House of Time, though the reverse is not true. It is why I can teach you, at least of Time."

Sam frowned. "Matter and Time sounds like a powerful combination." Perhaps connected to the lines he saw and knowledge of how events would occur?

"Yes," Wor Wobniar said. "Of the House of Matter, come inside and we will find what we can."

Sam followed the Nostelrahn's tiptoeing steps over vines growing across the steps into the building. He traced a finger along the pitted stone as he passed. It was old and volcanic, like pictures he'd seen of Hawaii. The thought of Earth brought a tightness to his throat. He could remember pictures and places, but not enough detail to make a portal. His home was here, in the Nether.

"How old is this place?" he asked, to distract himself. The bubble inside the Nether was close and comfy, though it contained a stone temple.

"I do not know," Wor Wobniar answered, turning so the flashing lights across xyr head were visible. Xyr serrated jaws ground in time with the lights. "It stores every piece of information from the House of Time. As far as I know, this building could have stood since the last Dissolution, or longer." The walls of the temple were thicker than Sam's arm was long.

Inside, there were hanging orange lights, which Sam recognized. They were majus-fueled lights, made from the Houses of Power and Potential. The same type illuminated the interior of the Spire of the Maji.

The building was one open room with a high ceiling, several stories above, and the lights cast long shadows across rows of shelves and stands holding items made of metal, wood, stone, and crystal. To his sides were racks of cubbyholes, each one holding a rolled sheet of sheer material. The shelves rose into the gloom of the ceiling, eight or more times his height.

Wor Wobniar spread xyr arms in three directions, claws clicking as xy gestured to the shelves and stands. "This is the collected knowledge of the House of Time." Xyr head flaps oriented on Sam. "You are the first I have shown this to. I have been the only one here since my mentor joined the web."

Sam's eyes roamed the interior. It was large, impressive, and ancient, but with a feeling of something hidden. He counted. Even if each cubby held a scroll or two of great importance, there didn't seem enough to account for thousands upon thousands of cycles. He was used to the data storage of computers. All this could have fit on one disc.

"This is...this is it?" he asked. He didn't want to give offense, but the chances of him finding meaningful records pertaining to his situation was low. He didn't think every answer of the Houses of Matter and Time would be laid out in front of him, but...

Wor Wobniar's mouthparts grated in a rough laugh. "This is the House of Time. Wait." Xy held up one claw.

Sam waited, eyeing the blocks of pitted stone stacked with no space between.

Wait for what? What is xy not telling me—

A wave of silver washed through the temple, leaving him dizzy. The blocks of stone were in the same places, yet not. Seams were at different heights. Colors were subtly changed. He stared at the Nostelrahn.

"Each cubby holds many scrolls, though not all are accessible at the same...time." Xy glanced around. "This iteration may hold for the next few minutes, or even a lightening. It is one of my favorites." These stone blocks were lighter, and a few gleamed with reflective material caught in their structure.

"I see." The weight of the collected knowledge pressed against Sam. Even the Symphony seemed more complex, with little ditties and solos spinning off from the main melody to spiral into their own music. It was playing faster than before the change. He bent his knees without thinking, his shoulders weighed down, his breathing becoming fast and deep.

"It's a lot," he said. "I can feel the age."

"It hits people differently at first," Wor Wobniar said. Xy waved a claw at a pair of stools set in front of a slab of stone. "Sit if you need, and get your bearings."

Sam did so, and breathed a little easier. It wasn't exactly a panic attack, but similar. His eyes wandered around the room. The scrolls must have been this facet's equivalent of books, though made of an unfamiliar fabric. He sat as Wor Wobniar busied xyrself in various nooks, picking up this scroll and that, searching through them and ultimately rejecting them all.

Then another curtain of silver passed, leaving Sam's stool wobbling in a different direction. This time, artifacts glinted from several shelves, and he realized many were made of Nether crystal. There was almost a physical weight in the building, pressing down from the history and records sitting silently in rows and columns. It had the feeling of a cathedral, dark, shadowy, and ageless.

"This place can teach me of the House of Matter?" he asked.

"I am certain there is information in one of the iterations," Wor Wobniar said. "There is plenty on the House of Time. Ah. Fortunate we are here now." Xy scuttled to a shelf now containing artifacts, xyr head flaps waving like a fish's fins. "I believe this iteration holds it. It has been here since my mentor... Ah. Here." Xy plucked something up in one claw and scuttled back to Sam. "This will help."

Sam accepted the object, which was warm to the touch. It was translucent, made of Nether material, and shaped in part like a ring, though with a section missing, like a "C". He slipped it on a finger. It fit, with other little nubbins cradling the fingers next to that one.

"What is it?"

"A focus tool." Wor Wobniar was silent for a moment. Lights flashed across xyr forehead, but the Nether didn't translate them. Then, "This belonged to my mentor, one of the Praveadi—the purple beings you saw." Xy gestured with a claw. "Ey taught me much, and one of ey's final acts was to take off the focus, shortly before ey left this reality. As far as I know, there are only two of these tools. You have some in your facet?"

The ring of crystal suddenly felt very heavy on Sam's hand. A promise. A burden. A responsibility. "I don't know where they would be." Around them, the House of Time wavered again, and these stones were black as night, sucking in what little the majus lights produced.

"Then you will need this one," Wor Wobniar said. Sam could hardly see xyr. "It aids in our perception of the *Vloeinkaal*."

"You've said that word before," Sam said. "What is it?"

Wor Wobniar waved xyr head flaps in thought. "It is like...a web of time. A sequence of cause and effect. A pool where an outcome may or may not happen. It is complex."

Sam sat up straighter on the little stool. It didn't wobble anymore. "Does it look like translucent lines, connecting everything together?"

The Nostelrahn's lights all flashed, in surprise. "You have encountered this already? It took me many cycles to separate it from the Symphony." Xy scuttled closer. "Perhaps because you perceive both the Houses of Time and Matter? We must study this."

"It was only for an instant," Sam said, "and it's only happened a couple times. I can't see it on purpose."

"Still, it means you are well-tuned to the House of Time."

"And the House of Matter?"

Wor Wobniar settled on xyr tripod of legs. "That is more difficult."

"Do you have a directory of information?" Sam asked. Another wave passed through—the last several had come quickly, one after another, as if the House of Time was showing off—and Sam squinted in the renewed light. There was a difference in this iteration, like a crack in the wall poured light through from elsewhere. Cataloging this place might well be impossible.

"The thirty-second prophet listed the information and artifacts in many of the iterations, though not all," xy replied, "and some scrolls have been moved since then. Still, it is a start."

Sam didn't want to ask the next question, but it boiled out of him. "How...how long will this take? Enos is still captive, and there are important events coming in my facet of the Nether. Inas and I need to get back..."

Wor Wobniar's head flaps oriented on him. "You must train for when the Dissolution arrives. Look around." Xy gestured to several cubbies in the temple and now Sam saw the scrolls there were...flickering, as if they didn't know whether they belonged in this reality or not.

"You see this?" xy asked, and Sam nodded. "One of the signs I reported to the Effature. The Dissolution is closer than it should be, interfering with the flow of time. I suspect that is why you have arrived here now."

"Like fate?" Sam asked. He didn't like an unknown force controlling what he did. "I came to the Nether by accident."

Wor Wobniar stood motionless. If xy was human, Sam thought xy would be staring off into the distance. The scrolls stopped flickering.

"Interesting. I suspect you will learn more when you can look into the *Vloeinkaal*. It told me you were here. It said the chime would ring and our facets were moving close enough together to cross. It pointed me toward the bridge between our facets, unused for more than a thousand cycles."

"Did it tell you *what* the Dissolution is?" Sam asked. "I've heard the name, but no explanation."

Wor Wobniar's head flaps fluttered. "It is a change to the entire universe, recomposing the Grand Symphony all at once, though perhaps an occasion we may live through? An end and a beginning at the same moment. That is all I know."

Sam frowned. Another event no one knew about. "What if Inas and I stay a day or so?" he suggested. He had to help find Enos. "Then we must go back to our facet." This was supposed to be a meeting between representatives. Except now Wor Wobniar wanted to keep him here and train him. If it was anything like what Majus Cyrysi did, it would be a matter of ten-days, months, or even cycles, instead of days.

"Hm. You will need to come back."

"Or you could come to our facet."

"That could happen." Wor Wobniar scuttled close, until Sam could smell xyr strange, spicy scent. "Make no mistake, the Dissolution is approaching faster than any of us anticipate. It should not be here for thousands of cycles yet, but the *Vloeinkaal* proclaims it to all who can perceive its wrongness."

Once again, the House of Time flickered and changed around them in a flash of silver.

Construction and Activation

- Our reality is not as simple as it appears. We well know there is a sequence of mathematically related vibrations underlying the fabric of reality—maji can tap into these to produce effects outside of normal physics. But though the maji claim dominance in this field, precious few go further than that. Are there other Grand Symphonies fueling different universes? Are there themes we are not yet aware of? This is what the Society of my youth protected against—the unknown unknowns. The older I become, the more I appreciate both the danger and the opportunity of these hidden safeguards.

Personal journal of Mandamon Feldo, Councilor for the House of Potential

"You really need all this old stuff for your device?" Gompt asked. He poked through a rack containing capped beakers of chemicals while Krat tapped her feet. Mandamon wasn't completely certain how Krat sensed things. The System Beast had no visible head or hands. But Krat seemed well aware of her surroundings.

The group had taken a quick break to get a midday meal, then met back at the abandoned house, and the tunnels beneath.

"It is hard to say," Mandamon said, and Gompt's head snapped up to watch him. His bright blue eyes bored into Mandamon from behind his glasses. "My plans for the device will work in theory, but to bring the design to fruition will take work. It will not be easy to usher a three-house majus back to this reality."

"That sounds ominous," the Festuour said. "I've seen you with a plan before. It's usually several cycles of effort, and lots of pain and suffering."

"This one will likely be no different." Mandamon raised his voice to get the others' attention, who were still poking around the detritus left from the previous Society. "If have finished your evaluations, I have an announcement."

<I am c-curious what you have in mind,> Touching Digits signed. <It still seems a strange time to revive the Society.>

"Not so strange," Mandamon said. "Between our ranks, we cover all six of the houses, in several combinations."

"Will any of our skills matter against the strength of a three-house majus, which you say is a source of great power? I assume such a being might have their own ways of returning to this universe," said Laryn I'Hon. Hir large eyes missed nothing.

"Indeed. Yet they contacted Slithen the Dreamer for aid, and I suspect the Dissolution draws near. I believe they might offer their help—but they need this to arrive." Mandamon grunted as he bent to retrieve a cylinder from a corner of the underground space. He unlatched it to produce the set of schematics he'd tucked safely out of sight. "I've had related concepts stored away for many cycles, but the Life Coalition's emergence, the talk of the Dissolution, the Aridori, and one strange young man led me to combine several ideas."

Gompt tugged the rolled sheaf of papers out of his hands and began flipping through them. He grunted. "You've made some improvements to the parts I recognize."

At a squawk from Krat, Gompt waved the papers over the arms and the tops of the legs, which seemed to satisfy her.

"Symphony may take exception to this design. Might also have unanticipated effects on local space-time," the Symphony Beast said. The two young Methiemum maji traded glances, and Touching Digits leaned forward, trying to get a look.

"There will be enough perturbation of the Symphony, if the Dissolution truly approaches faster than normal," Mandamon said. "A little more will do nothing."

"Perhaps not nothing," Laryn said. Zie had one sheet from Gompt and was studying it. "But then, not enough to matter, as you say." Zie looked up. "How long do we have to build it?"

Mandamon shrugged. "How long until the end of the universe? Sooner than we like. But if we work together, I think we can create a prototype in a month or so. I have waited too long, dealing with the politics of the Council. The faster we have a working prototype, the better."

"What exactly will this thing do?" asked the young female Methiemum—Emma. "Search out your mystical three-house majus?"

"Not precisely. Think of it as opening a door and inviting something through. We must assume the three-house majus waits on the other side," Mandamon answered. "So now we test our hypothesis. In fact Sam—the young man—gave me the idea to return to this project."

<How is t-that?> Touching Digits asked.

"He made me question the origin of the Methiemum. One who is biologically of the same species appears from a homeworld none of us have heard of. With so much lost in the Aridori War, I wondered what else has been hidden. What did the previous Dissolution change?"

"The previous Dissolution?" Gompt asked. "Wouldn't that have happened thousands of cycles ago, if the tales are true?"

"Tens of thousands or millions, more likely," Krat said.

"We do not know the exact time. It is our principal problem," Mandamon said. He spread his arms, palms out, to quiet the others. He was getting too old for this. "However, new technology I've dabbled in with Methiemum businessmen gives us the ability to date the life of certain objects. It takes a few notes from the House of Potential, and one can trace the ancestry of the elements in an item."

<What d-does this have to do with the Dissolution, or am I confused?> Touching Digits signed. His fingers bounced off each other as he signed.

"We've done preliminary tests on the oldest sites of Methiemum architecture and artifacts we could find. None are over fifty thousand cycles old."

"Then the Methiemum began their technological development only fifty thousand cycles past?" Laryn asked. "It makes sense, considering how much your species loves to innovate."

Mandamon sighed, and knuckled a knot developing in his back. Too much time standing the past several days. The others gathered here— even Gompt and Krat—had not been party to his investigations over the past four cycles.

"A valuable point, but not the one I am making." He took in a deep breath, then let it out, and panned his gaze over the assembled two-house maji. "There is no piece of Methiemum remains, as far as we can find, over fifty thousand cycles old. No dwellings, no tools, no split rocks, no painted caves, no bones. Nothing." Now the others were frowning. Good.

"What are you saying?" Gompt asked. "Were there no Methiemum at all that long ago? Did you folks just spring full-fleshed from the trees?"

"Or appeared due to effect of Dissolution," Krat added. Gompt's furry muzzle opened, his lips making an "O" shape.

Mandamon waggled a finger at the System Beast. She truly had the same intuition as Kratitha. At some point he must talk with her about her progenitor's programming. Could it be duplicated? Should it?

"You see why I have concerns about events if another is on its way. Is fifty thousand cycles the length of this sequence? How can we know, if it removes all trace of what it does?"

<Yes. If this event can wipe an entire s-species' history, or transplant them, w-what did it do to the rest of us?> Touching Digits fingers jumped as he stuttered, his middle fingers meeting more often than they should.

"Indeed." Mandamon looked at the assembled two-house maji, all professionals near the top of their field, none prone to over exaggeration or susceptible to night-stories. "Therefore I propose to build a device capable of splitting the veil between this realm and others that may exist." He waved a hand toward the sheaf of papers.

"Where the Life Coalition failed, we will succeed. We will invite a three-house majus who has transferred to another reality—one where I hypothesize the Symphony is quieter, or runs at a slower tempo. One where that universe's Dissolution may arrive only after its inhabitants have lived out their entire species' existence. This device will hold the veil open long enough to bring them through to share what they've learned. Perhaps, as the Sathssn legends say, they will have a source of great power to be used against the coming Dissolution. And if not, they may show us what happened last time, so we may prepare."

* * *

Mandamon looked up, blinking, from the collection of wires he was soldering into place on the main board. His eyes were getting too old to see this detail. Several wires ran to tubes with a vacuum inside, which would help regulate the current into the device, only opening gates when required by the programming. Krat had been invaluable in designing that architecture over the last several ten-days.

They'd expanded the cavern where Mandamon stored the equipment so it would accommodate all seventeen of them and their workstations. This area was close to the floor of the Nether, and a section near one wall reflected their lights in a faceted spray of crystal. The house they were under was near the intersection of two walls of the Nether, which loomed over the city of Poler. He suspected the floor structure of the Nether was like a giant bowl. The center depth was located around Gloomlight and the surrounding lakes and swamps, the crystal covered by several times the depth of earth in the shallows near the walls.

Each two-house majus was working busily on their own section of the design, in accordance with the aspects of the Symphony they controlled. They'd had several successes, and more failures, but overall, the splitting device was coming along. While each part worked by itself, it was unknown whether his design would reach through the veil between this universe and another. Assuming that was even the correct place. Moortlin's notes were incomplete on where the three-house maji secluded themselves.

The only way to find out was to build it.

"Gompt," he called, and Krat spun around with a clicking of her little feet, bringing Gompt's head around to focus on him. His glasses were pushed far down his nose and he squinted at Mandamon for a moment before pushing them back up.

"What is it?" he asked. "I've almost got all these blasted logic gates fitted in order. Smaller than the tits on a tree-louse."

"I need three additional gates over here if you have—" Mandamon jerked upright as a deep, sonorous chime sounded, seemingly everywhere at once. "What, by Shiv's magnificent eyebrows, is that?"

The sound kept on, destroying any possibility of work until it ended. The two-house maji, picked for their sense of innovation and curiosity, were also harder to rein in than a pack of weasels. They scattered to map the sound. In truth, Mandamon was just as curious. He'd heard nothing like this in all his cycles.

<It appears to be c-coming from the Nether crystal itself> Touching Digits—female today—signed, her fingers fluttering in the stutter. She pointed at the section of exposed crystal floor, her arms roped with alternating hoops of brown and yellow. Mandamon could barely hear

her changes in the Symphony of Potential. She manipulated the vibrational energy around them as the sound passed through the air. He couldn't hear the other half of it—the part in the House of Communication—but he tucked the technique away for later trial.

"Any thoughts?" he asked as the sound finally died. It had lasted for several minutes. The others shook their heads. He had found little in either of the Symphonies of Potential or Healing.

"Sensors detect epicenter on other side of Nether," Krat grated. "Perhaps in Imperium." She was standing in the corner, all her legs touching the surface of the crystal, Gompt taking notes while perched on her.

"And it reached all the way here?" Gompt asked. "Underground, in a cave beneath Poler? That's a powerful signal."

Emma poked her head down through the hatch in the ceiling. "I couldn't hear it at all up here. I think the sound only emanates near the walls and floor. Maybe not even all of them."

"She's right," Laryn I'Hon added. "The walls and floor of the Nether passed the signal along with little resistance. I can tell that through the House of Strength."

"Hm." Mandamon pulled at his beard—which usually soothed him. Another disturbance in the Nether. Was this the first sign of the Dissolution, or merely a repetition of events so long in the past no one had records?

"No damage to the equipment?" There was a round of negatives. "Then we carry on. More reason to complete this project. If the phenomenon repeats, we will attempt more measurements."

* * *

The deep resonant chime repeated in an increasing pattern as the days went by. First it would skip a day, then occur every day, and then twice a day. Every time it rang, Mandamon felt pressure build within him to complete his project. Surely meeting a three-house majus would reward them with a font of information about the universe.

But despite his feelings, Mandamon didn't let the others go haring off on side projects. Much. They discovered the sound only happened near the floor of the Nether in this region, but not through the walls. One majus snuck back to the Imperium and reported it was much louder in that region. Everyone could hear the sound, and the entire city was wondering what it was. In Poler, located in the opposite corner of the Nether, no one could hear it except for them. The sleepy city kept on as it always had.

Mandamon would have investigated further if he dared, but he had a growing feeling it would matter if they finished construction sooner rather than later. Some inner clock in his subconscious was ticking down, to what he didn't know. There were occasional chords in the Symphony of Potential giving him a sense of massive gears, turning beneath the surface of the universe, as if the Nether itself was reconfiguring to a new state, opening some door.

His design grew from day to day as they collected components, added notes to the complex System driving the algorithm, and tested aspects of the program. Acquiring the parts was another matter, often requiring trips to remote locations on Methiem, Festuour, and Loba, and one memorable trip to the floating city of Parasmenia, in the Sea of Fire, on Etan. It was the only location in the ten homeworlds that produced a crystal with just the right resonating parameters.

After a ten-day, they tested the dimensional tearing. Mandamon wanted to call it dimensional *shifting*, but Gompt was insistent.

"It tears the wall between dimensions, so we're gonna call it what it is." The Festuour waved a hand to the other maji, most of whom were watching their exchange. "If we bring one of these three-house maji through, there will be records and artifacts left over. You want future scientists blindly stumbling into making a tear so big the universe collapses? No. So we're labeling it like it is, and I hope we'll remember to use some caution."

They called it dimensional tearing, but they still tested it.

"Bring in more power," Mandamon called to an older Methiemum majus. "We're almost there!" He lowered his goggles. Gompt had insisted everyone have a pair.

With another surge of electric current, The Potential of the System rose to an exultant hum. "That's it! Gompt—throw the switch."

Krat scuttled to a giant switch on the wall and Gompt, his hands ringed in the blue of the House of Grace, hesitated, then lowered the lever. It was just as important to know *when* to activate it.

The half-constructed device, like the skeleton of a sphere, vibrated in the middle of the room, and collectively, the maji took a step back.

Mandamon peered through his goggles into the brightness in the center of the cavern. It was nearly as brilliant as the walls at midday—not that they knew what time it was down here.

"It's working!" he cried. "I can hear the chords of potential energy buckling. Just a few more moments and—"

Something exploded in a shower of sparks and the nearby maji covered their heads. Touching Digits ran forward with a blanket to smother the flames.

"Well, we'll need to find another fuse capable of handling that much current—or more," Gompt grumped. "That one came all the way from a special forger on Methiem. It cost a month's worth of my savings, and I'm on a fixed income."

"Contact them again," Mandamon told his old friend. "And get it fast. In the next few days if you can."

"It'll cost," Gompt said.

"I'll pay it."

* * *

The chime had come three times a day for the last four days. Mandamon unclenched his fists as the latest faded away. He itched to discover the meaning of the sound—was the Nether crumbling? Was someone drilling into it with the new equipment that explorer had discovered? Was it a cry of pain or a call for unknown action?

But they were so close, and he suspected time was short. Those deep chords in the Symphony of Potential were rising in key each day. It gave him night-terrors about the Nether shifting, grinding the Imperium to dust as the crystal walls slid to new configurations. The other two-house maji who could hear the music of Potential were also reporting restless nights.

They spent the days until the new fuse was ready adding more safeguards to the System programming, though all of the maji agreed the prototype was basically finished. It was a task to keep them from each other's throats.

Mandamon pushed his glasses up and looked over the results from the last trial. The level of kinetic energy storage was strangely high, like it referenced a part of the Symphony none of them had access to. He'd shown it to the other maji, in case one of them caught the source, but none had. The resonating frequency was higher, too. He was certain this energy came from a previously hidden portion of the Grand Symphony—detectable as their experiments probed farther through the veil between universes. Was it coming from an unknown pocket where a three-house majus had concealed themself?

All they needed was the fuse.

The next day the chime rang all day, completely disrupting their plans. It grew so loud at times they couldn't even communicate, and they constantly had to re-calibrate the finer components of the device. The vibrations coming through the ground were just enough to knock things out of alignment.

When it stopped, they let out a collective sigh of relief. Touching Digits squatted over the exposed Nether floor and tapped a quick drumbeat on it with her fingertips.

"Check the alignment, quickly," Mandamon called as he climbed the ladder to the abandoned house above. He could at least see if the Nether was caving in.

It was not, but he met Krat scuttling toward him from the front door. "Do you have it?" he asked.

Gompt held up a bulky cylinder with thick trailing wires. "Got it."

* * *

It took the rest of the night and the next morning to check over everything once more, align the finer mechanisms, and set up protective barriers between the watching maji and the circle inscribed in the middle of the device.

For once, he'd had a restful few hours of sleep. The emanations deep in the Symphony of Potential had ceased. The Nether had finished the alignment it had started. It helped his nerves not a bit.

Mandamon followed a set of tubes with his eyes through a maze of connections and into the module holding the main System. The base of the device was half as tall as he was, triangle-shaped to concentrate the tearing energy. Above, a rotating ring extended outward into three upright arms reaching nearly to the cavern's ceiling. They hummed imperceptibly, tuned to an inharmonic chord. It was ready, and so were they.

Touching Digits came around, holding a stack of tiny vials and signing with one hand. <For luck,> she said as she handed one to Mandamon, Gompt, and to Krat. She continued around to the others.

Mandamon sniffed at his. A pleasant aroma rose from the vial, with hints of pear, sandalwood, and rose.

<To luck!> Touching Digits signed, and the others saluted back to her.

"To luck!" They downed their vials. It burned the back of Mandamon's throat, and he took in a deep breath.

"Turn it on."

They'd adjusted the startup sequence so it drew power slower than last time. Gompt and Emma controlled that aspect, while Touching Digits and Laryn regulated the current to avoid spikes in the flow. Gretahn, the young Sathssn, ensured the biological membranes did not overheat.

The upright arms in the middle spun around the focal point, and Mandamon listened for the Symphony of Potential's key change that would signal when the barrier between this universe and the next was breached.

This time, the fuse held when Gompt threw the switch.

"It's opening!" Mandamon called as he pulled his goggles down. The glow between the arms was brighter than the walls. It would have burned his eyes if they weren't protected.

<I see something,> Touching Digits signed. <There is a new theme in the Symphony of Communication. A presence may be trying to come through.>

"Power fluctuating!" Krat rasped, and Gompt reached for the controls, rings of orange flowing down his arms.

"Hold it together!" Mandamon called. There was a flurry of movement on the other side of the rotating machine. Shapes ran to correct variations in the equipment. But in front of him a doorway formed. At first it looked like a ball of off-white substance, completely smooth, like a malignant egg. Where had he seen an object described in that manner? The report had passed through the Council recently.

The thought flew from his mind as the sphere modulated, transforming as if it were a cell dividing.

"There's a funny hiccup in the power requirements!" Gompt called. "It's pulling more than the new fuse should allow, but it's still working—somehow!"

<There is energy arriving from the other side,> Touching Digits signed.

"The base process is degrading," Laryn shouted. "It's collapsing."

"Keep it steady!" Mandamon called. He took several notes from his core, tentatively placing them where the Symphony of Potential vibrated so fast it was in danger of fraying the melody.

The bubble in the middle of the rotating arms grew, then shrank, then divided into two and four and eight. It was like a mesh of soap bubbles, roiling as if boiling in a pot of water.

Then the bubbles smoothed, and peeled away from the focal point. For an instant, Mandamon glimpsed a shape, or figure.

Then it was gone.

The tear in their universe snapped shut, and an arm broke with an earsplitting *crack*. Maji scrambled out of the way as the rotating machine flung the appendage across the room, embedding its length in a wall.

There was silence, save for the grunt of Gompt's heavy breathing and the dying whistle of escaping steam. The device tottered, lopsided and bent past easy repair. A valve slowly deflated.

"What happened?" Mandamon said as soon as he could breathe.

"Everything was on target as far as I could tell," Gompt said.

<The machine says it was s-successful,> Touching Digits stuttered. She eyed the arm stuck in the wall.

"Then where is the three-house majus?" Laryn asked.

"Stolen," Krat grated.

"What do you mean?" Mandamon barked. "Stolen by whom? *Where?*"

"Readings report tear opened, but redirected to different place," Krat said. "Whatever came through is loose somewhere in this universe."

CHAPTER EIGHTEEN

Seeds Will Bloom

- In all my studies of the Drains, there is only one consistency, and that is that they are not to be consistent. Though I do not know the starting conditions, save the one in the Dome of the Assembly, each Drain has reacted differently. The one the twins told me of consumed most of a merchant caravan, then appeared to depart. The one in Dalhni was destroying the town's center—a much greater area—and then was reported to lift off into the sky. Others have been smaller in scope, such as the very first one I encountered on one of Methiem's moons. Is there to be any true prediction what a Drain will do, or will I be doomed forever to chase their aftermath? Perhaps there is an underlying meaning or mechanism to the Drains, and the destruction they enact on this universe is simply a side-effect?

From Personal Journal of Origon Cyrysi, Majus of the Houses of Communication and Power

Rey stepped through his portal from the bridge where they fought Nakan to somewhere dark and musty. There was a smell like old oil and rusted metal. He could hear the others shuffling around, and Majus Ayama taking roll. Majus Hand Dancer showed up from her canceled concert in High Imperium just as Majus I'Fon found a couple maji of the House of Communication to take care of the Effature. Majus Ayama had strong words for them about taking the old man to the medical ward attached to the House of Healing. Rey couldn't imagine him being gone. He'd been around forever.

She had finally relinquished her charge just as Rey thought he couldn't hold the portal open any longer. Then his mentor arrived with six of the Effature's guards, all Lobath, who happened to be patrolling near the base of the House of Communication, and they'd all gone through.

Rey took the notes of his composition back and the portal imploded, colors fading, though they hadn't illuminated the dark room. The light and color created by changes to the Symphony was funny like that. It didn't touch real life, as if it were overlaid on top. He exhaled in relief, as his exhaustion dissipated. After the precious minutes they'd taken to follow Nakan, he was surely long gone from here. Wherever here was. It was dark as a cave.

"Panen?" Majus Ayama called.

"I am here," the Lobath majus said. "I will translate our words for the guards, as we share a dialect."

"Ori?" Majus Cyrysi answered her. "Rey?"

"Accounted fer," Rey said, and the majus grunted. Rey took a tentative step toward the noises. There were metallic rattlings. He remembered the guards having swords. His feet felt like they pushed against the ground too hard, and he bounced like a rubber ball. The ground felt like either dirt or rock.

"Then we're all here. I would have liked more, but that's what we have."

"Where, hmm, *is* this?" Majus Caroom said.

"I suspect we are on the asteroid orbiting near Sath Home—the Life Coalition's last hideaway," Majus Ayama answered.

"Yet we are not engaging the Coalition, as we agreed?" Majus I'Fon asked. Zie sounded worried, as well zie might, after fighting Nakan. That Snakey was formidable. "They must have many soldiers, especially if they are all here."

"Not if I can help it," Majus Ayama answered. "Our best course is secrecy, for now."

Rey rolled his eyes. Who'd put her in charge? She was a majus like the others now, no longer a councilor.

"We must find Enos and secondarily Nakan, if he is alone. Once we have details of their hideaway, we'll come back with the full force of the Effature's guards instead of six."

Rey had to admit the plan was sound. Maybe there was a reason Majus Ayama had been on the Council.

"Can anyone be seeing an exit from this place?" Majus Cyrysi asked. "I am to be wondering if we have arrived in a closed pocket of this asteroid."

"My aim weren't that far off," Rey said. He'd placed the portal exactly where Nakan made his. The information he'd gotten from Majus

Cyrysi was jumbled, but also very complete. The other portals he'd practiced with Majus Kheena didn't have nearly as much context—they depended on familiar tags in the Nether, from Gloomlight to Poler, to several places out in the farmlands. After being here a lightening or so, he'd be able to make a portal on his own, without piecing it together from multiple sources.

"Me, I see there is more illumination in this direction." That was Majus Kheena's voice. Rey's mentor sounded shaken, with good reason. They'd met a new species, seen the leader of the Nether possibly assassinated, and learned of new Houses of the maji, all in one day. In fact, it was near night in the Imperium. Rey wondered how those living here told time.

"How can you see— Oh, Sathssn eyes process more wavelengths of light, don't they?" That was Majus Ayama again.

"This light, you cannot see it?" asked Majus Kheena.

<I can see a little, though I think not as much as you.> That was Hand Dancer, presumably waving her hands about. Rey tried not to think about the translation implications. Even worse, they were no longer in the Nether. Any translation happening was because the strange crystal had gotten in their heads. Rey shivered. Yes, it was useful, but anytime he thought about it, he got the creeps. His imagination had fuel in this pitch dark.

"Then Kheena and Hand Dancer in the front, with the guards behind them," Majus Ayama said. "Let us know if you see anyone. Be ready." Rey heard her shuffle and grunt, moving nearer and testing her footing in the reduced pull. "Anyone else see anything?" There was no response. "Right, then Caroom, Panen and Rey in the middle. Ori and I will bring up the rear—we have more experience with this sort of thing. Feel around and call out when you're in place."

Of course Majus Ayama and the old Kirian had done something *just like this* back fifteen cycles ago, when they'd tracked down the legendary whatsit of whocares... He wondered if anyone else got tired of their bossy condescension.

"Follow," Majus Kheena said, and Rey heard the scrabble of hard boots in a step too long for the majus' legs. It sounded like a slow jump.

The hallway they entered was just as dark, but Majus Kheena and Hand Dancer directed them forward.

After bumbling around for several steps, Rey was already sick of the charade. "Oy," he called. "Can anyone make a light? Anyone got a light on yer?"

"Either Hand Dancer or myself could be making light with the House of Power," Majus Cyrysi said from behind him, "This would be permanently taking some of our notes to achieve, and if we are to be encountering forces of the Life Coalition—"

"Eyah, I get it," Rey broke in. "Yer not wantin' to waste yer notes."

"I have, hmm, a set of flint and tinder if one of this group has a combustible object," Majus Caroom rumbled. They were bumping down the corridor with as much noise as a troop of drunk sand slinkers.

<There are torches on the walls.> The disembodied voice floated in Rey's mind like a memory of speech and he winced. He could just see Majus Hand Dancer's outline, like a ghost, as she stopped.

There was more fumbling and a spark of light, revealing Majus Caroom with a torch on one side. Rey turned to see Majus I'Fon's wide surprised eyes to his other side, next to the guards. The wari Lobath looked uncertain, though it was hard to know with a Lobath's perpetually unblinking eyes. Hir skin was clammier than the guards. At least they had one majus who could counter Nakan in the House of Grace, though Majus I'Fon hadn't been able to hold him on the bridge.

"Are you certain you placed the portal correctly?" zie asked Rey as their group continued down the corridor. There had only been one passage so far, with no branches, stretching from the dead end where the portal opened.

Rey tried not to sigh. "I'm certain."

"It is only I do not wish to be trapped in an unknown place, with potential enemies on all sides. The Symphony has several odd sub-themes demarking what appears to be highly volatile—"

"What's that?" Majus Ayama's voice rang out behind. A cross-corridor loomed out of the dark a few paces ahead, and as they quieted, they could hear footsteps. "Back, and hide the light."

Majus Caroom and Majus I'Fon shielded the torch with their bodies as the group shuffled and bounced back down the corridor. The guards pressed their swords to their legs to keep them from rattling. When Rey looked back, he saw another light growing. Soon a group of black-cloaked individuals passed perpendicular to their path. Not one turned their hood to look in their direction, but he imagined the other group's torchlight would have blinded them anyway.

Rey's mentor grumbled under his breath. Majus Kheena had his cowl back and shook his head. Rey caught the end of what he was saying.

"...deserve to wear the clothes of my people."

After they passed, Majus Ayama grabbed the torch from Majus Caroom and peered down the three directions available to them. "Forward, away from that crowd, or after them?" she asked. "Where would they keep Enos?"

"That group may be traveling toward some place with more people," Majus Cyrysi said. "Do we want to be going there?"

"And instantly be captured?" Majus I'Fon asked, between translating for the guards.

"We may be able to pry information from them if we capture one first," the guard leader said.

"Secrecy, remember?" Majus Ayama said. "Let's try to avoid noisy fights."

"That group, they may also be heading *away* from a concentration of soldiers," Majus Kheena added.

<We are six maji, an apprentice, and a small set of guards,> Majus Hand Dancer signed. Fortunately, Rey could see her hands moving in the light, so he didn't have to hurt his brain trying to figure out where the words came from. <Surely, we are able to confront a larger group of non-maji, or even a few maji, if it is necessary? If all here are agreeable to that path, of course.>

"We, hmm, at least know we are in the right place," Majus Caroom observed.

"We must keep our element of surprise," Majus Ayama countered.

"And another group will find us here dickering if we wait any longer," Rey said. "Why not keep our same direction thataway, until we all ken what's happenin' here?" He threw a hand out in front of him. "This place can't be *that* big."

"He is having a point," Majus Cyrysi said.

"Fine. We go straight for now. But we'll need to follow Coalitioners at some point, if only to find where they are keeping Enos," Majus Ayama said, and set off without even waiting for the others to agree.

They were forced to keep up as she half skipped through the cross-corridors and along their original path.

They bounced through rough tunnels without seeing any others and Rey counted away the minutes. He realized this place was much bigger than he'd expected. Enos could be anywhere, as could Nakan. If they'd traveled this far in the Nether, they would have run into someone else by now. So where were all the Life Coalition members?

"Should this group, hmm, split up to cover more ground?" Majus Caroom asked, a little later. "These ones may find both Enos and, hmm, Nakan with this strategy." They had passed several more cross-corridors, a large dead-end room, and a set of closed stone slab doors on either side of the corridor. The guards had volunteered to check them, but found them all deserted and disused, as if the Coalition had hollowed this area out cycles ago, then forgotten about it. Perhaps they had expanded their base, but how long had they been here to do so?

"No—stay together," Majus Ayama answered. Rey agreed, this time. No telling where all these passages led. "If we can find Enos, excellent. If not, we might find an armory or Nakan's room, to discover what kind of weapon he used. If we find nothing in the next lightening, we memorize coordinates for a future portal and come back with more reinforcements."

<Then we may determine a way to save the Effature from his injury?> Majus Hand Dancer added.

"Us, we must also discover the Life Coalition's reasons for what they do," Majus Kheena said. "For them, there must be a reason to go through this trouble disrupting the Assembly. Before they are destroyed, we must know why—oof!"

Rey's mentor ran straight into another cloaked figure, emerging from a cross-corridor. They must have heard the discussion and come running. The figure held a barbed club and swiped at Majus Kheena, who fell back.

Majus Ayama sprinted forward, the guards to either side of her with swords drawn, as more Coalitioners poured from the tunnel. A white and olive green aura erupted around the majus' arms and legs, and she was in the group's midst before Rey could even react, throwing punches and kicks like an angry dust storm. Cloaked figures grunted and fell, and metal clanged against metal in the confined space. Majus I'Fon was nearly as fast, and the wari Lobath went sliding around the group, which Rey could now see was ten or more strong. Some were obviously not Sathssn, by their height or width.

The pressure in the cavern dropped and Rey shook his head to clear it. Majus Cyrysi had both hands out, ringed in yellow and orange. Two more Coalitioners dropped to the ground. Rey hadn't even moved, and there were only a few left upright. Majus Ayama, Majus I'Fon, and the guards had taken out the rest.

The last two ran, yelling, and Majus Kheena growled, rings of brown coalescing around his hands. Rey heard his mentor change the galloping pace of the energy the fleeing Coalitioners put into the ground. The music became a soft echo of what it had been, and their steps grew smaller, as if the ground resisted them moving. Majus I'Fon caught up to them, and did something complicated with the House of Grace, waves of blue moving with hir arms. The two slumped to the floor.

"That were right impressive," Rey told his mentor. "I'll be usin' it in the future, if yer don't mind."

Majus Kheena gave him a long look. "In the Symphony, it is easy to be destructive. The most elegant changes are those that create."

"Still, it's right useful in a pinch," Rey said, and his mentor nodded reluctantly.

"Were we getting all of them?" Majus Cyrysi asked. He peered down the dark corridor where the group had emerged. "I am not seeing any other lights, but there may be a bend in the tunnel."

Majus Caroom was already picking up fallen Coalitioners, slinging one over each of their massive shoulders. The guards helped, pairing up to lift other prone bodies. "Then this group should, hmm, make certain these ones are not found," they said.

"Good idea," Majus Ayama answered. "I don't want to split our group to investigate if anyone got away. Best to move from here quickly, and hope the sound didn't alert anyone. There were doors around the last bend the guards said were empty."

After a minute of searching, Majus Hand Dancer signed, gesturing to a stone slab, propped open to reveal darkness. <This one is a room big enough for all of them.>

"Perfect. Put them in there," Majus Ayama said. "I'll make sure the ones still alive won't wake up for a bit." She touched each Coalitioner on the forehead, bestowing a ring of white and olive.

They pressed faster now, and Rey attempted to remember how many cross-corridors they had passed. How big was this place? It had been a lightening at least, maybe two, and they had seen nothing like the army that attacked the Dome, and no maji. Just two small patrols that could have been guarding the outskirts of the base.

"Oy, hows about bouncin' back the way that group came from?" he suggested. "This tunnel just keeps goin' and I think it curves a bit. Is it just a giant circle?"

"Me, I have noticed this as well," Majus Kheena said. "Perhaps the cross-corridors lead to the interior of this tiny homeworld and we are circling the exterior. This, it would explain why these corridors are mostly deserted."

"Which means there will be more Coalitioners that way," Majus Ayama said. She stopped at another crossing and looked down the dark tunnel. "This place is a maze. We won't stay lucky."

"Yer took care of that last group easy enough," Rey said.

"More encounters will, hmm, increase chances of this group's failure," Majus Caroom said.

Majus Ayama thumped a fist against the rock wall. "I need to find my apprentice," she said. "But if they overwhelm us..."

A similar frustration boiled up in Rey. He wanted satisfaction for Nakan's assault on the Effature. He'd been the one to finally open the portal here, and the Life Coalition was nowhere to be found.

"Ori—what do you think? Keep on or call it off?" Majus Ayama waited a moment, then snapped her fingers in front of the Kirian's lengthy nose. "Are you with us?"

Majus Cyrysi shook his head, his crest flaring. "I am to be hearing familiar chords. Since we stopped, I am finding it in both the Symphonies of Power and Communication."

<Will it keep us from turning away from this journey?> Hand Dancer signed. <Can you point the phrases out to me?>

Majus Cyrysi's hands rose, as if trying to cradle the air. "This music is reminding me of...the Drains."

"But the voids have, hmm, no melody in the Symphony," Majus Caroom said, and Majus Cyrysi made a face, his crest falling.

"I am knowing that, but it is familiar, still. Connected."

"Could it be linked to Nakan's knife?" Majus Ayama asked. "Is it their armory? Can I hear it, Ori?"

"I think you may," the old Kirian answered. "There is to be a strange subset of false harmonics lurking in both Symphonies I hear."

<Excuse me, but I can recognize this as well,> Hand Dancer signed. She had been turning different directions, waving her hands, since Majus Cyrysi first spoke. <It takes control from the principal theme of several melodies, but only for an instant. I have never visualized anything like it.>

Rey wondered how the Lobhl perceived the Symphony. The odd species did not hear well. The guards shuffled nervously at the maji's discussion. They wouldn't be able to understand without Majus I'Fon translating.

"I've got it," Majus Ayama said. "Oh, that is weird. I see why you say it's like the voids. It almost like the silence after one, but...not. It's different. I bet if we find it, we find how the Life Coalition created the voids, even if they've professed to change tactics. Perhaps it's close to where they keep their prisoners."

Rey turned inward, listening to chords of the Symphony of Potential. The structure of the music was off, but he couldn't place how. He hadn't learned all the advanced theory a full majus would know. He turned to his mentor. "Do yer hear it?"

"This disturbance, yes, I hear it," Majus Kheena said. "Listen to the reoccurring theme deep in the energy structures of the planetoid itself."

Rey concentrated on the music playing underneath reality. The more he listened, the more he found little incongruities popping up, where the music would dip into another key for a second, then be back to normal the next. In other places, it was as if there was a different piece of music playing over the Symphony, but he could only hear single notes from it—not enough to get a sense of what it was.

"One believes, hmm, it is stronger in this direction," Majus Caroom said. They stumped to the next cross-corridor and turned left. Majus Cyrysi was right behind, and Hand Dancer behind both of them, waving her hands like she was trying to play three different harps at the same time.

<The interruptions in the major theme are stronger here. Do you detect the missed fourth note in the chromatic scale?>

They were all hurrying now, no longer sneaking.

"Shiv's teeth!" Majus Ayama swore, and Rey nearly ran into her when she froze. "There's a different theme in the Symphony of Healing. Movement—a lot of movement—coming from that direction." She pointed to the left.

Rey looked down the passageway snaking away, and took in a quick breath as he saw a flash of torchlight.

"Us, we must have missed one," Majus Kheena said. "Stand and fight, or follow the discrepancy?"

"Away from the soldiers," Majus I'Fon replied. Hir breathing was ragged, hir rubbery skin sweaty. "If we are fast enough, we can lose them." Zie translated to the guard leader.

"Leave it to us," the guard said, and all six drew their weapons, standing their ground. "You must report what you've found to the Assembly."

Majus Ayama looked like she might argue, then gave the Lobath guard a little bow. "Go with Brahm."

Majus I'Fon translated and the guard saluted hir.

The maji took off down the corridor at a run and soon heard a clash of steel and shouts from behind them. The sounds contrasted with the disturbance in the Symphony.

Rey winced with the rest of them as a particularly discordant phrase interrupted the Grand Symphony. The disruption was growing, though he doubted it was because they drew closer. It battled against the organic frequencies, like someone was playing with the Grand Symphony in a way that wasn't natural, tearing a hole through the melody.

"Faster!" Majus Ayama urged. A light was growing behind them, and they could hear voices calling for them to stop.

"The guards were not successful," Majus I'Fon said, hir voice dropping in sadness.

"Let us hope they were to be captured," Majus Cyrysi answered.

"You, help me aid Majus Caroom," Majus Kheena told Rey. The Benish was stumping along, but falling behind. "Us, we will give their steps more energy." His mentor crafted a change in the melody as they ran, and Rey marveled at the finesse. He tried to make a parallel change, a different melody but achieving the same result. It was like what the majus had done to the fleeing Coalitioners, but in reverse.

They gave their chords to Majus Caroom, slowing as the Benish sped up. Rey pumped his arms, trying to run faster. The voices were getting louder, and this didn't sound like ten. It sounded like an entire squad. A troop. A company. The guards would have had no chance, but they might have delayed the Coalitioners enough for the maji to escape.

"This way!" That was Majus Cyrysi, his crest askew, as he turned a corner at speed, his robe rising to show off a glimpse of a spindly ankle. "The disturbance has a resonance in the Symphony in this direction."

The discord grew as Rey ran, gritting his teeth and panting. How could any majus stand listening to this noise? If it was the armory, no wonder it was far away from everyone who lived here. He'd be nursing a migraine if they stayed here much longer.

Majus I'Fon spun in place, running backwards, and flipped hir hands out, rings of blue cascading back the way they'd come, ice growing on the floor. There were answering yells behind them and the sound of falling. But there were regular footfalls too. That hadn't stopped all of them.

Another turn left, then one right. Majus Cyrysi pointed out each turn as they ran. The changes—corruptions—in the Symphony grew stronger. Rey wanted to cover his ears, but that wouldn't help.

"What is this racket?" he shouted. "Something from the Life Coalition?"

"No idea, but it can't be good," Majus Ayama shouted back. He wondered what the soldiers behind them thought, at them shouting over silence.

"It must be connected to how they are to be creating the Drains," Majus Cyrysi yelled back. His crest looked like he'd been struck by lightning. "Perhaps there will be a weapon."

They turned a last corner, and Rey almost plowed into Majus Caroom, halted in front of a stone slab embedded into the wall.

<It is behind here!> came Majus Hand Dancer's frantic signing.

With an echoing growl, Majus Caroom plunged their hands into the rock wall, spikes of green paving the way for their fingers. Sounds of tearing wood clashed with the shriek of metal and rock. The door broke into sections, falling away.

They piled through the opening, and Rey spun to see the Lobhl and Majus Cyrysi exchange words and signs before thrusting their hands out.

A wall of yellow and orange burst out from them, shimmering in the door like a webspinner's nest reflecting morning dew.

The voices behind them crescendoed and several dark cowls smashed into the solid wall of air. There was confusion, and yells and curses as their pursuers fell in a tangle of limbs. Several more stabbed at the seemingly empty doorway with pikes and swords, and Rey fell back. But the maji's shield held—for now.

"What in the name of all the gods—?"

Rey turned at the exclamation. Majus Caroom and Kheena were gawking.

The room was filled with flickering silver shards, which vanished and reappeared like snow crystals. They were the size of both of Rey's hands held together and hung in the air, all at different heights, as if they had never finished falling to the floor.

It was also a dead end.

"What is this?" he yelled. The music was like being in the middle of ten noisy orchestras, all playing different pieces.

"If I had to guess—" Majus Ayama began.

"Drain seeds," Majus Cyrysi called from the doorway. His head was half turned toward them, while his body faced the angry mob of Coalition soldiers blocking the only exit. "This is the method they were to be using to create the Drains. This is what we saw shot from the cannon at the Assembly."

"Why have those ones not, hmm, continued making the voids?" Majus Caroom rumbled, like trees creaking in a storm. "The Life Coalition has plenty of ability."

"Maybe they are waiting for a certain time, or event," Majus I'Fon called. Zie had hir long fingers in hir earholes.

"Look, here," Majus Kheena had one hand to a chart on the wall. There was a list of voids and dates, with lines connecting them interspersed with detailed coordinates.

"The void at the Assembly, it was the culmination of all others they created. Two on each homeworld. This, it is why they stopped. Them, they would have had to work again from the beginning, but the Assembly knows of their methods."

"Now that Sam moved their void," Majus Ayama added. "So these are extras, stored far away from the rest of the Life Coalition."

<Excuse me, but we have limited time to decide what to do before these soldiers break through our barrier,> Hand Dancer signed. A pike stabbed at the empty air above her head, but bounced off the wall of color. <Some have already left to alert others. Also, I feel I must question why the Coalition has asked to become part of the Assembly, and why they started acting with honor before attacking the Effature. This makes no sense.>

"They also kidnapped my apprentice, and are probably torturing her," Majus Ayama grumbled. "Which is why we need to find her."

"An' we may not get the chance, if we don't get out of here," Rey said. "Anyone else notice there's no other exit?"

"I believe it is the time to make a portal from here," Majus I'Fon announced, and held hir hands up, rings of blue running down hir arms.

"Not yet!" Majus Ayama called, but Majus I'Fon stumbled back from a pop of color.

"It won't open!" zie cried. The nearest seeds wobbled in their trajectories, drifting first closer to the Lobath and then away. Majus I'Fon shook hir head and took a hasty step back.

"Those crystals are, hmmm, interfering with the Symphony," Caroom rumbled. They twisted with a creak as a sword *pinged* off the doorway. "This group needs, hmmm, more options."

Rey looked to Majus Cyrysi and Majus Hand Dancer, both sagging under the continued abuse from the crowd of soldiers, and to the room full of glistening objects. There was an empty rack against one wall, and he pointed. "I'll bet my granddame this is where Nakan got that knife from." The others looked at him, and he ducked his head. "Just think. It makes no sense he'd attack when the Life Coalition is suin' for peace. So mebbe they're not all walkin' the same path." That made a lot more sense considering the talk he'd had with the leaders.

"Then you, you wish to explain this situation to those outside the door?" Majus Kheena asked. Rey hadn't heard his mentor snark so before.

"Majus Caroom wanted options. This is a place where they might be weak, eyah?" Rey opened his hands.

"I don't care what they think," Majus Ayama said, her voice ringing oddly off the hanging shards. "Every Coalitioner can go burn for all I care. I want my apprentice back, and I want to get out of here."

Majus Caroom stepped toward the two holding the door and landed a huge hand on their shoulders, the green of Strength flowing into them. Majus Cyrysi straightened, and the Benish stepped back. "Then what does this group, hmmm, do with this knowledge? How does this group leave? Is it possible to, hmmm, bargain with the Life Coalition for the return of Rilan's apprentice?"

"Still want to talk to them?" Majus Ayama asked Rey.

He grimaced. She didn't need to rub it in.

"Whatever it is we are deciding, I feel it will need to be soon." Majus Cyrysi's voice was strained.

"Can we throw a seed at them?" Majus I'Fon asked.

"Do not be touching them," Majus Cyrysi called. "We are not knowing what they will do."

Majus Caroom grunted, and extended one thick finger with a creak like a branch swaying in the wind. Where they pointed, behind the glimmering shards, was the metallic outline of a cannon. It was the one the Life Coalition had used to create the void at the Assembly.

"Well, we know these things'll create one of them voids, somehow," Rey added. The Kirian stared at him, and Rey waved a hand. "Fine, fine, I'll nay say anything more."

"No, I think you may be on to a solution," Majus Cyrysi said. His voice and crest were rising with excitement. He stepped away from the wall of air just as a soldier—a beefy Methiemum—threw his shoulder against it. Rey thought the mass of orange and yellow bent inward.

"You can't be serious, Ori," Majus Ayama called back.

"What else are we to be doing? We cannot leave through a portal. These soldiers will be tearing us apart before we have a moment to explain. And, we are having a member of each of the six houses here," the Kirian said, his crest wild. "This is how they were represented when they fired the one in the Assembly."

<You wish to set off a void here?> Majus Hand Dancer signed. The flip of their fingers denoted incredulity.

"A Drain may be destroying the other seeds contained here, and give us the leverage we are needing to escape. If it does not, we can be holding the seeds hostage, and threaten to set the rest off if they are not returning Enos and giving us Nakan." Majus Cyrysi was shouting over the yells of the soldiers and the discord in the Symphony. The disturbances were getting more frequent, and Rey waggled a finger in his ear.

"What about Enos?" Majus Ayama crossed her arms.

"We'll have a better chance of rescuing her than we do now," Majus I'Fon said.

"Before this group attempts anything, hmmm, hasty, perhaps these ones should determine why the fluctuation, hmm, in the Symphony occurs." Majus Caroom rumbled. "It will affect changes."

An aura of blue grew around Majus I'Fon again and the Lobath squatted close to a sliver, hir head-tentacles dangling. "There is a path connecting these pieces to the tremors in the Symphony," zie called over hir shoulder. "It is nearly complete—only a few notes missing. I believe we may be in danger of a void occurring here, even if we do nothing."

<Then is this melody deliberate to disrupt the Life Coalition? Who is creating it?> Majus Hand Dancer's signing was frenetic.

"Unknown, but I'm starting to agree with Ori," Majus Ayama said. "Enos is in as much danger as we are. The Life Coalition has never been honorable—ask anyone in Dalhni." She turned to Majus Cyrysi. "This is a chance to cripple them, if we survive. Ori, what do you think? Drains grow slowly, don't they?"

<I wish not to be a part of this. The choice is not one of integrity,> Hand Dancer signed.

"My integrity won't mean much if I'm dead," Majus I'Fon snapped.

Majus Cyrysi waved a hand. "We can be connecting the last part of the music between the discord and the Drain seeds here. The soldiers will be backing away at the sight—" He winced at the screech of metal on metal. They were attempting to dig through the wall. "And in the confusion we attempt to rescue Enos, and take Nakan, if possible." He looked around at the others. "Panen? Caroom? Kheena?"

Majus I'Fon rose from hir squat. "I have seen enough suffering from the hands of the Life Coalition, and we have few other options. If we can make them stop attacking for a moment, we may be able to get far enough away for a portal to open. I will help."

Majus Caroom's eyes glowed brightly for a moment as they thought. "One would normally never do such as this, but one was also at Dalhni. One has seen what the Life Coalition, hmmm, does when that group is not pushing for peace. One is also concerned about the effect of this disturbance on the Symphony."

"That's a yes?" Majus Ayama asked, and the Benish nodded their head with a snap and a creak.

Now the others looked at Majus Kheena.

"These people, they are my species, though some of them do wrong," he said, his voice pitched over the dissonance. He snuck a look at the doorway, still filled with dark cloaks and weapons. "They have come forward to talk, even if under strained circumstances. Sabotage, is this method really best? Is there no other option to negotiate?"

"Are you willing to risk your life for a chance to negotiate?" Majus Ayama asked, but Rey's mentor was already shaking his head.

"Me, I cannot, in good conscience, do this," he said.

Something swelled up in Rey and he stepped forward. "Then I will. They attacked the Effature. Whoever created all these weapons, they need to be taken down." He speared a hand at the floating seeds. "Mebbe out of what's left, will be sommun willin' to deal. Let's give 'em sommat to deal about while we find Enos." He looked around at the others, daring them to say anything.

"Then will this Drain be that much greater, when it is absorbing all the other Drain seeds?" Majus Cyrysi asked. No one had an answer. "We may need to push with extreme force if the soldiers do not move when the Drain opens."

"Without the option of a portal, I am willing to engage these troops, if needed," Majus Kheena offered.

"Good idea," said Majus Ayama. "Ori, let's have an escape plan ready for after we start this madness. No diving into it like usual."

Majus Cyrysi jerked his hand back from a sliver. "That is to be the most sensible course."

"Uh huh." Majus Ayama raised an eyebrow. "Those participating in this...thing, stand here. Will the shield hold?"

<I will keep it stable while you engage in other activities,> Hand Dancer said, and turned for the door.

A spear pierced the wall of air and stabbed into the Lobhl's shoulder. It retracted as fast as it had thrust out.

Hand Dancer made no sound, but fell back, her hands wavering in what was translated as a scream of pain.

Majus Amaya started to her, but Hand Dancer waved her back, cradling her arm close. Pink blood dribbled down her arm.

<Activate the Drain seeds,> Hand Dancer signed curtly. <I will ensure they do not come any farther.> She was breathing heavily, eyes tight. Another pike hit the wall of air, but this one stuck, as if in a pool of honey.

Majus Ayama gave the Lobhl a terse nod. "Quickly," was all she said. Majus Kheena went to apply pressure to the wound.

Rey joined the rest of the maji. Even over the commotion in the hall, the interruptions and corruptions in the Symphony were like a swarm of insects buzzing around his head.

"Find the fundamental note of your house," Majus I'Fon told them, then looked to Majus Cyrysi. "Or houses. That is the note we must connect between the seed and the disruption in the Grand Symphony."

"We have no way to know how fast the Drain will expand," Majus Cyrysi added.

"Best hope those soldiers know what a void is," Rey mumbled. Was it worse to confront an angry mob, or a mob scared because a giant death-sphere was behind you?

There was silence, save for the tortured Symphony. Then, "Ready?" Majus Ayama called.

Rey felt deep within, finding a note from his core matching the high whistle of the Symphony of Potential.

"Ready," he said to Majus Ayama, as the others did the same.

"Which one, Ori?" she asked, and the Kirian pointed to a sliver near them.

"This one, when it is phasing back in," Majus Cyrysi shouted as the sliver vanished.

They gathered around, careful not to touch anything else, and waited. The din of weapons bouncing off walls and thickened air drifted to them. Rey swallowed, wondering if he'd made the right choice. Were they any better than the Life Coalition, for starting one of these things up in their stronghold?

"Now!" Majus Cyrysi called, and as the sliver reappeared in their midst, Rey leaned in, an aura of brown surrounding his hand. Majus Caroom shone green for the House of Strength, Majus Cyrysi with one hand in yellow for the House of Communication and the other ringed with orange for the House of Power. On Rey's other side, Majus Ayama held a ball of white light in her hand for the House of Healing, and Majus I'Fon's fingers had an aura of blue for the House of Grace. The note was pulled hungrily from his being, sucked into the nascent void, joining the chorus of dissonant interruptions in the Grand Symphony.

As the connection formed, the jangling disturbances in the Symphony ceased and Rey groaned in relief.

"Move!" Majus Ayama yelled, but Rey was already heading toward the exit. Even as he wove through the other glimmering slivers, the temperature around him dropped. He made it to the door of the room and chanced a look back. Just as in the Assembly, a ball of putrid substance grew in the center of the room. It would intersect the next sliver in three. Two. One...

The soldiers at the wall were silent, watching, their weapons sagging. They recognized the void.

"Drop the shield," Majus Ayama said to Majus Cyrysi and Hand Dancer.

<No need,> Hand Dancer signed with one hand, clutching her shoulder. The yellow and orange covering the doorway fractured and dissipated before the Drain. Suddenly, Rey could hear the Coalitioners breathing. One made a strangled sound.

Majus Ayama grabbed for Rey's arm. "We need to leave. It *will* kill you."

As she pulled him backwards, the perimeter of the void touched the next sliver, and...bent. The Symphony curdled like old goat milk in his mind.

"Wait," he said, and jerked his arm free from Majus Ayama. As if in slow motion, the maji were flowing past him, toward the now retreating soldiers, auras flaring. Then Majus Cyrysi stopped too, looking where he did.

"Oh ancestors," the Kirian said. "That is different."

"Press them back," Majus Ayama shouted. She was halfway out of the door, hands up as if ready to tackle all the soldiers by herself. "We must find Enos!"

"There are more Coalitioners coming," Majus Kheena called from next to her. "We are trapped."

"We can push through. We can find—," Majus Ayama started, but Majus Cyrysi waved a robed arm back at her.

"Look at this," he said. The void intersected a second sliver. The first still resisted the growing sphere, pressing in, like a pin against the skin of a soap bubble. The soldiers shuffled and backed away. A few ran off.

"It's slowing down," Rey said. The blob had expanded rapidly until it intersected the first shard. Now it oozed around the restriction. The cold wasn't as bad as everyone said, either. Hadn't Sam said he almost froze? This was nothing like that.

Majus I'Fon held hir arms out, ringed with blue, facing down four of the remaining Coalitioners. "They are gathering reinforcements. We have only moments."

"This Drain is not to be performing as other Drains have," Majus Cyrysi said. He took a step forward, but Rey grabbed his robe.

"Woah there. Let's not call yer granddames down on us just yet, eyah?"

With a tiny *pop*, the void engulfed the first sliver. They winced at the spike of discord that rammed through the Grand Symphony, like a pen slashed through writing paper. The void contacted more slivers, which pressed in like spearpoints poking an overgrown loaf of dough. The place where the first sliver disappeared fractured, wobbling and dividing into another void, before that was swallowed up, and the void divided again.

Now Majus Ayama came closer, the threat from the soldiers dissipating. "What's it doing?"

"Nothing that it should be," Majus Cyrysi said.

"I can tell that because I'm not dying," Majus Ayama answered. "What does...oh Shiv, that's not good." It swallowed another sliver and the void went into permutations. "Can you *hear* that?"

"So this is not what yer were expecting?" Rey asked. Another sliver absorbed, and the void bubbled and wobbled. He wanted to hold his head. The dissonance had its own dissonance.

"Not at all." Majus Cyrysi said. There was a creak behind them, as Majus Caroom shouldered a Coalitioner out of the way. They backhanded a lethargic stab with a pike.

"The Symphony is, hmm, becoming unstable," they said.

"We know," they all answered.

The thing engulfed another, and then another sliver, and the maji winced. The surface of the void was no longer smooth. It roiled and split, each new sliver adding more chaos to the vista and to the Symphony.

Once again, Rey heard the tromp of boots coming down the corridor. They had wasted their window of surprise.

"I've no idea what it's doing either, but I donna trust what's happenin'" Rey said. He winced as the Symphony howled and dipped in his mind. "Mebbe we should be on our way." They turned as one to the doorway, but Majus Hand Dancer was upright, one arm dangling as the other hand pointed into the bubbling chaos.

<Something is coming through,> she signed.

CHAPTER NINETEEN

Emergence

- Me, I was given this vision to share with you all, my followers: In a waking dream, I found myself within the holiest of holies—the crater at Thlissen, where the Ideal Form was first revealed. Save here, there was no statue of the Form. Instead, me, I saw a clear box with no entry, surrounding a bulbous globe of white. As dreams go, I was suddenly inside the box, reaching for the pale glow of the sphere. In my hand, there was a knife reflecting strange light, and I parted the skin of it, the edges blackening and curling away. From within, there emerged a golden tablet, inscribed with instructions, which burned themselves into my mind. The tablet, it was the words I give to you. It is the instructions of the others, which show how to bring them to us, with their promise of great power to sustain and heal not only our people, but keep the entire universe from harm.

From the holy revelations of Slithen the Dreamer, paragraph five, first chapter.

The next morning—according to the Nether crystal surrounding the House of Time—Sam rose early to continue his search. They'd had little luck the night before finding references to the House of Matter. Wor Wobniar was deep in study of a scroll when he awoke, as if xy hadn't moved from xyr spot overnight.

The temple shifted as Sam reached for the oldest scroll he'd seen. It vanished, replaced with a much younger one, just as the lines opened up before him.

"What...?" He stepped back, hardly able to see from the influx of direction and intent clouding his vision. Everywhere, signs connected and crossed, showing actions that would occur soon, or later, or maybe not at all. He spun, but it was as if a plate of glass surrounded him, etched with what would be.

"I see them too," Wor Wobniar grated from nearby. The colors on xyr head were flashing bright. "The *Vloeinkaal* is never so intrusive."

"What does it mean?" Sam asked. The swirling impressions and lines were giving him vertigo and he stumbled back, reaching for a handhold.

"Look for the deepest threads," Wor Wobniar said. "At their conclusion lies the eventual Dissolution."

But the Dissolution was supposed to be far off. Sam's thoughts turned to Enos, stuck with the Life Coalition. Could he see where she was, in the flowing lines?

Wor Wobniar's jaws closed with a snap like rock breaking. "No!"

"What! What is it?" Sam stared into the lines. The easiest ones to follow showed actions he and Wor Wobniar were doing. Xy must be looking at the fainter, deeper layers.

"This is not the Dissolution, but it hastens its coming!" Wor Wobniar said. "The event unfolds, changing the direction of what is to come."

"Where?" The lines had never lasted this long. Sam hardly dared blink. The Symphony transitioned in his mind to a higher key, ringing almost supersonic. It was like crystals colliding, buzzing, and shattering. But the rhythms corresponded to the movements of the lines. He couldn't concentrate on both at once.

"The Symphony," he began, "I've never heard it like this."

"It is the House of Time," Wor Wobniar said. "Do not change the notes. It can cause dangerous diversions to the flow of time itself."

Two Symphonies swirling in concert, creating a gigantic portal in the Dome of the Assembly. He'd manipulated time before.

The *Vloeinkaal* only grew more intense, and pressure built in Sam's head. He raised a hand to his temple. "When does it stop?"

"Usually long before this. A massive event swims through the *Vloeinkaal* to our time." The Nether added strain to the translation of Wor Wobniar's words. "It is huge. A disruption so immense—"

The center of the crystalline melody cracked.

Sam put both hands to his head, wincing against the shards of music that stabbed through his brain. If music could have sharp edges, this did. His knees buckled and he leaned against the cool stone of the House of Time.

"Are you sure it's not the Dissolution?" he shouted over the melody.

"I do not believe so," Wor Wobniar's lights flashed bright in response. "Though nothing has ever caused so much disruption. Yet this is localized...somewhere. I cannot tell."

"I can," Sam said, with sudden conviction. He was of the House of Matter *and* the House of Time. If he could locate an event from screeching music and ghostly lines—well, he might be hallucinating, but he would try.

He clenched his hands, finding rhythm in the horrible screech of the music, tracking the lines as they carved its visual interpretation. It was painful to comprehend, but Sam forced against the agony, his molars grinding against each other. It was very far away—not in the Nether, or on Methiem, the only two places he'd been. Was it on another homeworld? There were familiar presences, as if he'd memorized some of the notes.

"It's Enos," Sam said, "and Majus Ayama, and Majus Cyrysi. There are others too. Lots of them. I don't know what's happening, but I have to get to them. I have to get bac—"

The *Vloeinkaal* vanished, and the music of Time with it. As if someone had jerked away a crutch he leaned on, Sam pitched forward, sliding down the wall. He grabbed at the stone, fingers gliding down polished marble, past a cubby with ancient parchment. Wor Wobniar tottered on xyr three legs, like a top about to collapse.

No attack. Not now. Push it away. This is a safe place. There's no need for anxiety.

Sam breathed into his center, sinking to a squat. He closed his eyes and felt his body, existing. He'd been through too many unfamiliar things. He'd stood under an expanding Drain and fought the Life Coalition with music. He'd traveled to a new facet of the Nether. He would survive this.

The shakiness subsided, and Sam swallowed, then pried his hands apart. They were freezing cold and he rubbed them on his shirt. It was a new blue one he'd had the tailor—Hapt—make last ten-day. He looked up to find Wor Wobniar's head flaps all pointed at him.

"You are well? Such a powerful presence of the *Vloeinkaal* is hard to recover from." Xy looked shaky, and put out two of xyr arms to brace on a wall.

Sam pushed to his feet. "I'm used to having attacks like this. But I have to get back."

"You are used to the stress of the House of Time? How is this?"

"No—I'm used to panic attacks, which you called a 'defect.'" He realized what he thought was a panic attack was instead caused by seeing the lines, or perhaps from hearing so much of the Symphony of Time. He stared defiantly back at Wor Wobniar. "Maybe it's not such a defect to those of the House of Time."

The Nostelrahn's head flaps wavered, then shifted away. Xyr claws clicked in what the Nether told him was embarrassment, mixed with acceptance. "Possible."

Sam shook his head. "It doesn't matter. My friends are in danger and I need to be there for them. I think the others found Enos—Inas' other instance. He'll come with me." Sam backed toward the door as the House of Time shifted to blue stone with deep imperfections reflecting the light into a thousand sparkles.

Wor Wobniar held out two of xyr claws to the scrolls around them. "What of our research? You have been here only a few lightenings, and the Dissolution comes, hastened by this new event."

"It has to wait. This is more important," Sam said. He almost added 'I'm sorry,' but stopped. He wasn't. His friends *were* more important. "Can you show me how to pass through the wall again?"

Wor Wobniar bowed xyr head, and xyr lights flashed in acceptance. "If that is your choice, I will show you from the House of Time. The token I gave you will make changes easier within the House of Time." Xyr head flaps wavered, as if xy expected to find the House in ashes around xyr. "I hope we continue soon. This was not the Dissolution, but sign it progresses even faster than I anticipated. There is much to prepare."

"I know," Sam said. The lines flashed through his memory, pathways burned into place. Many of the lines simply stopped. The Dissolution *was* coming. He closed his hand; the C-shaped ring xy had given him pushing into his skin.

"My friends can help us, and they'll want to know all about this facet of the Nether."

Wor Wobniar's head flaps waved back and forth in resolution. "Yes. With two in the House of Time, both facets may face the Dissolution together." Xyr three legs drew in, making xyr taller. "The Nether itself shows we must work together, by shifting our facets closer, and ringing the chime to meet. Back to your friends, and we will continue your training soon." Xy seemed to have made peace with the decision, and scuttled forward.

Sam barely restrained his surprise. *Another revelation, though it makes sense the Nether can move its facets. I know so little about this place.*

They exited the House of Time and traipsed through the verdant growth in the little pocket inside the wall. Sam followed Wor Wobniar's musical dance through the notes of the wall, and the ring of Nether crystal smoothed his work, blending the composition more evenly with the natural passages of the Symphony.

They exited at the rear of the Effature's palace, the passage through the wall less disconcerting this time. Sam's mind whirled through the implications of the *Vloeinkaal*. What had happened, and on which homeworld? Was it the Life Coalition?

Crominu Vaevicta, in her Aridori form, was having breakfast with Inas at a little table, basking in the morning glow from the wall. Sam's stomach growled in protest. When was the last time he'd eaten?

"There you are," Vaevicta said. "What have you learned, Wor Wobniar?"

"The Dissolution closes in," the Nostelrahn said, xyr jaws grinding together.

"You have said this for many days," the Effature said. She seemed unconcerned.

"Something big happened on our side," Sam told Inas. He was up in an instant, coming to take Sam's hands. "It's on one of the homeworlds, but I think Majus Ayama and Majus Cyrysi might have found Enos."

"That's excellent!" Inas' eyes widened as he pressed a pastry on Sam. "These are tasty. You have to try one. The Effature has been showing me ways to control the emotion from changing. She knows so much. She was about to take me to meet the other Aridori."

Sam took a good look at his friend. No, his *boyfriend*. Inas looked...happier. The cloud hanging over him since Enos rescued him was not gone, but was reduced. Talking with another of his species—one that wasn't a prisoner of the Sathssn—had obviously helped him.

Inas' eyebrows drew down. "Controlling things requires concentration. It will take a long time to master." But then his face cleared, and he looked up at Sam, his face unfolding in a lopsided smile, like the ones when they'd first met. Sam felt a weight he didn't know he'd held melt away. The doom he'd felt from the *Vloeinkaal* was less, now he was with Inas.

"That's wonderful, Inas," he said, squeezing his hands. "How do you feel?"

"Much better." Inas leaned in and Sam accepted the kiss. It was warm and firm, tasting of the jelly on the pastry, completely unlike when Inas backed him against a column in the palace. "She told me what was wrong with my hand, too." He let go to roll his wrist in the air, and Sam saw the way his lithe fingers opened and closed, no longer jumping in length and width.

Sam darted a look to Vaevicta, who was watching with what he thought was a proud smile. His eyes drifted to the diadem sitting atop her head. Just like Palmoran's. Were they a sign of the Effature, or of the Aridori? "What was wrong?" he asked.

"The Aridori from Gloomlight left a piece of themself with me," Inas said. Sam tried not to pull back, but Inas must have felt him tense. "It is safe. Well, better. I know it's there."

"It's still there?" Sam tried to keep the agitation out of his voice. There wasn't time to discuss. They could talk when they found Enos. "Never mind. We have to return to our facet. We can—or I can—bring others here to meet with the species in this facet. But for now..."

"What is it?" Inas' eyes roved over his face. "What happened?"

Sam just shook his head, and took his hands back. "It's big. We have to go."

"Give my regards to Palmoran," Vaevicta said, and now her face was dark. "I feel a change deep within, as though what you speak has affected him. It is faint, as our connection barely exists any longer. Our instances are too separate." She stood, opening her scaled hands. Sam's eyes found the green and purple scales of her front. So like Effature Palmoran's robes. How had he been so stupid? "Please, if you get the chance, bring him through the wall. It has been many centuries since I have seen my other instance."

Sam looked to Inas, whose face was tight with concern. He couldn't imagine separating from Inas and Enos for that long. "I will, ma'am," he said.

The trip back to the bridge was uneventful, but Sam fidgeted at the time it took. He fixed landmarks in his memory, but only by habit. Inas' warm hand was on his shoulder, and Sam's anxiety was chased away by the scale of what he'd heard in the Symphony and seen in the *Vloeinkaal.*

They passed Nostelrahns, tripod-like Praveadi, Caraakn lumbering past, and Lufvurn floating overhead. He even glimpsed a pair of Aridori turn from a side street with a careful glance both directions. Inas stared after them, greedily taking in their movements and interactions.

Four more species the Assembly had never met, and one thought extinct. They'd need an ambassador, after Sam learned what the *Vloeinkaal* was trying to tell him.

"Will you come with us?" he asked Wor Wobniar at the wall, but xy flapped xyr head flaps in a way the Nether translated as negative.

"You've passed through the wall twice on your own. You know how, and the ring of crystal will help you. I must stay here and research. Too many portents and signs are coming to pass. I will read the scrolls, and share what I find. Come back as soon as you discover what happened, and we may continue training."

"I'll do that," Sam said. He pulled Inas closer. "Come on. I can take you through this time."

"I trust you," Inas said, and leaned up for another kiss. His lips were soft, and Sam closed his eyes and relaxed into the feeling. His Inas was, if not whole, then at least better than when they entered this facet. He needed to come back with Enos so they could meet others of their species—ones who weren't captured and tortured by the Sathssn.

Sam waved to Wor Wobniar, whose lights flashed in acknowledgment. He felt for the Symphony, weaving his notes so they danced through the rhythm of the wall. He found Inas' rhythm in the Symphony and made a bridge between their songs, mirroring the way their fingers twined together. The crystal slid around them with all the colors of the Symphony as they entered the wall.

* * *

Enos blinked as the world boomed around her. She groaned and pressed a hand to her belly. It came away red, and the pain intensified.

What is happening? Nakan had slashed at her. That was where the pain originated. *Then why is everyone running around?*

Shapes flitted past. Nakan was gone. Had he meant to finish her off and been stopped by the strange rumbling, or had he meant to leave her there, bleeding? How long had she been unconscious?

Bleeding? Do Aridori bleed?

Another voice addressed her. *We only bleed if there is a need. Close your wounds. Use the excess you have inherited to rebind the flesh.*

She concentrated on her middle, but the wound resisted. The Symphony was wrong. There was a ragged triplet of notes, then the music stopped, left hanging where the skin and muscle on her belly gaped open. Two clean cuts, through skin and into muscle. The music continued on the other side of the wound.

How do I fix this? She'd never been attacked like this before.

Putra's head appeared in her view, their large Kirian eyes narrowed. "Very bad. This knife is cruel for us. Nakan has threatened before, but never used it. We were too precious. But now, maybe not? Use the substance you took from the big one, child. You still have some left." They took a quick step to one side as the cavern rocked.

What is going on?

Enos tried to slow her breathing. There was pain from the belly wounds, though not as much as she expected. Then the Symphony struck a wrong note, and she winced. The knife couldn't have done that much damage.

Forms in dark cloaks ran by as the cavern shook. Enos tried to lift her head, but grunted at the pain. Flakes of rock drifted from the ceiling, oddly slow in the lessened pull of this place. The chairs in a line in the middle of the room were empty, most of the Coalitioners gone. Whatever the leaders had been trying to communicate was forgotten.

Another person ran past, calling back over their shoulder. "—room with the void seeds. Something's gone wron—" They disappeared through another doorway.

"Focus." Putra's hand slapped her cheek and Enos started. Yes. The pain. The wound. Fix that first.

Enos closed her eyes, groping inward, listening to the ragged Symphony as she took count of her body. Her front was damaged, but could she move that mass elsewhere? Somewhere less dangerous to her health?

She experimented, pulling notes from her core and bridging them between the different melodies. Then she changed form, to migrate the slashes from her belly to…where? She needed her legs, her head, her chest. Down one arm? It would be uncomfortable, but easier to work one-handed if she had to. Maybe she could grow another arm. She giggled.

There was a *tsk*ing sound and Enos opened her eyes. Putra was still standing over her.

"Heal quickly. Soldiers say something is happening in the caves above us. The ones they do not let us go in. Zhaddi wishes to explore. We have an advantage we have not had in centuries."

Enos concentrated. The discord in the Symphony was distant, back near their room. There was other strangeness in her wound. Why did the music fracture?

She dragged her thoughts back to the slashes. Had Nakan poisoned the knife? No. Keep on track.

She focused on the wounds, then looked at her finished work. There was a single ugly slash from her left bicep to her forearm. It stung, but the edges were closer together than on her belly. Enos dived into the Symphony of Healing, moving notes to connect two codas. The very ends of the cut drew together and became soft scar tissue, but the rest of the wound resisted, like fingers pulling the wound open from inside her body.

Enos drew in a deep breath, suddenly exhausted. If she took any more notes from her core, she wouldn't have energy left to move, and whatever was happening was big.

A rock the size of her fist landed next to her head and Enos flinched. Her belly didn't hurt, and her arm did, but she could move without crumpling into a ball.

"I'm ready," she told Putra, who nodded and gestured to Zhaddi and the others. As Enos pushed to her feet, she saw they were standing nearby in a clump. The rest of the room was deserted save for a few guards still at their post, halberds pointed in their direction. She could see the weapon staffs shaking. She sniffed, and found she could smell their fear. It was exhilarating.

Putra leaned in toward her. "There will be a little blood," they whispered. "This is always my favorite part."

Then they were gone in a whirl of claws and teeth. Zhaddi and the others changed, faster than either Enos or the poor guards could follow.

One of the nameless ones took the top from a halberd with one swipe of a massive paw. The second strike took the head from the Lobath who held it. Then Putra and Zhaddi were in front, dismantling guards like sides of meat.

Enos realized she was running forward, the drive to assist the pack rising in her. She skidded to a halt, bouncing across the hard floor.

No!

The voices inside her moaned in disappointment, and Enos looked away before she saw what caused the horrible squishing and crunching noises. There were barely any screams.

I won't be like them.

A hand touched her shoulder and Enos jumped. Zhaddi was there, wiping away a smear of blueish blood from their mouth with one hand. Their long tongue came out and cleaned off the rest.

"We are ready," they said. "There is opportunity today. You can take us away with a portal, yes?"

Enos thought furiously. These people should not be among others, not as they were. She'd been locked in the same room and they had taught her, but she fully believed they would tear her to shreds if given a chance.

The little voices jabbering excitedly in her mind were temptation enough, and she hadn't been abused by the Sathssn for a thousand cycles. Putra, Zhaddi, and the others of her people needed special care, not freedom. There was no way she was giving them the chance to ravage an unsuspecting Assembly, especially not with the Effature dead or dying. She must find a way to keep them here, but how, when they knew she could change the Symphony?

"I have to learn of this disturbance first," she said, then stepped sideways as the whole room rocked. The others watched her, prowling closer, flanking. It reminded her of when the big Aridori had come after her. She swallowed. "The Symphony is unstable from these tremors. I'm not even certain I can open a portal." It was getting more and more discordant, in truth. Very much like when the Drain had appeared over Dalhni.

Someone mentioned void seeds. Is there a Drain here? Will I be forced to take the Aridori away? Even if they should have been dead centuries ago, that doesn't mean I should cause them to die now.

Enos put on the face she'd used for cycles, dealing with customers of her family's caravan. Let nothing show. Keep the family safe. Visions of Sam and Inas, Majus Ayama, and the others flashed through her mind—her new family.

Putra and Zhaddi looked at each other for a long moment, and Enos wondered if they had a hidden means to communicate.

"We will come with you," Putra said. "We wish to see what is happening—" the cavern rocked again, violently this time, and they all fought to keep their balance. "—but then we want to leave. You are the key to our escape." They said nothing more, but the promise of what would happen if she didn't cooperate hung heavy.

Enos only hesitated for a second, then nodded. "Come with me." She'd figure out what to do with them later.

Once out of the cavern, they ran into Coalitioners who hurried along, taking little notice of their group.

"Why aren't...oh." Enos looked back to see a group of dark-cloaked figures followed her instead of a band of Aridori.

They ran for minutes, sliding around other groups. Enos listened to the Symphony while she ran. It was fracturing and disintegrating like it had in Dalhni, except...not completely. Was this not a Drain? Did the Life Coalition have another weapon? It sounded like the Symphony was pushing back, keeping the Drain from growing. Had someone found a way to stop them? Who had set it off?

They crossed the bridge over the gaping chasm at a run. Finished rooms were on this side, but the corridors were rough stone on the opposite. The dissonance was painful in Enos' mind, but as she ran through stone tunnels, the discord ceased, though the walls still shook.

Is that good, or bad?

A turn left, another right, and they ran down a straight passageway. They had to be close.

Then they ran into a tight-knit bunch of cloaked figures—soldiers—packing a passageway. There were at least twenty of them, and she guessed the source of the disruptions, Drain or not, was past them.

The Aridori flowed forward as soon as she stopped, before she could say anything. Two of the guards disappeared in a flash of black cloth, their remains shoved behind the Aridori. More guards went down silently, and hands pulled Enos forward, stumbling across gaping wounds and loose entrails. She gritted her teeth, trying not to look at the slaughter.

The rank of soldiers wavered and flowed. There were muffled grunts, but within seconds Enos was surrounded by black cloaks not made of cloth, but of Aridori flesh. The whole attack had taken almost no time. As she watched, one of the Aridori, and then another, grew an extra cloaked head from a shoulder, making their group look larger than it was.

There were only six Coalitioners left—the leaders, and they hadn't even noticed, too intent on the doorway opposite them. Any others who had stood here stared with sightless eyes and dripping wounds, hidden behind the Aridori. Enos grabbed at the nearest cloak.

"Don't hurt anyone else, or I won't help you," she hissed to Zhaddi, or possibly it was Putra. She saw a flash of purple eyes under a cowl. Putra, then. Their false second head stared forward resolutely.

Enos looked to the Coalition leaders, staring at the entrance to a room from which a strange glow emanated. If this was a Drain, why wasn't it cold, and why was no one yelling or running away?

Then Nakan—she could tell it was him just by how he walked—pushed forward.

"You who call yourself leaders, you cannot decide who will speak, so I will." He crossed the hall, and Enos almost shouted with joy as Majus Ayama emerged from the doorway of the room.

* * *

Rilan stood face to face—well, face to hood—with Nakan, daring him to act. The soldiers had backed away, letting the group that was obviously in charge through. Ori and the others had wasted too much time watching the void and now they were trapped, again. Opening a portal was impossible with the void's interference and the Life Coalition blocked the passage.

"As much as I'd like to rip your head off," she began, "we have a bigger problem. You should be thankful I stabilized the Effature, or we wouldn't be talking." The bones of her knuckles creaked as she made a fist, watching the little Sathssn. "This void is acting strange. We think there's something, or someone, trying to use it as a doorway."

She watched Nakan shift infinitesimally to his right, trying to get a better angle. She moved one foot out, countering him. They had both been trained by Zsaana—who she suspected was lurking with the other Coalition leaders—she in *Fading Hands*, and he in *Dancing Step*. There was no glow of blue around Nakan, and no aura of white around her. Neither changed the Symphony.

"Your group, they come to our home and threaten us. Why should we not remove you from our way?" Nakan said. Over his shoulder, others came forward. Rilan guessed Nakan was not acting fully in accord with them. So had they called for the attack on the Effature or was it Nakan's idea? The Sathssn shifted forward again.

"A fair trade for your actions on the bridge, isn't it?" Rilan bared her teeth. "But the time you take to fight us means whatever comes through will have the advantage on you. Better to fight those you know, or a complete unknown?" Rilan stabbed a thumb backward, taking the chance to move again, keeping her stance equal with Nakan's.

"Rilan, be attending to the Drain, rather than this petty rivalry, yes?" Ori murmured behind her. She didn't take her eyes off Nakan, but she knew Ori's crest would be sticking out at all angles. She ignored him.

"You want to fight, or talk?" she asked Nakan. She kept her eyes on the triangle between his shoulders and navel. She would see any twitch of his hips or shoulders, be ready for his attack.

"Us, we have not yet had our rematch," Nakan purred. "Twice, I have achieved what I wanted, in the warehouse and on the bridge. You, you think you can stop me?" Out of her peripheral vision, Rilan saw the soldiers shuffle forward. If they regained their courage, she would move back. The doorway was a good chokepoint, and she adjusted so she was just inside the opening.

"It is, hmm, still growing," Caroom rumbled behind her. "The object is, hmm, bigger than a Pixie now."

"We've taken away most of your void seeds," she told Nakan. "In the time you take to fight us, the void will destroy the rest. I bet those take a while to create."

"Many cycles," Nakan grated. His left boot slid back as Rilan slid hers forward, making no sound on the rough, compressed dirt of the tunnel floor. "Yet our organization, we can make more."

"All this, none of it matters," interrupted a voice behind Nakan, and another figure pushed to the front, forcing Nakan to lose his position.

Rilan frowned, and relaxed. Talking it was. She loosened her fist slightly. Nakan would not get away with what he'd done. "And who are you?"

"Me, I am Janas, leader of the Life Coalition. You may have detonated the seeds, but you have only furthered our plans." The speaker peered around Rilan's shoulder to see the pulsating void behind.

That got Nakan's attention. "Me, I have not heard this." Finally, he looked away from Rilan and she rolled her shoulders to release their tension.

"If you attended all our meetings you would know," Janas retorted. "You maji, you have achieved what we thought lost. If only us, we knew setting off all seeds at once would start the reaction we tried for cycles to achieve. Careful planning replaced by simple luck of the crater's pit."

"You are knowing of the one coming through the Drain?" Ori asked, pushing Rilan aside. She growled, trying to monitor Nakan. But he could no longer engage her, and Rilan's attention shifted to the void. The thing inside was a dark shadow, closer than before. Better to fight the unknowns.

Another Coalitioner pushed Nakan ever farther to one side. "This, it is what we meant to do with the void in the Assembly—open the bridge to a place of great power. The other, they will give energy to solve the problems of Sath Home and have enough left to bring peace to the Assembly."

<Peace? Your actions have not brought peace so far. How do you justify this change in honor now?> Hand Dancer's fingers raced as she signed, and the Coalitioner stepped back at the normally placid Lobhl's vehemence. Blood dribbled down her arm from her shoulder.

"Sacrifices, they must be made for true peace," the cloaked figure said. "Us, we have been directed for over a century by the original plan of Slithen the Dreamer. The Dreamer, he was the first to contact the presence on the plane of great power. He brought us here."

"Them, they will not understand the revelations of Slithen, Iano," Janas said.

"This is the first we've heard of them," Panen said. Zie was keeping one eye on the void.

"Now, let us through, and we will show you the power of our prophesy," Janas said. She took one step forward, but Ori came abreast of Rilan and intercepted her path.

"There is to be no such thing as prophesy," Ori growled, his crest low. "Everything can be proved by study."

"Then us, how did we come to this small body in the space above Sath Home?" Iano asked, his gloved hands spreading. "We came where no majus has been before, and founded this fortress. This, it has been the stronghold of the Life Coalition ever since."

"Luck," Ori said, but Rilan moved toward the void. The Coalitioners knew more about what was happening than they did. Did they really have some prophesy?

The shadow was growing faster, and had replaced the Life Coalition as the greatest threat. "As fascinating as it is, we may have to shelve this discussion," she said, and pointed. Everyone turned to look.

"The bringer of dreams, they come!" Janas shouted, and pushed forward. Rilan batted at Janas' gloved hand as the Sathssn thrust her aside. "If only my parents were alive to see this! Slitho and Harha, they worked so long for this goal!"

Caroom brought their hands up to trap the Coalitioner, but Rilan shook her head. They would all see this person the Life Coalition claimed would bring peace to the Assembly.

The shadow was obvious now, large and bulky inside the void. It looked like nothing so much as a giant gestating cocoon, the bubbling convolutions hiding what was inside.

Without speaking, the other Coalition leaders flooded into the room. Their chokepoint of the doorway was gone, but Rilan doubted a fight was coming, at least not with the Life Coalition. A hooded figure nodded to her and Rilan frowned at the creaky motions of the figure. He was obviously an old Sathssn, but still graceful of movement.

"Our last meeting, it was many cycles ago," the figure said. "Me, I keep up to date with the work you did on the Council. You were a satisfactory choice to replace me."

Rilan's eyes widened, "Zsaana?" she asked and the figure gestured acceptance. So he was here. "I thought the apprentices were mistaken when they said you took up with this bunch. But you were always a close-minded old hard-ass, weren't you?"

"Yet one who will be proved correct in his choice of side," Zsaana said, and nodded toward the void. "The prophesied one comes."

Ori sidled next to her and reached for her hand. Rilan took it. Nothing in her adventures with him or her time on the Council had prepared her for this. She stroked her thumb down the back of his hand. She would face it with him.

The skin of the void split like a rotten melon, and Rilan had a glimpse of a reddish, featureless plane before a body eclipsed it.

The thing which came through was pitch black with vivid orange stripes running across its body. It moved in a sinuous line, hundreds of little orange cilia on its sides rippling to propel it forward, like a brightly colored and poisonous millipede. Several people took a step back at its wavelike motion, like a shark swimming on land.

The creature was as long as Rilan was tall, and its body narrowed on both ends, but she could find no face, or even a head. A fleshy fin on top of the body rippled in the same way the sides did, a wave of threat.

We/I are come/searching to receive the tribute/payment of energy/power offered by the Dreamer, it said, though Rilan could see no mouth. *Where is it/will it be?*

She frowned over at Janas. It was almost as if the creature said two different things at once. But the Life Coalition's leader said the creature would *bring them* boundless energy, not that it was looking for more. Janas' hood was cocked in surprise, and Zsaana took a step back, his hand rising to press to his chest.

They hadn't expected the creature either. Rilan clenched her free fist again. She wondered if there would be a fight after all.

CHAPTER TWENTY

Congruence

- With Councilor Feldo missing, many of Speaker Oscana's remarks lack their usual insight, and the Council of the Maji seems lessened. I have nothing against the Head of the House of Grace—she is of my species, after all—but I do not believe the Council is acting in concert. The heads of the Houses of Power and Healing are new, still finding their place, and the heads of the Houses of Communication and Strength are, well, I shall say they have not contributed greatly in the past few cycles. With all these disruptions, we must depend on the quiet leadership and wisdom of our Effature, Bolas Palmoran, while dealing with the demands of the Life Coalition and the revelation of the Aridori's continued existence. I do not know what we would do without his guidance and advice.

News article quoting Rabata Liinero Humbano, Head Speaker for the Etanela

Sam inhaled a ragged breath as he exited the wall with Inas, and heard his boyfriend do the same. They hadn't needed to breathe in the wall, but now his lungs screamed.

"There's no one here," Inas said. Sam looked around. The bridge—turned to steel by his work—was empty. He could feel his notes boosting the music into a different key. They resonated in the crystal ring that now graced his left forefinger. He'd left that portion of himself here. So many of his notes were missing—a mistake to leave them.

Sam reached to take the notes back and a wave swept through the bridge, steel shifting through colors until it was once again stone. The surge ended below his feet, and Sam straightened, energized.

Inas watched the transformation, gripping Sam's hand as if to keep his balance. "I heard parts of the bridge's structure changing," he said. "But if I tried that with the House of Strength, the music would have been ridiculously complex." His eyes were drinking in Sam's face. "I didn't know you were so strong."

Sam shrugged, oddly embarrassed. "I don't know if strength has anything to do with it. My house seems to have a lot of overlap with the others. Majus Ayama and Majus Cyrysi also heard parts of what I changed."

"What could we do, working together in the Symphony?" Inas said. He squeezed Sam's hand. "Even more when we get Enos back." His face screwed up in sadness. "We could almost hear each other's music sometimes, though Majus Caroom said that was impossible."

"We will get her back," Sam said. He stared into Inas' eyes. They were dark, with little flecks of a lighter green or hazel around the edges of the irises. It almost matched the color of the House of Strength.

Sam forced himself to peer over the side of the bridge. The area was deserted. "We've been gone almost two days, and something big happened while we were in the other facet. I think Majus Ayama and Majus Cyrysi went after Enos, but they left no one here to meet us?" The certainty that no one *really* wanted him around rose up, but he quashed the thought. Inas was right beside him.

"We were the first to pass through the wall in centuries." Inas said. "Vaevicta wanted us to report back to our Effature."

"The Effature." Sam looked to Inas, his eyes widening. This Effature, Bolas Palmoran, was an Aridori like Crominu Vaevicta. He was her other instance, like Inas and Enos. "Yes, we have to find him."

They tried Majus Cyrysi's room first because they were halfway up the House of Communication. It was empty, no note. Not that he expected one. Maybe from Majus Ayama, but not from his absent-minded mentor.

"We could see if Majus Caroom is home," Inas suggested. "I have barely seen my mentor since..." He looked away, and Sam rubbed his back. There was more—much more—Inas needed to work through with those memories, but Sam knew how long it could take. He'd be there to help Inas out.

But Majus Caroom was also not at home and the grounds around the houses of the maji were deserted. Usually, other maji would be out wandering the paths.

"What's going on? I'm getting worried," Sam said. They stood in the gardens of the Spire, alone. He tried to push away the panic climbing up his throat. "*All* of the maji didn't go to find Enos. Where are they? Can you feel anything from her? "

Inas shook his head again, his black hair trailing across his shoulders. "I...do not know. I felt nothing when she connected with me. Perhaps she excels at it. But the Effature must know more and I need to speak with him. About a lot of things."

"Then we'll go to the palace." Sam said the words decisively, but the old fear rose at walking through the Imperium again.

No! I've been through the wall of the Nether. I've visited the House of Time. Stop being afraid!

It didn't help completely, but he took a step forward, gripping Inas' hand.

Inas bumped his shoulder. "I'll stay close." He leaned in and Sam tilted his face down for another kiss. The lack of anyone else around made it seem like a secret they shared.

He stopped, a breath away from Inas' lips, as someone *did* turn the corner at a run. He was an older, round, and pale-skinned Methiemum, who looked familiar. He wiped sweat from his forehead.

"One of the apprentices said they saw you wandering around," the man said, gesturing to Inas and Sam. "Come quick. He's been asking about you, and I don't want to be away from him for long."

"Who?" Sam asked, as he fell into step behind the man. Inas was right beside him. "Majus Cyrysi?"

"Majus Caroom?" Inas asked at the same time. The man shook his head.

"The Effature. Where have you been? Everyone's heard of the attack. The Assembly is losing their minds. Most of the maji are there now, except for the ones trying to break down my door."

"The attack?" Sam said as Inas said, "The Effature? What happened?"

Was this what he'd felt in the House of Time? An event big enough to scatter the maji and injure the Effature?

The man stopped walking, turning to peer into their faces. Then he spun away and walked even faster. "He can tell you better than I. I just helped work on him. Strangest operation I've seen. The knife scrambled his melody. Almost as if he weren't Methiemum anymore. If that Vish-cursed circlet he wears hadn't interfered with my music, I could have healed him, but he refused to take it off."

Finally Sam remembered the man's face—Majus Szaler, the new head of the House of Healing. He'd taken Majus Ayama's place on the Council. He would have been able to detect the Effature's true species, wouldn't he? Sam traded a look with Inas, who shrugged one shoulder, as if to say 'don't press the question.'

They hurried through the House of Healing and into the medical facilities that had grown up beside it. It was not quite like a hospital from Earth, but there were fast-moving doctors and nurses, the occasional long-faced person, standing by themselves, and the smell. That was ubiquitous, it seemed.

Four of the Effature's guards were lined up outside the door the surgeon led them to, along with a group of maji who all vied for Majus Szaler's attention. He waved them away, and hustled Sam and Inas through the crowd.

"He's insisted he talk with you, but he's barely stabilized," Majus Szaler said. "Do not tire him out." The surgeon pressed the door open and gestured them through to a sizeable room—larger than any hospital room Sam had seen, with several writing desks, a bed, a table with six chairs, and a large couch circled by more chairs. More like a meeting room than a hospital room.

I guess when you're the leader of the Nether, you get special circumstances.

The Effature was lying on the low couch, wearing the same clothes he always did, the circlet gracing his head. Aside from a bandage around his middle, he could have been taking his ease, but his face was pale—almost gray.

"Come in, please," he said, gesturing with both hands, but the movement was weak. "That is sufficient, Szaler," he called. The round man grumbled, but shoved his way back out. Sam could hear him arguing with the maji outside.

As soon as they were alone, the Effature's face drooped, and deep circles appeared under his eyes.

No, those aren't circles. His skin's turning black, growing scales. Like an Aridori's face.

"You are with friends, sir," Inas said. "We met Vaevicta. She sends regards and much love to her other instance. She wants you to visit her." He reached out. "If I may?"

Sam watched his friend. Inas had a sad smile on his face. What had he learned from Vaevicta while Sam had been with Wor Wobniar?

Inas and the Effature clasped hands, their fingers melding into each other's hands, and both closed their eyes. It was what Vaevicta did with Inas when they met.

The Effature sank deeper into the couch, and his features became plastic, sliding between those of an old man, and of another creature entirely, with a long black scaly snout.

It was only a few moments before Inas and the Effature opened their eyes. The old man's features returned almost to normal, save some scaliness around the sides of his face and in his hands.

"Thank you for sharing," he told Inas, who bowed his head. "I see my other instance has kept her memories better than I."

"She urged you to change more," Inas said, but the Effature waved his words away.

"That is not pressing at the moment." He looked to Sam. "Did you discover more of the Dissolution from Prophet Wor Wobniar?"

"I did," Sam said, "though something is happening with Majus Ayama and the others. Wor Wobniar thinks it will bring the Dissolution even sooner. We both saw..."

He trailed off as the Effature and Inas stared at him. Sam hadn't told even his boyfriend yet.

He quickly recounted what he and Wor Wobniar had done, even including details about the hidden and shifting House of Time.

"And an event so pressing occurred—here?—that it alerted both you and the prophet?" the Effature asked.

"Yes," Sam said. "Was it the attack on you? Wor Wobniar wanted me to stay and study with xyr, but the lines—" He shook his head. The others wouldn't understand. "That is, it seemed I needed to come back immediately."

"You see my injury." Palmoran gestured to the bandage around his middle. "I was attacked by one of the Life Coalition, dissatisfied, I suspect, by how his fellows were proceeding with the Assembly."

"Can you not..." Inas asked, waving his hands vaguely.

Bolas Palmoran shook his head. "I have not changed enough recently. Healing of wounds I might have done in my youth, if dire enough, but no longer." He repositioned, his face pinching in pain.

"There was a foreign agent in the blade. As if the wielder knew how to damage my—our—species." He included Inas with a look.

"And the maji went after the Life Coalition?" Sam asked.

"I believe so," the Effature said. "The cloaked figure moved with great speed and grace. Majus Ayama seemed to know the individual, though I was not conscious for the journey from the bridge to the medical ward. Maji were directed to bring me to Joban Szaler. They said Rilan Ayama's group traveled through a portal."

Sam slammed a fist into his other palm. "Nakan. It has to be him, especially if all the maji present couldn't stop him. But that means Majus Ayama figured out the portal to the Life Coalition's location."

"Nakan," Inas hissed and Sam watched him warily.

"He controls the Aridori the Life Coalition hold prisoner." Inas' face drew down into a sneer. "He's a vile person, and his assassins are nearly as bad. They're as old as you, sir, or older." Inas nodded to the Effature, who frowned at the information.

"We have to follow them," Sam said. "They have Enos, and we can help..." He broke off, and stared over the others' heads at the rotating oblong of pitch black growing in the room's corner. It was ringed with brown—the House of Potential.

"Someone's coming," Inas said, and Sam caught the slightest glimmer of worry on the Effature's normally placid face. "Who would know to make a portal here?"

Majus Ayama stepped out as soon as the portal was formed.

"Sam!" she called. "Inas! You're back." She turned to the Effature. "And I see you are still alive. I'm glad. I knew if Szaler couldn't save you, no one could."

Majus Cyrysi was right on her heels, closely followed by Majus Caroom, Majus Hand Dancer, then Majus I'Fon, hir head-tentacles in disarray, then Majus Kheena.

So he wasn't the one who opened the portal.

Majus Ayama frowned at the Effature. "I hope you're up to some negotiation, sir. Whatever we expected from the Life Coalition, it wasn't...well, you'll see." She opened a hand to the portal as the first black-cloaked figure stepped out.

Sam tensed. He sensed unease from Majus Ayama, and the Symphony grew complex as another followed the first figure, and another, until there were ten or more, crowding the room. Extra notes hung around the newcomers, as if they'd been near an explosion, but the music was...off, too. Sam squinted. There were reverberations in the Houses of Matter and Time, like little vibrations that, over years, could cause a building to collapse into rubble. He absently rubbed the ring Wor Wobniar had given him. It was buzzing like it would jump off his finger.

The maji arranged themselves near the door, while the Coalitioners took the other side of the room, the portal opposite the Effature's couch.

Then the portal seemed to bulge, and tiny legs curled around the edges, pulling another creature through with effort. A low sinuous body appeared, bright orange and black, like a clownfish but slithering over the floor in a sinuous wave. As the rest of it pushed through the opening, it moved fast and low, like a shark on land, and a fin on its back twitched toward one side and then the other. As the fin tilted to either maji or Coalitioners, they stepped back. The creature emitted a wave of *other* and Sam wrinkled his nose. There was a new theme in the Symphony, a bulky loping melody throwing the other themes off their timing, as if it shoved the music away.

"What is tha—ugh." Sam clutched at the pain in his head.

THIS IS MY EMISSARY.

Sam thought that voice had disappeared forever, vanished into the giant Drain he'd banished from the floor of the Assembly. It had taken the combined might of the Life Coalition to summon it the last time, and now it accompanied one creature?

The *Vloeinkaal* popped into existence for a single instant and lines shriveled and died around the creature, just as they did around a Drain.

He grasped at the echoes of the voice, but it faded like dew in the sun, leaving nothing behind.

Sam straightened, catching sight of someone even more important, half hidden behind the Life Coalition guards. He circled around the menace of the creature, which squatted in the middle of the room.

Enos.

* * *

Enos watched the Aridori masquerading as the guards of the Life Coalition leaders, but looked around as Inas ran toward her with a shout. Sam wasn't far behind.

She realized he'd felt *present* since she stepped through the portal, but she'd been too focused on the assassins, free to do as they wished.

"Enos!"

They collided, and she breathed in the scent of her other instance as he crumpled her in a huge hug.

"You are in danger," she whispered, clutching him tight. Over his shoulder she saw Majus Ayama introducing the Coalition leaders to the Effature. Her mentor's eyes twitched toward her, but there had been no time for them to even speak to each other.

"The others are here." Inas tensed in her arms, but his eyes went to the disguised Aridori, picking them out though the Coalition leaders still hadn't noticed. One hood swung in their direction, then back to the creature that had come through the Drain.

"Where is the biggest one?" Inas whispered back. How could he tell that one was missing? He leaned back to study her face. "You've changed. You're taller. One of your eyes is different." He looked at the gash on her arm. "And you're injured."

She dismissed the gash with a shrug. A problem for another time. "I'm not just me anymore," she whispered back. She caught his eye-flick to the Aridori and nodded. "The big one attacked me. I...finished the fight."

Inas pressed her hand between his, and Enos relished his warm touch. It had been too long since they were together. But then his flesh flowed around hers, soothing the angry voices inside her. Why would he freely offer himself? She began to accept his body, as the urge to soak him up like a sponge sopping up water rose through her. Then she shoved it away.

I am in control.

"The other Effature taught me some tricks. I can help you mesh the new parts," Inas said.

Enos blinked. That was not what she'd expected him to say.

"Wait—*other* Effature?"

"Some odd things happened," Inas said, his old smile tugging at the corner of his lip, but he didn't get to continue, because Sam was there, pressing into their embrace, and it felt like the days of confinement with the Aridori prisoners fled at his touch. His presence was as welcome as that of her other instance.

"I missed you," Sam said, and pushed his forehead against hers. She leaned up, breathing him in, running a hand down his shaggy hair.

A *need* surfaced, the drive to feel all she could, to search for new sensation. It came from changing too much. But knowing that made it manageable. She channeled the desire into a fierce kiss, pressing Sam back with its force, taking all her breath away with it. His arms encircled her, and Inas hugged both of them, his ever-present warmth like a small star. They were complete again.

Then Sam pulled back from her lips, sniffed, and swallowed. His eyes bored into hers.

"We're in danger," he said, and Enos would have laughed at the echo of her words if he hadn't looked so serious.

Sam peered over his shoulder at the creature that had come from the Drain, which was debating with Majus Ayama. There was a communication barrier, even though they were in the Nether.

"The voice came with it," Sam said. "The one that removed my memories of Earth."

Enos' stomach dropped at his words, and Inas looked as concerned as she felt.

"He told me while we were in the other facet," her other instance said. Their heads were close together, and they spoke in whispers.

"It's connected to that creature, and it's incredibly dangerous," Sam said. "It said the creature is its emissary. I think the voice is behind whatever is really making the Drains. This isn't just the Life Coalition. This is connected to the Dissolution, somehow."

* * *

"We have no extra power. These idiots told us you would bring the way to peace with you, whatever that is." Rilan pointed at Janas as she stared down at the sinuous orange creature. It felt wrong, as if the Symphony itself was rejecting it. She couldn't get a fix on its biology with the House of Healing, much less anything to do with how it thought.

The creature hadn't introduced itself, but kept demanding power. Or maybe energy. The Nether wasn't very clear in its translation, for once. The words appearing in her memory wavered and changed, as if they could mean multiple things.

We/I am must have/want/find a concentration/the source of/new types of power/energy.

"I don't know what you want," she said, and looked to Ori, who shrugged, then down the line of the others. Rey, who'd just closed the portal he made, scowled at the Coalitioners. He was standing close to them, just past the knot of bodies made from Sam, Inas, and Enos. Rilan wanted to rush to her apprentice, but there was no time. She thanked all the gods Enos had made it away from the asteroid.

They'd come here at agreement from both the Life Coalition and her group of maji, as the room of void seeds was vibrating as if it would collapse the cave in the little homeworld. The Nether, where everyone could communicate, was the best place to meet a new species. It had been so ever since the Assembly was founded.

And here she could bring Nakan to an accounting. His fellow Life Coalition members didn't seem to like him either. Out of the corner of her eye, she saw Sam, Enos and Inas turn to face them. What had the Sathssn done to her? She looked...taller. Had they made her use her Aridori abilities to change shape?

Rilan shook her head. No one would appear and offer a source of free power, so what did this disturbing creature want? It seemed to watch her, eyeless, its fin cocked toward her.

"If you, you do not give power," Janas said, "then do you seek a representative or leader?"

The creature squatted, its cilia-like legs spreading out as if feeling the floor.

We/I search/come for great power. We are/I am the Elgynerdeen. We have been shouting/communication/pleading for much time.

<Pleading? Do you need assistance?> Hand Dancer signed.

"Our leader can negotiate with you," Rilan said, gesturing to the Effature. "He is currently injured, but can help when he is healed." She glared at the Coalitioners, and hoods turned to Nakan. So there was another story there.

"I am always eager to meet new species," the Effature said. His voice was weak, and Rilan could see signs of stress around him. Ripples of darker coloring passed along his face, as if Nakan's knife still affected him. What had it done?

The creature slithered over to him, the fin on its back waggling. It made Rilan's spine itch and she forced her shoulders to loosen. Something was very wrong about *all* of this, but she didn't know what.

"Greetings from the Assembly of Species," the Effature said. "Please forgive my state. I have been—"

"You still live." Nakan stepped out of the Coalitioners, shaking off the hands that had held him back. "Me, I thought I was rid of you."

Rilan shifted her feet, ready to fight the majus. There were so many who could hear the Symphony in this room they'd trample all over each other if they started changing notes.

"Not as yet," the Effature said, and shifted to a more vertical position. His voice was as harsh as she had heard from the old man.

There is not peace/conflict/danger here, the Elgynerdeen said. Was that its name? Or its species?

"Yes, there is conflict," Rilan told it. The fin on its back twitched toward her and it swung around. She took a step back.

Conflict/disorder is not best/optimal. Peace/silence/finality is more efficient.

"This being, it is one who sides with the philosophy of the Life Coalition," one of the cloaked forms said. "We also seek to bring peace to all."

This is negotiable/different/misunderstood, the Elgynerdeen said, swinging its body the other way, and the Coalitioner who spoke—she thought it was Janas—took a surprised step backwards. Rilan smiled grimly. So their prophecy didn't predict everything.

The Elgynerdeen twirled in a circle, though without a recognizable head, Rilan wasn't sure where it was facing.

We will share/enact our peace/silence/transformation.

"While that is a possibility, we must negotiate our terms," the Effature said, then sucked in a breath, holding the bandage on his side. That was when the Elgynerdeen moved.

Quicker than she thought possible, it was at the Effature's side, slithering halfway up the low couch he rested on. She'd only taken one step during the same time.

Negotiation/peace/silence/not peace will become one. The creature was on the Effature's chest, then melted into him. The Effature choked out a surprised cough, his wide eyes sinking back into his head, his body falling back in a heap. Rilan realized *he* was melting too, falling into nothingness.

"No!" she called, as everyone rushed forward. Time slowed and she glimpsed Sam clutching his head, Enos and Inas gathered around him.

She reached the Effature's side at the same time as Nakan, but even as the Symphony whipped through Rilan's mind, she could already tell it was too late. Chords fused into a sludge of notes, everything playing at once. The Effature and the Elgynerdeen flowed together like melting snow, into a pool of color, then nothing. A crystal circlet rolled down the couch and onto the floor. It looked like it had legs, or prongs. How had it been attached to the Effature's head?

Rilan swiped a hand across the bare sofa. It wasn't even warm.

"What happened? Where is he?" She spun to the Coalitioners, her braid spinning in a spiral.

* * *

Rey stared at the place where the Effature had been. His gut clenched, his skin cold and clammy. This wasn't right. He'd known it from when the weird critter had trouble going through the portal. Had to pull itself through, like it didn't belong in either place.

The others rushed forward, though the old man was already gone, along with the repulsive creature who'd come through the void.

His eyes found Janas and Zsaana, who he'd spoken to what seemed like cycles ago. If he hadn't talked with them, would this have happened? Would the Effature be gone? Would Inas have deserted him for Sam? He clenched a fist. So many things wrong. He should have stayed on Sureri—never left home.

The Life Coalition had spoken in their prophesy of access to great power, but they were clueless. Now they'd killed the Effature. He'd tried to understand. Tried to rationalize with all these aliens. No one paid any attention to him. The Assembly was stupid, the Council of the Maji useless. It was far past time for them all to stop fighting.

Rey moved behind Janas, listening to the Symphony describe the energy around her. He could do—

"You think like one of the Blessed, I can tell," said a voice behind him. Rey jumped and spun. It was a guard, but bright blue eyes peeked out from under the cowl. What—?

"It is such a simple thing. I will show you." The figure reached out with arms that were too long, and Janas made a small noise as they captured her head, squeezing. What were these creatures?

"Only a little kick to the back of her boots," the not-guard whispered. The other Snakeys weren't even watching. All eyes were on where the Effature had been, but Rey's voice was frozen in his throat.

The person snapped out with one leg and Janas' full weight was transferred to the joint between her neck and her body. Rey could hear the crescendo in the energy and there was a sharp crack, lost in the noise the others were making over the Effature.

Not even the other Coalitioners noticed. Not even Zsaana, who should have been able to tell with the House of Healing. Janas fell limp.

"Hold this." Rey caught the body, falling back with her, out of the line of sight of the others and closer to the guards. None of them had reacted. Weren't they supposed to be *guarding* her?

Then they turned to him, as one. They *had* seen. Rey swallowed, cradling the small body.

Vibrant purple eyes stared out from another hood. These were no Snakeys. As he watched, a shadow of fangs grew. A gloved hand lifted and nails lengthened into knives.

Aridori.

"You know the ways of the Blessed, of silent death, though you are not of our species." The shape glided forward and Rey pressed back against the wall of the chamber, still holding Janas' cooling body, very very unsure now of what had happened. He had only *thought...* He hadn't...

"We also wish to take our vengeance on those who have imprisoned us." The voice was like silk, laced with poison. These were the ones who'd been tortured with Inas. The Aridori assassins. "Such initiative has a place with us, should you wish it. There is great power to be had."

"I...I..." Rey could only stammer.

One of the other hooded figures looked back, then made a small signal.

"We must go now," the voice whispered. "Bring the body. It will be valuable fuel."

The group surrounded Rey, pulling him to his feet, bustling them from the chaotic room like a line of shadows crossing a wall.

* * *

The voice screamed in Sam's head about power and time. It was too much and his body was shutting down. Enos and Inas were next to him, but everything was going wrong. Pain cascaded up his legs as his knees hit the floor.

MY EMISSARIES WILL DRAW ME TO THIS PLACE AS I WAS UNABLE TO DO BEFORE.

The voice was stronger, like music blasting at full volume.

I stopped you, Sam thought back. *You were gone.*

NEVER GONE. ONLY HIDDEN. BUT NOW THE CONDUIT IS CONNECTED, NO MATTER THE LOCATION. WATCH.

Majus Ayama and Nakan were still arguing next to where the Effature had been. Sam struggled to his feet against the oppressive voice, and turned, with horrible fascination, as a skin like rancid pus bloomed into view. His eyes fixed on it, even as others jumped out of the way. There was a hole in the Symphony where notes split and died. It was like a Drain, but also unlike it.

The skin split open and two more orange and black-striped creatures exited, scattering Life Coalition and maji alike. Then the Drain collapsed behind them into a pile, like a leftover shell.

We are/I am the Elgynerdeen, the creatures said in tandem. *We will compose/share/enact our silence/peace/equality with this place.* They swarmed forward, one climbing up the robes of a Coalitioner, and both of them faded to nothing.

"Get out of here!" Sam yelled at the maji. "Majus Cyrysi—make a portal. Anywhere!"

Majus Ayama whipped around as Majus Hand Dancer spread her hands and a portal bloomed, circled with orange and red. Majus Caroom and Majus Kheena tumbled through and the others followed.

In the back of the room, another Drain swirled out of nothing, shedding three more creatures in moments, blocking the path to the maji.

"We're going a different way," Sam called, making a split-second decision. "We'll meet up at Dalhni." It was the first place he thought of not in the Nether, because he was almost certain this place would not be safe for a long time.

Hand Dancer gave him a slow roll of her fingers in acceptance, pushed a frowning Majus Cyrysi and Ayama though. Sam caught the hasty bandage on her shoulder as she turned and stepped through her portal. It closed with a snap.

"They're coming through, and we can't stop them," he told Enos and Inas. "But I know where we have to go."

The Elgynerdeen, like enraged millipedes, swerved around the remaining Coalitioners, trying to catch one. Auras of white and green and brown sprang up around them, but they were diminished, in the presence of the invaders.

"Wait!" Inas called, and dashed through the room. Enos called to him, but he jumped over a chair and snagged the Effature's circlet from where it had rolled under a table. One of the creatures swerved behind him, passing over where the Nether crystal had lain, instants before.

The Symphony blared in Sam's mind, chaotic and shifting. The Elgynerdeen ate holes in it as they moved. He gritted his teeth and forced his notes between the music here and another place, fresh in his memory. Was it far enough? How did one count the distance through the Nether wall?

Like stretching a rubber band over an object far too large for it, Sam strained to keep his notes in place. The C-shaped ring buzzed hot on his finger, *cleaning* the notes somehow. Before him, a tiny portal opened, ringed in silver and gold. It was just big enough for a person to squeeze through.

"Go!" he shouted, as Inas panted back to them, his prize clutched in one hand. They fled, diving though his portal, Elgynerdeen on his heels.

Sam looked up into the open jaws and waving head flaps of Wor Wobniar. The Nether told him, unneeded, that xy was surprised.

"I know how the Dissolution will start," he said.

Redirection

- All our calculations were right on target, or so we thought. Mandamon assumed the three-house maji all passed to the same place on this other plane we were accessing, and no one questioned him, even Krat. But, the way to see your own tail is to look over your shoulder, as they say. Why would a being with the ability to rewrite half of reality bother to come back and help us against the Dissolution? I also don't know if Mandamon's thought about that if these supposed three-house maji can pass through the dimensional tear, what's to stop something else from doing the same?

Journal of Timpomitnob Gompt, Watcher, majus of the Houses of Grace and Potential

Mandamon picked through the wreckage of his dimensional equalizer with the other two-house maji. They'd been able to get some readings on what happened, but not nearly enough. He clenched a hand and pounded his thigh with it.

They were supposed to access a three-house majus. They had accessed *something*, but with no physical confirmation, it could have been anything.

Krat and Gompt trundled up, his friend scanning down a list of the last musical signals recorded by the System.

"Wherever that thing appeared, it was definitely not here," he said.

"Arrived at unknown coordinates," Krat added.

Mandamon let the machined arm he was holding fall to the floor with a clang. They could fix the machine, but it would take time, and he was no longer certain it was worth the cost.

"Why?" he asked. "When they could have simply walked through the pathway we opened? Is the Dissolution not actually a threat?"

Gompt shook his furry head, the tips of his long ears wobbling. "It was a portal, but it didn't connect all the way from our side. It was— what would you call it—exploratory?"

"Did not know precise landing location of other end," Krat said.

Mandamon frowned. "You mean it opened an unanchored portal? One end fixed here and the other just—" He waved a hand through the air. He'd never thought of his dimensional equalizer as opening a portal, but it did, in a way. And portals had to have two endpoints to open.

<Another first,> Touching Digits signed, approaching from the other side of the wreckage. He had stated he was male, for tidying the mess and analyzing their final readings. <Truly this was an honorable endeavor. The first b-breach of the walls of this universe, the first unanchored portal, and the first contact with a completely unknown form of life.>

"Well, not quite first contact," Gompt said. "Not any contact, since whatever came through went elsewhere."

<Another topic I wish to discuss,> the Lobhl signed. He held a long list of equations between one thumb and a finger. <The fundamental frequency inside the event was substantially different from that of the Grand Symphony. I believe we can conclusively say this was a *different* Grand Symphony, and therefore a different universe.>

"Then we succeeded," Mandamon said.

Touching Digits held up one finger. <However, the frequency is getting fainter, even in the short time we accessed it.>

"Fainter?" Mandamon asked. "Meaning?"

"End of song," Krat said, and Mandamon peered over his glasses at the System Beast.

"Do you mean what I think you mean?" he asked. If true, this was bad. Very bad.

Touching Digits flipped his hands in agreement. <Correct. The Grand Symphony of this other universe is coming to an end. It is dying.>

"Then we need to find out where this being came through and how we can help," Mandamon said.

END OF BOOK 2

Don't you hate cliffhangers? So do I. Fortunately, you don't have to wait! Just look for book three, *Fall of the Imperium*, to read the conclusion to the Dissolution Cycle.

If you enjoyed this book, please leave a brief review at your online bookseller of choice. Thanks!

Wondering about Origon's early adventures? You can sign up for my mailing list at www.spacewizardsciencefantasy.com and get a free short novelette: *The Five Hive Plateau.*

Appendix: The Houses of the Maji

- For uncounted cycles, the six houses of the maji have worked together to uphold the Great Assembly of Species. They control the only means of transportation in and out of the Nether and between the homeworlds, and thus have a great responsibility to the non-maji members, who far outnumber them. As such, every majus has a say in the Assembly, a concept some non-maji are not comfortable with.

Houses of the Maji, often attributed to Ribothari Tan, Knower, later of the Council of the Maji

- Each house of the maji can hear and change one section of the Grand Symphony and thus affect reality, by the individual applying the notes that make up their own song. This application can be seen by other maji in a visual representation of color, often accompanied by a secondary color, personal to the individual majus. It is said each house's Symphony is based on a certain frequency or note.

From "Memoirs of Yaten E'Mez," Highest of the House of Communication and Speaker for the Council, 379 A.A.W.

House of Strength

The color of the House of Strength is bright emerald green, and the areas of the Symphony it affects often have to do with constitution, defense, strength, and growth, as well as soil and rock. A large portion of these maji have jobs as herbalists, veterinarians, or naturalists, though as with any house, the possibilities are nearly endless. Their Symphony diverges from the sound of a baritone resonant string.

House of Communication

Members of the House of Communication are the most common councilmembers chosen to become Speakers for the Council of the Maji. Their house color is pure yellow, and they affect quick thought, speech patterns, as well as air pressure, weather systems and avian creatures. Many of the House of Communication serve as diplomats of the maji, working less with the physical changes in their Symphony than those of interplay between the species. Their Symphony's fundamental tone is that of a low reed.

House of Power

The House of Power deals with the play of politics, movement of societies, personal relationships, as well as power generation, and simple heat. Their house color is fiery orange. They can as easily be found in the industrial districts of the Imperium and the homeworlds as in clandestine meetings and national assemblies. Their Symphony's base melody is of a sounding horn.

House of Grace

Those of the House of Grace are often subtle, with their control of liquids and ice, as well as efficient movement, cooperation, and coordination. Their house color is sapphire blue, and they work around transportation systems, food distribution, diplomatic intermediaries, and engineering positions. Many members are fond of kinesthetic movements such as dance, athletics, and martial arts. The founding tone of their Symphony is a passionate tenor.

House of Healing

The members of the House of Healing are best known as skilled physicians and surgeons, as the brilliant white of their house color seems to indicate. However, there is much more to the specializations of the house, including plant and animal breeding, psychology, profiling information on individuals, and even archeology through residue of living creatures on ancient artifacts. Their Symphony's fundamental tone is a high ringing of struck metal.

House of Potential

The House of Potential is the most directly tied to science and engineering. Its members are responsible for many of the technological improvements of the ten species made in recent cycles. Their house color is a rich rusty brown, and they are, at the very simplest, concerned with energy transfer. They are known to work with the House of Power on fuel and work generation, and the House of Healing on ancient history, describing energy paths of artifacts. They deal with kinetic movement as the House of Grace does, transfer of force as the House of Strength, and energy of the weather with the House of Communication. Their members can also create Systems, or long-lasting changes in the Symphony, driven through a store of energy. Their Symphony starts with the shriek of whistling air.

The Society of Two Houses

This shadowy organization only recruited members able to hear two aspects of the Grand Symphony, though it was dissolved in 953 A.A.W., around fifty cycles before current events. There are rumors of individuals asking about these types of maji again, though the ability is regarded as a curiosity nowadays. The Society named the combinations of abilities the two-house maji exhibited as below, with examples of practitioners:

Negotiator: Strength/Communication (Laryn I'Hon)
Overwhelm: Strength/Power
Pressure Point: Strength/Grace
Biologist: Strength/Healing (Moortlin)
Fabricator: Strength/Potential
Connector: Communication/Power (Origon Cyrysi)
Dancer: Communication/Grace (Yutirei Janerea Retina)
Psychiatrist: Communication/Healing
Innervater: Communication/Potential (Touching Digits)
Engineer: Power/Grace (Kratitha, Emma)
Geneticist: Power/Healing (Gretahn)
Computer: Power/Potential
Surgeon: Grace/Healing
Archeologist: Grace/Potential (Timpomitnob Gompt, Watcher)
Investigator: Healing/Potential (Mandamon Feldo)

Appendix: The Species of the Great Assembly

- The number of species in the Great Assembly varies over the cycles. Currently it resides at ten, including the recent addition of the Lobhl. The founding members are those who, according to tradition, started the first Assembly when the maji of their species discovered each other in the Nether.

From the notes of the Effature, Bolas Palmoran, 983 A.A.W.

- All members of the Great Assembly share basic similarity in form and function, though the species are physically spread far across the universe. The Nether helps to form connections despite differences, to the point where some scholars wonder whether the Nether has some impact on the species that find it.

From "Assumptions on the Nature of the Nether" by Festuour philosopher Hegramtifar Yhon, Thinker

Methiemum

The Methiemum homeworld is known as Methiem, and hosts a species well known as traders and decent scientists. They were one of the first to discover the Nether, as they are entrepreneurial and prone to adventure, though perhaps at the expense of long-term planning. However, this cannot have affected them greatly, as the common trading tongue of the ten species is derived from one of their dialects. In addition, they were the first to suggest an Assembly of all species who discover the Nether, probably to secure trading rights with the others. They are the most prevalent species of the ten, of medium height and coloring ranging from a dark mahogany to very pale peach, even with cases of albinism. They often have fine hair restricted to the tops of their heads and sporadically over the limbs and torso, more so on the males. Common Pronouns: he/him, she/her, they/them.

Kirian

The inhabitants of Kiria are known for their philosophy, debate, and ancestor worship. They were another species to discover the Nether early and became a founding member of the Great Assembly. They make fine statesmen, though they have a convoluted natural dialect in many of their nations, which does not translate as well inside the Nether as other species. Kirians do not let this stop them from expounding on any subject they know of, and some they do not. The males of the species favor long colorful robes in many cultures, while the females prefer to leave their arms and legs bare to show off their fine feathering and delicately curved nails. The species is generally tall, with wrinkled, liver-spotted skin, and feathers creating expressive crests on top of their heads. Males may also cultivate moustaches and thin beards, and both are sparingly feathered on the torso. Their pointed teeth can be unnerving when bared in smiles, though their dentation is mainly for gripping in their diet of grubs, beetles, and other slippery creatures. Common Pronouns: he/him, she/her, they/them.

Lobath

The Lobath are often looked down upon by the other species as dull and uninteresting, much like the prevalent mushroom farms on their rainy homeworld of Loba. However, Lobath are found at every level of society, from the menial to the most intellectual, and are one of the founding members of the Great Assembly. Consistently, they are defined as hardworking, compared to the other species, and tend to fill more physically demanding jobs. They are usually savvy with technology, especially new inventions. Other species may joke of the permanently surprised expression on the Lobath face, arising from their unblinking silvery eyes. They have a large range in coloring, from yellow, to orange, to red and brown, but are more easily identified by their squat neck-less bodies and three head-tentacles sprouting from the crown of their heads. The tentacles are often braided or tied together in certain styles. Males may have small rubbery growths above and below the mouth, while females have thinner head-tentacles and wari, the third gender, are generally of slighter, taller, build. Common Pronouns: he/him, she/her, zie/hir.

Sathssn

The Sathssn are unusual in that over eighty percent of the culture of Sath Home subscribe to various sects of the Cult of Form, based on perfection of the physical body. This invades every aspect of their society, from dark cloaks, robes, and gloves, to marriage rites, where the participants must be examined by other family for any illness or disfigurement, to livestock, bred to only descend from the most reputable lineages. The inhabitants of Sath Home are especially prone to cancers and tumors, and their winnowing practice began as a necessary response. Like many such things, it became religion. A notable exception is the Southern Coastal Coalition, a nationality where scales are allowed to be shown, and some may even go about without cowls and gloves and in short sleeves, to the dismay of the rest of their species. In the rare occasion skin is shown, the Sathssn body is covered in tiny scales, ranging from yellow to green. Sparse hair may be present on the head and face, and eyes are red with yellow slitted pupils. Some Sathssn antisocial tendencies have caused interspecies conflicts in the past, yet they remain in good standing as a founding member of the Great Assembly. Despite their almost worldwide religion, many become scientists or statespeople. Common Pronouns: he/him, she/her.

Etanela

The long-lived Etanela are described as inherent pacifists, though the planet of Etan provides its fair share of malcontents, adventure seekers, and revolutionaries to the Great Assembly, of which they are a founding species. The Etanela typecast comes from their love of music, painting, sculpture, and literature. Many accepted great works were either created by an Etanela, or funded by one. Lots of educated Etanela are gifted speakers, and love to argue. Physically, they are the tallest of the ten species, with the largest individuals rising head and shoulders over even Kirians. Their skin tends to light blue, revealing aquatic origins, also noted in their large eyes and long fingers, and small, streamlined noses. The only hair the species exhibits is in a mane surrounding the head, often left to trail to the shoulders. The species is largely divided into four genders, with both dominate and subordinate versions of those who carry young and those who do not. Their mating rituals are often obtuse to those not of their species. Common

Pronouns: he/him (dominate), he/him (subordinate) she/her (dominate), she/her (subordinate).

Festuour

Festuour can be hard to pin down to a stereotype. They thrive in the variability of professions and are well known for their philosophers, gourmands, mechanics, scholars, tailors, and explorers. On their homeworld of Festuour, once a member of the species finally discovers their chosen path in life, it is appended to their name permanently. Their inclusive friend-based society encourages members to do anything they set their minds to, with cheery acceptance. Children are reared communally to give the best options for advancement of themselves and society. Physically, Festuour are stout, covered in coarse greenish-brown hair. Their faces have long snouts with large noses, and nearly all members of the species possess piercing blue eyes, though a common failing is nearsightedness. The hairy Festuour do not often wear clothes, instead preferring accessories such hats, glasses, gloves, belts, and bandoliers with many pouches. They were the last of the founding members to convene the Great Assembly, though they have the distinction to be one of two species to share a galaxy, the other being the Methiemum. The two are often staunch allies politically and many of the Methiemum's customs and idioms have bled over to Festuour culture. Common Pronouns: he/him, she/her, they/them, zie/hir.

Benish

Even longer-lived than the Etanela, the Benish were the first newcomers welcomed by the newly created Assembly of Species. Most still live on their homeworld of Aben, and they are the least populous members both in the Nether and in the Assembly of Species. Cautious by nature, Benish are studious to a fault, often observing a situation from all sides before making even a preliminary decision. Little is known about their home cultures, save that the species is genderless, and propagates by a form of budding, where the parents, however many, share and mix memories, arranging parts of their history before dying to produce a new child or children, who inherit the progenitor's memories. Physically, the Benish are one of the most different species, with flesh made of a substance closer to plant than animal. They have no well-defined bone structure, and each member is varied in coloring, skin tone and roughness, and placement of internal organs. Common Pronouns: they/them.

Sureriaj

The Sureriaj are the most xenophobic of the ten species, surpassing even the antisocial tendencies of the Sathssn. Their culture is entirely founded on the concept of family, going so far as to have, instead of independent nations, major family lines that matriarchally govern their homeworld of Sureri. There is also a large group consisting of the disgraced—those who have lost their right to their family name—known as the Naiyul. Names are very important to the Sureriaj, and each individual has a hierarchy of names, the most secret known to progressively closer family members. Physically, the Sureriaj are tall and gaunt, with proportionally long legs. They have fine hair covering the entirety of their body, through which the skin can be seen. Their faces are not always appealing to other species, and that, with their aloofness, is the basis of the species slur "gargoyle." Their society is two thirds male, and two males and one female are required to create a viable offspring. The Sureriaj have the second lowest birth rate of the ten species, just higher than the Benish. Common Pronouns: he/him, she/her.

Pixie

This warlike and competitive species was the second to last to join the Assembly. To others, some of their members seem less intelligent to the point of an animal intellect, though this may be explained by their descent from a hive mentality, as well as their careful breeding of a fierce warrior caste, at the expense of progression in other areas. For each sufficiently courageous deed a pixie completes, a letter or syllable is added to her name, and many go by shortened nicknames. Pixies are short, blue to gray in coloring, with black compound eyes. They are capable of short flights with their gossamer wings, though often they will lift from the ground when speaking to another species, as if in recompense for being the shortest of the species. There are reports of members of another gender, hidden deep in their enormous city-hives, but all individuals who interface with other species are identified as female. Common Pronouns: she/her.

Lobhl

There is no proper spoken name for the Lobhl homeworld, so it is titled as the members name their species. The Lobhl have been members of the Great Assembly for only fifty cycles, and caused controversy when they joined for the amount of money spent on social restructuring, especially in the rotunda of the Assembly. Because the Lobhl have no vocal chords, they communicate entirely with complex hand gestures, and expensive visual displays were added in many areas to cater to them. Lobhl faces and heads are nearly featureless, leading to small problems in communication, even in the Nether. Lobhl hands are the points of reference for the species, widely different between individuals, and often tattooed. Each hand has seven digits, two of which are thumbs on opposing sides of the hand. Generally the Lobhl species is talented visually and mathematically. They also have a great love of what they define as music, though most is visually experienced. Their names are translations of actions they routinely perform, and their gender roles vary with the individual and the social situation. Their young are raised communally, and are neither carried in the body, nor in eggs. Many Lobhl worship the god of music, an incorporeal concept of light, like a personification of the Symphony, and most of their other religions focus on vision over sound or language. Common Pronouns: he/him, she/her, they/them, zie/hir, it/its.

Aridori

Little is known about this species. They were rumored to be one of the founding members of the Great Assembly. However, many records were lost in the Great Aridori War, when the entire species suddenly turned on the others, often taking the forms of old friends, or even close family members. They were eventually eradicated, with many renegades hunted by teams of trained Sathssn commandos, but legends of their shapeshifting prowess and patient, long-term deception have provided generations of nighttime stories to scare children. Only recently, there has been a resurgence of interest in this species, as the Sathssn have revealed there are a few specimens left in captivity, undergoing unknown training and restrictions. Common Pronouns: he/him, she/her, they/them.

Appendix: Timeline of Major Events

A.A.W = After Aridori War

0 A.A.W. – End of Aridori War

686 A.A.W. – Moortlin Leads The Society of Two Houses

726 A.A.W. – Pixies Species Enters Great Assembly

919 A.A.W. – Formation of the Life Coalition

927 A.A.W. – Mandamon Feldo Born

939 A.A.W. – Origon Cyrysi Born

952 A.A.W. – Lobhl Species Enters Great Assembly

953 A.A.W. – The Society of Two Houses Falls

962 A.A.W. – Rilan Ayama Born

964 A.A.W. – Methiemum-Sathssn War of Trading Rights

972 A.A.W. – The Five Hive Plateau Insurrection

984 A.A.W. – Origon Cyrysi's Brother Murdered

985 A.A.W. – Sam van Oen Born

999 A.A.W. – Sureriaj Baldek Plot to Sterilize Methiemum

1003 A.A.W. – Origon Cyrysi Pilots the First Space Shuttle

1003 A.A.W. – Sam Arrives in the Nether

1003 A.A.W. – Life Coalition Attacks the Dome of the Assembly

1003 A.A.W. – Journey to the Top of the Nether

1004 A.A.W. – The Chimes Begin in the Nether

ACKNOWLEDGEMENTS

Well, this is the Second Book. I've written, and published, a lot more than two books, but this is significant as a milestone for me because it is the first time I've written the second (and also third) part of a single story. If you read the dedication (you didn't, did you?), you'll see I've recognized Writing Excuses, an award-winning podcast run primarily by Mary Robinette Kowal, Brandon Sanderson, Dan Wells, and Howard Tayler. The first episode I ever listened to from them was about writing the Second Book, and it was basically a list of everything I'd done wrong at the end of my then first book, The Seeds of Dissolution, and what I needed to put into this one. That was seven or eight years ago, but I haven't forgotten that advice, and I hope I've used their advice well.

This is my third time using Kickstarter, though it was a weird one, right in the middle of the COVID-19 pandemic. That said, I am once again blown away by the friends, family, and strangers who were willing to help me fund this project. The Kickstarter helped pay for not only a new cover for The Seeds of Dissolution, but also covers for this book and the next, as well as six amazing illustrations by Cory Godbey, between this book and the next. You can find his other work at corygodbey.com. I've once again used the awesome map by Damijan in the front. Lastly, thanks to my excellent copy editor (and wife), Heather Tracy, who has helped in so many ways it's impossible to count, including just putting up with me.

Many others have made this book a reality, and a big thank you goes to my alpha and beta readers: Reese Hogan, J.S. Fields, Robin Duncan, Sara Cordair, Katie Cordy, Natalie Ingram, and all the folks at Reading Excuses for critiquing my submissions.

Of course, much of this wouldn't have been possible without my backers on Kickstarter. In no particular order, they are:

Dorian Graves, Hannah, Mike A. Weber, Brett M Guth, Ashley Capes, Jeff Lewis, Reese Hogan, Leon Fairley, Alex Claman, Maxime van den Berg, Tami Veldura, Lucas Cooperberg, Mitchell S., Ryan.e, Robert Claney, Robert Tienken, Tyler Bletsch, Bunny & Timmy, Stephen Ballentine, Cristov Russell, Anaxphone, Robin Hill, Nathan V., PJ Kimbell, Russell Ventimeglia, Skywings14, Dave Kochbeck, Jay Quietnight, Allen Gibson, John Mierau, Daniel Lin, Dean Heller, Cen, Jesse & Michela Brown, Jennifer Tifft, Margaret Lamb, Mike Goffin, J.S. Fields, Christy Shorey, Scarlett Letter, MS Manning, Ian Fincham, Becky Barnes, Robin Duncan, Natalie Ingram, Adam Nemo, Sara Codair, Ross Newberry, Courtney, Josiah, Ezra, and Elias Brooks, Dyrk Ashton, Steve C. Boykin, Fernando Enrique, Arioch Morningstar, Connor Cassie Thomasson, Katie Cordy, Matt Cote, Wayne Mathers, Ashley, Tim Mushel, Kerry aka Trouble, Ian Chung, Andromeda Taylor-Wallace, Alex Kuhlman, Stuart Turnbull, Matt Burris, Daniel Eavenson, Chris Nash, Zak, Cass, and Emma McClellan, eSpec Books, Crys Cain, Melissa Sweeny, and the Doubleclicks.

Thanks to all of you, and I hope you enjoy reading!

ABOUT THE AUTHOR

William C. Tracy writes and publishes queer science fiction and fantasy through his indie press Space Wizard Science Fantasy (spacewizardsciencefantasy.com).

His largest work is the Dissolutionverse: a space opera with music-based magic including nine books and a TTRPG. He's also published Fruits of the Gods, an epic fantasy with seasonal fruit magic, How To Operate Your Body, a nonfiction book about body mechanics and correct posture, The Biomass Conflux, a sci-fi trilogy with colony ships and a planet covered by a sentient fungus, and The Shifting Lands, his current work, which is a progression fantasy series about martial arts and moving islands.

William is an NC native and a lifelong fan of science fiction and fantasy. He has a master's in mechanical engineering, and has both designed and operated heavy construction machinery. He has also trained in Wado-Ryu karate since 2003 and runs his own dojo in Raleigh NC. He is an avid video and board gamer, a beekeeper, a reader, and of course, a writer.

You can get a free Dissolutionverse novelette by signing up for William's mailing list at spacewizardsciencefantasy.com

Follow him on Instagram, Facebook, and Threads at spacewizardpress and Bluesky at wctracy.bsky.social for writing updates, cat and bee pictures, and thoughts on martial arts.

Please take a moment to review this book at your favorite retailer's website, Goodreads, or simply tell your friends!